Reaper

BOOK 1
THE SECRET OF ALBA

Lindsey Winsemius

Get an exclusive sneak peek of *Patrician*, Book 2 in
The Secret of Alba Series by visiting
www.lindseywinsemius.com/my-books

Published by ApogeeINVENT
www.apogeeinvent.com

ISBN 9780692481042

First Edition July 2015

Cover Design by Andrew Frey

For my husband, who taught me that real love isn't about romantic gestures; it is about trust, and finding someone with whom you can truly be yourself. Thanks for telling me to take the risk.

And to all the readers who took a chance on a new author: Thank you.

Chapter 1

"Every action has its pleasures and its price." - Socrates

Aerina Delacroix took a deep, shaky breath as she walked gracefully up the familiar steps into the open courtyard of the Capitol. Her large blue eyes scanned the gathered crowd surreptitiously. Most of the voting class of Alba had gathered to watch the pre-dinner show. She noticed many familiar faces in the group, seated with their backs to the sunset—the Consul, her parents, all her friends. It was Founder's Day, and the Patricians were celebrating by watching the Pleb dance troupe perform an interpretive dance of the founding group's escape from war-ravaged Los Angeles.

Her gaze sought out the dark shadow not far behind Consul Julius' seat.

Marcus.

Her already pounding heart skipped a few beats and resumed at an even quicker pace—her typical reaction to catching a glimpse of the Virmortus leader.

The marble steps were cool beneath her bare feet. Nerves made her slender legs weak as she stepped into the open space of the courtyard. Brilliant rays reflected off the smooth white surface, making it shimmer like a mirage. Behind the gathered spectators, crimson spread like blood from the setting sun across the horizon.

If she were caught, her life would be forever changed.

Strangely, she was more nervous about performing than being caught masquerading as a Pleb. She'd practiced and performed with this group many times, but never could quell the nerves that rose before each performance.

The troupe's vivid scarlet costumes contrasted brilliantly with the unrelenting white of the majestic structure and the clothing of the gathered Patricians.

The Capitol overlooked the Pacific Ocean on the steep

coastline near the ruins of old San Francisco. The massive building was a feat of architecture, with its towering pillars and endless white marble.

From her place in back of the group, Aerina focused on the expanse of ocean stretching to meet the still-luminous sky. She was careful to avoid direct eye contact with any familiar faces. Her long hair was tucked under a red turban-style headdress. Dark eye makeup and costume jewelry completed her disguise. She had taken on the appearance of many different castes over the past few years. But she had never dared be so bold as to appear before her close friends and family in the guise of another class.

Then the music began, and Aerina forgot her fears. Her slender body moved in a fluid motion to the sound of the music, bending, dipping, and then leaping. The wind from the ocean blew over her heated skin. It was heaven. She could never feel this free in her role as a Patrician.

She was in the middle of a spin when a scream cut across the courtyard. Onlookers and dancers alike froze. Everyone looked towards the dais where the Consul was sitting. One of the dancers had drawn a knife and was rushing the marble platform. The setting sun hung over the ocean behind their leader's seat, nearly blinding Aerina as she stared in shock at the scene unfolding.

While everyone stood in frozen horror, one figure detached from the shadows of a pillar behind the platform. Dressed in black, he was a panther approaching his prey — silent, swift, and instantly deadly.

The dancer dropped without a sound, a small pool of deep red almost the exact color of her costume forming beneath her prone body.

Before Aerina could move, more black-clothed figures emerged from their positions, rushing towards the remaining dancers. She watched in horror as the next dancer was cut down. And the next. The entire troupe she had practiced with, laughed with, primped and dressed with, were being killed before her eyes. Not just killed.

Executed.

Her eyes met those of the dark figure turning towards her. Him. He had killed the assassin. And he would kill her, too. In this moment, she was just another Pleb dancer. A dancer thought to be part of an assassination attempt on the Consul. All the privileges and rights she had as a Patrician were stripped away in this moment; sacrificed by her bored whimsy.

Fear spread through her; real fear she'd never had a reason to experience before. It was nothing like the adrenaline rush she normally sought. This was a sick, dark oil that flowed from the pit of her stomach, filling her body and threatening to close her throat.

Aerina ripped her headdress off, letting her hair tumble down around her shoulders. From a distance, she heard several gasps spread through the crowd of horrified onlookers. She was a recognizable figure on the Capitol Terrace with her long, unusual golden-red hair.

As Marcus drew closer, realization spread through her in a crushing wave. He knew it was her. He had already known. Her last hope drowned beneath the oily fear. He didn't care.

He met her bold sapphire gaze, so full of life. She didn't try to turn or run. It would be futile.

"Please, Marcus," she spoke tightly, forcing the words past the fear that filled her throat. She tried to keep the panic from taking over completely as she took a step back. He didn't rush, just kept striding towards her without pause. He was large, powerful. His dark brown hair was cut short, his eyes a dark promise of retribution. She met those familiar eyes, desperately searching for a sign of...anything. But they were as icy and emotionless as always. The eyes of death. She wondered a bit hysterically how many people died with those eyes as the last thing they saw.

His hands moved quickly, pulling out a small garrote coiled in a metal band on his muscular wrist. Before she could run or even duck, it was around her neck.

First was a stinging pain, and then the pressure around her neck became excruciating. The world faded around her to a hazy red. She gasped but couldn't draw in any air. Her hands instinctively flew to her neck, but the flexible wire was so tight she couldn't grasp it. The wire cut deeper and her hands became slick with her own blood.

This is all your fault.

It seemed unreal; impossible that this was actually happening. She wanted to meet his eyes, look at his familiar face. He was now behind her, his large frame pressed to her back. Panic filled her as she continued to try and draw a breath, to fight against him. It was impossible. He was hopelessly strong. Darkness seeped into her peripheral vision, and a buzzing filled her ears. Her panicked eyes met those of her father as if through a tunnel. He stood with her mother, watching the scene in horror. They would be shamed. But she wouldn't have to worry about becoming an outcast. A Jana. She would be dead…

All. Your. Fault.

"My debt is repaid." The low voice cut through the cloud that had sunk upon her senses. Suddenly the pressure left her throat, and the ground rose quickly to meet her. Blackness descended.

Marcus let Aerina's body drop to the cool marble at his feet. She was unconscious but alive. He tamped down the rage that flowed through his body, keeping every emotion in check out of long habit.

As he stepped back from her prone body, no one moved. His eyes scanned the scene, checking for any remaining threats.

The threat was eliminated. All the dancers were dead.

He didn't let his eyes linger on their scarlet-costumed bodies, strewn about the white marble like the fallen petals of a rose.

Nothing matters but your job.

Silence hung over the scene of violence, broken only by the occasional gasping sob of the Patricians witnessing the Virmortus ferocity.

He'd done his job. The assassin was neutralized. The Consul was safe, absent now from the grisly scene.

His eyes dropped again to the small form laying before him on the cool marble. What was her involvement? Would he be forced to kill her after all?

He would do his job, no matter how distasteful. No matter how much he wanted to keep her alive.

When she had entered with the troupe, he had instantly recognized her. Unexpected anger had begun to burn below the surface at her audacity. Yet he had remained immobile as he watched.

As the scene had unfolded, his instinct had taken over. Protect the Consul. Neutralize the threat. A threat he was trained to always expect, to always be ready for.

The moment he had dropped the assassin, he had gone for her, the helpless rage building in him. As the leader of the Virmortus, it was his responsibility to identify and defuse all dangers to the balance of Alba and her millions of inhabitants.

He would kill anyone who posed a threat. It was how his men had earned the name *Reaper*; one only saw a Virmortus when death was imminent.

The last thing he had wanted to do was hurt Aerina. But he had no choice. Her act of rebellion, a mere whim to her, could now cost her life.

She'd saved his life years ago. He'd repaid the debt. Their connection was severed as certainly as the garrote had cut into her neck. Her fate was now in the hands of the Consul.

Chapter 2

"The only true wisdom is in knowing you know nothing."
- Socrates

Aerina came awake with a gasp, her hands going to her throat. It was burning, and too painful to move. The pain meant she must still be alive.

She could feel bandages. She sat up slowly, recognizing the white and pale blue drapes of her own bedroom. The dim light from the moon cast a pale glow on her bed. Night had fallen, but she could still see faint light glowing along the horizon.

She turned her whole body slowly, slipping her legs from under the white cotton sheets and setting her feet on thick woven carpet. Also white.

Unreasonable anger burgeoned as she looked at the unrelenting white. White for balance. White for peace.

Perfection.

This is all your fault.

Stupid. It had been stupid. *She* had been stupid. And she was going to pay for it.

Her mother entered the room as she was slowly rising from the side of the bed.

"Aerina, darling, you must rest." Even after the dramatic end of the evening, her mother was perfectly groomed. Her shiny blonde hair was carefully styled just below her ears. Her elegant white gown had been traded for a casual pencil skirt and matching white blouse.

"I'm fine," Aerina muttered, wincing as she slowly tilted her head from side to side. Rest? Rest until the burning went away and the scars faded from her neck? Or rest until everyone forgot about her dissension. Sometime in the next ten years or more.

Raina sat down beside her daughter, clasping her hands in her lap.

Aerina almost wished her mother would chastise her; tell her what an idiot she was so she could justify her actions. Explain herself. Apologize.

But her mother didn't give her the opportunity, keeping her normal cool distance.

"The Consul has decided to forgo any further punishment. You are very fortunate, Aerina. The Alpha Virmortus could have killed you; *should* have killed you. But he has advised the Consul that you were not normally part of that troupe, and were unaware of the assassination attempt." Raina's voice was quietly reproachful.

"I had no idea," Aerina finally spoke, her eyes fixed on the dark ocean far below. She still couldn't believe that the quiet girl from the troupe had tried to kill the Consul. Of all the ways she had imagined the evening ending, of all the things that could have gone wrong, that hadn't even been a scenario.

"I know, darling," her mother replied softly, her hand hovering for a moment uncertainly before coming to rest on Aerina's tousled hair. Aerina leaned into her, taking rare comfort from her normally detached mother. Raina stroked her daughter's hair awkwardly for a moment. "I am afraid that while you may not be punished further by the Consul, things will be different now. I am sure you remember Jana Littleton?"

How could she not? Every Patrician knew the story of Jana. When Aerina had been a girl, she had heard of the University student who had run away with the family gardener. An Aggie. The scandal had spread through the Patrician Caste, and Jana had become an outcast overnight. The Aggies wouldn't accept her and she had returned home, but the damage had been done. The other students avoided her. She was no longer welcome at gatherings, and when graduation had neared, no one had tried to recruit her to a voting sector. Even her parents had distanced themselves, concern for their younger daughter forcing them to turn their backs on poor Jana Littleton. Unable to handle being a social pariah, the girl had eventually taken her own life, throwing herself from the Capitol balcony.

Aerina had already known the penalty if she were caught. She just hadn't worried about it overmuch. Posing as other castes had given her a sense of freedom, a release from her personal demons. In the moment, the high had seemed worth any risk. The repercussions had seemed distantly improbable.

Now they were her reality.

Her mother stood, and Aerina lowered her head into her hands, her neck screaming in agony at the movement. In the low lamplight from the hallway, she stared blindly down at the scarlet wisps of the costume she still wore. The bright red of the material made the darker red stains of her own blood barely visible. In the unrelenting white of her room, the brilliant color was a stark reminder of her new status. It might as well have been a scarlet letter; her neck branded with Marcus' garrote.

"We need to determine if the assassin worked alone, or had accomplices." The Consul steepled his fingers, his eyes going from each Senator to rest on Aerina's father. Antony had been the Senator of Society for over fifteen years, and was confident he held the trust of the Consul.

"Antony, Marcus has convinced me that your daughter had nothing to do with the plot. The death of the innocent Plebeians is unfortunate and we need to ensure that it is kept quiet to avoid any possible fallout." Julius again scanned the group, waiting for each one's nodded agreement. "As always, our main priority is to keep the peace. To maintain balance." He focused his direct gaze on Antony. Antony met Julius' eyes calmly, refusing to let the others see his anxiety. "We need to know if your daughter has any useful information, and convince her to keep her silence. Marcus has graciously allowed you to speak with her in his place."

Antony looked over to where the Virmortus leader stood silently against the wall near the door. Like the devil himself, the black-clothed figure was not always seen but was always present. Antony knew Julius would do whatever was necessary to preserve the balance in Alba. He was reasonable; fair. A good leader. Antony trusted the Consul with his life. But the Alpha Virmortus scared Antony. He wasn't ashamed to admit it; most of the other Patricians felt the same. The leader of the elite assassin group was cold, unreadable. Untouchable.

Antony had known Marcus since he had been a boy in the Training Grounds, if one could even call the young warrior a boy. Antony doubted the intense man had ever truly been a child.

As if he felt Antony's gaze, Marcus turned towards the Senator. Their gazes met for a moment. Antony fought back the dread that slid down his spine, trying to hide his involuntary shiver from the large man's watchful gaze.

"I will speak with her," Antony promised, his eyes still on Marcus. No way did he want that man near his only remaining child.

"Good." Julius sat back in his chair, narrowing his eyes slightly. "I have full confidence in Marcus and his men. There has been some concern expressed about the assassin searching for the Technology. This is doubtful, but will certainly be addressed. Any questions?"

Julius scanned the faces of the eight Senators as if searching for dissension. There was none. These eight were privy to information about the State that no other citizen would ever know, and that information would be protected unto death. They were bound together by their commitment to the preservation of the State, and the secret of their founding ancestors.

When the six men and two women had shaken their heads negatively, Julius nodded his own again.

"I think this meeting has concluded."

Marcus forced himself to wait patiently as the Senators rose, gathering their holoreaders. They kept their gazes averted from Marcus, subconsciously giving him a wide berth as they exited. Unlike Julius, he didn't trust any one of them. Everyone had a weakness; a breaking point. They'd give up any secrets if pushed hard enough. Or if the incentive was great enough.

Their fear was equal parts amusing and irritating. The only person, besides the Consul himself, who had ever seemed unafraid was Aerina.

And all that would change now. Now that he had almost

killed her.

"Have you found anything?"

Marcus brought his attention back to the issue at hand. Julius remained seated in the white wingback chair at the head of the table. He leaned back slightly and the soft leather folded around his lean, athletic form.

"No, sir," Marcus reported tersely. "No evidence of collusion was found in her living quarters or on her Com devices."

"What do you think?"

"I believe someone else is involved. My guess is Alban."

Julius' face twisted for a moment in a savage grimace before settling back into its normal serene expression. He nodded once before rising and walking over to the glass windows running the length of the room. Every room in the Capitol had been built to capture the stunning views of the coast below. He looked out over the rugged coast to the left, and the lower terraces to the right.

"Control requires a delicate balance, Marcus." Julius continued to look out over the city-state he ruled. At this moment, the slight yet fit man looked all of his sixty years. It wasn't physical as much as the weariness in his eyes, the lines etched on his face, which spoke to an excess of experience. Of stress and perhaps more sorrow than the average person.

"Too much control, or too heavy of a hand, and people rebel." Julius spoke quietly, as if to himself. "Too little control, and too much power in the hands of people, and no decisive action is ever taken and anarchy arises. Like we saw nearly a century ago in the Second Civil War. Balance is everything in life."

Marcus nodded his head in acknowledgement. He understood the basis of their state politics. It was taught in elementary classes. Many other regions that had survived the Global War adopted similar philosophies, although their execution varied.

Marcus also knew the control required to keep that balance sometimes required men like himself to cross a line; to become more of an assassin than a soldier. Like he had years ago at the request of Julius. When he secretly executed the man's own wife to protect the city's most valuable secret from their biggest enemy.

Julius had called it a necessary execution, but to Marcus, it had felt more like murder.

Nothing matters but your job.

It had been Marcus' first act as the Alpha Virmortus, and the secret had bonded the two men together better than any bond of blood or friendship ever could.

"Thank you, Marcus. Keep me informed," Julius finally said, his eyes still studying the city that stretched below.

As he left the Capitol and headed towards his small villa, Marcus couldn't stop his gaze from wandering over to the northern side of the Capitol Terrace. To Aerina's villa.

It was like many of the others—simple yet elegant, made of marble and granite with towering pillars and a flat roof that was often used to enjoy the views. It had a high wall surrounding much of the back, and he could see the trees of their private Serenity Garden over the top of the stone wall.

He walked down the center of the mist-shrouded street. It was empty but for the Armati that patrolled in response to the earlier threat. The Patricians were no doubt huddled in their homes, discussing the shocking events of the Founder's Day celebration. Afraid to go out. Afraid of further chaos. He thought again of Aerina. Would tonight's violence dampen her vivacity? Would her fearlessness be replaced by the same restraint bred into other Patricians?

It doesn't matter, he told himself again. She was nothing to him. Any connection they had was over now that he'd paid his debt.

Out of long habit, his dark eyes scanned the night, looking for anything out of place. Inconspicuous street lamps glowed eerily in the mist that blew off the ocean. Everything felt damp and the air was heavy. Taking a deep breath of the thick, wet air, Marcus rolled his shoulders. He had spent the morning training recruits, and the fighting had been intense. He needed another few bouts to work off the lingering frustration, he thought, his eyes again going to the darkened villa where Aerina recovered.

Turning away from his own villa, Marcus strode to the Training Grounds where his men slept.

It would be a long night for all of them.

Chapter 3

"Freedom is the right to tell people what they do not want to hear." - George Orwell

Aerina sat staring in the Serenity Pool, her holoreader in her lap. She had been doing her university classes from home, viewing the material and dictating any homework. Besides a short, secretive conversation with her best friend Lina over their holoreaders, Aerina hadn't had contact with another Patrician since "the Incident". That was how her parents euphemistically referred to her near-death and subsequent exile.

It had been nearly two weeks and she was already going crazy with boredom. Sighing deeply, she clicked the button that neatly folded her holoreader to a small square that attached to her bracelet. The Engineer Caste had become quite clever with their gadgets.

Idleness was contrary to her nature. The whirl of social activities, classes, and occasional subterfuge had come to an abrupt end. Marcus may not have killed her, but he had very effectively murdered her social life. She'd even been avoiding her foolhardy yet exciting adventures to the lower terraces. Now she was just staying home and slowly expiring from boredom. A much more diabolical punishment than public execution, she thought wryly. Too much more of this, and she really would end up like Jana Littleton.

From her window that morning she had seen some great waves crashing against the coast. Several Plebs had been carrying their boards down to catch the waves before going to whatever menial labor awaited them, and even a few Patricians had joined the sport. Before The Incident, she might have been one of them.

The day had passed uneventfully. Just like the day before, and the day before that. She had eaten the evening meal with her parents before wandering to the gardens to try and get more homework done. Which was pointless. She couldn't focus. State politics. History. It was all seeming so meaningless to her.

With a sinking feeling, she acknowledged that her chances of becoming an active voter were slim. Who would recruit her now?

She'd taken her status for granted; flaunted her defiance of the State's traditions and laws. And now she was paying the price.

She knew she should consider herself lucky she hadn't paid the ultimate price, as the other dancers had. The pressing sorrow that filled her at the thought of the other dancers was like a weight in her stomach that at times rose in her throat, threatening to choke her.

Why hadn't he killed her?

Her hand drifted to her neck at the thought of the leader of the assassins. It still bore evidence of his assault. A no-doubt lasting scar that marked her forever as a deviant; an outcast from her aristocratic peers.

This is all your fault.

The burden of shame had followed her from childhood. From one bad decision that had altered her life. It seemed that every time she tried to elude the weight of regret, it only grew worse. Her life changed yet again. And she had no one to blame but herself.

A defiant spirit rose from the crushing weight of self-blame. This didn't have to be her future. She could be Jana. Or she could be free. It was still her choice. She was still alive.

The great burden of abject desolation seemed to lighten. Yes, she'd lost a lot. But she needed to focus on what she still had. In a way, besides her life, she had nothing left to lose. This was a chance for her to forge a new life. Perhaps even start over.

To have a life she'd always thought impossible.

Aerina walked slowly down the softly lit street. The neat cobblestoned ways were nearly empty at this time of night on the Capitol Terrace. In the distance, the quiet hum of an e-car partnered with the soft flow of headlights. It turned away, the hum fading away in the calm night. The streets were once again deserted. Aerina glanced around quickly, feeling unusually nervous. Security was always around, unseen. She'd never been as aware of that as she was tonight.

She had worn a simple white top that fastened on each shoulder and draped delicately down in front to band low on her hips. The back was bare. She had put on tight white pants that hugged her slender legs—what she felt was her best feature. Because of the chill brought in with the mist, she had grabbed a light ermine jacket that fit snuggly around her rather modest chest and small waist.

It was also white.

It always baffled her that the founders hadn't been a little more selective in choosing a symbolic color for the ruling class. A royal purple would have been nice, and much easier to keep clean.

She did have to admit the unrelenting white was striking; intimidating, even. And on a moonlit night like this, her white stood out conspicuously against the dark backdrop of the well-manicured neighborhoods.

The hand-laid cobblestone streets were lined with stone sidewalks connecting each villa. Most villas glowed from within as the inhabitants of the Capitol Terrace went about their evening activities. Aerina picked up her pace when she passed the familiar villas of classmates or her parents' friends. For all her brave thoughts earlier, she wasn't ready to face anyone yet.

It didn't take her long to reach Marcus' small villa. The head of the Virmortus lived on the southeast part of the terrace, near the Training Grounds. Before she could have a second thought, she knocked on the heavy door.

A few errant butterflies took flight in her stomach as she waited, the dim, misty night seeming even more foreboding as she stood before his unlit door. What was she doing? What would she say? *I've come for you to finish the job?*

Then the door swung open silently and she was standing face-to-face with her almost-killer. It was too late to turn back now.

The object of her secret fantasies, and a few nightmares, stood before her, as intimidating as ever. His large, well-honed form filled the doorway. Broad shoulders blocked most of the light from within, nearly the breadth of the frame. He was still dressed in his Virmortus attire, minus the armored weapon vest. The black pants and snug t-shirt only further emphasized the power he radiated even without any weapons. Like all the Virmortus, he was clean shaven and his hair clipped short. His face was square, his nose blunt and slightly crooked, as if it had been broken a time or two. She had noticed over the years new scars that appeared on his cheek, forehead, and a few that disappeared under his clothing. But what caught and held her attention, as always, were his dark eyes. A deep brown that was nearly black, his eyes were always watching, cataloguing, judging. They revealed nothing; masking so much. She *ached* to learn what lay behind those shadowy orbs.

His inscrutable gaze dropped to her neck, and it was all she could do not to cover the fading bruises and abrasions with her hair. Instead, with the familiar brash confidence she used to cover her insecurity, she tossed her loose hair behind her back and took a small step forward, almost touching his chest. She had to tilt her head up, way up, to meet his eyes.

"Admiring your handiwork?" she asked flippantly. His dark eyes flew to hers, still unreadable. *Just like always*, Aerina thought with an inward sigh. If she had hoped to garner a reaction, she was going to be disappointed.

"Can I come in, or are you going to have to strangle me again if I am caught *fraternizing* with you? After all, I might pose a threat to your, um, person," she finished, her eyes scanning his form with deliberately insulting slowness. The perusal had been meant as a joke, but the rebel butterflies in her stomach began doing summersaults as she studied the hard chest before her nose.

After a long moment, Marcus stepped back. She was forced to brush past him, and a tingling awareness spread from where she came in contact with his muscular form.

She walked slowly into his villa, her eyes taking in the small and perfectly neat space. His villa was one large area with only pillars to divide the immaculate rooms. She saw stairs in the back that led to the roof. No Serenity Garden softened the white stone. The back of his villa was built into the cliff.

The silence stretched between them, but surprisingly Aerina did not find it uncomfortable. Charged, certainly. The energy crackling between them felt as if it could ignite the dry tinder in the real stone fireplace.

She stepped further in, absently picking up a game piece from a chess board set out on the kitchen table. Scanning the board, she moved the piece forward.

"You're in check," she stated, glancing at him, wondering if he caught the double meaning.

His eyes gave away nothing, although he did take a moment to study the board. He advanced slowly. She refused to take a step back as he approached, standing her ground until he was almost touching her. He leaned forward and she forgot to breathe. His dark eyes were so close she could see green-gold specs in their nearly black depths.

He smelled glorious, like the evening mist, weapon oil, and the slight musk of a man who's worked hard. She could feel the heat from his body, and a thrill that was part fear and part excitement shot through her.

Closer still came his harsh, roughhewn face and then… he reached around her. And moved another piece on the board. She let out a breath she wasn't aware she'd been holding. Her heart beat rapidly, and he was so close, she was convinced he could feel it. If his mouth was just a few inches lower…

"Your move." His words, the first spoken that evening, brought her back from her moment of fantasy. She shot him a sideways glance, ruefully acknowledging his own double entendre. *Touché.* She looked back at the board. He had moved his knight to protect the king, and she would need to retreat or lose her queen.

Frustration began to overcome her serene facade. "I didn't come to play chess," she said, moving away from the board, averting her face from his knowing eyes. She was afraid his close scrutiny would reveal the turmoil beneath her blasé demeanor.

Her searching eyes glimpsed a massive bed in the room beyond. An image of his powerful body relaxed in sleep popped unbidden into her mind. The heat she'd felt at his nearness settled a little lower. *What's wrong with you?* She chastised herself. *This man almost killed you.*

But he didn't.

"I wanted to thank you. For not killing me." She met his eyes again, those perpetually empty pools showing no sign of emotion. *And I want to ask you why.* She wasn't bold enough to ask the question plaguing her for the last weeks.

She could feel his gaze, feel it penetrating her false bravado, delving beneath her carefully crafted mask. But he said nothing. After a long pause, he nodded his head once in acknowledgement of her thanks and walked slowly to the door, opening it.

"Ok, I can take a hint." With a jerky movement, she moved a piece on the board before walking out, her low heels clicking on the tile floor. She didn't look back.

Marcus watched Aerina stride boldly towards her villa, her white clothes making her a beacon in the dark mist. The gentle rhythm of her body revealed her years of genteel upbringing. He took a deep breath to calm his over-heated body. Just proximity to the brazen little Patrician made his blood heat with frustrated desire.

He closed the door with a barely audible click. Every action he made was measured, careful; silent. Repeatedly taught over his years in training to become a Virmortus, it was now part of his nature.

He studied the chess board. One dark brow lifted when he saw the move she chose to take. It sacrificed her rook, but would allow her to take his knight. Her near-death experience hadn't reformed her at all. Satisfaction moved through him slowly at the realization. He squashed it quickly.

Her visit had caught him off guard, an unusual occurrence for him. He'd gotten the sense she wanted something from him, but he wasn't entirely certain what. It didn't take a highly intuitive individual to surmise that she was feeling the effects of the blatant rejection by her caste.

But why come to him?

He was the last person who would be able to help her; to reinstate her to the former charmed position as a Senator's daughter.

One thing was certain—she was dangerous. A ray of light in his perpetual night, she threatened his carefully cultivated control. He'd meant it when he'd said it was her move. And she'd left, not quite running in the opposite direction, but close enough. He should be glad he had gotten rid of her so easily.

But he wasn't.

Chapter 4

"You cannot find peace by avoiding life." - Virginia Woolf

"I still can't believe you never told me about moonlighting as a Pleb," Aerina's best friend Lina repeated for the fifth time. She seemed more upset about Aerina's secrecy than her association with other castes. Lina had agreed to accompany Aerina on a trip to the beach on the condition that they met early on the Ferry instead of the Patrician tram. The entire ride down through the terraces, she had vented her frustration about being kept in the dark.

"I told you, I didn't want to make you an accomplice or force you to lie for me." Aerina repeated absently. *And I knew you would try to talk me out of it, and then accidentally tell someone*, she added silently. She leaned back on her beach chair, watching the surfers cutting through the spray with envy. Studying her friend, she let the lingering resentment fade away. Lina was risking her own social standing just by being with her.

As Lina continued to chatter, her mind drifted to the night before; to Marcus. She still felt the heat of embarrassment over showing up at his house uninvited and basically being asked to leave.

Embarrassment wasn't the only type of heat she felt thinking of the excitingly dangerous man. The near-death experience hadn't altered her fascination with the Virmortus leader. She opened her mouth to tell Lina about the evening, but snapped it closed again from long habit. Some things she couldn't even share with her best friend.

Desire for the State's head assassin was one of them.

She looked over at her friend with affection. They had been friends since nursery school, despite their differences. Lina was Aerina's physical opposite—her hair dark brown and Patrician-short, her figure tall and curvy. Voluptuous was the word Aerina used, but a less kind individual might say *chubby*. Her personality was also the ying to Aerina's yang. Quiet, unassuming, and sometimes overly cautious, she had such a kind heart that everyone couldn't help but love her. Aerina's own brash nature tended to offend many of the Patricians.

"I suppose I forgive you. But honestly, you almost *died*, Aerina. Watching that Reaper put his hands on you...I thought..." Lina shook her head, her eyes misting. "I don't think I could survive being a Patrician without you."

"I feel the same about you, sister." Aerina rested her head for a moment on her friend's sun-warmed shoulder.

The private beach reserved for Patricians was nearly empty this early in the morning. Only the diehard surfers and a few runners braved the mist to enjoy an unexpectedly warm September morning.

Aerina pulled her wide-brimmed hat down lower over her face, which was partially covered by her largest pair of all-purpose glasses. In the bright sun, they had automatically darkened to hide her eyes and face from view. For her friend's benefit, she had dressed incognito. She felt like a pre-war celebrity, hiding from the paparazzi.

"Are you going to be able to finish University on time?" Lina asked, throwing her light blanket off as the sun burned the mist away.

"Yes, I've been doing my work at home and watching the lectures remotely on my holoreader."

"You turn 21 in a few months and you'll need to choose your Voting Sector. Have you been recruited by anyone yet?"

"Not yet."

Lina looked over with sympathy. "You specialized in Intelligence. But I am pretty certain after your recent actions, the Peace Sector is not going to recruit you."

Aerina smiled to herself. That was a huge understatement.

"Your father will probably take you into the Society Sector."

Aerina felt anxiety rise, nearly choking her. She stood and picked up a shell, tossing it into the surf. "I don't think I could survive living my life to vote on issues like penal codes, curfews, and proper garbage removal procedures."

"Society is important—it keeps us structured and preserves the peace." Lina sounded like she was quoting their socioeconomic textbook. Aerina shot her friend a wry glance.

"I know it's important. It's just so damn *dull*." Aerina's eyes followed a Pleb surfer as he caught a wave, riding it almost all the way to shore. He broke from the water and grabbed his board. As he walked towards the designated Pleb beach, his eyes slid over Aerina admiringly. Her white bikini suit emphasized the golden hue of her skin, and tiny gold threading shimmered like the highlights in her hair. She returned his gaze boldly, arching one golden eyebrow above her glasses as if daring him to say something.

"Then what are you going to do?"

Aerina looked away from the passing surfer to meet her friend's concerned gaze.

"Before all this, I was hoping to talk to the Consul about joining the Outside Emissary."

"Aerina, you know the Emissary rarely takes on apprentices. The Consul doesn't use him often enough."

"That is what I wanted to change." Aerina dropped back onto the sand, gesturing animatedly. "I want to make contact with more of the Post-War cities and learn what the rest of the world is doing. Perhaps even establish trade—"

"Our isolation policy has kept Alba successful for nearly a century. Why fix something that isn't broken?"

"Don't you ever wonder what is out there?"

"Sometimes, I guess. Mostly I just don't think about it."

"Wouldn't it be exciting to find out? To learn more about the world that exists all around us?"

"A world that is dangerous, and could ultimately bring us back to the state our founders wanted to avoid—war." Lina shook her head with confused disapproval. "Aerina, I can't believe you are arguing against the basic tenets of our society. Even a Pleb or Aggie learns that lesson in their schools."

"The world needs to change to survive. People need change. We can't exist in a state of limbo forever," Aerina stated quietly.

The breeze off the ocean picked up, blowing her unbound hair around her face. Lina pushed back her much shorter locks in annoyance.

"I understand what you are saying. But I still think we shouldn't rock the boat. Let the Consul and his Virmortus worry about the balance. We just need to do whatever job we are assigned."

"It doesn't matter now. I'll be lucky if I get to vote on garbage removal at this point," Aerina said half-jokingly. She didn't agree with her friend, but she also knew they would never see eye-to-eye on this issue. She ached to go outside — to see what the world was like beyond the Alban walls. The world was out there, waiting to be discovered. Explored.

And perhaps it would find its way inside Alba, whether the Patricians liked it or not.

The day at the beach with Lina was relaxing once they steered away from discussing contentious subjects like politics and Aerina's sad future. She was surprised how good it felt to spend time with an old friend that didn't sneer or turn away in disgust. Lina had dropped her off before heading out to the Theatre with a group of their university friends.

"I would invite you, but I'm pretty sure they would refuse to sit with you," Lina explained apologetically. Aerina forced a smile and shrugged. Forget them anyway if they were such shallow friends.

So she'd done more homework in her bedroom, watching hologram files of debates and the process of new protocol implementation.

Boring. So. Very. Boring.

Rolling onto her back on her bed, she held up her *white* pillow and screamed in frustration into the downy fluff.

"Are you alright, dear?" Her mother stuck her head around Aerina's door, a look of concern on her delicate features, so like Aerina's.

"Yes, just relieving a little stress," Aerina said with a wan smile.

Her mother stepped into the room, concern in her pale blue eyes. She sat on the edge of Aerina's bed, wearing her normal work outfit of a white pencil skirt and tidy blouse.

"I know it is difficult. But people's memories are short. The scandal will fade in time and soon everything will go back to the way it should be," her mother said reassuringly.

"That's what I am worried about," Aerina muttered under her breath. Her mother's eyebrows drew together in alarm.

"Aerina, I worry that you don't properly appreciate the position of privilege and responsibility you have been born into."

Aerina sighed, sitting up in her bed. She could see the lights of a large fishing boat heading towards the docks far below. The dockside bars would be packed tonight with crew and the girls that serviced them.

"I probably don't appreciate it like I should," she admitted. "I try, I truly do."

"Your father and I just want what's best for you. For you to find your place; the role that you are meant to fill." Aerina looked at her mother's impeccable hair, perfectly tailored clothes, and tranquil features. *That will never be me,* she thought in near despair. Where did she belong? Because it certainly wasn't here, in this world of perfection. And it wasn't with the Plebs; she'd learned that lesson painfully.

"Can I ask you something personal?" Her mother nodded encouragingly. "Why did you never have another child, after — "

"Your father and I felt that it would be best to focus our attention on you," her mother cut her off, as she always did, when Aerina was about to mention the forbidden word in their household.

Max. Her little brother.

"But why not adopt? The Law of Two says — "

"I am quite familiar with the basic laws of our State," her mother interrupted again, more coldly this time. "If you ever have a child of your own, you will understand the depth of despair a mother feels after losing one." Her voice was thin, as if she were trying to fight back tears.

This is all your fault!

Aerina immediately felt the familiar crushing guilt rising to the surface.

Why can't you love me like you did before? Why can't you be proud, or disappointed, or angry — something that shows me you care? All those questions rose inside her, threatening to outpour from her trembling lips.

"I'm sorry, Mother," she said quietly instead.

Her mother took a deep breath, continuing on a little more calmly. "We have been encouraged to adopt a child born to parents who have already used up their allotted two and whose third child applications have been rejected by the Population Control Sector. But the law never requires partners to have two children."

"I know," Aerina said softly. "I just wondered why you didn't choose to have another child. I suppose I don't want to be your only chance at having a perfect child. Because I'll probably fail."

Raina looked at her daughter chidingly. "Now Aerina, your father and I just want you to find your place. To be content with your status. We certainly don't expect perfection."

Aerina forced a smile, tamping down her self-protective flippancy with an effort. The words hurt.

"Thanks Mom. I guess it has been a little more difficult than I realized to be an outcast," she admitted ruefully. Her mother smiled reassuringly.

"The one thing you can count on is that things will change." The older woman patted Aerina's hand gently, studying her. "Perhaps if you cut your hair, it will be a way to show that you are changing. That you are accepting your place as a Patrician," she said encouragingly, picking up a heavy curl.

Cut her hair? Aerina instinctively pulled the silky strand from her mother's hand, turning it in the light, watching the crimson highlights gleam. Her hair was part of who she was — what she wished she could be. Free, wild, and untamed. She wasn't sure if she was ready yet to let go of that part of herself.

"I'll consider it," she told her mother instead. "Thank you."

"That's a good start," her mother replied approvingly, rising.

"Just think about it."

No amount of contemplation could change her circumstance. And no amount of meditation could cure the restlessness in her soul. Several hours after the disheartening talk with her mother, Aerina stepped out onto the stone patio in the front of the villa. Night had fallen, and she could see the brightly lit Theatre several blocks away. All her friends would be there, enjoying the latest show. Her parents had gone with their friends, also not inviting Aerina. It seemed everyone was there but her.

She turned in the other direction and meandered slowly down the darkened street. She knew one person on the Capitol Terrace who wouldn't be at the show. One who was as much an outcast as she.

Marcus' villa was dark when she strolled up the walk. She knocked on the door anyway. The only sound was the distant crash of the surf and some overactive birds nesting in the cliff above. She knocked a second time and waited an extra minute. He was either waiting her out or gone. Since he didn't seem to be the type to hide in his villa, it was probably the latter. Turning away with a disappointed sigh, she almost ran into a large form gliding up the walk.

She gasped in fright. "Do you have to sneak up on me?"

"Sorry," Marcus said in a tone that wasn't at all apologetic. He passed her, waving his hand quickly before the scanner to open the door. A muted beep was followed by the lock releasing, and the door sprung open. Not willing to sit on his doorstep like a recalcitrant pet, she followed him inside.

"Would you like to come in?" he asked sardonically as he turned on a light.

"Why yes, thank you for inviting me," her response was equally dry as she studied his broad back. For once, he seemed a little rough around the edges. His normally neat suit was dusty and had a slight rip on the shoulder. When he turned to face her, she saw a fresh cut on his cheek that looked as if the blood had been swiped away with an impatient hand, leaving a red streak through the dirt on his skin.

"Are you alright?" she asked after a moment of studying him.

"I'm fine," he replied without looking at her, setting a small pack down in the hall closet. She rolled her eyes, her gaze falling on the kitchen table.

She smiled in delight when she saw the chess set still on the table, untouched from her previous visit except for a counter movement from Marcus.

"You knew I would come back," she stated, glancing up at him with minor consternation mixed with pleasure.

He just raised one brow. "I believe in preparing for the worst case scenario," was his impassive response as he turned towards the bathroom. She narrowed her eyes at his retreating back. The man had a sense of humor. That was definitely a joke.

Or he actually disliked her. Pushing aside that thought, she chose to believe the former.

The sound of running water came through the wall and a moment later he came back out, shirtless. He had washed his face and neck, and stray water droplets trickled down the deep grooves that delineated each muscle on his chest and abdomen. She watched, fascinated, unable to glance away.

Heading towards what looked to be the newest model of Wardrobe, he hit a button and a new shirt popped out. As he turned away, she gasped at the sight of his back. A huge purple-black bruise spread from his shoulder to mid-back, emphasizing old scars covering the muscled expanse.

"What happened?" she asked as he pulled the clean shirt over his head.

"It's Friday," he said shortly in response.

"Ok...?"

"Haven't you ever heard the saying about curiosity and the cat?" he answered her unspoken question in a quiet tone she assumed was meant to sound intimidating.

"What, are you going to kill me for asking too many questions?" she replied scornfully, unimpressed with his not-so-subtle threat. "Haven't *you* ever heard the one about the boy who cried wolf? Your constant threats of death have lost their sting."

His mouth quirked at the corner in an almost-smile. She couldn't stop her own answering smile, a feeling of exaltation spreading through her. She'd been the one to bring a smile to his perpetually grim face.

He nodded, as if giving her that point. He lowered himself to the couch slowly, but dust still wafted from his pants. He probably wanted to take a shower, she thought. She should politely excuse herself so he could shower and relax, as he obviously needed to.

But the thought of the empty house that awaited her was too much to bear. *It's not like he couldn't shower while I'm here, if he really wanted to...* she thought, only slightly ashamed of the excitement that thought engendered.

"On Friday, I take the new recruits out to the desert so they can test their skills," Marcus finally answered her question, much to her surprise. Aerina turned a kitchen chair around to face him in the living room, leaning forward.

"Did one of them catch you unawares?" she asked after a long silence.

Marcus' mouth quirked again in his almost-smile. "They would wish that were the case. I'd never hear the end of it. No," he shook his head in disgust. "One of them triggered a rock slide. I got hit by a boulder grabbing him and another recruit as they tumbled down the hillside."

"That seems rather dangerous." Marcus just looked at her mutely. It *had* been a stupid comment; they were Virmortus. "Should you go see a Medella?"

He raised one brow.

"Fine. Men of death don't visit the doctor."

"Was there a reason you came here tonight?" he asked finally, leaning his head back on the couch and watching her through narrowed eyes.

She opened her mouth, but no reason popped into her head. Her mind searched desperately.

"The assassin. I just wondered if you made any progress in the investigation. I need to clear my name, you know." It sounded pretty convincing to her ears. She was an outcast now, but it was doubtful that discovering the motive of the attack would change that.

He raised one brow again in that annoying way of his, his gaze assessing. She squirmed slightly. Of course he knew she wasn't being totally honest. But what did he expect her to say, the truth?

I came here because I can't stay away from you. Even after you almost killed me, kicked me out of your house, and practically rebuff any advance I might consider making, I'm infatuated with you like some adolescent. Yeah, that would go over well. He'd escort her to the door even faster than he did last night.

"Nothing new," he said shortly, casually rolling one shoulder. It must hurt like hell, she thought.

"Do you have some Num ointment? I could put it on—"

"I said I am fine," he delineated each word carefully.

"Hmm, prickly when we're in pain, aren't we?" she said beneath her breath, glancing back at the chess board. Narrowing her eyes, she studied his move. It was a good one. Either he'd worked up some skill playing against himself or he had someone to play against. Of course the leader of counterintelligence would be good at chess.

He was probably also good at poker.

But she was pretty good herself at the game of strategy. Leaning over the back of the chair, she moved her piece forward, leaving her finger on it until she was satisfied with her move. Glancing back to where Marcus lounged on the divan, she noticed him still watching her with half-closed eyes.

She suddenly wished that she'd spent a little more time on her appearance. Her white lounge pants and fitted short-sleeve button down were fine for doing homework, but probably wouldn't be helpful at attracting a man. Particularly this man, who didn't even spend more than a few moments looking at her.

Aerina underestimated her appeal. Marcus sat on the couch, watching her light up his villa with her vivacity. Her hair fell in waves around her shoulders, her casual clothes only serving to highlight her willowy form. And her feet were bare. Why that was what he found the sexiest, he couldn't say. He'd never cared about women's feet one way or another, but something about her painted toes and delicate arches...

He forced himself to relax, resisting the urge to shift to a more comfortable position to accommodate the new fit of his pants.

She was so blithely unaware of what he really was. If she fully grasped the depths of his sins, knew the violence he was capable of, she wouldn't be sitting so casually in his home. He should be disgusted by her naiveté; her ridiculous ideals. Instead, he found them charming. Her passion was refreshing, even if it was a little misguided. When she found something that she cared about, she put her whole self into it.

He wondered what it would be like if she decided to care about him.

Immediately he pushed the unwelcome thought from his head. Thinking like that was dangerous for both of them. He knew what he was — he had accepted it. Romance had always ranked low on his list of priorities. Even lust could be controlled. But there had always been something about her that had stirred him.

And now she was here. In his villa. Her eyes told him that she was willing to give in to the powerful attraction between them. With very little effort, he could probably have her, however he wanted. He was tempted to take what he wanted from her and get her out of his system. Once it was over, he could go back to focusing on things that mattered.

But instead of taking what he wanted, he sat on the damn too-small divan his decorator had selected and drank in the light of her presence. Because for all his control, he couldn't force himself to kick her out again. Not yet.

"Besides playing chess with yourself, what do you do in the evenings? You know, for fun," she asked, leaning back in the tall back kitchen chair.

"Sleep," he replied, not moving.

"Is that a not-so-subtle hint?" she asked in amusement. "Come on, you must do something. The theatre, bars, sport complex.... Brothels?" she threw in the last suggestion quickly, and he almost smiled at her transparency.

"I work hard," he replied quietly. "I don't have a lot of time for frivolity." Her face became shuttered, as if she understood the slur he had intended. A twinge of guilt rose inside him; so unfamiliar an emotion it took him a moment to realize what the uncomfortable sensation was. Her smile increased in wattage, becoming dismissive. It was an expression he'd become familiar with from her. He held back a sigh.

She was right about one thing. He hurt like hell.

He watched as she jumped to her feet and began to wander around his villa. She absently fondled some of the objects the decorator had selected. He hadn't paid much attention to what the woman had put in his home. It was comfortable, and the earthy color scheme suited him. That had been all that mattered. Although, the divan really was too damn small.

He found it fascinating how she couldn't be still for a moment. Or quiet. She was always moving, always fiddling with something, always curious. And her curiosity was dangerous. It had almost killed her once.

Her lithe body moved easily around the room, her hair shimmering in the low light as it slid over her shoulder.

"You used Penelope Strat, didn't you?" she asked, studying a framed print.

"Excuse me?" he said, his mind working quickly to understand the direction of her thoughts. She caught him off-guard more than any other person.

"The designer. She's only the most famous Pleb decorator. I recognize her touch. She redesigned my parents' house after... several years ago." Aerina had paused briefly before finishing.

After her brother had died, he figured she was going to say. He remembered the incident; hadn't given it much thought at the time. No one had discussed it then, and certainly not now.

Death was not something anyone liked to talk about, but the Patricians particularly avoided it.

It seemed strange to him. Perhaps it was because he dealt in death all the time, but everyone had to face death at some point. Their own and those around them. Why it was such a taboo subject was a mystery to him. His men learned to accept death, not to fear it. It was the most valuable lesson he could teach them. A man who didn't fear death was, in a word, fearless. And then the possibilities were endless.

"Yes, she did decorate it," he answered her question.

She finally turned to face him, a wry expression in her large blue eyes.

"I should go. You probably need to rest." Waiting a moment for him to respond, she headed towards the door, slipping into her delicate white moccasins. He stood politely, but didn't trust himself to get close enough to walk her out.

She walked out without a backward glance. He collapsed back on the couch. She'd be back.

If she had known of his confidence in her weakness towards him, she might have forced herself to wait longer to return. She was over the slight pique she felt at his apparent disinterest by the time she'd returned home that night. And now that she'd broken the ice, she couldn't seem to stay away. Instead of terrifying her, something about him made her feel calm. Comforted.

And so she found herself at Marcus' door the next night, the need to see him almost desperate after a particularly trying day.

She'd returned to the University in an act of rebellion. To show them she wasn't cowed; that she wasn't humbled. No one had actually forbidden her from attending class. So she'd dressed in her shortest tennis skirt that flared gently at mid-thigh, a woven shirt with intricate beading, and her tallest white pumps. A few swipes of make-up and she'd felt invincible.

It had been even worse than she'd feared.

She'd entered her first class early, and the few students in it had stared at her as if she'd contracted leprosy and lost a facial feature.

Then some had gotten up and left. Once the first wave had broken the ice, the entire class trickled out until just the Magister stood in front.

"I'm sorry, Aerina, I'm going to have to ask you to leave,"

he'd said snidely. As if she'd done something to offend him personally.

It took everything in her to keep her expression polite. "I'm so sorry I'll have to miss today's lecture," she'd murmured sarcastically, a gracious smile plastered on her face.

Mentally shrugging off the first class as a fluke, she'd sat in the University's large serenity garden with a latte, waiting for the next class.

The first student to notice her, a formerly friendly acquaintance, Katy, did a double take before hurrying in the opposite direction.

A small group of classmates wandered in, giving her looks that ranged from surprise to horror. Like she was the one who had murdered the entire dance troupe and their blood was still on her hands. *Was this how Marcus felt every day?* How awful it must be to live one's life like this. No wonder he had developed such thick skin.

"I can't believe she has the nerve to show up here," one of the girls said in a low voice to the group.

"I know," another agreed in an audible undertone. "I would think she'd at least have enough respect of this institution to stay away."

At that, Aerina stood, sauntering over.

"I can hear you, you know," she said dryly. "And it didn't take that much nerve to show up here. Once you've been strangled by a Reaper, this," she waved her hand to include the group and the school, "really pales in comparison."

Someone in the group gasped in shock at her boldness.

"You broke the Law of Segregation, and —" one of the boys began hotly.

"Spare me," Aerina interrupted, her deep blue eyes scanning the group contemptuously. "I'm the daughter of a Senator. I know the laws as well as you. I follow the spirit of the law if not the letter. Just as you do, Lance, when you visit the Pleb brothel every Friday. Or you, Becky, when you sneak around with your gardener. If that's not a pre-war cliché, I don't know what is," Aerina said in derision. Becky ducked her head, her cheeks flushing. Lance's unofficial match and girlfriend looked at him in fury, her own face getting as red as Becky's. "At least I have the *nerve* to display my mark, unashamed," Aerina finished quietly, flicking her hair back so the thin scars on her neck were visible.

The group immediately split, all talking at once. Lance's girlfriend was shouting. Aerina watched them scatter like cockroaches under a light with satisfaction. It was petty, she knew, but still gratifying. The feeling faded quickly, leaving behind the emptiness of a hollow victory. Turning with a sigh, she almost bumped into the men who had come up behind her.

Marcus stood with Consul Julius and the Outside Emissary, who was also a Magister of Social Studies. Aerina smiled sickly, forcing a higher wattage.

Only the Emissary seemed shocked by her behavior. The Consul regarded her thoughtfully, and Marcus had the tiny quirk at the corner of his mouth that indicated amusement.

Laugh it up, she thought in annoyance, directing her discomfiture and anger towards Marcus' impassive face. *You'd probably love it if Julius tells you to strangle me again. Then you'll never have to suffer my presence again.*

"Aerina," Consul Julius murmured politely in greeting, nodding his head. His light eyes crinkled in amusement. At least he didn't look as if he was going to sic Marcus on her. The Outside Emissary just stuck his nose in the air and looked past her. Lina was right—she'd lost any chance of working with that pretentious man.

Marcus said nothing, as always. The men then passed on without another word, leaving Aerina standing alone in the garden. Still an outcast.

She'd gone home, knowing the outcome if she were to try and attend another class. She'd caught sight of Lina across the University campus, but hadn't tried to greet her. She didn't think she could take public rejection from her best friend, and it wasn't fair to put Lina in that position.

The day home, alone, had only increased her desire to wallow in self-pity. To wrap the cape of rejection around herself. But moping about was so alien to her nature, she couldn't keep it up for more than a few hours. Then she ate the always-delicious dinner their cook had prepared. She shed the self-pity like an ill-fitting skin and decided to abandon the empty house.

She found herself outside Marcus' door, debating about knocking or just heading back home to give self-pity another try. Was she really ready for another rejection by the man who both fascinated and frightened her? Before she could remind herself that self-pity wasn't really her style, the door opened.

"Are you going to stand there all night?" Marcus asked in his normal expressionless tone.

"I was just out for some fresh air and happened to be on your street," she lied unashamedly. "I thought I would find out what your good buddy the Consul thought about my excursion to the University today."

Marcus fell back a step, leaving the door open in an unspoken invitation. "I don't think he cares one way or another." He walked back towards the coffee table where he had what appeared to be a weapon completely deconstructed. He picked up two pieces and carefully fit them together, glancing up at her as she closed the door behind her. "Although he did find your lecture amusing."

"Hmm. And you?" she asked, watching him through narrowed eyes as she stepped down from the entryway into the living room.

"I found you as stimulating as ever," he replied evenly, not looking up from his work. Aerina crossed her arms over her chest, not sure how to take that statement. Then his eyes flicked up for a moment, not traveling any higher than the long length of golden thigh exposed by her short, flirty skirt.

A small smile made its way across her face. He wasn't as immune to her as he pretended to be.

"You can wipe that smug smile off your face and sit. Help yourself to a drink," he commanded. She smiled even wider as she went to the Dispensare and selected sparkling juice.

"Do you want anything?" she asked as she picked up her glass.

"No thanks." He snapped the weapon together with amazing

swiftness.

"What is that?" she asked curiously, sipping the cold juice.

"One of the latest weapons from the Engineers," he said, fitting the cover over the front.

"What does it do?"

"It's a wireless detonator. The Armati plant explosives. The location of any enemy within one hundred yards will then appear on this screen," he showed her a small 3-D screen, "which can be used to select when and where the explosives should detonate. It also works with electrical currents that will pass through the ground to specified sectors on the map," he explained.

"May I?" She held her hand out and he placed the square-shaped device into it. She turned it over in fascination. A screen popped up with a holographic grid of the city.

"Electrical weaponry is popular now, isn't it," she asked, using her hand to twist the grid, studying the city's layout.

Marcus nodded. "Now that we've created a basically inexhaustible way to generate electrical energy, the weaponry is easy to create. It's cleaner, more efficient, and much more accurate than ballistic weapons." He plucked the weapon from her hand, shutting it down while walking to the back of the villa. His lean fingers quickly typed a lengthy code into his safe and he carefully stored the weapon amongst the impressive assortment that filled it.

Aerina turned towards the table, settling in to the chess game.

"My turn, I see." She rested her hand on her chin to study the move he had made since the previous evening. She crossed her legs, letting the skirt ride high on her thigh.

Marcus walked slowly up behind her, looking at the game over her shoulder. He was so close she could feel the warmth from his thighs against her back. She resisted the urge to lean back further. It was amazing how comfortable she felt with him, as if they had played chess together in his home for years.

Aerina made a tsking sound, moving her bishop to take his rook. "Bad move, darling. That was your last rook." Marcus said nothing, leaning over her shoulder. Aerina breathed in the scent of him, that familiar spicy musk that made her heart beat faster. His forearm brushed her cheek as he leaned forward, and she wanted to run her hand lightly over the fine dark hairs covering the sinewy muscle.

Her stomach clenched, those familiar mad butterflies taking flight. The fact that those arms could wrap around her and squeeze the life from her with little effort didn't alarm her as it should. The raw strength was coupled with an incredible control.

She was so absorbed in the essence of him, she almost missed his move. Her move had opened up a space for him to take her queen.

"You distracted me," she accused, studying the board in disbelief.

"I wasn't the one hiking my skirt up to my waist," was his cool retort.

"What?!" she exclaimed, a light flush covering her cheekbones. Damn, of course he would notice her pitiful attempts at flirtation. She resisted the urge to smooth the skirt lower. "The game isn't over yet," she muttered, studying the board with renewed vigor.

Marcus stood behind her for a moment longer, and she could swear she felt a light hand brush down her hair. And then he was moving away, leaving her to believe the touch was imagined.

"I am still looking into the attack at the southern outpost of West Ryan. It was most likely a raid." Marcus stood before the Consul the next morning, giving his daily report. "I've heard from my man in the Republican State of Texaco. There is still no real government control, and raiding has become a major problem. These raids have been coming closer to our region. Just last week one of the outpost towns near old Los Angeles was hit." Marcus' holoreader projected a 3D map grid of the region, the towns hit by raiders highlighted in red.

The Consul smiled slightly. "The return of the Wild West, is it? I trust you can deal with that threat?"

"Of course. I am going to enlist several more Pleb and Aggie youths to the ranks of the Armati each month as a defensive safeguard. They are being trained on the new line of weapons just released by the Engineers. But the raiders are poorly armed and their transportation still depends on oil-based fuel, which is in low supply in this region. I don't consider them a great threat."

"Are they still using ballistic weapons?" Julius asked.

"Yes, they haven't updated to any of the new weaponry." Marcus paused, considering. "Ballistic weapons have so many disadvantages, particularly against the EMW and chemical technology. But I have to admit, speaking purely of psychological warfare, they are a good way to terrorize smaller settlements. The sheer volume of sound and gore can be quite intimidating."

"I'm fairly certain those hillbillies aren't thinking as far as that. They just like the boom and blood," Julius said in disgusted amusement. Marcus nodded his agreement. Julius paused a long moment, then asked: "Have you heard any news about the Southern Empire recently?"

Marcus resisted the urge to roll his aching shoulders. He had spent another long night in the sparring ring after Aerina had gone home. One of his newest recruits seemed to be particularly promising in hand-to-hand combat. Worst of all, it hadn't taken the edge off the sexual tension caused by close proximity to Aerina. The desire was becoming more and more difficult to control.

"Nothing recent. News of the Southern Empire is rare. For many years after the Global War, they kept a low profile to stay under the radar of the European Alliance. But after the European uprising a few decades ago, the outpost towns have begun spotting a few scout vehicles. Rumors of their weaponry has spread. If they ever did decide to attack, the ballistics of the Texaco rebels would seem like children's toys. Fortunately, the scouting vehicles haven't been seen in several years."

"No news is good, then. And the internal threat?"

Marcus debated for a moment on how much to tell the

Consul about his concerns. The assassination attempt was more than just a group of unhappy citizens. Something bigger was going on, but without any facts to back up his suspicions, he wasn't ready to alarm Julius.

"I am still looking into it," he answered briefly, closing up his holoreader.

The Consul pursed his lips before nodding slowly. He obviously didn't care for Marcus' answer, but he knew the young man well enough to know that he would share any information he thought pertinent.

"Very well. Keep me informed."

Marcus nodded briefly before turning to exit.

"Marcus?" The Consul's voice stopped him, and he turned back.

"I trust you know what you are doing with the Delacroix girl?" Julius was leaning back in his chair, studying.

"Not really, sir," Marcus answered evenly. The Consul smiled at that, leaning forward.

"I was going to warn you to be careful, but I can see that isn't necessary." Julius stood and wandered over to the large windows looking out over the terraces far below. "She's a fascinating girl. A little misguided, perhaps, but with some maturity, she will make a great Senator. She's a natural leader; not afraid to ask questions, not apologetic for her decisions. I like that."

Marcus' brows rose at that. He would have expected the Consul to be a little more disapproving of Aerina and her careless flaunting of valued Alban laws.

"I'm glad it wasn't necessary to kill her," Julius added, turning back towards Marcus. "I hope you will help her see the side of Alba that she needs to better understand. I see a bright future for her."

Marcus nodded slowly, understanding that Julius was giving his approval, whether Marcus required it or not. They both knew Marcus only answered to the Consul because he chose to. As the revered leader of the Virmortus, Marcus held considerable power. Perhaps even more than the Consul himself. The day might come where that power was put to the test. But Julius seemed content to share it for now, which would no doubt change in future generations.

Exiting the Meeting Room, Marcus came face-to-face with the next generation of leader. Niko, the Consul's son, had been obviously lingering outside the room, eavesdropping. He wore his perpetual sneer.

Marcus stepped aside politely to let the heir enter the Meeting Room. Niko brushed past him without a word, intentionally bumping his shoulder against that of the larger man. Marcus remained immovable and Niko bounced further back, hitting the door jamb. Marcus watched the younger man impassively, although he mentally rolled his eyes at the childish behavior.

Niko glared hotly as he straightened away from the door, an inexplicable hatred burning in his blue eyes. The young man's bodyguard, a Virmortus that had trained alongside Marcus, followed his charge into the meeting room, nodding to Marcus respectfully.

Marcus turned away, hiding his own disgust. The heir to the Consulship was a complete idiot. He wished Julius would make more effort to groom his son to take over the position.

After the death of Julius' wife, Marcus had tried to drum up sympathy for her son. But Niko spent most of his days whoring, drinking, and living the life of luxury with his equally useless friends. Sympathy had been difficult; understanding damn near impossible.

Nothing matters but your job.

The day Niko took over the Consulship would be a sad day for the people of Alba. Marcus knew his own job would become much more difficult. All Marcus could do was wish Julius continued good health. And plan an unfortunate accident to befall the heir, if necessary.

Pushing those thoughts from his head, Marcus strode swiftly down the long hallway towards the courtyard. He had enough present problems to deal with without worrying overmuch about the distant future.

A group of Patricians passed him in the hallway, respectfully moving aside to give him plenty of room to pass. His black uniform, made of tightly woven metallic wool that was resistant to puncture yet lightweight, contrasted sharply with their white attire. He was like the shadow of a shark moving through a wave of light.

Everywhere were small reminders that he didn't fit in here. He'd felt that since he was small; since he'd lived with a father who couldn't stand the sight of him. Becoming adept at disappearing into the shadows had been a matter of survival. Now he spent most of his life there. It was what he was good at. He was a born hunter.

It was time to exercise his talent.

"I'd like to speak with you, Aerina." Aerina looked up sharply as her father walked into their family Serenity Garden. She was just finishing up her University project for graduation— her thesis on Balance and Evolution.

"Of course," she murmured, shutting down her holoreader. It folded itself into a tiny square, and she clipped it to her ivory bracelet.

Her father was dressed in a lightweight white business suit, attire that most Patricians wore while working. He sat down elegantly, twitching his slacks so they fell neatly over his white leather moccasin-style shoes. Patricians emphasized a careful balance between class and comfort in their attire.

Balance. Everything was about balance.

She tucked her own sandaled feet beneath her on the bench, letting the simple white dress she wore fall over her legs. She had only put on a light cardigan to ward off the slight chill of evening, and the cool ocean breeze spread goosebumps across her skin.

Antony motioned to the Pleb who was carefully pruning a shrub nearby. The young man nodded and left the garden. Antony turned towards his daughter.

"I need to know everything about the dance troupe you joined." Antony looked intently at the pool as he asked.

Aerina paused in surprise. It was not what she expected. She had thought her father was going to discuss her upcoming graduation and choosing a Voting Sector from her sadly limited options.

They hadn't discussed 'The Incident' at all. Both her parents were content to put it behind them and hope that Aerina had learned her lesson; that the Patricians would eventually forgive if not forget and the whole situation would just go away. Until then, they went about their lives as normal, preferring to pretend the unfortunate incident had never occurred.

Aerina wished her parents *would* chastise her. *Maybe then I would know they cared.* As soon as the thought entered her mind, she pushed it out. She knew they cared about her in their own way, but ever since her little brother... they hadn't been a family.

This is all your fault.

Focusing her attention back on her father's question, Aerina frowned.

"I don't know much. A friend of mine asked me to fill in, so I trained on the dance, but I didn't know any of the dancers well." Aerina twisted her valuable ivory bracelet absently. It had been a gift from the Consul on her sixteenth birthday. It was from the outside, which made it even more valuable to her. "What did you want to know?"

"We need to learn as much as we can about the assassin and her attempt to kill Julius. It is important that you remember as many details as possible."

"I normally would visit the dancers with an acquaintance, Julia, who is a professional dancer. She taught me the basics, and I danced in a few small performances at the Trinity Theatre, just the small one on the south side of the Theatre District on the Pleb terrace."

Antony nodded encouragingly for her to continue. His carefully cultivated expression didn't seem shocked or disgusted, as Aerina expected. Although her father hadn't become a Senator by wearing his heart on his sleeve, either.

"Julia is the one who asked me to fill in for the dancer who was sick; the girl's name was Mychel."

"Do you know how to find this Julia or Mychel?"

Aerina hesitated. She didn't want to get Julia in trouble — the girl worked hard to support her younger sister after both their parents were killed in a warehouse fire. "I'm not sure. I can find out."

Her father watched her intently for a moment before nodding. He understood.

"Do it quickly. The Consul, and the Virmortus, are eager to get this situation resolved."

Aerina nodded. She understood, too. He was warning her that the Virmortus were involved. *As if I hadn't noticed*, she thought, touching her neck absently. If only he knew how aware of the Reapers she actually was. At least one particular Reaper.

But he was right to warn her. The Reapers didn't care about caste or explanations. Their sole duty was to protect the Consul and preserve the peace in the city of Alba at any cost. They answered to no one but the Alpha Virmortus. All classes had learned a healthy respect for the power of the assassin caste; to fear the Reapers.

"I have a meeting. I hope you have been considering your choice for Voting Sector. You will be eligible for recruitment soon." Antony rose and offered her his hand, pulling her lightly to her feet.

"Yes, Father, I have been thinking about it."

"Good. We can discuss it further later." With a nod, he strode out through the garden gate, heading towards the Capitol.

She could see the Capitol above the villa, gleaming palisades and a golden dome with the Alban flag flying. The white stag. A symbol of peace and balance.

It would be dark soon. And the Plebs would be heading out to play after their long days at work.

She needed to warn her friend. The Reapers were hunting.

Chapter 5

What the ancients called a clever fighter is one who not only wins, but excels in winning with ease." - Sun Tzu

Aerina walked to the Ferry. Night had recently fallen, the dark horizon still awash in purple and blues. A strong wind from the east kept the mist at bay, and the nearly full moon gleamed brightly in a clear sky.

The familiar feeling of being followed sent a shiver down her spine that had nothing to do with the cool of the evening.

With one final look over her shoulder, the wind whipping her unbound hair across her cheek, she slipped onto the Ferry.

She made her way slowly through the large lower platform that was for vehicles to the top level, which was glassed in and had padded seating for passengers. Beside the private Patrician tram, this was the only route between the terraces, unless one was a mountain climber.

The attendant walked among the passengers, checking ID chips that connected each citizen to the Network. He didn't give her a second look, merely scanning her wrist and moving on. It wasn't unusual for Patricians to travel on the Ferry, and it was the only way get a car to the other terraces.

She was just thankful no Patricians had chosen to take the Ferry tonight. They would be bound to recognize her. Being a Senator's daughter that had nearly been executed made her infamous.

Aerina glanced over to where an Armati stood. His dark uniform, close cropped hair, and rigid stance made the soldier stand out from the other passengers. He was looking at her.

She gave him a small smile and slid her gaze away. *Play it cool. You're not doing anything wrong.* She was used to stares from soldiers and the working class alike. She wasn't conceited, but she knew it wasn't just her Patrician status that gained her second looks. Her delicate features, slender body, bright sapphire eyes, and long golden hair with hints of crimson combined to make her an attractive package. It also made her more memorable.

She hoped her ID wasn't being monitored. Aerina absently rubbed her wrist where the device lay, unseen, below the skin as the warning buzz sounded to indicate the Ferry was leaving.

The large tram slid down the hillside, stopping on the Merchant Terrace. From her high perch in the glass box, she idly watched the elegantly dressed Merchants and Engineers going out for the evening to their theatres, restaurants, and nightclubs. A few tired-looking Plebs entered, staying on the level below her, and in a few moments the transport ferried them towards the lower terrace.

The Plebeian Terrace slid slowly into view as the lights of the Merchant Terrace disappeared above them. Here, the buildings were packed together, and built high. A small park at the center, brightly lit now, was the only green in a jungle of brick building and cobblestone streets. The streets were packed with people, a few e-cars, and several work vehicles making late-night deliveries from the Agriculture Town.

Plebs in work uniforms heading home for the night mingled with skimpily clad girls heading out to the nightclubs. This terrace was the largest, spreading out to the beach and back towards the farmlands that covered the valley.

It was loud, chaotic, colorful, and Aerina loved it.

She exited the Ferry with only her light canvas pack, avoiding eye contact with the two Armati who stood guard at the entrance. She felt their eyes on her as she headed out towards the busy street, her heeled pumps catching on an uneven cobblestone and nearly throwing her to the ground at their feet.

Real cool, Rina. She stole a quick glance up to see them both trying to hold back smiles. Neither moved to assist her. Straightening, she picked up the pack that had fallen. Tossing her hair over her shoulder, she nodded coolly at them. *Thanks for nothing, assholes.*

Damn Pleb heels were much taller than her normal sandals.

She weaved through the throng filling the sidewalk. An

Aggie truck honked its horn loudly and repeatedly, causing the crowd to slowly part so it could makes its way down the narrow street.

She turned into an alley and ducked quickly into a restaurant through the side door, heading straight to the back. The pungent aromas of curried sauces filled her nostrils, making her stomach rumble lightly to remind her of the dinner she had skipped.

A small but clean restroom gave her the privacy she needed to change into her Pleb guise. She pulled off the white wrap-around dress and stuffed it into the dark blue pack she carried.

She now wore a black sheath with gold trim around the low neckline. She left her hair down, to match the popular Pleb style, and put on imitation gold teardrop earrings and a matching necklace. Hesitating, she decided to leave on the ivory bracelet with her holoreader. She wanted to be able to call someone in case of emergency.

She stood on the toilet and stuffed the pack on a high ledge in the bathroom.

As she walked down the lively street, the breeze picked up off the ocean, bringing in salty air. Her hair began to curl around her face, and she wished she had worn a dress with sleeves. Even though September was warm here on the Pacific coast, the nights were always cool.

After walking down several brightly lit blocks, she came to the Trinity Theatre. It was a large brick building on Lombard Street, named for a particularly well-known street in old San Francisco.

Heading around back, she glanced once over her shoulder. A few young men in an array of battered slickers leaned against the outside of a bar. Dockworkers, she thought. They manned the fishing boats, and were known to get rowdy.

One of them looked at her and nudged his friend. He smiled, and from across the street she could see his stained yellow teeth.

She slipped inside the Trinity's back door with a sigh of relief. The familiar worn wood floors smelled of polish and the muffled sound of music settled like a blanket on her frazzled nerves. Habit brought her to the large practice room. Julia was there, as always, preparing for the evening show.

The young woman who managed the Trinity's dance troupe was petite, her high cheekbones and almond-shaped eyes giving testament to her Eurasian descent. But what she lacked in stature she more than made up for in sheer presence.

"Step, step—no Bruce, higher. You need to throw her higher. Perfect. And again!" Julia moved in rhythm with the song, calling out counts as her troupe performed. They were spectacular.

"Take five!" Julia called and turned, noticing Aerina.

"Aerina!" Her shocked gaze darted around as if checking for Armati. "Come with me," she said quietly, taking Aerina's arm and ushering her into a tiny office.

"Sit down," she gestured to the single chair in the cramped space. Aerina shook her head.

"You sit; you look like you've been on your feet for a while."

With a shrug, Julia dropped into the battered chair. It gave a protesting creak as she leaned back. Aerina perched on the edge of the small desk.

"I'm sorry about the dancers," Aerina said quietly. Julia remained silent for a long moment.

"I just can't believe they're all dead. What a horrible tragedy. Mychel is still in shock." Julia shook her head. "To think she would have been caught in the fire had she not been ill."

"Fire?" Aerina repeated. Then realization struck. "They told you the dancers all died from a fire?"

Julia gave her a strange look. "Yes, I was told they all died in a dressing room fire—all of them except you. When they never returned, I sent someone to find out what had happened. The Capitol Medella wouldn't give me any information. Then later, a representative of the Patricians came and told the families that all the women had been killed in a fire."

"Oh Julia," Aerina breathed, shocked at the cover-up. "They were killed by Reapers."

Julia just looked at her, her dark eyes wide. She ran a shaky hand through her long black hair. "Why? I knew the story sounded odd. Fires are rare here with all our precautionary measures." Julia tapped her foot and then rose to her feet, obviously agitated. "What happened?"

Aerina told her the story of the attempted assassination and subsequent execution of the troupe. She then went on to tell her about her father's questioning.

"They are going to be looking for you, at least for questioning. Mychel too," Aerina warned her. "I'm sorry it took me so long to come and talk to you. I didn't realize they would be suspicious of you. And I guess I was too caught up in my own situation," she finished apologetically.

"Damn." Julia rubbed her hands over her eyes. "I had heard rumors about a Reaper execution on the Capitol Terrace, but we always hear rumors. I never thought... Damn," she said again, slumping further in her chair.

The door opened suddenly, making both women jump. Aerina smiled widely at the young girl that entered. She was like a smaller version of Julia.

"Jamia!" She hurried over to hug Julia's little sister.

"I haven't seen you around for a few weeks. How's life on the Capitol Terrace?" Jamia asked, squeezing Aerina back tightly. The open affection was always a welcome change from the more reticent greetings of the Patricians.

"Just as 'unbalanced' as ever," she replied, sharing a look with Julia.

She glanced at the clock, straightening quickly. "I've got to get my dancers on stage. Can you meet me later, after the show? Our usual place, at the Surfside Bar?"

"Sure," Aerina agreed, proceeding Julia from the office.

Aerina stayed to watch the show with Jamia and a few of her school friends. After seeing the younger girl off home, she walked with the group of dancers to the bar down the street. Plebeian Terrace was relatively safe, but Aerina couldn't shake the feeling of being watched.

The dancers talked excitedly about the show, which was more popular than most, and had been running for some time. They'd even attracted some Merchants and Patricians to the

Trinity.

Julia had told Aerina she'd rather her dancers not know the truth about the executed dancers. They were having a difficult enough time dealing with the loss of their colleagues.

The Surfside was near the docks. It was loud, crowded, and its clientele ranged from dockworkers to Aggies, and a few slumming Merchants.

Aerina slid in the booth beside Julia and ordered a fruit drink. Patricians generally abstained from drinking because of the negative side effects. Apparently it was difficult to retain one's sense of serenity and balance when intoxicated. Of all the new experiences Aerina had been tempted to try, consuming alcohol hadn't been one of them.

The bar was dimly lit but it couldn't hide the grime coating the booths, and Aerina felt her dark pumps sticking to the floor. She didn't care. She loved the excitement, the loud chatter, and occasional bursts of laughter. Usually there was a space cleared on the floor for dancing, and the windows were always open to let in the ocean breeze to cool sweaty bodies.

This was how life was meant to be experienced — in all its filthy glory.

"Tell me more about the girl; the assassin," Aerina shouted in Julia's ear.

"Her name was Cassandra." Julia leaned close to be heard over the noise. "She was the daughter of an Aggie. But she worked really hard to join Mychel's troupe. They often performed at Patrician events and at the Serenity Theatre."

"What would make her willing to do it? She must have known it would lead to her death."

Julia just shook her head in bewilderment, tucking a strand of silky black hair behind her ear. "I didn't know her well. You should talk to Mychel — she worked with Cassandra." Julia glanced quickly around the room before leaning in again. "She should be here soon; her show runs a little over every time."

Just then, a loud commotion drew their attention to the back door. A group of men were shoving their way into the bar. They scanned the room and their gazes fell on Aerina. One nudged his friend and motioned to her.

"Shit. Trouble," Aerina muttered, more to herself than to Julia.

"Do you know them?" Julia's eyes followed the men as they worked their way through the crowd towards their table.

"No, but I noticed them noticing me back at the Theatre. I have something they want, and I don't think it's my rockin' body." Aerina lowered her hands below the table, wishing again for long sleeves, this time to cover her valuable bracelet.

"Oh, don't be modest. You know you have a body to kill for," Julia joked to cover her concern. Her eyes were scanning the room for the bouncer or perhaps an Armati that would be willing to help. The Armati presence had been heavy on the streets but was conspicuously absent here near the docks.

"Can I buy you ladies a drink?" The first man bellied up to their high table. Julia carefully moved her drink away from his protruding gut. He rested muscular forearms on the table, leaning forward with a grin that showed yellowed teeth. His watery eyes remained fixed on Aerina. Aerina did her best not to grimace.

"We're all set, but we appreciate the offer," Julia told him politely.

"We insist," said a second man, his eyes also on Aerina as he waved over a server. He was a little cleaner than his friend, but in a shifty, drenched-in-cologne kind of way. Some of the other dancers looked at each other in discomfort.

"No really—" Aerina placed her hand on Julia's to stop her. Their best strategy would be to just accept the drinks graciously and hope the men would leave.

Twenty minutes later, that hope was crushed. The men had settled in, one even squeezing in next to Julia in the circular booth. The big gut one with bad teeth.

One by one, Julia's dancers were excusing themselves. Some were dancing on the crowded floor, while a few left the bar completely until only Aerina and Julia and the group of men surrounded the high top table.

A few minutes later, two Armati walked in, the crowd

parting before them as they made their way over to talk with the bartender. Julia looked at Aerina, who nodded. This was their best chance. The dockworkers wouldn't try anything with soldiers in the bar. Everyone knew that to mess with an Armati would bring a Reaper to your door.

"We really appreciate the drinks, but I think we should probably be going. Early morning tomorrow." Julia smiled as she swiped her wrist on the table scanner for the bill, pressing the button to confirm her purchase, and grabbed her purse.

"Sure," the man sitting next to her said congenially, sliding out to let her pass. Aerina murmured her thanks and slid out behind Julia. The man's hand trailed 'accidentally' across her breast. She held back a shiver of revulsion. The two women made their way towards the exit.

"They're not following," Julia murmured. Both women exited the bar with relief.

"Let's go back to the Theatre. We can talk there. I'll call Mychel and see if she can stop in," Julia said.

Aerina walked quickly with Julia back towards Lombard Street, looking back over her shoulder a few times. The streets were still filled with people enjoying the nightlife, but the evening had taken on a sinister undertone.

"I never used to feel so jumpy. This whole situation must be affecting my nerves," Aerina said. Her feet hurt from walking in the heels, and the evening had gotten even colder. She hugged her arms close, goosebumps following the breeze across her skin.

"I know what you mean," Julia agreed. "They were probably just dockworkers looking for an easy lay." They turned onto Lombard Street. The Theatre was dark now, but the bar across the street was still busy.

Aerina felt a prickling on her neck and glanced quickly back. She thought she saw a shadow scuttle into an alley behind them, but couldn't be sure in the dim light.

They headed down the side alley to the back door of the Theatre. Most of the light from the street was blocked, and Aerina jumped at the skittering of tiny feet. Yuck, rats.

Julia glanced back and laughed. "You get used to it." She was about to turn back towards the door when her eyes went wide. Aerina's heart skipped at the expression on her friend's face. A heavy hand fell on her shoulder, grabbing and flinging her to the ground.

The shadowy world swirled. Aerina hit the cement with a gasp, catching herself on her hands and knees. Before she could recover, a booted foot kicked her in the chest, sending her sprawling.

Aerina coughed, trying to get her breathe, the pain shocking. She had never been hit in her life. She felt disoriented, staring in shock for a moment at the boots in front of her face.

She heard Julia scream as another man stepped into her narrow view, shoving her small friend against the unopened theatre door.

"Give us the bracelet and no one gets hurt," the man standing over Aerina said harshly. His words seemed to echo in the silent alley. She looked up from her prone position. It was the big gut man who had sat next to Julia at the bar. He was close; so close she could smell the sweat and fish stink that clung to his slicker.

Aerina cursed her decision to keep the bracelet on. It was extremely valuable, and these men could undoubtedly sell it to a wealthy Merchant or even a Patrician.

Aerina considered running, but knew she couldn't leave her friend behind. With a shaky hand, she unlatched the delicate bracelet. The man grabbed it from her.

"Thanks, lovely. Now that we've concluded our business, how about a little fun?" His friends detached from the shadows, laughing in agreement. The one holding Julia ran his hand down her breast and shoved it between her legs. Julia knocked back against the door, staring at him stoically.

Aerina felt rage burning in her, overcoming her immobilizing fear. Adrenaline pumped hotly through her, giving her much-needed courage. Her frozen limbs melted from the heat, tensing in preparation. Big Gut had turned to look at his buddy molesting Julia. Taking advantage of his distraction, she slowly removed her pumps.

Everything happened quickly, from a distance, as if she were watching a holofile of someone else. Holding the shoe tightly, she launched herself past Big Gut at the one holding Julia, slamming the sharp heel as hard as she could into his temple. She felt the thin heel break through flesh and hit bone with a sickening yet satisfying thud. The man cried out and collapsed to the ground, but his friends closed in quickly.

"That little bitch just took out Jax!" one of the men said in disbelief.

"She'll pay," Big Gut sneered, smiling evilly. "And then we'll get paid for the fun we're about to have. He said he wanted her dead. He didn't say how or in what condition to leave her body," he added with relish, practically licking his lips in anticipation.

Aerina heard the words, but in the moment the meaning barely registered. She faced the group, holding her bloodied shoe at ready like a weapon. The only weapon she had. She'd even left her sica blade at home. How ignoble. They would find her body here, clutching a damn shoe. Julia moved to stand beside her, holding her own sica blade in a trembling hand.

She braced herself as Big Gut suddenly charged. And then the night seemed to explode before her.

A large, deadly shadow flowed through the group, dropping her attackers as if in a holosimulation. Aerina watched in a mixture of awe and horror at the macabre dance unfolding before her.

The first man went down with his neck broken, his head hanging at an odd angle. Aerina caught the quick glint of a sica blade in the lamplight before it disappeared into the overly-cologned man's chest. The shadowy figure whirled, still in a gruesome death dance, to meet three large men who had been hovering in the background as if deciding to fight or run.

They ran out of time to decide. He broke the closest one's neck with a quick twist of his large hands, and then tossed the dead weight towards the two other frozen men. As they collapsed beneath the body of their dead companion, the Reaper turned towards two more men that Aerina hadn't even seen in the shadows. He pulled out a blade longer than a sica blade and without pause, sliced the air so quickly Aerina didn't know he had slit both men's throats until the blood gushed forth. The men seemed frozen in shock before their bodies slumped forward slowly, collapsing to the ground nearly simultaneously.

The man holding her bracelet had turned to run, but before he could take more than a few steps, the assassin's garrote had tightened around his throat, cutting deep until blood flowed freely. The Reaper stepped back, letting the final body drop to the ground. He bent and scooped up her bracelet in one fluid motion.

He turned towards the women, his eyes familiar emotionless shadows.

Marcus.

She'd known it was him before the first man had fallen; that familiar fluid movement, large body, black uniform. It was the Marcus she'd seen in the courtyard the day she'd almost died. Not the Alpha Virmortus, a respected leader, but Marcus the Reaper. Killer. Man of Death.

He strode towards them, stepping over bodies without a glance. Julia shrunk back in fear, her eyes flicking quickly from Marcus to the gruesome scene before them and back again. Like she wasn't sure what horrified her more.

"Get in the car." His voice was low, controlled. His dark eyes were shuttered, his body still. The very level of tight control made Aerina nervous. He was furious.

"Marcus—"

"Now." He didn't raise his voice but Aerina nodded. He flicked his eyes over Julia and dismissed her. Pulling a squat black weapon from his belt, he turned and fired in one easy motion. A nearly invisible blue arc flew from the weapon's mouth, dancing over the bodies of the two men on the ground who were still alive. Their backs arched, fingers curling in the rictus of death.

Marcus stepped over them, heading towards the front of the alley.

"I'll call you tomorrow," Aerina murmured to Julia, pressing her friend's hand quickly before turning to hurry after Marcus. She didn't dare defy him now. The other woman seemed frozen in place, barely nodding in acknowledgment. She glanced back once as she turned the corner from the alley, a last view of Julia surrounded by broken bodies.

Marcus' sleek black car was parked down the street. He had opened her door, closing it with a controlled snap behind her. She saw him converse briefly with an Armati, who looked towards the alley, nodding once. Cleanup crew, no doubt. She hoped Julia would have the sense to have disappeared inside the Theatre.

Marcus said nothing as he entered the car, swiping his ID to start it. The silence stretched between them as he expertly navigated the small vehicle down the teeming streets towards the Ferry. He drove like he did everything else—with perfect control. Not a single movement was wasted or unplanned. He didn't fidget, didn't shift in his seat. His complete and utter control was unnerving, and Aerina couldn't imagine the kind of training that made him that way.

She shifted in her own seat, trying to adjust her short dress. It hadn't seemed so risqué when she'd bought it at the Pleb store. Marcus' eyes remained fixed on the road.

"Wait," Aerina finally said as they neared the Ferry, "I need to get my—"

Marcus reached back and shoved her blue pack into her arms.

He had known all along.

Aerina absently rubbed her sore ribs as the Ferry ascended. How could he have known where she was? And her stuff? Did he follow her? A chill went through her at the thought. Had he been the one she felt watching her?

She glanced sideways at Marcus. He faced ahead stoically, one large hand resting on the wheel. Her eyes were caught by the blood on his hands. Strangely, she wasn't appalled by the sight.

She had blood on her own hands, she realized, still clutching the bloody pump. And he had *saved* her. This time, it wasn't her blood.

She opened her mouth to thank him.

"Don't speak," he said in a low, measured voice. She snapped her mouth closed, looking over at him. He was definitely furious. No matter how hard he was fighting it.

Sighing, she leaned back in her seat. They were nearing the Capitol Terrace. The attendant waved them on as they exited, not stopping to check their IDs. Marcus was a well-known figure in Alba. A much-feared figure.

The streets of the top terrace were nearly empty, the quiet startling after the clamor she had just come from.

Aerina's heartbeat accelerated as Marcus passed her villa. Where was he taking her? She hadn't done anything wrong. Possible scenarios flew through her head. When an image of Marcus wrapping his garrote around her neck popped into her mind, she knew she was getting hysterical. *If he was going to hurt you, he could have just left you for the dockworkers.* When he pulled off into his own carport, her heart slowed slightly. Perhaps he just wanted to talk. She grabbed her bag as the charger automatically rose to connect. Both car doors lifted.

"Inside," Marcus commanded.

"Yes, sir," Aerina murmured sarcastically, slightly irritated in spite of herself at his high-handed demeanor. She knew she should feel nervous. This *was* the man who had almost killed her only a month earlier. What did he plan to do with her now?

Aerina walked through the side door into his kitchen. Her bare toes curled on the cold tile. She was still chilled, and felt exposed in the tight, overly revealing black sheath. Her hair was a mess, and she had scrapes from her clash with the unsuccessful thieves. The now-dead thieves, a small voice warned her.

"What the hell did you think you were doing?" Marcus' harsh question made her jump. She turned to face him defiantly.

"I was just meeting with an old friend."

"Are you completely stupid?" Aerina stiffened, taking offence at his rude questioning.

"That's enough, Marcus."

Marcus stared at Aerina, struggling to control the rage that had been building in him since he saw her walking towards the Ferry earlier that evening. Her white dress had been a damn beacon, proclaiming to everyone what she was up to. She had nearly been executed for treason less than a month ago. Did she think no one was watching her?

She was in danger, and she was either too ignorant to know it, or too ignorant to care.

She looked so small and helpless standing there in her bare feet and mussed hair. Her leg was bleeding and a dark bruise was already purpling the golden skin on her arm. The rage burgeoned anew, and he turned away.

He didn't care. *Nothing matters but your job.* The phrase from his youth was burned into his mind, but it was getting harder and harder to convince himself of that.

"No, it's not nearly enough." His voice was low and controlled. He washed his hands meticulously in the kitchen sink, wiping them dry with a deep brown towel. He hesitated a moment, fighting the urge to fling it down, before folding it and carefully placing it back.

He was unflappable. Emotionless. And suddenly, Aerina couldn't stand it anymore. For years she had watched him, fascinated by him. Attracted to him. Now she was finally here, with him, and he still wouldn't open up. Wouldn't show her even a tiny glimpse of the real Marcus.

"If you're done insulting me, I have things to do tonight," she said coldly.

"The only thing you are doing is going home."

"If thinking that will make you feel better, go right ahead and delude yourself. Can I have my bracelet?" She held her small hand out.

"I'll return it to you tomorrow. Go home." Marcus braced his legs apart and crossed his arms. If he was trying to look intimating, it worked. In that position, his muscles were clearly defined under his black armored suit, and she had to tilt her head back to meet his eyes.

"I'm not a child." Aerina felt childish just saying that. Damn, this man got under her skin. *Balance and serenity bring peace*, she recited the calming mantra. She took a deep, calming breath and tried again.

"Listen, Marcus, I appreciate your help, but—"

"If I hadn't found you, you would be dead right now. You have no business going down to the Pleb city. Didn't you learn anything?" His hand went to her neck, hesitating a moment as if he might be afraid to touch her before tracing the nearly healed scar left from his garrote.

Heat spread from where his hand touched her skin. A familiar wild, sick butterfly fluttered to life in her stomach. She'd never seen him hesitate. Was he nervous? She marveled at the thought. Touching his scarred hand with her own, she continued more softly.

"I knew you would find Julia eventually. I had to warn her. To find out if she knew anything that could help," Aerina explained, meeting his eyes boldly. His rough hand dropped away from her neck, breaking contact. She ignored the sense of loss she felt.

"'Find her eventually?'" he repeated with cold disdain. "I already knew everything I needed. I know she's danced for ten years, that she supports her little sister. That the fire that killed her parents was started by a faulty wire the Merchant who owned the warehouse was too cheap to fix." Aerina opened her mouth to ask how he knew so much, but closed it again at his forbidding expression.

Marcus stepped back as if he didn't trust himself so close to her. Aerina narrowed her eyes. He looked tense, and a slight muscle twitched in his jaw as he clenched his teeth. She wondered if he was aware of that tell in his normally inscrutable poker face. She'd never seen him so angry. It was both frightening and exciting at once. But he wasn't finished.

"Do you have any idea the danger you are in? This isn't a game to relieve your boredom."

"I know it's not—"

"Forget it," he interrupted her protest in his infuriatingly low, even voice. "Your kind will never understand."

Aerina saw red. "My 'kind'? I am the daughter of a Senator. I've been trained since birth in the ways of our State; the dangers of unbalance, and the importance of each class's role in the survival of our society. You are nothing but the tool of the

Consul to enforce the rules created by 'my kind'."

Marcus turned around and grabbed her arms so quickly she didn't have time to do anything but let out a frightened squeak. He pulled her up on her toes so they were face-to-face.

"You know nothing about me and what I do." His voice was harsh and low.

The very ignorance of the Patricians infuriated Marcus. He thought of the years of training he had undergone as a youth, of barely being able to drag his broken body out of bed in the mornings. The mental and physical tortures he had been forced to endure.

But worse than what he had experienced was what he had witnessed.

The scenes of destruction he had seen outside the city of Alba were indelibly etched in his memory. Of entire towns annihilated by warring cities; the groups of raiders that thrived on destruction; the sick perversions they practiced upon innocent people. On children. The dictators that followed no laws and killed indiscriminately. The Patricians lived a life of luxury, with little knowledge or concern to the world outside. Even the world within the walls, they took for granted. The protection they assumed was their birthright.

Marcus had never known luxury. He'd fought for everything, taking each beating and punishment without a cry for help. Because he'd known that in the end, no one would help. No one cared what happened to him. The only person he could depend on was himself.

And he'd never forgotten that lesson.

"Then tell me. Help me understand." Aerina's soft voice brought him back from the past, her large blue eyes meeting his. He knew he should feel disgusted by her—her entitlement, her lack of understanding, her poise and beauty that represented everything he wasn't. Everything he'd never have. But he couldn't. He couldn't help but want everything she was. To want her for himself. To keep her safe, by his side, for his sole enjoyment. To bask in her luminosity; drink from her effervescent joy of life.

He knew she could never be his, yet he still couldn't manage to stay away from her. He wanted to grasp each stolen moment, knowing it was only the tragedy at the Capitol that allowed him even this. And when she was no longer an outcast; when she no longer needed him, she'd go back to her perfect life and he'd have these moments to get him through the long, dark years ahead. Without her.

Aerina felt ashamed of her outburst. He was right. She didn't understand; couldn't begin to fathom his upbringing and what his role now entailed. She could feel the strength in his hands; in his arms holding her up almost effortlessly, but strangely, she wasn't afraid. Tingling spread from where his hands gripped her bare arms to her very core.

For a moment, she forgot the argument. She wanted him to kiss her, to touch her in passion and not anger. Her eyes dropped to his lips, taunt with anger and control. Involuntarily, she licked her own full lips. She saw his eyes follow the movement, and for a moment she thought he was going to fulfill her wish.

Then he set her down gently and his hands dropped away. Disappointment spread, crushing the butterflies of passion with its heavy weight. She rubbed the spot where he had gripped her, missing the heat.

"You don't *want* to understand." His voice was calm. He'd gotten himself back under control.

Aerina pushed aside the overwhelming frustration. She'd almost broken through his shell. For a moment, she'd thought he was going to open up to her, just a little. His mask was firmly back in place, his temper back under control. With Angry Marcus, she felt like she could get somewhere; she might find a chink in his armor. But he was back to his implacable self, the always-controlled leader. Taking a step back, both physically and figuratively, she kept her own voice calm. "Ok. Then tell me what you know about Cassandra, the assassin. And who told those men in the alley to kill me."

Marcus leaned back against the kitchen counter and crossed his arms, eyeing Aerina thoughtfully. He unclipped his holoreader, setting it on the center of the table.

The reader opened and Marcus scanned a card. Aerina watched interestedly, noticing that once again he didn't scan his ID chip like other citizens. *Hello Marcus,* the life-like female voice welcomed him. He instructed it to pull up the file for Cassandra Redding.

Aerina watched as photos, transcriptions of conversations, call logs, and other personal information hovered over the device. A strange grid with moving dots, one in red, appeared and Marcus immediately minimized it.

"Reader, tell me Cassandra Redding's personal history," he instructed. *Here is Cassandra Redding's personal history, would you like me to read it?*

Marcus answered in the affirmative, and Aerina listened to the holoreader outline Cassandra's heartrending story, while images from her past were projected in holographic form. Surveillance camera images, family photos, and school projects all showed as individual files that they could select to play. Everything on the Network that connected everyone in the city-state was available to Marcus. He left the files closed, letting the reader recite the summary.

She had been young, the same age as Aerina. Born an Aggie, she had worked in the fields outside the city on a dairy farm. As a youth, she had traveled with her father to the warehouse in the city when she had been raped by a group of men.

Still too young for an anti-pregnancy shot, she had become pregnant.

Her family had refused to let her abort the child, and so she went to the city for the procedure. Rather than return home to face her family and the strict Aggie community, she started working for one of the legal brothels on the Pleb Terrace. She worked both the brothel and as a dancer for several years before joining a dance troupe. The year before her death, she had quit the brothel to work full time for Mychel's dance troupe.

To hear her story told in the cool feminine voice of the holoreader made it seem all the more tragic. The poor girl had struggled and suffered, only to be reduced to a holograph file on a Reaper's reader.

The holoreader went silent. Aerina stared at the table for a long moment before meeting Marcus' stony gaze, her own eyes misty.

"I had no idea…I only met her a few times and she barely spoke…" Aerina couldn't seem to find the words to explain how she felt, an unusual occurrence for her.

She was shocked at the tragedy of the girl's life.

"All Patricians are sheltered," Marcus stated matter-of-factly as he clipped his Reader back on his belt. "It helps you make political decisions that aren't swayed by emotion."

"Individual stories should be taken into consideration when making important votes," Aerina said hotly. Marcus shook his head.

"It is too easy to use one emotional story that is the exception, the outlier, to sway someone's sympathy, and can result in a decision that has long term negative impacts on the society as a whole." He sounded as if he were quoting a textbook. Did he really believe what he was saying?

"I don't agree. I think the human factor is essential in being able to make a decision."

"Are we going to argue political theory, or did you want to discuss Cassandra?" Marcus asked dryly.

Aerina opened her mouth and then snapped it shut. "You're right. So what are you going to do next?"

"Find out who she came in contact with."

"Being alone and emotionally fragile, she would have been an easy target for someone to manipulate," Aerina said softly. Marcus nodded, watching her carefully.

"I would think you'd be more concerned about your own situation," he said finally.

Aerina met his gaze. "I thought it must be you or your men following me, watching me. Tonight I realized if you were following me, I'd never know it. Then when those men attacked, one said something. Something about getting paid for my death. I knew it wasn't you."

Marcus remained silent, waiting.

"Who would want me dead, beside that assassin? He, or she,

must be worried I know something. When you let me live, it threw off their plan. Whoever is responsible knew how Virmortus operate. They wouldn't have expected anyone to survive."

Not bad, Marcus thought. With access to the same information he had, she might be able to come up with the same conclusions as he.

"Now you see the importance of remaining close to home," Marcus replied, to her annoyance. "It is much easier to keep an eye on you, and keep you safe."

"Are you following me?" she asked bluntly.

"I am kept apprised of your whereabouts," he replied vaguely. Her ire continued to rise at his half answers. If that was how he wanted to play it...

"I'll do my best to make your job simple," she answered with saccharine sweetness. Let him take that however he wanted.

Chapter 6

"In three words I can sum up everything I've learned about life: It goes on." - Robert Frost

Aerina called Julia on her way to meet Lina for lunch. Julia was already at the Theatre, warming up. Aerina could see beads of sweat on her friend's forehead in the small image that popped up from her holoreader. She quickly explained about Marcus taking her home and that both Julia and Mychel were cleared from suspicion. She could see Julia's relief.

"Are you ok, after the mugging I mean?" Aerina asked her.

"I am fine. You're the one who took the hits," Julia replied. "How are your ribs?"

Aerina stretched and winced. "Still a little sore. But I'll live."

"Thanks to your Reaper friend. Must come in handy to have friends like him," Julia said, only half joking.

They said their goodbyes and Julia's face winked out. Aerina was relieved her friend seemed unscathed by the previous night's events. And still willing to associate with her. A more cautious individual might assume trouble followed Aerina. More than just trouble; a certain Reaper.

Aerina snapped her reader back onto the bracelet Marcus returned after walking her home.

He hadn't lingered, and Aerina had a feeling he'd had other things on his agenda before he would return to his own villa. But the short walk in the cool night had almost seemed romantic, even if he had been still piqued with her. He'd given her his coat to wear, and she wasn't ashamed to admit, at least to herself, that she'd slept wrapped in its masculine scent. Marcus' scent.

Even with the horrific events of the evening, she couldn't but feel a little elated. Last night he had most definitely been the Reaper. But she'd also glimpsed the man. The impossible control he exerted over himself could waver. Emotion, empathy, passion; they hadn't been completely expunged during his training. She just needed to find the right triggers, and an ocean of patience, to uncover the man that lived in the killer.

She shook her head at her own foolish thoughts, feeling like a moon-struck youth, fantasizing about him while she should be doing other things.

Like finishing her thesis for University.

Lina had invited her over so they could work together on some final projects, and critique each other's work. She'd been surprised that Lina was willing to risk censure by allowing Aerina in her home. And that her straight-laced mother wouldn't object. But she wasn't going to question her good fortune. Perhaps this was a small step to being reinstated in her caste.

Aerina parked her family's e-car in front of Lina's villa. The home was very similar to Aerina's in size, shape, and color. It belonged to Lina's mother, a Magister at the University. Her father, in the Economics Voting Sector, had his own house. The Law of Marriage didn't allow for divorce, which apparently had been pretty common in pre-war America, but couples didn't need to live together.

Aerina knocked and walked in without waiting for a response; Lina's house was practically a second home to her. She also secretly didn't want to give them a chance to have second thoughts.

Voices drifted from the Serenity Garden. Walking through the open central courtyard, she could see two people in the garden.

"You didn't tell me *she* was going to be here." Helen's sharp voice cut through the meticulously groomed serenity of the garden. The words also cut a tiny wound into Aerina's heart.

She moved into the garden and sank slowly onto one of the many white chaise lounges surrounding the Serenity Pool. "Sorry to taint you with my presence. I know how appalled everyone is by my behavior. I didn't expect anything less," she said calmly.

"Not *everyone* is appalled," Lina said soothingly, shooting a guilty look at Helen. "Some of the students are envious that you had the nerve to associate with Plebs. I mean, it's not as if we haven't all thought about it once or twice."

"We just had the sense not to actually do something so ridiculous," Helen cut in. "No offense, Aerina, but I have been working for an offer from the Legal Voting Sector, and you know how strict they are." She sat stiffly on another lounge, pulling her pencil skirt over her knees.

Helen was small, fit, and had hair that was so blonde it was almost white. Aerina suspected it was not naturally that pale. Not that she would ever say anything.

She waved one hand dismissively. "I understand."

"Now, Helen, she really didn't do anything wrong. Her curious nature got her in trouble, but as her friends, it is our responsibility to stand by her. Everyone will forget that unfortunate incident soon." Lina grimaced apologetically at Aerina.

"She broke the law," Helen said tersely. "Without proper segregation, the balance of the entire city is at risk."

Aerina was barely able to keep from rolling her eyes. "I hardly believe a little mixing between the castes is going to be the ruin of Alba," she responded calmly, opening her holoreader. The welcome screen projected above her hand and she swiped the virtual button to open her thesis. The multimedia report, consisting of video, images, voice recordings, and text, popped up. "I personally worry more about the Law of Death, myself."

Lina snorted in an attempt to cover her laughter. Helen was less amused.

"I don't understand how you could have been brought up with the same ideals we have and still have no concept of their value," Helen said disapprovingly, seeming genuinely flabbergasted.

"I understand the value of balance and control. I just think a little change every hundred years can be a good thing."

"Those laws have made our city survive for those one hundred years."

"What about when survival isn't enough? We can't exist in a bubble forever. Not if the rest of the world is expanding. 'Change is always imminent; if you don't seek out change, it will find you unprepared'."

Aerina and Helen had both leaned forward during the argument, Lina standing between them with a worried expression.

"Is that your thesis? What has happened to you, Aerina? You used to be so...normal. Your father is a Senator, for serenity's sake. I'm sorry, but I cannot conscionably spend the afternoon here," Helen finished quietly, packing up her things and heading towards the door.

Aerina watched her go, trying to ignore the hurt spreading through her at her friend's blatant rejection. She should have kept her mouth shut; held her unpopular opinions to herself. Lina looked as stricken as she felt, and the hurt was alleviated slightly.

"Don't worry about her," Lina said, "She's worried about the Final Examinations, and being selected by Legal. She only came today hoping to see Stephen, anyway."

Aerina forced a smile, shrugging as if it didn't bother her.

"Lina, is something wrong with Helen? I saw her rush off..." Both girls turned to look at Lina's mother as she trailed off, her eyes on Aerina. The older woman turned to Lina. "Can I speak with you, please?" The cold tone was so unlike her normal friendly demeanor that Aerina winced.

Lina hurried after her mother, leaving Aerina sitting on the lounge alone.

I suppose I'd better get used to this feeling, Aerina thought, unable to keep the self-pity at bay. Slowly she gathered up her things, knowing what was coming.

A few moments later, Lina reappeared, her gently rounded face repentant.

"I'm sorry, Aerina, I guess today isn't a good day after all to work on our final projects," she said awkwardly, not meeting Aerina's eyes.

"Sure, no problem," Aerina replied with forced cheerfulness, hurrying towards the garden's back exit. The only thought on her mind was disappearing before Lina could see the tears that had sprung, unbidden, to her eyes. She slipped quickly through the garden door, exiting the same way a Pleb might after working in the villa for the day.

And for once, being a Pleb didn't seem so wonderful.

As evening fell, Aerina couldn't help but wonder what Marcus was doing. Her world had narrowed considerably since The Incident. The people who had once been peripheral—Julia, Marcus—were now her sole companions. What would her "friends" think if they knew she had turned to the Reaper who had almost killed her for companionship? No doubt they would be even more horrified than they already were. They'd think she was crazy.

Which she probably was.

As she drove home from the disastrous afternoon at Lina's, she found herself taking the long way around, near the cliffs. The way past his villa.

The small villa showed no signs of life as she cruised slowly past. Parking the car in the cul-de-sac, she walked down the wide cobblestone street slowly. The other villas here were small like Marcus', probably belonging to other high-ranking Virmortus. They all looked equally empty, which she was thankful for. She'd never visited him in daylight before. It felt a little strange; forbidden.

She knocked lightly on the door, unable to stop herself. After the rejection of the afternoon, she needed to see him. Somehow, through the heavy mist that had settled over her life of late, he had become the beacon; the one unchanging force she could focus on when everything else felt obscured.

There was no answer. She could have scanned her wrist to leave a virtual calling card, but shied away from the idea. Did she really want him to know she had stopped over again? He must think her pathetic—she couldn't stay away.

She would just make sure he wasn't in the shower or something. Feeling like a voyeur but unable to help herself, she peaked in his carport window. Empty.

Disappointed, she returned to her own e-car. It was still

early. He was probably at the Training Grounds, or at the Capitol in a meeting. Carrying out important State business.

Another wave of self-pity rolled over her. Her life felt pointless; trivial. She just wanted to do something that mattered, for once to feel truly *alive*.

This is all your fault.

Resting her head on the steering wheel, she fought the urge to beat her fists against the soft leather. Patricians did not lose control. Patricians did not express strong emotions.

Damn.

Swiping away the tear she'd been unable to contain, she started the car with a wave of her wrist. The heavy mist was turning to a light rain, so she headed back towards the Capitol to pick up her parents after work.

Aerina pulled into the large turnaround in front of the Capitol. The University was next to the Capitol, and Aerina saw her fellow students leaving their classes. She pretended not to notice the stares and whispering that ensued when some noticed her. She slouched a little lower in her seat.

She didn't see Marcus' e-car. Unlike her own white four-seat electric car, Marcus' was low and wide, built for speed. His was also black, the standard color for all military vehicles.

Even their e-cars were segregated.

She saw Niko walking with his group of cronies, the silent and ever-present bodyguard trailing behind him. When he saw her, he gave her his familiar sneer and said something to his friends. They all laughed.

I can't wait until he becomes Consul, she thought sarcastically. The Consul held important veto power and command over the military. She could only imagine how Niko, so petty and self-absorbed, might run the city. Consul Julius had always been fair, if strict, as a ruler. After his wife had died tragically, he'd become a little more withdrawn, not appearing in public as frequently. But his style of rule did not change.

Things would be much different with Niko as ruler. But laws were laws, and the Consul was always appointed by the previous Consul. Julius had made it clear that his son was next in line.

The city's daytime alabaster glow became a crimson stain as the sun settled low on the horizon. Nothing stayed the same forever. Not even Alba.

That night, Aerina again found herself standing in front of Marcus' house. The rain had subsided but the air was heavy with moisture. Moonlight gleamed off the damp cobblestones, the white villas shining in the low lamplight.

She couldn't help herself. She couldn't stay away. As the day had turned to night, the urge to be near him, to see him, had grown so pressing she couldn't ignore it.

His villa was still dark, and the carport empty. There weren't even wet tracks inside, indicating that his car hadn't been there all day.

The crushing disappointment she felt was a little surprising, and very scary. How had she become so attached to him in such a short time?

Being with Marcus was quickly becoming a habit. A dangerous one. Aerina weighed her options. She could wait, hoping he would come home eventually. Or she could visit the Pleb Terrace to see Julia's new show. Or go home alone. Every option just made her feel a little pathetic.

Instead she wandered down the street to Balance Park. Fewer lights here made the shadows longer, and the trees rippled eerily in the damp air.

She looked up above her. It had been years since she'd visited the large recreation area. Mount Diablo rose high above the city to the east. The top terrace had been cut back into the mountain. Sheer cliff-face rose up on three sides, the mountain behind to the east and the ocean on the west side far below.

Besides the park that had hiking trails and small wildlife, and the private beach below, the Patricians rarely spent time elsewhere than the Capitol Terrace. It had theatres, libraries, game rooms, a sport complex, and the Circus track, where Aggies brought horses or dogs to race.

She knew some Patricians visited the legal brothels,

although none were on the Capitol Terrace. It was accepted as a necessary evil of society, and most brothels catered to both male and female clientele.

Tonight, none of the accepted forms of entertainment sounded even remotely appealing.

She wanted out.

Out of the city. Space to think. Space to feel free.

Without another thought, she began climbing the cliff. She frequently used the rock wall in the sports complex, and considered herself a good climber. The closest outcropping was less than twelve feet above her.

When she finally pulled herself onto the small ledge, she had changed her mind about the difficultly level. Her nails were chipped and bleeding, she had scratches everywhere, and her white slacks and thin jacket were dirty and snagged. Climbing this cliff without equipment would be near impossible.

She leaned back against the rough, cool surface of rock behind her. She'd have to wait until her arms stopped quivering before attempting to make her way back down. It was embarrassing, really, how weak she was.

She thought back to the attack of the previous night. She'd felt terrified. Helpless. If Marcus hadn't been keeping track of her, the night would have ended very badly for her and Julia.

He'd saved her again. It probably didn't improve her image as a privileged Patrician, unable to fend for herself. Sighing, she leaned forward and scanned the brightly lit terraces far below her perch.

The founders had chosen their location well. But, Aerina thought as she sat contemplating the dark ocean far below, the city would remain safe only as long as the rest of the world lived like Alba. Isolated. Self-sufficient.

A noise below interrupted her contemplation. She pressed back against the jagged outcropping behind her, hoping to remain unnoticed. Fear rose, making her breathing jagged. Why had she been so foolish to ignore Marcus' warning? Had they followed her here?

The figures were too far to make out their faces or words.

One figure, obviously a large man, had come from the back of the park. Another from the park's entrance. She leaned forward, trying to catch a glimpse of them, but the clouds shrouded the moon, and very little light shone on that section of the park.

A loose stone went clattering from beneath her foot and Aerina threw herself back, her heart pounding in her ears. Both figures turned quickly to look in her direction. Laying down away from the edge, Aerina held her breathe, listening. Footsteps approached, crunching on gravel.

"See anything?" a low, unrecognizable voice asked. The other man answered negatively.

"I'll see you in three weeks, then," the first voice said, and she heard the muted sound of retreating footsteps. She waited, afraid the remaining man, the large one, would hear her carefully measured breathing.

After what felt like an eternity, she heard the second man retreat, his footsteps stopping after a few feet before he continued out of earshot.

Aerina waited another long minute, then several more. Slowly she raised her head, staring hard into the dark recesses of the park. Was he still there, lying in wait? Watching to see who came down from the precipice? She climbed down shakily, her heart hammering, afraid that any moment someone would grab her from behind.

Once her feet hit solid ground, she rushed towards the park entrance as silently as possible, not breathing normally until the park was far behind her.

Distance made her feel as if she might have imagined the danger. Maybe she was really losing it. Until tonight, she'd never felt unsafe on the Capitol Terrace.

As soon as she saw him, she would tell Marcus her concerns. He would know what to do.

Chapter 7

"Only in the darkness can you see the stars."
- Martin Luther King Jr.

"I'm heading down to the beach, Mom. I might have dinner with Lina tonight, so don't worry about waiting for me." Aerina's mom waved to her through the door of her office, not stopping her dictation into her holocomputer.

Aerina slipped on her white sandals with delicate gold chains running over the top of her foot. They matched her white bikini with gold latches on the side of her hips and between her breasts. She had put a thin knit dress over top that fell just above her knees and loose sleeves that fell to her elbows.

The day was warm, the bright sun burning the mist off early. She walked to the Patrician tram, taking a deep breath of the salty ocean breeze. Sometimes at this time of year they could smell smoke in the air, as the strong warm winds in the south would start brush fires from the outpost towns or a lighting strike.

Today the air smelled fresh. A perfect beach day. She stepped lightly onto the tram, smiling at the attendant who was working hard not to stare as he scanned her wrist. He hit the button that sent them lowering slowly, a slight flush on his cheeks. Several of the glass panes were open, letting the breeze in, fluttering golden curls around her face.

It stopped directly on the private beach, and she waved as she exited, eliciting another blush from the young man. She walked slowly down the boardwalk to the beach, watching the surfers. She itched to join them, but rather than heading to the small cabana that housed sports equipment and other beach paraphernalia, she headed north across the boardwalk towards the Pleb beach.

Scanning her wrist, she rented a bright red umbrella. Opening it, she sat down in the sun to wait. It wasn't long until she was joined by Julia and Mychel.

"Sorry we're late," Julia said breathlessly, dropping into the sand. Her lean dancer body was encased in a pink and orange maillot. Mychel flaunted her own fuller curves in a deep blue bikini. Aerina glanced down at her own modest white bikini and sighed.

"No worries, I haven't been here long," Aerina replied, pretending not to notice the whistles from a group of surfers passing by. She subconsciously straightened her spine in the beach chair, crossing her ankles demurely. Julia waved absently to good-naturedly acknowledge the catcalls before grabbing a bottle of sunscreen from her tote.

Mychel settled back on her towel with a groan of satisfaction.

"I needed this. I haven't taken a day off in over a month." She stretched her long legs out, wiggling painted toes. She had silky red hair and accompanying white skin dusted with freckles. Aerina watched her casual abandon with envy, wondering absently if she was going to put on some sun screen.

"I hear you," Julia agreed. "We've taken on a few new performers at the Theatre and I've been busting my ass to get them up to speed. Kevin has no concept of the work required to carry out a perfect performance."

"Owners never get it," Mychel agreed. "But they deal with the finances and security, so I don't mind."

Aerina kept her mouth shut. Compared to these women, she lived a life of leisure. She had her university classes and studies, which hardly seemed like work. But she couldn't stop the twinge of jealousy that stole through her at their sense of purpose and dedication.

She looked out over the ocean at the surfers and swimmers. Not far in front of them, a family with two young children played, building a rather lopsided sandcastle. She smiled as she watched the two children's antics.

She felt a sudden sadness watching the little boy playing with his older sister. The perfect little family. That had been hers, once. Would things have been different if her brother had lived?

This is all your fault.

"Care for some company?" The deep voice drew her attention from the playing children and her past to two men dripping water on her towel. Both gripped surfboards. Not in the mood to mingle, Aerina glanced over at the other women.

Julia opened one eye and shrugged. Mychel pretended to sleep. Aerina glared at her uncooperative friends.

Turning back to the men, Aerina smiled apologetically. "Maybe another time. We're just trying to relax today."

"So are we," the other man said, dropping his surfboard onto the sand and sitting on it, resting his arms on his legs. Both men were attractive, lean and tan with light sandy hair. But Aerina couldn't help but compare them in her mind to Marcus' dark looks and toned physique. He had earned every muscle and scar the hard way. Compared to him, these were mere boys.

"You must have misunderstood. 'Maybe another time' was my polite way of telling you 'No'. Is that clear enough?"

"Yeah, ok," the man said after a long moment, rising again and brushing the sand off. Grabbing their boards, they stalked off.

"I swear, that haughty air of command you have is bred into you," Julia laughed once the men were out of earshot. "You should teach me how to do that someday."

"It would come in handy," Mychel agreed. "Although a can of pepper spray will do the trick in a pinch."

Aerina smiled. "I believe that is illegal, my friend."

"A sica blade isn't very useful against a group, but you can buy yourself time with a can of spray."

"You've had to fight your way out of a group of assailants?" Aerina was horrified, thinking of the night she and Julia had faced the group of dockworkers. Was that a regular occurrence in the Pleb city?

Mychel shrugged. "No, never anything that severe, thank serenity. But there are times the dockworkers get out of hand. It's nice to have something to threaten them with."

"What about the Armati?"

"They are around and will step in, but generally prefer to

keep a low profile. On the plus side, they also tend to turn a blind eye to women carrying pepper spray," Julia commented, joining the conversation.

"You work so hard and then have to defend yourselves, too. It doesn't seem right," Aerina said indignantly.

Both Pleb women laughed.

"Your concern is sweet, but honestly, we love our work. We choose to work so often because we want perfection from our troupes. And security around the Theatre is great," Julia explained. "What happened the other night was a rare exception."

Aerina sat back, considering what Julia said.

"I guess I've been under a false impression. I've heard…concerning…stories." She explained what she had learned about Cassandra.

"I can see why you have a bad impression of the Pleb city," Julia said quietly. "That was a horrible but unusual event. The Reapers took care of the men who did it. Bastards had left Cass for dead, thinking no one would ever know. It was a miracle she survived, as badly as she was beaten. Poor Cass had a hard time dealing with it, and the resulting pregnancy. I don't think she ever got over it," she finished sadly, sitting up to stare out at the water.

"She certainly never talked about it," Mychel chimed in. "I knew her for years and if I hadn't heard the story from other girls at the brothel, I would have never known."

"How did she come to work with you?" Aerina questioned.

Mychel grimaced. "You're starting to sound like the Reaper who came to question me after she…died."

"Marcus?" Aerina asked in surprise.

"I don't know his name. But I can tell you he was the most terrifying thing I've ever come in contact with. A mere can of pepper spray wouldn't have even slowed him down. I'd rather meet up with a whole crew of dockworkers than that man in a dark alley." Mychel shivered in the heat of the sun, rubbing her hands on her pale arms. "He was big and dark, but what was the most unnerving was how he was so… controlled. Like he was a machine and not a man."

Sounds like Marcus, Aerina thought wryly.

"What else did he want to know?"

"If I knew anything about who she was seeing romantically, or why she would have tried to kill the Consul," Mychel responded sardonically.

"And?"

Mychel shook her head. "I told him I didn't know anything about either, and thank serenity he believed me. I'm sure he's come up with some pretty inventive interrogation techniques."

"You should have seen Rina's Reaper kill the men who attacked us in the alley by the Theatre," Julia interjected. "He *was* a machine. It was a group of large dockworkers and he took them out like he was swatting flies. Honestly, I blinked and it was over." Julia waved her hands for emphasis as she regaled Mychel with the gory details. "His hands moved so fast with that wire, it was amazing."

Aerina's hand went to her neck, and both her friends' gazes followed.

"Sorry, Rina, I forgot you felt it yourself. After seeing him in action, I'm pretty sure he didn't intend to kill you. If he had, you'd be dead," Julia commented ruefully.

"He was repaying me," she murmured, her mind lost in the past.

"How does a Reaper owe you?" Mychel asked, her curiosity evident.

"I saved his life once, when we were young. From the Consul heir himself."

"That little shit threatened a Reaper?" Mychel scoffed.

"He knew Marcus couldn't fight back. I stood up for him until the Consul came and intervened. Niko is a bully, but a dangerous one," Aerina answered grimly.

"The day he takes over, this city is going to hell," Julia muttered in agreement, glancing around as if afraid someone might hear her. Mychel nodded, flopping over onto her stomach. Aerina noticed the redhead's stomach was as bright as a cherry.

"Are you sure you don't want sunscreen?" she asked.

"I'll never get any color that way." Mychel's voice was muffled by her towel.

"So we're back to square one with Cassandra," Aerina said in disappointment. "I was hoping you would know something."

"Sorry," Mychel said. "I wish I could help. I know you'd like to clear your name."

Aerina considered that. "I don't think it would matter one way or another. My real crime, it seems, is in impersonating a Pleb; stepping out from my own caste. Even if the motive is uncovered, I'll still be an outcast. I just need to come to terms with my new status. Besides the rejection from nearly everyone I've ever known, it's not so bad," she finished wryly.

And I would have never gotten to know Marcus if I wasn't an outcast, she thought silently, not ready to admit even to her Pleb friends how she felt about the Reaper who had both nearly killed her and saved her life.

"The real reason…I think someone wants me dead. Someone who thought I'd be killed with the other dancers."

Mychel was silent, and Aerina regretted bringing up what was surely still a difficult subject for her. The troupe had been like family to her.

"Oh Aerina, are you sure?" Julia gasped. "Are you ok…?" Aerina smiled at the worry in Julia's voice; the first genuine concern about her safety outside of Marcus. Julia asked more questions, but Mychel remained silent.

"I know who her parents are," the redhead finally said, her voice still muffled by the towel. "I could take you to see them. I know it's a long shot, but they might have some information."

Aerina hesitated, thinking of Marcus' warning. Visiting the Aggie town would leave her more exposed than ever. Leaving the city might give the killer the chance he or she had been waiting for. But Cassandra' parents might have information that would lead her to the killer.

She had to try.

"Let's do it."

They borrowed Kevin's e-car to drive out to the Agriculture

Terrace. The owner of the Trinity Theatre was reluctant to part with his ancient machine, but Julia was wonderfully persuasive. She had to stay behind to prep for the evening show, so just Aerina and Mychel slid into the low vehicle.

Rain began to fall lightly as they left the city through the north gate. Armati guards scanned their wrist IDs before waving them through. Aerina thought she saw one of the soldiers talking into his military-issue Com device, but she was also a little paranoid. It might have been her imagination. *Relax, girl. The last time Marcus knew what you were up to, it was a good thing.*

Her fear from the previous evening in the park had faded in the light of day. Perhaps she should just forget about it. It was the Capitol Terrace, for serenity's sake. Nothing ever happened there. She would just need to be hyper-vigilant outside of the Patrician sanctuary.

Mychel drove. She had been an Aggie before moving to the city and was familiar with the route. The cobblestone streets became gravel and the small car bounced lightly with each pothole. Aerina rode shotgun, watching the city fade away and the countryside open up around them.

She'd never left the city before and it was at once frightening and exhilarating. The late summer wildflowers were still in bloom, the grasses tall and thick. As they got further from the city's stone walls, dense trees towered over the road.

A large truck carrying what looked to be potatoes passed them, nearly pushing the small car off the narrow, mud-slicked road. Mychel honked good-naturedly and the Aggie waved.

The dense woods disappeared and the land flattened into a huge green valley below them. The Agriculture Terrace.

Fields stretched for miles, dotted by small yet neatly kept houses. A small lake gleamed to the far north, with livestock barns nearby. A small town and a series of large silos and warehouses were at the center of the farmland.

"It's beautiful," Aerina said, leaning forward as they drove down the steep hill toward the town.

"I couldn't wait to get out when I was a girl," Mychel admitted. "Coming back, it *is* kind of nostalgic. The Aggie town has a certain charm. But I would still take the city any day."

Before long, they were slowing down to pass through the quaint little town and heading towards the lake. Mychel pulled the small car into a dirt drive.

Aerina got out slowly, her eyes going over the small house with wooden slat siding. Flowers in the front still bloomed brightly, and a long wooden deck welcomed them to the front door. The air smelled of dirt and manure, but Aerina didn't find it distasteful. It smelled natural. Earthy.

As they approached the steps on the deck, the screen door opened with a small creak.

"Can I help you?" an older woman asked, her expression welcoming but wary. She had her hair drawn back in a tight bun, and wore tan woven slacks and a blue blouse. Her face looked weary, as if sorrow was not an unfamiliar visitor.

"I'm sorry to bother you," Mychel began, "I'm Mychel and this is my friend Aerina. I was a friend of Cassandra's." Aerina waited with baited breath for the woman she assumed to be Cassandra's mother to react.

Her eyes darkened but she stepped back. "Please, come in."

Mychel and Aerina followed her in the house.

"I'm Tammy. This is Jeff, my husband." An older man seated at the kitchen table rose and nodded politely. "We are—were—Cassandra's parents."

"I'm so sorry for your loss," Aerina said, impulsively clasping the older woman's lean, work roughed hand. Tammy seemed surprised, but smiled at Aerina.

"Thank you, dear," she responded, gripping Aerina's hand in both of hers for a moment before moving further into the room.

"We were about to eat dinner, would you like to join us?"

"We don't mean to intrude—" Mychel began.

"We insist," Jeff spoke up gruffly.

"Then thank you, we'd love to," Aerina said quickly before Mychel could protest again. She found herself craving more information about these hard-working people. The bitter tinge of guilt rose slowly in her. Why had she never talked to the Aggies working in her home? She'd barely spared a thought for them over the years, so accustomed to having them as a fixture in her life. Like the furniture in her home. It was uncomfortable to realize she hadn't been living the ideals she talked about.

They talked about light topics during dinner. The meal was delicious, the atmosphere relaxed. Aerina asked questions about the Aggie lifestyle, and the farm the couple ran.

Jeff pushed aside his empty plate after polishing off a huge piece of berry cobbler—which Aerina found to be the most delicious dessert she'd ever eaten. He leaned back in his chair and opened the topic on everyone's mind.

"So how did you know our Cassandra?"

Aerina wondered for a moment if they thought she and Mychel were from the brothel. They were awfully friendly, if that were the case.

"Cassandra was a dancer in my dance troupe," Mychel said quietly, setting down her own spoon suddenly as if her appetite had fled. "I knew her for several years. She just began dancing full time with my group the few months before her death, but she joined us part time before that. She was very talented, and is greatly missed."

Tammy nodded with a grateful smile, pressing a trembling hand to her mouth. Her hazel eyes were watery with unshed tears. Jeff just looked at his clasped hands, gnarled with arthritis.

Aerina swallowed her last bite past the lump in her throat, taking a sip of water. She'd felt sorrow over the death of all the dancers, but being here with Cassandra's family, seeing their pain, made it all more real. Tammy turned to look at her, waiting to hear her response.

"I was there when she...when she died."

"You're a Patrician?" Tammy looked shocked, and Jeff raised his head quickly. Aerina looked down at her clothes. She had borrowed a pair of black slacks and a tight short-sleeved sapphire sweater. "Or you were there as a dancer?"

"Yes, I am a Patrician. And I was there dancing." She could tell both Tammy and Jeff were uncertain how to react. Tammy finally sighed shakily, as if it didn't matter how Aerina fit into the situation.

"We'd heard about the fire and were already mourning. Then the Reapers came. At first I thought..." Tammy's voice trailed off, her eyes meeting Jeff's. "They told us what had happened...what she had done. The leader himself asked to see any belongings or things she might have sent us. I have so few..." Tammy's voice broke, and she visibly pulled herself back together.

"I don't understand why she did it...I knew she was lost to us, after what happened to her. But she seemed to be coming around. She even sent us a few messages. I showed them to the Reaper." Tammy rose, opening the drawer of a small lamp table and pulling out an old model holoreader, one of the first to have a virtual keyboard. Swiping her wrist to unlock it, she pulled up the messages.

"May I?" Aerina asked. Tammy nodded, and Aerina very gently swiped open the first message. Mychel talked quietly with Tammy while Jeff listened, telling the couple stories about Cassandra's dancing, her kindness to others, what she enjoyed doing in her free time — like knitting, of all things. Tammy smiled at that.

"I taught her to knit. She complained horribly, saying she was never going to knit once she moved out," Tammy reminisced. "My little girl always dreamed of moving to the city."

Aerina scanned through the messages quickly. Most were about dancing, mentioning some of the shows and fellow dancers. Cassandra asked about old friends, and commented on the weather.

The final message seemed different from the others, more excited. Cassandra even mentioned coming for a visit, to stay for bit. *I might need to get out of the city for a while*, she wrote. *Perhaps things can be different then.*

She had planned the assassination. But why? What would drive a quiet girl like Cassandra to kill the most powerful man in Alba? She seemed to be improving, even happy.

What had pushed her over the edge? Aerina furrowed her brows, staring blindly at the holoreader in her hand. The door burst open and a young woman rushed in.

"Whew," she exclaimed, tugging off a bright yellow rain slicker, spraying droplets of rain all over the entrance. "Quite the rainstorm and it isn't even close to the rainy season." She glanced into the dining room and stopped.

"Oh, I didn't know you had guests," she said, her warm voice frosting over. She hung the slicker up and moved into the dining room.

Tammy made the introductions. Cassandra's sister Cynthia was a younger version of Tammy but for her eyes. The hazel orbs gleamed with hostility and suspicion as she greeted the women.

"Food's in the kitchen," Tammy told her daughter, sitting back down.

They chatted a little longer while Cynthia ate her dinner in silence, wary eyes continually glancing at the uninvited dinner guests. Aerina ignored the girl's stare, feeling relaxed in a way she hadn't in some time. The small fire that burned in the fireplace lit the room in a cheerful glow, and smelled slightly of smoke and pine sap. The scent mingled pleasantly with the lingering smells from dinner.

"We should probably go before the road turns completely to mud," Mychel finally said, rising. Aerina rose too, giving the surprised Tammy a hug.

"Thank you for dinner, it was wonderful," she told the older woman, smiling at Jeff to include him in her appreciation. "You have a lovely cozy home; I enjoyed our visit. I'm just sorry it had to be under such sad circumstances."

Tammy smiled at Aerina, clasping the younger woman's smooth hand with both of her well-worn ones. "Thank you, both of you, for sharing your memories of Cassandra. I had hoped that one day... well, it doesn't matter now. I am just glad she had such good friends." She reached for Mychel's hand to include her, clasping it tightly for a moment before stepping back.

"I'll walk you out," Cynthia spoke up, rising from the table. She still wore her damp jeans, spotted with mud, and a simple yellow blouse. Walking with them to the door, she grabbed her slicker again and pulled back on her boots. She also pulled two umbrellas from the hall closet, handing one to each of the women before pulling up her own hood.

They walked slowly to the small e-car, picking their way carefully through the muddy drive.

"Why are you asking about Cassandra?" Cynthia asked bluntly as they neared the car, stopping to face the women. Aerina clutched her umbrella as rain dripped off the front. She could see rivulets of water trailing down Cynthia's slicker and into the mud at her feet.

"I just want to understand why she did it," Aerina said finally when Mychel remained mute. "This isn't over. I don't think she acted alone; if I can learn her motive, perhaps we can end it before someone else gets hurt."

Cynthia stared at her for a moment as the rain pounded steadily around them.

"You have no business coming here, heaping more sorrow on my parents. Don't you think they've been through enough without a privileged little bitch like you sniffing around, trying to *investigate*?" Cynthia hissed, her words barely audible above the pounding of the rain.

Aerina stiffened, the heat of shame threading through her despite the cold rain dripping around her and soaking into her shoes.

Your. Fault.

Mychel opened her mouth to defend her, but Aerina held up her hand.

"You're right. I was only trying to help, but I suppose there isn't much I can do now to alleviate your parents' pain. I'm sorry."

"Your apologies mean nothing to me," Cynthia spat, ignoring the rain that ran down her face like a river of tears. "Stay away from my parents. You don't belong here. The next visit won't end so well for you. Don't come where you aren't welcome again." She turned away, sloshing back into the house without a backwards glance.

Aerina stood, immobile, in the pouring rain. After a long moment, she felt Mychel's hand on her arm.

"Let's go, Rina."

The ride back to the city was done mostly in silence. Besides a few comments about the poor condition of the road, both women kept their own counsel.

Aerina watched the Aggie town pass with much less excitement. The small wooden shops and empty boardwalks looked less welcoming in the dark rain.

Perhaps Cynthia was right. What did she think she was doing, investigating Cassandra's death? Marcus had made similar comments about her interference. Her *privileged* life. Maybe she *should* stay where she belonged. If only she could figure out where that was.

Wiping a stray rain droplet, *not* a tear, from her cheek, her resolve hardened. It was her life in danger, after all. It wasn't her fault that Cassandra had made the choices she had. Life was a series of choices—some small, some big—that set a course.

They were nearing the large gate to the Pleb city when she noticed a large Aggie vehicle lumbering up behind them. Aerina dragged her gaze from the rain-streaked window to glance back as the truck approached quickly. Too quickly.

"What the hell—" Mychel began, looking in the rear camera. A moment later, she was shouting profanities as the truck connected with their rear bumper. The small car shuddered, the proximity beep sounding, and Mychel struggled to maintain control in the slick mud.

Aerina gripped the dash tightly, looking behind them, trying to get a view of the driver. All she could see was a dark figure in the driver's seat. And then the truck was again upon them, the second hit knocking her teeth together.

Looking wildly at Mychel, she saw her friend gripping the wheel intently, bracing for the next hit.

"If we go off the road, get out and run into the woods," Mychel instructed brusquely. "This is a targeted attack, and my bet is they are coming after you."

Aerina felt a fresh wave of fear. They weren't giving up.

The third hit caused the little car to fishtail wildly, Mychel bringing it back under control by sheer force of will.

"Just a few more yards. A few more yards," Mychel was muttering, accelerating slowly after the last turn. Aerina realized she was gripping the seat with bruising force when pain began shooting through her hands. Hope flared in her chest as she saw the large gate come into view.

Looking behind, she saw the truck had fallen back. The next time she looked, it was gone. The driver couldn't risk being identified by the Armati guards at the massive city gate.

The Armati soldier who came down to verify their IDs was young, not much older than Aerina. She seemed shocked, and a little uncertain, when Mychel told her of their attack. But she drew herself together quickly, motioning to the other guards. Soon Aerina and Mychel found themselves being interrogated in a small room in the gatehouse, questions fired at them quickly and succinctly.

Aerina was hesitant to tell them her reasons for visiting the Aggie Terrace. She didn't know how much the Virmortus shared with the regular soldiers about investigations. When she explained she was looking for closure around a traumatic event, the young Armati looked at her differently; recognizing her.

Aerina shifted from foot to foot, hugging her arms around her cold middle. Her clothes were damp, her white half boots destroyed by mud. But the cold in her gut came from fear. Someone was trying to kill her. It hadn't felt real until this moment.

She couldn't help but wish for Marcus' calming presence. As angry as she knew he would be, she felt safe with him.

The soldiers took down all the information about the truck she and Mychel could remember. It wasn't much.

"We should be able to identify the attacker," an older Armati said. "This kind of thing is rare, but it does happen. If we can't locate the perpetrator ourselves, we'll pass the case along to the Virmortus. Haven't had a case they couldn't solve yet," the grey-haired man marveled. The younger soldier nodded her agreement, her star-struck eyes still on Aerina.

She met Mychel's gaze. Neither woman mentioned their

concern — that this was more than just a random attack. Someone was targeting Aerina.

She thought of Cynthia's parting words. *The next visit won't end so well for you.*

Was that a threat? Had she come after them, or sent someone? Perhaps she blamed Aerina for Cassandra's death in some way, or was just angry because Aerina had lived and her sister had died.

The Armati wrapped up their questioning, promising to contact the women with any updates. They thanked the soldiers, getting back into Kevin's damaged car. Aerina made a mental note to offer to pay for repairs.

Mychel turned in her seat to face Aerina. "You'd better go straight home and tell that Reaper friend of yours about this."

"I don't understand why they want me dead; if I was going to share information, I would have already done it." Aerina was at a loss. Did she know more than she realized?

"As long as you're alive, you're a liability. Perhaps you saw the others involved and they're afraid you'll remember something. And now you're asking questions; talking to Cassandra's family." Mychel turned back, swiping her wrist and typing in Kevin's password to start the car. "Just be careful. Until your Reaper solves this case, you're in danger."

Mychel dropped Aerina off at the Ferry with a wave and headed back towards the Theatre District.

The Ferry was almost empty; a few late-night workers were heading to their posts and two well-dressed men got off on the Merchant Terrace. Aerina sat in the back, her blue eyes watchful. She kept her hand in her coat pocket on the handle of her sica blade, her back pressed against the seat.

By the time Aerina exited the Ferry on the Capitol Terrace, the rain had slowed to barely a sprinkle, but the evening air remained heavy with moisture. Her damp hair curled around her face, and she pulled her light jacket tighter around herself. She'd changed back into her white clothes in the car, but they were more suited to a beach day than a cool Northern Coastline evening.

The terrace was mostly dark, lit only by the soft glow of the pseudo-oil lamps that lined the streets. Rather than turning towards her own villa, she headed towards the towering dark cliffs to the west. Towards Marcus' home.

She couldn't keep herself from continually scanning the streets, her ears straining for the sound of anything out of place. The serenity of the Capitol Terrace had been shattered.

As she approached the cobblestone street that ended before the edge of the cliff, she didn't see any lights in his villa. Looking over her shoulder at the still-empty street, she walked to his carport and peeked in.

Empty.

He was still gone. After a moment of hesitation, she picked up her holoreader and looked him up on the Network phonebook. Marcus Trent. No names were listed in the Network as his nearest kin.

She quietly instructed her reader to call the number. Immediately, she heard the digitized voice asking her to leave a message. That meant his phone was either off, or he was out of range from the ComTower.

Sighing, she clicked her reader back onto her bracelet, ignoring the twinge of worry and growing fear she felt. It had been a long day and her feet were killing her. She would head home, warm up with a shower, and sleep.

Turning back, she gasped at the dark figure standing on the walk behind her. Gripping her sica blade tightly, she stood, shaking.

"What do you want?" she demanded, surprised the words came out past the fear lodged in her throat.

The shadow glided closer and she stepped back, holding up the blade.

"Relax, Ms. Delacroix. Mr. Trent asked me to follow you. I know about your accident; my partner just briefed me. I wanted to be sure you were alright." The man stepped under a streetlamp, revealing his Virmortus weapon vest.

"Where is Marcus?" she asked sharply, not relaxing her

guard.

"He asked me to give you this," the slim man, surprisingly small for a Virmortus, held up a black-gloved hand. Aerina glanced down, seeing the chess piece he held. It was her king. "And he said 'checkmate'," he finished, his voice even.

Aerina lowered her blade. If this Virmortus was trying to kill her, he could have done so already. Stepping forward, she took the piece and slipped it into her coat pocket.

"Thank you," she murmured, her normal snarky attitude absent.

"I'll walk you home," he said in a voice that didn't allow for argument. Aerina warmed slightly. She should be annoyed at Marcus' high-handedness, but all she felt was relief at this point.

Chapter 8

"No one is so brave that he is not disturbed by something unexpected." - Julius Caesar

Aerina woke to the muted chime of her holoreader, indicating a call. She scrambled around on her end table, searching for it, an excitement building in her chest. Marcus was calling her back.

Her heart sank when she saw Lina's face project from the reader, but she took the call.

"Hey, sleepyhead. I can't believe you're still in bed. My brother says it's a perfect day for surfing. What do you think?"

Aerina was surprised Lina's brother Stephen was willing to be seen with her. She felt a surge of renewed excitement. Perhaps her exile was coming to an end. Then she remembered the previous night. Perhaps she *should* stay close to home...

"I don't know if I'm up for it today, Lina. And I thought you hated surfing?"

Lina's smile looked more like a grimace even on the transparent projection. "I don't *hate* it. I'm just not very good. And feel like I'm drowning half the time. But I don't mind it, really."

Aerina rolled her eyes. "Yeah, ok." She knew her friend was trying to find ways to bring Aerina back into the caste. After the past few weeks, surfing with Stephen seemed like a lifetime ago.

But it would help her relax. What could possibly happen in the middle of the day, anyway?

"Let's go."

"Meet us at the Patrician tram in twenty minutes," Lina instructed before disconnecting. Aerina rolled out of bed and grabbed her short-sleeved wet suit. She scrubbed her face, threw her long hair into a ponytail, and headed towards the tram.

Lina, Stephen, and a few of his buddies were waiting. Aerina groaned inwardly when she saw Todd. Her parents had mentioned him as a possible candidate for a marriage arrangement, which Aerina had immediately rejected. He still made awkward overtures every time she saw him. Maybe her new status would have crushed his infatuation.

She wasn't that lucky. In the small glass tram, Aerina positioned herself in the back corner next to Lina but Todd still managed to wheedle his way between the girls. Aerina shot daggers at her friend while Lina pretended not to notice.

"I've missed seeing you around lately," Todd said, putting his foot in his mouth with his opening statement. Aerina sighed as the older boy blushed, realizing his faux pas.

"Yeah, too bad you got busted running with some crazy Plebs. I thought for sure the Virmortus was going to take you out," one of the other boys, Anthony, said goadingly. Aerina opened her mouth with a scathing retort, but Stephen cut her off.

"Leave her alone," he said quietly. Aerina shot him a grateful look. He'd been as much a big brother to her as he had to Lina over the years. The subject changed to the look of the ocean—the waves were decent, not too choppy with a long roll.

They all selected boards, even Lina, and paddled out through the surf into the deeper water. Aerina straddled her board, content just to ride the waves, enjoying the sun beating down on her head and the cool water lapping at her bare legs.

She watched the others. A few of the boys caught a nice-sized wave, riding it to shore before it capped and knocked them off. Lina, at Anthony's goading, tried to get up as a large wave came rolling through. She lasted barely a second before the board tipped one way and Lina splashed the other way, limbs flailing. Aerina fought back a smile. Lina would never be a good surfer.

Her blue eyes scanned the horizon, squinting against the glare of the sun, magnified by the light haze hovering over the water. From the corner of her eye, she caught sight of Todd paddling over. With an inaudible groan, she looked for a wave, any wave, that would carry her in.

A good one rolled through and she was up, the board wobbling precariously in a moment of uncertainty before she got the rhythm of the wave, riding it towards shore. The spray felt cold yet refreshing, the board buoyant beneath her feet. She gracefully slipped into the water as the sand sped towards her, grabbing her board and rising from the surf.

She glanced over to see Stephen walking beside her, carrying his own board. They dropped down on the sand, side-by-side.

"How have you been," he asked, resting his lanky body back on his elbows. He was tall and dark like his sister, his love of sports keeping him lean. Becoming a technology geek hadn't slowed him down at all.

"Fine, really," Aerina replied, not wanting to bore Stephen with details of her emotional turmoil. "It was a little boring at first, but now..." She trailed off with a shrug.

"Lina tells me you're investigating that dancer, the one that tried to kill the Consul?" His voice held both disapproval and concern.

Aerina tamped down the twinge of annoyance. Couldn't Lina keep anything to herself?

"I just wanted to learn a little about her." Aerina glanced over at Stephen as a thought struck her, her eyes narrowing thoughtfully.

"I know I'm not the only Patrician who is spending time with the Plebs. Lina tells me you like to visit some of the brothels on the Pleb terrace."

Stephen stiffened, a slight tint of red staining his cheekbones. He watched Anthony attempt to help Lina get up on her board, narrowing his light brown eyes as his friend "accidentally" brushed his sister's bikini-encased bottom.

"How would she know that?" He sounded disgruntled.

"Well?"

"None of your business."

"Stephen, I know you don't agree with what I'm doing. But I need to learn more about Cassandra. She worked at a brothel, and if I could just talk to some of her—er—coworkers, I could learn valuable information about what happened." *And who is trying to kill me*, she added silently. "Would you take me to the—"

"No, absolutely not," Stephen interjected, knowing Aerina well enough to figure out where her question was leading.

"Just once. I just want to —"

"No."

Aerina thought quickly. Todd was giving them long looks and she knew it was only a matter of time until he joined them.

"Helen. I know you like Helen. I can help you." Stephen looked over at her quickly, his eyes narrowing. He knew she was bluffing; Helen would never listen to her now. She smiled encouragingly. "Come on, Stephen. Women go to the brothels, too. I suppose I can just go on my own…"

That threat did the trick.

"Fine. I'll take you. Once. We'll go tonight and get it over with."

"Thank you!" she squealed, giving him a hug. "Whatever you do, just don't tell Lina."

Aerina waited impatiently for evening. Her attempts to reach Marcus were futile; his device remained off or out of range. She didn't bother leaving a message.

On the way back from the beach, she'd watched for the Virmortus that she knew was trailing her. Even though she hadn't seen him, she was still certain he was there. The knowledge was strangely comforting.

What he would think about the little evening jaunt she was about to undertake? What would Marcus think when he found out?

She decided to worry about that when it happened. She dressed carefully in flowing white pants and a short sleeve knit top. The urge to wear dark clothes was strong, but she worried about looking out of place. Best just to play it cool; like she told Stephen, women visited brothels. She was just another Patrician, out for an evening of fun.

She met the boys at the tram again, the same group minus Lina. Anthony winked at her lasciviously, while Todd refused to look at her. Stephen grinned.

"Shall we go?"

The tram slid to a stop on the Plebian Terrace. Aerina could already feel the excitement of the lower city pumping through her veins. She couldn't help but smile with exhilaration as they made their way through the active streets.

She felt more conspicuous now than ever in her Patrician white. Her eyes darted around, trying to catch a glimpse of the man shadowing her. Was he there? Another more sinister thought followed. *Who else was following her?*

They came to the entertainment district, adjacent to the theatre district, which had brothels, casinos, and a sport complex. Aerina walked next to Stephen, feeling the glances of the Plebs milling around. Neither Stephen nor his friends seemed uncomfortable. They walked blithely forward, comfortable in their status as superior. She relaxed slightly; this wasn't a lonely muddy street outside the walls. This was the heart of the city.

A sign gleamed up ahead. Aerina couldn't help but smirk at the name. *Finding Serenity.* The brothel entrance was guarded by two large men looking suspiciously like ex-Armati. They nodded to Stephen and opened the door, scanning ID chips for the cover charge. Aerina followed the boys inside with a mixture of curiosity and discomfort, holding her own wrist to be scanned. She could feel the guard's eyes on her and worry began to take over. Did he recognize her? Did they have access to the same secret data that Marcus did, and was her chip flagged somehow?

Aerina tamped down the rising panic. She wasn't doing anything wrong.

"This brothel caters to Patricians," Stephen murmured as the group was escorted forward by a young woman dressed in a simple white gown.

The entrance was grand in a subdued way. A large staircase went to the upper floor, supported by graceful columns that left the main floor open. The interior was decorated tastefully in white with gold accents. Aerina could see why Patricians would feel comfortable here.

The women were dressed in variations of the flowing white gown, some quite sheer, others with golden chains holding much of the outfit together. A few of the women approached the newcomers with welcoming smiles, their movements graceful and unhurried.

A young man, looking to be the same age as Aerina, spoke briefly with the hostess before approaching her. He smiled, holding out a slender, tanned hand. He was fit but very lean.

She took his hand hesitantly, looking back at Stephen. He quirked a brow as if to ask if she was sure, and she nodded, waving. He turned back to the woman at his side with a smile.

As Aerina followed the young man to a low couch in the back, she couldn't help but wonder if Marcus ever visited brothels. Virmortus didn't marry. He must find some way to relieve sexual tension.

"I am Aquilus," the young prostitute said quietly, his hand resting on her shoulder, moving in slow circles.

"Aerina," she replied, moving slightly until his hand was barely touching her. He was too feminine for her tastes. She favored large men. With dark hair and eyes.

"Aerina, tell me what you like. What makes you happy?" his voice was gentle, like his touch. Aerina again thought of Marcus, imagined his large, rough hand rubbing her shoulder, down her back, like this man was. Immediately a spark of desire ignited.

She cleared her throat.

"You want to know what would make me really happy?" she purred. Aquilus leaned in with a smile, waiting.

"If you could tell me about Cassandra Redding."

Immediately the young man stiffened and moved away slightly. His hand fell away. Aerina thought she detected a glimmer of fear in his light green eyes.

"I'm sorry, who?" he asked unconvincingly. Damn. She should have been more subtle.

"She was a friend of mine. She worked here, and I know she still came here to meet her lover. Please, can you tell me who she met here?" Aerina asked imploringly, gripping his smooth hand.

He extracted his hand gently from her grip.

"I'm sorry, but I am afraid I will not be able to please you tonight," he said with false regret. "I will send someone else."

Aerina waited, her frustration mounting. She doubted the

next person would be any more helpful. A young woman approached. She sat down with Aerina.

"I am Camila. Aquilus tells me he is unable to please you. Can I be of service?" the young woman asked, taking Aerina's hand in hers. Damn, her hands were as soft as Aquilus'. What was their secret?

"Did you know Cassandra Redding? She used to work here." As soon as she had said Cassandra's name, she could see the girl's eyes go flat. She wasn't going to learn anything from the workers. Camila politely denied knowledge of Cassandra several times before rising herself.

The woman Aerina assumed to be the manager of the brothel approached next with a large man she hoped was security and not the next prostitute sent to "please" her.

Aerina groaned inwardly. She was about to be thrown out of a brothel. But, after nearly being publicly executed by the man she secretly desired, she supposed this wasn't so bad.

It was all about perspective.

"I'm sorry, miss, but we are going to have to ask you to leave," the tastefully dressed older woman murmured politely, gesturing towards the back door. Aerina sighed and stood, looking over to where Stephen and his friends had been. They had disappeared, no doubt up the large stairway. At least their evening was ending better than hers.

She headed towards the back door, her elbow held firmly but politely in the giant man's grip.

"Thank you ever so much," she murmured sarcastically as he held the back door open for her. The door closed behind her and she stood for a moment, debating what to do. Should she try and get a message to Stephen or just walk back herself?

Deciding that Stephen would probably prefer not be disturbed, she was turning away as an e-car pulled around the back. Instinctively Aerina stepped back into the shadows to watch with a mixture of embarrassment and fear.

Her nervousness faded, however, as she saw Niko and two of his friends exit the car. The door was immediately opened by the manager herself and the Consul's slim, flaxen-haired son was escorted in. He was obviously a regular. Not that she was surprised, knowing what a complete wastrel he was.

Turning, she walked slowly back towards the street. Perhaps she'd stop in and visit Julia and Mychel at the Theatre since she was already here. She might be able to catch them between shows if she hurried.

Chapter 9

"Don't wait. The time will never be just right."
- Napoleon Hill

Marcus was gone for over a week.

Aerina worried. After returning from the failed attempt at interrogating the brothel employees, she had staked out his house. She needed to talk to him. To tell him everything. When two more days went by with no sign of him, she became increasingly concerned.

What if something happened to him? No one would ever tell her. She might hear of it eventually, but what if he was injured? Or what if he was on the outside and hadn't returned?

What if he was avoiding her? She rejected that last thought quickly. Marcus would tell her off before he would avoid her.

After worrying over these questions for a long day, she couldn't take it anymore. She had to know.

Taking her parent's e-car, she drove towards the far end of the Capitol Terrace to the Training Grounds. Set apart from the rest of the terrace, the grounds were cut back into the mountain. The entrance was small, unassuming on the east side of the road. To the west was steep hillside that dropped down to the ocean below.

The road ended at the cliff's edge. Aerina parked her car and walked towards the heavy steel door slowly. The door opened into a tiny building that appeared to be an extension of the rocky wall behind it. Some of the building was built over the precipice's edge, with large steel beams braced to support it. She'd seen them from a distance many times, but she'd never actually been close to the Virmortus headquarters. And certainly never attempted to breach them.

She shivered, but not from the cool ocean air that slipped through her thin coat. Gooseflesh covered her arms. Clouds hung low and dark in the sky, predicting rain and adding to her feeling of foreboding. Straightening her shoulders, she pulled every bit of hauteur she had gained as the daughter of a Senator around her for courage.

The door was, unsurprisingly, locked. She scanned her ID card to no avail.

"Do you need something?" barked a voice loudly in her ear, making her start violently. An intercom, she told her racing heart. It didn't seem to care, racing on.

A small button next to a tiny camera eye and speaker was obviously how she could communicate. Depressing the button, she spoke clearly into the small box. "Yes, I'm looking for Marcus Trent. I need to speak with him."

"He's not here."

Thanks, you're so helpful, Aerina thought sarcastically, saying instead, "Can you tell me where he is?"

"No."

Aerina set her back teeth. Did they teach poor communication as an interrogation tactic? Marcus certainly had that skill perfected.

Shooting the tiny eye her best aristocratic look, she tried again. "It's important. My name is Aerina Delacroix. I need to speak with whomever is in charge."

A long silence followed her demand. A minute passed. And then another. Hopefully he was checking on her request, because she would feel awfully stupid standing here, waiting, if he wasn't.

She tried not to fidget as she waited. It was tough, particularly when she imagined one or more of them watching her through the tiny camera lens. What would Marcus do? Scale the wall, hack into the ID system, and force his way in? Unfortunately, none of those solutions were an option for her. All she had were her good looks and Patrician arrogance.

She was here. She'd already made an idiot of herself. She wasn't leaving without talking to *someone*, dammit.

She was considering flashing the camera to see if that got a reaction when there was a buzz and click, followed by a curt command.

"Come in."

What am I doing? she asked herself as she wrenched open the heavy steel door. How many people had come through these doors unwillingly?

And how many of them didn't leave again?

The hallway was short and unrelenting white. A second door opened in front of her, and filling the frame was a large, black-uniformed figure.

"Miss Delacroix. Please come in," the Virmortus greeted her in a deep, even voice. He was big, his muscles bulging and straining the tight armored shirt, a weapon belt buckled around a lean waist. His skin was dark, nearly ebony, and it made his light grey eyes all the more disquieting.

"Thank you," Aerina murmured politely as she slipped through the second heavy door, hearing it closing behind her with a distinct click. She ignored the slight claustrophobic feeling that settled around her.

Trapped.

These were the Training Grounds. Her eyes quickly took in the scene before her. A vast room built into the mountain, lit by numerous electric lights, spread nearly two floors down below. Everything was stone and steel; an unrelenting grey arena. She shivered again. This was where Marcus had spent his childhood.

Several men dressed in black fought savagely below, and she stood, transfixed, watching them. Their speed was impressive, as were the wounds each had on them. *That explains Marcus' scars.* Her eyes darted to the large man next to her. He was watching her, as if waiting for her reaction. She did her best to school her features into a look of unconcern, but was sure he could see her horrified fascination.

"This way," he said finally, turning and walking to the left. Aerina tore her eyes away from the violent scene, following him down a cool stone hallway.

They walked into an office, which looked as if it could have been a Patrician's office in the Capitol. The contrast to the stark hallway was startling.

A large desk dominated one wall. What caught her eye was the screen which made up the other wall. It appeared to project a topographic grid of the city with millions of tiny moving lights, under which a long meeting table stretched, accompanied by several plush chairs. Aerina's eyes narrowed as she studied the odd grid, trying to determine what purpose it served.

"What is this?"

The large man, who had yet to introduce himself, clicked a button and the grid suddenly went dark. "You're tracking people, aren't you?" she asked in horrified fascination, large blue eyes meeting the cold grey of the Virmortus. It would be easy; everyone had an ID chip. That explained how Marcus had conveniently known where she was the night he had saved her.

They had always known what she was doing.

Aerina unflinchingly met the large man's emotionless gaze, raising one brow in question. She wasn't going to let him intimidate her.

His eyes seemed to lighten slightly, perhaps with humor. Ignoring her question, he finally introduced himself. "My name is Ramus Grim. I am Marcus' second in command." Aerina's fought to control an instinctive smile. Grim? Was that really his last name, or did he make that up? Sort of like a stage name?

"Mr. Grim," — she was proud she'd said it with a completely straight face—"you know I'm looking for Marcus. If you could just tell me his whereabouts, I will be happy to quit pestering you. I'm sure you're a very busy man." She turned up the wattage in her smile, flipping her hair lightly before she could stop herself.

"Please, call me Ramus," he answered, still studying her thoughtfully from his too-observant grey eyes. "I think now I understand," he added quietly as if to himself.

Aerina's forehead wrinkled slightly in confusion, but she waited. She was beginning to regret the rash impulse that had driven her here today. What was she really going accomplish?

"I'm afraid I cannot tell you where Marcus is currently, but if you give me a message, I will be sure to share it with him when I speak with him next."

"I can leave a message on his Com device," Aerina replied, slight frustration seeping into her voice despite her best effort to keep it contained. "Or with the man he has following me. Do you know when he will be back, or is that top secret too?"

Grim—excuse her—*Ramus*, lifted an eyebrow at her sarcasm. "Unfortunately, I don't know," he replied politely, then waited expectantly. She began to wonder if he was deliberately baiting her.

If he was trying to raise her ire, it was working. She was getting nowhere. Why had he even agreed to see her? It no doubt would have been highly amusing to have left her standing out there until she tucked tail and walked away.

"Is there anything you *can* tell me?" she asked, injecting a note of pleading into her voice.

"You know," he answered instead, settling his large frame easily into the office chair, "I believe you are the first visitor to these Training Grounds without an express invitation."

"I can't imagine why, after the warm and friendly welcome I have received," she answered sardonically.

Ramus let out a bark of laughter, seeming surprised by her comment. He stared at her in fascination, leaning forward and resting massive forearms on his equally massive quadriceps.

"Tell me, Miss Delacroix, does your mouth ever get you into trouble?"

"Not as often as my dancing." Ramus laughed again, and this time it sounded a little less rusty. It was Aerina's turn to watch him in fascination. It was like they were two completely different animals, studying one another on a first encounter. Wary, but not yet having a reason to be afraid.

And hopefully it stayed that way. Ramus looked congenial enough, but he was also a giant. And if those two guys she had witnessed trying to kill one another in the pit were any indication of the training he had undergone, he was deadly.

"Is this Marcus' office?" She turned the subject, hoping to glean a tiny bit of information about the object of her interest.

"It is the office he uses when he is here, yes."

"So he spends a lot of his time here?" she inquired casually, her eyes running over the desk. She badly wanted to open some of the drawers, and check out the holocomputer.

"At times," was the answer from Captain Vague.

Aerina coughed a couple times as if her throat were dry. She smiled. "I beg your pardon. I don't suppose you have anything to drink?"

Ramus' return smile didn't quite reach his grey eyes. He stood suddenly, and it was all Aerina could do to keep from jumping. His smile widened as if he knew how nervous he made her. He pressed a small button on the wall, speaking into an intercom she hadn't noticed before.

"Could you bring us…" he raised his eyebrows in question.

"Water is fine," she murmured, doing her best to hide her disappointment.

"Water, Nemo." He stepped back, watching her. So much for that plan. He'd seen right through it.

A moment later, the automatic door slid open and a wiry young man entered, carrying a tray with a pitcher of water and two glasses. Aerina smiled, thanking him. He stared at her for a moment before ducking his head. She thought she saw the red stain of a blush on his prominent cheek bones, but he turned away quickly before she could be sure.

"Where did you come from, Ramus?" she asked, sipping the water he handed her. If he seemed surprised by her question, he hid it well.

"I was the third child of a merchant family," he said finally, drawing the words out slowly, as if just remembering himself.

"Many Virmortus are third children, aren't they." The question was more of a statement. It was a sad fact that families caught giving birth to a third child without a permit from Population Control, rather than killing it, were often forced to give up the child to the Armati, who then pushed them through the Virmortus training. Not all survived the intensive program, according to rumors.

Thankfully, third children were rare, and third children born without a permit even more so. Most Albans understood the importance of population control.

"Some are," Ramus answered with another annoyingly vague response.

"Is Marcus?" she asked innocently, taking a dainty sip of water, watching him with wide guileless eyes over the top of her cup.

"Marcus' story is his own to tell," Ramus replied softly, chidingly. Aerina sighed. She was getting nowhere.

She set her water glass down on the desk with a snap.

"Since you aren't going to tell me where Marcus is, or turn your back for a moment so I can go through the desk and peek on the holocomputer, or accidentally divulge any interesting or personal details, I might as well stop wasting your time," she said candidly, tired of the subterfuge. Guile had never been her strong suit. Ramus' eyes widened for a moment, a sign she had truly caught him off guard with her frankness.

"I'm sorry I couldn't be of more help," he answered with only the lightest of sarcasm, "but I'll be sure to let Marcus know of your visit." Ramus opened the door, motioning for her to precede him. She stood for a moment, considering refusing to leave. But the look on *Mr. Grim's* face suggested that would be a poor choice.

"Do me a favor and don't," she muttered instead, preceding him back down the hall. In the large pit below the hallway, the two men were no longer fighting. One was being examined by what looked to be a Medella, while the other was listening intently to a third man, perhaps the instructor. Both men were a mess, clothes torn and covered in blood.

She shivered as she entered the small hallway leading back outside. What kind of person came from an upbringing in which such casual violence was accepted? It was difficult for her to pair civilized, intelligent men like Marcus and Ramus with the violence she knew they must have endured. She had even witnessed the violence Marcus was capable of, and still had trouble wrapping her mind around the fact that Marcus was a trained killer.

She needed to remember that the man and the Reaper were one. A wild beast was never completely tame, no matter how gentle it might appear.

Chapter 10

"You can discover more about a person in an hour of play than in a year of conversation." - Plato

The remainder of the week passed with painful slowness. So painful, in fact, that Aerina almost wished the would-be-attacker would resurface just for a little excitement. Almost.

Aerina spent much of the week alone, lost in her own thoughts. Lina was busy with her "acceptable" Patrician friends, Julia and Mychel had their schedules full practicing for a new weekend show, and her parents were their normal absent selves. The only contact she'd had was when Stephen had checked in to make sure she'd made it home safely after the brothel.

As another day passed, she came up with one reason after another for Marcus' absence. Rather than focusing on preparing for her Final Examinations, her mind concentrated on Marcus.

Ridiculous, she told herself. How could she be so completely crazy over a Reaper? And not just any Reaper — their leader. The man was a trained killer, and had in fact inflicted a nearly mortal injury upon her. On top of that, he had never shown any interest in her. Besides as a potential victim.

Then why couldn't she get him out of her head?

Because I know there is more to him than the Reaper everyone else sees. The veiled sense of humor; the man who excelled at chess. The hero that had rescued her from a dark alley when there was no benefit to himself. The man who honored a decade-old debt by letting her live when she should have died.

Something about his hard demeanor, his aloofness, made her want to crack his shell and see what lay underneath. She'd only caught glimpses of the real Marcus; the man beneath the killer's garb. But what she saw, she liked.

Probably liked too much, in fact.

She was heading home from the sports complex when she caught a glimpse of his car in the Capitol drive.

A mixture of relief, fury, and another emotion she wasn't yet ready to name filled her at the sight of his familiar black cruiser.

She wanted to storm right up to him and demand answers, but she knew he had gone straight to see the Consul. Instead, she waited impatiently at home, watching for his e-car to pass on the way to his house.

It was almost dark by the time she caught a glimpse of the familiar dark vehicle cruising slowly towards the east side of the terrace. Tossing aside the book she had been pretending to read, she grabbed her jacket and walked towards his villa.

She had showered and changed into a pair of tight white pants and a blue t-shirt—a Pleb gift from Julia—that hugged her modest curves. In her rush, she'd only bothered to slip on her white leather moccasins and a thin coat.

Anticipation built in her chest as she neared. The week had seemed like months.

He answered on her first knock, his hair damp from a recent shower, wearing black drawstring pants and nothing else.

She couldn't help but stare for a long moment at his perfectly sculpted upper body. Muscles like that should only be real in paintings, she thought, her hand itching to trace the grooves and hollows. Then she noticed the scars, several crisscrossing his abdomen, one over his shoulder, and many small ones on his chest and arms.

Her eyes flew to meet his. He was watching her, one brow quirked as if daring her to say something.

She wanted to ask, almost as much as she wanted to touch. But of course she did neither.

"Can I come in?"

"Tonight isn't a good night," he responded quietly, not moving aside. She noticed his eyes seemed more shadowed than usual and slightly bloodshot.

"Where have you been?" she demanded with less heat than she had originally intended. Something about the weariness in his face made her feel the urge to comfort rather than chastise.

He quirked his brow again. "I didn't realize I was supposed to keep you apprised of my whereabouts."

She narrowed her eyes, the urge to comfort growing smaller. "I was worried." That was an understatement.

"I'm fine. Now you can go."

"I need to talk to you. To tell you a few things," she said, pressing her palm against his bare chest and pushing lightly. To her surprise, he stepped back, letting her enter.

He suddenly gripped her wrist, his hold light but unbreakable. "I told you tonight is not a good night. I don't have the patience to deal with you right now."

That hurt. Aerina knew they'd had a brief and tumultuous relationship. If their association could even be called a relationship. And he *had* been forced to save her life twice now. But she thought he felt more for her than just tolerance. That he felt at least a little of the electric connection she did.

Her eyes fell to where her hand was still pressed to his warm, damp chest. Unable to stop herself, she curled her fingers slightly, feeling the light hairs against her fingertips.

A slight shudder passed through his frame. "I hope you don't regret this as much as I'm going to," he rasped, pulling her against him, his hard mouth covering hers, swallowing her gasp of surprise.

It was as good as she had imagined. Better.

His lips were hard and firm as they moved over hers. His tongue swept inside to explore the moist inner folds of her lips. This was not a gentle kiss; it was a kiss of craving and possession. He was devouring her. And she wanted more.

He gripped her upper arms, lifting her up on her toes, pressing her against him. She could feel the firm contours of his chest brushing against her breasts through the thin t-shirt, and his muscled thighs pressed to hers.

He was just hard. Everywhere.

She was melting into a boneless mess. If he hadn't been holding her up, she would have collapsed. Drowning in his kiss, liquid heat spread through her body and pooled at her core.

Years of longing had culminated into this single kiss. She ached for more, pressing her body closer, her hands running over his bare chest, his flat abdomen. His muscles contracted and he gripped her arms even tighter. She was going to have bruises but she didn't care.

As quickly as he had grabbed her, he let go and turned away. He leaned one strong hand against a pillar, breathing heavily, fighting to control himself.

Aerina leaned back against the doorframe, raising a shaking hand to her still-moist lips. Her heart was pounding, her breath coming in short gasps. Her core pulsed with heat; with unfulfilled desire. She felt cold without his burning length molded to hers.

"Get out," he finally said in a low, harsh tone. Aerina stiffened at the command, the hurt she felt at his words immediately alleviated by his next statement. "I haven't slept more than a few hours this past week. I'm exhausted, and I don't know if I can stop myself again."

"I trust you," Aerina said softly, closing the door behind herself and moving slowly through the entranceway into the living room. She almost hoped he wouldn't be able to keep control of himself.

But she knew he would. Even if he didn't have faith in his ironclad will, she did.

"Dammit, Aerina—"

"You just got back from...wherever. You're tired and you must be hungry. I'll make you something to eat and then I'll leave you alone," she offered cajolingly.

She knew he wanted to say no, but finally he sat down at the kitchen table, saying nothing. He broodingly stared at the game of chess still on the table while she checked what food was available in the Dispensare.

Entering a recipe using the ingredients listed as available, she waited for it to cook before setting the simple stir fry dish before him, then joining him at the table.

He had set up a new game, having claimed her king. She pulled the piece from her pocket, setting it on the remaining empty space. The game began, each move planned in silence.

Aerina nudged her rook forward, countering his last move.

"You never do what I expect," he finally said quietly, moving his own piece.

"Good, I would hate to be predictable." She studied the board. It seemed like a straightforward move. But nothing about Marcus was straightforward.

They played chess while he ate in companionable silence. The anxiety that had hovered the past week seemed to lift with each moment she spent in his presence. And he seemed at ease, more relaxed than she had ever seen him. Maybe he was just too exhausted to maintain his normal aloofness.

Whatever the reason, she liked it.

Marcus watched Aerina study the chess board, idly pushing back a strand of long strawberry-blonde hair. Her latent energy burned beneath the surface, apparent in every quick motion and open expression. Being around her was both torture and heaven. He wanted her more than he'd ever wanted anything. She made him *feel*—anger, passion, even joy. And he couldn't remember the last time he had felt anything. He'd thought all the emotion had been drained from him in his childhood.

He did his duty, fulfilled his responsibilities. But that's all it was, all it had ever been. He had pushed himself hard the past week, for the first time *wanting* to return to the city. Not because of any pressing duties. Because of her. She gave him something to look forward to. The eleven missed calls on his holoreader had lightened his mood when he'd come back into range of the ComTower. He'd known she was thinking about him while he was gone. No one had ever done that before.

She looked up from the board, giving him an inquisitive smile. She was so beautiful—small yet strong, full lips, big blue eyes, and handfuls of silky hair. More than that, she was bold, curious, and full of life. He almost couldn't believe she was here in his kitchen. Unafraid. Happy just to be with *him*.

"Where were you all week? I asked around and no one seemed to know." She broke into his thoughts, leaning her chin on her hand.

He considered for a moment how much he should tell her. Finally, he said, "Outside. I did a routine check of the outpost towns."

Aerina's eyes widened. "Really? How exciting! What is it like? What did you learn?"

Marcus straightened slightly, tensing for another battle. He couldn't tell her, didn't *want* to tell her, what the world was like. And his role in it.

"Never mind, I get it, top secret stuff, right?" Aerina brushed it off lightly, making her next move. "I have some news for you."

Marcus relaxed imperceptibly, surprised at her easy acceptance. His Aerina was normally like a bloodhound when something caught her curiosity.

His Aerina... What the hell was he thinking? She'd never been his. She never could be.

Nothing matters but your job.

Aerina seemed impervious to his inner turmoil, moving on quickly to a new subject. "I did a little investigating while you were gone —"

"I heard," he interrupted, the reminder erasing the pleasure of the evening. He'd been briefed of her activities upon his return, much to his angry disbelief.

Aerina drew her knee up to rest her chin on it, not quite meeting his eyes.

"What are you going to do about it?" He stared at her, his eyes dark embers. She tried to meet his gaze, but glanced back down at the chessboard after a moment. He felt a small amount of satisfaction at her uneasiness.

When he sat forward quickly, she couldn't help but flinch. She tried to hide the motion with a flip of her hair as if trying to appear unintimidated.

"This is a serious investigation. You're like a child with a new favorite toy, playing at being a Virmortus. Do you know how stupid that is?" He bit off each word carefully, trying to keep his anger under control, forgetting that only a moment ago he had been relieved to have avoided this exact kind of argument. Without even trying, she knew how to get under his skin.

He was angry, but even stronger was fear for her safety. This thing was big, bigger even than he already suspected. And suddenly just doing his job wasn't his priority. Keeping her safe was more important. She shouldn't matter so much. He shouldn't be distracted.

But she did. And he was. And now he had to juggle both.

"I believe you've mentioned before your opinion about my intelligence. Or lack thereof," she muttered sardonically.

His voice was hoarse when he finally spoke, bringing himself back under control with effort. "This isn't a game. You are putting yourself in danger, and I can't have you stumbling around, potentially affecting the investigation."

"You know who it is, don't you?" she asked in angry frustration. "How?" Shaking her head in disgust, she continued, "Forget how. What I want to know is why didn't you tell me? You knew I was in danger. Why do you have to be so damn secretive!" She rose quickly, her chair tipping back and crashing to the floor.

Marcus sat back in his seat, watching her with his *infuriating,* unreadable eyes.

"It's my job to be 'secretive', Aerina," Marcus responded quietly. "Perhaps you should consider focusing on your own responsibilities."

Aerina's back stiffened at the backhanded reprimand. Graduation was approaching and she still hadn't been recruited by any sector. Of course he would know that. She might not *have* a job to do come January.

Aerina watched as Marcus' jaw flexed. Once. Twice. He was angry with her, that she didn't doubt. But did he trust her? She'd been nothing but honest with him, and she couldn't tell how much he was keeping from her. Probably everything. And that hurt. Dammit, she wanted him to trust her.

Swallowing her angry arguments, she got her emotions back under control.

Small steps, Rina. The man needs to learn about trust. It isn't going to happen overnight. Focus on the small steps. She *was* here in his house. They were talking. He hadn't thrown her out.

And he still hadn't put a shirt on, which was extremely distracting.

"Perhaps you're right," she allowed, turning her attention

back to the chess game, moving her pawn forward absently.

"Checkmate." Marcus followed her move with a quick one of his own. His large form lounged back in the chair he dwarfed as he watched her face. Her bright eyes narrowed, studying his move, then groaned. He had her king. Damn! He won again.

She looked up to demand a rematch, only to see him run a tired hand over his eyes. Immediately, she felt contrite for having kept him up so long and rose to clear the table. The discussion would have to wait.

"You should go to bed. I'll clean up and let myself out."

He stood slowly, stretching his large frame. She tried not to stare at the muscles that rippled on his still-bare chest.

"I'll walk you home," he said. Aerina opened her mouth to argue, then shut it.

"Fine. Why don't you rest on the divan while I clean up?"

Surprisingly, he didn't argue. He sat down slowly on the chocolate-colored divan, his eyes following her movements as she washed and dried the dishes. By the time she had put the last dish away, his eyes had closed, his breathing slowed.

He was asleep.

She moved towards him slowly, not wanting to wake him. Contrary to the cliché, he looked no less vulnerable in sleep. His powerful jaw, slightly crooked nose, and angled cheekbones made him look just as dangerous asleep as he did awake. Just as powerful.

She got a blanket from his bed and placed it over his sleeping form, gently easing him down until he lay flat on the couch.

He must trust her, to fall asleep with her in his home.

Little steps.

She sat beside him for a long moment, her eyes moving over his face. What had this man experienced to give him the terrible scars she had seen on his body? And the scars he carried inside? She was hungry for information that would bring her closer to understanding him.

He was completely and utterly fascinating. She couldn't explain the strange infatuation, it had just always been, since the day she'd first seen him.

She'd never dated or been interested in other boys, because next to him, they'd been just that: boys. And now she was afraid that her childish infatuation was maturing into something more. But what future could they have? They might both live on the Capitol Terrace, but there was an ocean of differences between them.

Brushing her hand over his short-cropped hair, she gently traced the square jaw shadowed with several days' growth of beard, the hollows of his cheek, over his lips. She flushed, feeling like a molester. The man was passed out from exhaustion, for serenity's sake.

Unable to help herself, she leaned in slowly, breathing in the glorious scent of soap and musk that was him. She brushed her mouth gently over his, delighting in the feel of the rough stubble against her soft lips.

Tucking the blanket around him, she rose and walked quietly out. Tomorrow would be soon enough to get the information she wanted from him.

Marcus heard the door shut behind her and released his pent up breath. She'd be safe enough walking home with the guard still following her. He had awoken when she placed the blanket on him, and had to fight not to grab her when she touched him; kissed him. Thankfully she hadn't noticed the obvious sign of his arousal tenting the blanket below his waist.

Adjusting the drawstring pants, he got up and collapsed on top of his bed to sleep off the urges he didn't know if he could fight much longer.

Chapter 11

"When love is not madness it is not love."
- Pedro Calderón de la Barca

It was late when Aerina slipped into bed that night. Both her parents had been sleeping, which she was thankful for. She didn't feel like offering up any explanations for her recent absences.

She couldn't sleep. Her room faced the ocean, but the mist was so thick she couldn't see the inky depths far below. The sound of the surf carried through the still night air, and if she listened closely she could hear the bustle of the Pleb Terrace.

Tossing and turning, she finally threw her sheets off. She couldn't get her mind to settle. She kept thinking of Marcus and the evening. The kiss.

It was just a kiss.

But it hadn't been. It was a turning point, metamorphosing their strange connection into something more. Could it be a relationship? More importantly, would *Marcus* consider their association a relationship?

She gave up on trying to sleep, getting up and padding quietly down the stairs to the kitchen. Grabbing a glass from the cupboard, she turned towards the Dispensare.

"Couldn't sleep?"

Aerina gasped, nearly dropped her glass, as she spun towards the voice from the shadows.

"Dad, you scared me," she said, pressing a hand to her racing heart.

"Sorry," he chuckled. He sat at the small breakfast nook with a glass of tea, just enough in the shadows that she hadn't noticed him.

Aerina selected ice water, waiting while the nearly silent hum was followed by running water. She filled her glass and slid into the slingback chair across from her father.

"What are you doing up?" she asked him, studying her ice cubes intently, unable to meet his eyes.

"Just my age," he responded. They were both silent for a long moment. Antony broke the silence.

"You surely have a lot on your mind?" The statement was more of a question.

Aerina smiled a little self-deprecatingly, pulling her knee up to rest her chin on. "Mostly the situation I have brought upon myself."

Antony stared at her thoughtfully for a moment. "You don't seem as regretful as I expected you to be."

Aerina considered how to answer her father. She decided to be completely honest. "It was hard, especially at first. But being forced out of the social group that I've always been a part of has...opened my eyes to what else there is. I guess you could say it's shown me a side of Alba that I hadn't seen before, even though I had tried." She looked up at her father, willing him to understand what she couldn't put into words.

His striking blue eyes, so like her own, reflected his acceptance of what she said. "I think anyone who has the potential for greatness must first question everything they know, and decide for themselves what is real," he finally said. "You aren't accepting what you are told about the world. You are finding out for yourself. That takes courage in the face of such staunch disapproval."

Aerina smiled faintly, feeling the pleasure of her father's approval spread through her, warming her.

"However," her father continued, "I believe your days of being persona non grata are almost over. We received an invitation to the annual Patrician Graduate Ball. Your name was included."

Aerina had thought she was used to her new status, but found herself feeling inordinately pleased at her father's news.

Things might have changed—*she* had changed—but to be accepted again by her peers and not suffer the sting of rejection... It was more than she had hoped for.

Draining her glass, she rose and set it beside the sink.

"Thanks, Dad. That is good news. Goodnight."

"Aerina?" She turned back at the serious note in his voice. He looked older than she remembered, sitting in his neatly pressed white pajamas. The lines in his face appeared deeper in the shadows, and the grey in his hair gleamed in the blue light of the Dispensare. He seemed to waver uncertainly for a moment, as if considering his words carefully.

"Be careful. Trent is more dangerous than you can imagine. Just because he let you off easily once, it doesn't mean he will again under the right provocation."

Aerina nodded once before heading back upstairs.

She appreciated her father's concern, but she knew Marcus. He wouldn't harm her. She was certain.

Almost.

The morning of the Graduate Ball was rainy and dark. The air was cold even for early October. Rather than spending the day primping, she wanted to put on her comfy clothes and lounge. Preferably with Marcus.

But he was working, of course, busy preparing security for one of the biggest events of the year on the Capitol Terrace.

The week had passed slowly; the days dragged by because Aerina lived for the nights. Feeling like a pathetic hound waiting for its owner at the window, she couldn't help but watch for his familiar vehicle to pass on the way to his villa. Then she would force herself to wait, sometimes staring at her untouched holoreader, taking dinner with her parents, or even going to the sports complex to be snubbed by her former friends. The shadow that followed her was a constant reminder of the threat hanging over her head.

No matter how hard she tried to talk herself out of it, each evening ended at Marcus' villa. The evenings spent with him were wonderful and painful at the same time. He was careful to keep his distance, and the sexual tension between them was at an excruciating level. The shadow waiting outside for her to walk home kept her visits brief. Marcus still walked her home each night, and even knowing they were being watched, she had a difficult time keeping her hands to herself.

She wasn't sure if she waited until dark because of pride, or because she was still trying to be somewhat secretive about their relationship. What little hope she had left of regaining her place as a Patrician would be completely crushed if everyone learned of her relationship with a Reaper.

A part of her didn't care; she wanted everyone to know that she was with Marcus. That she was falling madly in love with a man of death. But another part, the more rational part, warned her that Marcus might not return her feelings. That he might one day decide to quit humoring her and her world would fall down around her. Without the Patricians, without Marcus, what would she have?

Aerina fought to drum up excitement about the upcoming event. This was what she had wanted — to be accepted again by her caste. To no longer be an outcast. *Being an outcast brought you close to Marcus,* her inner voice reminded her. Reinstating her status as a Patrician might be the end of any chance she had at forging a real bond with Marcus.

Putting aside those depressing thoughts, Aerina took a quick shower. She was supposed to head over to Helen's after lunch to get ready. Helen had deigned to allow the soon-to-be reinstated Patrician into her villa.

Aerina called the taxi service, since it was raining and her parents had taken the car to the Capitol early to help oversee the ball preparations.

She carried her dress over her shoulder as she ran from the taxi to the house, scanning her credit chip quickly to pay for the ride.

"Aerina!" Lina squealed when she met her at the door, face alight with excitement. She had some white goop covering her face, so Aerina didn't lean in for their normal kiss on the cheek.

"Lead me to the torture chamber," she said wryly as Lina grabbed her wrist and dragged her to the large sunroom in the back of the house. Helen was seated on a stool while Korinne, their normal stylist, worked on her hair. A beautician Aerina didn't recognize waited to inflict on her the same disgusting treatment as Lina.

Her friends adored getting ready for events, so Aerina suffered in silence. Lina and Helen kept up a constant chatter, making Aerina's input unnecessary.

"I'm ready for my parents to decide on a match for me, but I haven't gotten any offers from the right people," Lina complained. "Ouch, Korinne!" she complained as the stylist pulled tight a strand of her thick dark hair.

"Sorry, miss," Korinne murmured.

"Well, my parents are considering the proposal from Burrus, but they hinted there might be another proposal forthcoming. I can't imagine who..." Helen trailed off, her brow puckered in consternation.

"I think I can guess who," Aerina murmured with amusement, thinking of Stephen's hesitant interest. Her own parents hadn't said a word about marriage. She had received a few match requests before all this, but felt certain none of the interested parties would consider her a worthy match now. She didn't care. The only proposal she'd ever wanted was from a man who couldn't marry.

"Well?" Helen said impatiently and Aerina realized she'd asked her a question. She wanted to know who was interested, of course. Aerina met Lina's eyes.

"Ask Lina," she responded as she got up to wash the white goop off her face. She left the room to use the sink in the bathroom, leaving Lina to face Helen's browbeating. Poor Stephen. If he managed to win over Helen and her family, he wasn't going to have an easy time of it.

But who could explain love? It could draw together seemingly mismatched couples.

You would know, accused her inner voice as she scrubbed her face clean of the gritty, unknown substance. She wasn't in love with Marcus. And perhaps if she reminded herself of that often enough, she could believe it.

"Did you hear about Valentina?" she heard Helen asking Lina salaciously when she returned from the bathroom. "She's petitioned to partner with an Engineer. Can you believe it?" She sat back, watching Aerina and Lina, waiting for their reaction. Lina, at least, didn't disappoint her, gasping in shock. Aerina glanced uncomfortably at Korinne and the beautician. What must they be thinking about Helen's comments? She was ashamed to think it wasn't too long ago that she would have joined the conversation.

"Valentina?! I would never have imagined... And how would she have met an Engineer?"

"I guess he designed her car," Helen said dismissively. "I can't imagine actually wanting to marry another caste. I think I'd rather be single. Forever."

"Aren't we taught that each class serves an important role in our society? That all are necessary for the survival of our state?" Aerina asked quietly, settling down on the divan in Helen's room. Korinne focused on finishing Lina's hair, and the beautician, Dianna, stood tight-lipped, stoically applying makeup to Helen's eyes.

Helen cast Aerina a disgusted look. "For a moment, I forgot about your penchant for slumming."

"Yes, some of the people I spend time with can act pretty disgusting." The pointed comment was lost on Helen. Lina shot Aerina a warning look, which Aerina returned with studied innocence. She'd almost forgotten how pretentious the Patricians could be. It was going to be a long evening.

"You've really outdone yourselves, ladies," she complimented the two women whose hard work had transformed her into a princess. Korinne and Dianna smiled as Aerina admired her own reflection in the mirror. As much as she hated the preparation, she had to admit that they had worked magic.

Her strawberry-blonde locks gleamed, teased into perfect waves that fell down her back, held only by a diamond clip over her right ear. The waves framed her delicate features and golden skin. Her eyes looked huge; luminous.

Her dress was ice blue with silver accents, breaking slightly with tradition of white with gold accents. It was simple but elegant, a single off-the-shoulder sleeve revealing her toned, elegant shoulders, hugging her curves past her knees where it flared out in a mermaid style.

"You'll steal the show," Korinne said with satisfied pleasure. "No one will remember little over a month ago you were thought a traitor." Korinne blushed as soon as the words left her mouth but Aerina waved them off.

"They'll remember. But this look will tell them I don't care."

Aerina walked up the Capitol steps slowly. It was difficult to do anything *but* walk slowly in the fitted dress. Nerves were getting the best of her. She was glad the event wasn't going to be held in the courtyard. The scene of death was still strong in her mind.

The rain had abated but the air was still heavy with moisture. Even through the thick haze, Aerina could see the top of the Capitol gleaming in the darkness.

The globe topping the Capitol was in fact golden stained glass that encased the large ballroom. An impressive chandelier of gold and crystal hung in the center, and it glowed from the lights of a thousand faux-candles scattered on candelabras throughout the room.

She hesitated outside the large entrance doors. What would the Patricians' reception be? Squaring her shoulders against whatever awaited her inside, she swept through the doors and into the brightly lit ballroom.

As she walked down the small marble staircase, she felt all eyes turn towards her. The laughter and chatter faded to near-silence. Aerina paused at the bottom of the steps, fixing a cool smile on her face. This was what she had expected, but she was still unprepared for the absolute awfulness of it. Refusing to let her discomfort show, she lifted her chin a fraction, scanning the room boldly.

Marcus stood in the back, his eyes taking in the scene. He couldn't help but feel a rush of pride at Aerina's cool, unaffected demeanor in the face of such stark censure. Her large sapphire eyes stopped on him briefly before taking in the rest of the tableau.

Pride wasn't the only feeling that spread quickly at the sight of her. Desire rose, as it usually did at the sight of her deceptively fragile beauty. She looked like a golden goddess, and he couldn't take his eyes from her. Her dress hugged her body, swaying gently which each graceful move. Her hair shone brilliantly in the soft light, lighting up the room like a sunset; the last stand of light before the fall of night. But it was her face that caught and held his attention. Her eyes gleamed with cool amusement, as if the Patricians were gathered for her personal entertainment. Her delicate features were held in the perfect combination of aloof disdain and quiet humor. She was elegant, beautiful, and untouchable.

Forcing himself to look away, he noticed that he wasn't the only male in the room affected by her beauty. He wanted to throw her wrap over the form-hugging dress. He wanted them all to know she was his.

But she wasn't.

Control. Nothing matters but your job. He forced his eyes to focus forward, getting his errant thoughts, and his overheated body, back under control.

Aerina walked into the center of the ballroom, letting everyone get their fill. She resisted the urge to do a little spin.

Amusement bubbled up unexpectedly at the invisible force field that appeared to surround her on all sides. *Just a few hours,* she told herself, sipping a glass of champagne. If Marcus could live this every day, she could last an evening.

He was here. Even though he did an excellent job of blending into the shadows, she would recognize his dark form anywhere. He had traded his normal armored black uniform for a tailored black suit that somehow made him look even more dangerous. A wolf in sheep's clothing.

He stood with his legs lightly braced, his hands clasped behind him. His watchful gaze moved continually. She knew he was on alert for another attempt on the Consul's life. Several other Virmortus stood in dark corners, and a few moved amongst the guests.

The Consul entered the room, and everyone turned towards him. He strode confidently down the steps, pausing to greet people. The crowd pushed closer, hoping to get a moment of his attention. But he had a goal in mind and continued to move forward.

He stopped directly in front of Aerina. She looked up to meet his amber gaze. He grasped her hand, his surprisingly rough, and pulled her close for a light kiss on her cheek.

"I'm glad you're here," he murmured in her ear, his eyes on the far wall where Marcus stood. Then he moved on. By that simple motion, Aerina had been absolved.

Lina and Helen approached her first.

"Whew, I thought we weren't going to be allowed to speak with you. How awkward that was," Helen said. Aerina couldn't help but feel a small level of irritation at her friends. They could have helped break the ice by approaching her immediately.

Sighing, she forced a small smile for the girls. At least they had included her when the rest of the Patricians had completely shunned her.

Her gaze traveled the room until it again fell on Marcus. She drew comfort from his presence. She met his gaze and gave him a small smile. He nodded almost imperceptibly. Her heart raced, and she watched his muscular form weaving fluidly through the crowd. The Patricians all glanced at him warily, careful to make room, avoiding his eyes.

Stephen, Todd, and Anthony came to join the girls. "You look beautiful tonight," Stephen said graciously, including all three girls in his gaze. Helen blushed, a sight Aerina had never seen before. Perhaps he had a chance with the prickly girl, after all.

She looked over to see Todd staring at her. She pretended not to notice.

The dancing started, but it was quite unlike the dancing at the Pleb bars she frequented. A quartet played classical music, a mix of ancient composers like Beethoven to newly composed pieces by Alban musicians.

Aerina loved both the beautiful fluidity of the classical and the energy of the Plebeian Pop music. Her body swayed in rhythm to the music as she watched several couples take to the floor.

Anthony pressured a reticent Lina out onto the floor. As he pulled her friend, still protesting, away from the group, Aerina groaned inwardly. Stephen was bound to ask Helen, and that would leave her alone with Todd.

Sure enough, a moment later she was left alone with her aspiring suitor. When Todd asked her to dance she couldn't think of a proper excuse, letting him lead her to the dance floor. As they moved smoothly through the room, she again sought out Marcus. His familiar frame was absent, and she looked back at her dance partner with disappointment.

Todd was watching her, his eyes slightly narrowed. Funny how she had never noticed that his eyes seemed a little too close together, and his handsome features were soft and boyish.

She had become partial to a face that told a story; scars, broken nose, and all.

"What are you thinking about?" Todd asked, his voice sounding a little sharp.

"Just glad to be back," Aerina answered quietly, forcing a smile.

"I almost thought Consul Julius was going to confront you, rather than welcome you," Todd confessed with a laugh. Aerina forced another smile, not responding to the awkward comment. He continued, "I'm glad that wasn't the case, though. I would have hated to see you leave. It's been dull without you," he added hastily at the end, his hand tightening on hers.

Then why didn't you try to see me? Aerina bit her tongue to keep the annoyed question from coming out. If she had really meant something to him, her exile wouldn't have kept him from her. She wondered how much of his pursuit was pressure from his parents to partner with the daughter of a Senator.

Aerina directed the conversation to meaningless small talk until the song ended and she could excuse herself. She still couldn't see any sign of Marcus. What if something had happened? The Consul was still mingling with the guests, but that didn't mean Marcus hadn't discovered something.

Telling herself she would just peek in the hallway, she left the ballroom through one of the side doors. The long white hallway was empty, the lighting muted. It was a relief to be away from the judging looks and curious stares.

She was heading towards the elevator when suddenly her shoulder was grabbed roughly from behind and she spun around, landing against the wall.

For a moment she thought it was Marcus and her heart quickened in excited anticipation. But she recognized Todd's sandy hair and boyish features before she felt his clammy lips on hers.

"Todd!" she exclaimed in disgust, pushing him away. He tripped backwards at the force of her shove, his boyish face set in determined, petulant lines. As he leaned forward again, she backhanded him lightly, trying to knock some sense into him. "Get away from me!" she hissed, not wanting to attract attention through the open ballroom doors.

"So *he's* good enough, but not a Patrician?" Todd asked angrily, rubbing the cheek where she'd struck him. "I just want what you've been giving to that damn Reaper."

"I don't know what you're talking about," she responded coldly.

"Everyone knows you've been to see him. Do you think any Patrician family will consider you for marriage now that you've been a Reaper whore?"

Aerina gasped at the maliciousness in Todd's voice. She had always thought him quiet; harmless. Anger filled her at his unexpected attack.

"I'd rather be a 'Reaper whore' than your wife. What does that say about you, Todd?" she answered tauntingly. His face flushed dark red and he stepped forward, shoving her back against the wall. The force of the shove caught her unprepared, and the fit of her dress made it impossible to catch herself. She fell hard, her head cracking against the white marble. Pain exploded, making her vision blur.

Struggling back to her feet, her shocked gaze caught sight of

Marcus striding toward them, death in his eyes, from a room at the end of the hall. At the same time, a small group of laughing Patricians came from the ballroom into the lobby.

The moments seemed to slow as disaster loomed closer. Aerina thought quickly, taking a step that put her between Marcus and Todd. She resisted the urge to rub the knot forming at the back of her head.

"I'm sorry you have to retract your proposal, Todd, but I understand. I'm sure you will find a lovely wife," she spoke quickly, soothingly. Todd seemed taken aback for a moment, but then he too noticed that they had drawn a crowd. He might be angry, but he wasn't about to jeopardize his own reputation. His hands dropped limply to his sides.

Marcus stopped, the tick in his jaw the only sign of his controlled anger. The group of Patricians stood around the corner and couldn't seem him. Aerina's eyes went from Marcus to the group in a warning.

"Thank you for your understanding," Todd said stiffly, stumbling quickly back into the ballroom, his eyes on Marcus the whole time. The larger man stared back at him with dark eyes of death. The Patrician seemed to realize he had narrowly avoided a dangerous encounter.

"Aerina, I was surprised to see you tonight. Is it true that you've been hanging out with the Virmortus?" one of the young women asked, her voice deliciously scandalized. Aerina recognized her from her University classes.

Aerina couldn't look at Marcus. He stood absolutely still around the corner from the small group. "I don't know if you would call it 'hanging out'," Aerina murmured, edging away slowly. Enduring the condescending stares in the ballroom was preferable to this.

The girl continued, pressing closer. "There is something exciting about them, but honestly, they are *killers*. Aren't you afraid? Or are you into that sort of thing?" The group giggled salaciously. "So tell us, what is it like with a Reaper? Do they like to tie you up? A little BDSM?"

Aerina felt a small flush spreading on her cheekbones, very

aware of Marcus standing not more than five feet away. He could hear every word. She didn't want him interceding and creating more of a scene. She needed to just get them to leave as quickly as possible, preferably without any further gossip fodder.

"That's ridiculous. Of course I don't associate with Reapers. Unless it's with their garrotes around my neck," she joked, trying to draw their attention away from the subject.

"Then how come some of our friends saw you going into his villa?" one of the boys asked.

"I needed some information—I wanted to make sure I was absolved from the...unfortunate incident. Reapers are surprisingly useful. If nothing else, they are good for information. Why else would *I*, a Senator's daughter, be associating with a Reaper?" She injected the right amount of derision in her tone.

"So you aren't in love with a Reaper?" The first girl looked disappointed.

"No," Aerina lied firmly, looking her in the eye. "I have absolutely no relationship with any *Reaper*."

The girl stared at Aerina for another moment before shrugging. The group turned the subject, losing interest. Aerina finally looked over at Marcus to mouth an apology. All she saw was his back as he walked away, stiff and remote as always. She couldn't help but feel as if she had lost something important that she didn't even know she'd had.

I didn't mean it, she wanted to shout. But he was already gone.

She walked back into the ballroom, the magical evening ruined. She felt like Cinderella at the ball, except she'd turned back into a pumpkin right in front of everyone. Including her prince.

And she had no one to blame but herself.

She left early, telling her parents she had a headache. Which wasn't a lie; after the confrontation with Todd and the group of nosy Patricians, her head had started pounding.

Todd and his friends had kept their distance, and the rumor

that he had withdrawn his proposal, the one she had already rejected, spread through the crowd quickly. Everyone whispered it was because of her fall from grace. She didn't care. She had desperately tried to catch Marcus' eye, but he hadn't acknowledged her.

Ignoring the taxis parked in the Capitol's drive, she walked through the drizzle. Her heels sunk into the damp grass and she impatiently pulled them off. She walked slowly down the tree-lined streets, letting the light rain ruin her perfectly coiffed hair and professionally applied makeup.

Not surprisingly, she found herself standing in front of Marcus' small villa. It was dark, his car missing from the carport. She sat on his front step to wait.

A light wrap was all she had to ward off the evening chill, and she began shivering. It seemed an eternity before she saw his black car cruising down the dead-end street. She continued to study the cloudy night sky as she heard him park, his door shut quietly, and his light steps on the walk. Then he was standing before her, his suit-encased legs filling her vision.

She still didn't look up, just pulling the wrap closer.

For once, he broke the silence first. "Aren't you afraid of being seen here. With me." The question was asked in a monotone but she sensed the underlying cynicism. When she still didn't say anything, he cursed under his breath in a rare display of sentiment. "Get inside; you're not dressed for this weather." He pushed the door open, pulling her to her feet and stepping aside. The cold made her clumsy and she stumbled forward. He caught her, but immediately released her.

Marcus looked away from her bedraggled form, refusing to let her past the barriers he had reconstructed. Her words replayed in his mind as he grabbed a change of clothes for her. *Why else would I, a Senator's daughter, be associating with a Reaper?*

"Put this on." He threw a shirt at her. She gripped the black t-shirt, glancing towards the bathroom. It was the only place that offered privacy. Shrugging, she wrenched the zipper down, struggling out of the ruined gown there in the entryway.

Marcus turned away quickly as her golden skin was exposed

inch by delectable inch. Did she think he was made of stone?

"Thank you," she murmured, and he turned back cautiously. She was covered from head to knees with his shirt, but the sight of her in his shirt, touching her naked skin, fanned the fire already burning in him.

"Marcus..." she trailed off, unsure of what to say. He ignored her, moving about the kitchen with hyper-efficiency. He soon had a mug filled with steaming tea. He set it on the table without a word, then prowled into the living room to start a fire in the fireplace.

Aerina sighed, sitting down and warming her hands on the side of the large black mug. At least he hadn't kicked her out yet. She'd half expected him to step right over her shivering form on his front step and lock the door behind him. After what she had said at the ball, she wouldn't have blamed him.

He finally sat down across from her, the room flickering cozily in the light from the fire. He'd removed the jacket of his suit and unbuttoned the top of the dress shirt but was otherwise fully dressed. She felt exposed wearing nothing but a T-shirt and underwear that amounted to little more a few scraps of knitted lace.

"Do you have any pants?"

He got up without a word, pressing a few buttons on the Wardrobe before tossing her the pair of grey drawstring pants that appeared. She pulled the pants up over her hips. They were huge. Tightening the drawstring, she sat back down at the kitchen table. She wasn't leaving until she had a chance to explain. And apologize.

"Did you need something else?" The hidden meaning in his question wasn't lost on her.

Reapers are surprisingly useful.

"Yes," she answered quietly, looking at him with her eyes wide. "I need to say I'm sorry. I didn't mean those—"

"Forget it. I don't want to hear it," he cut her off coldly.

"Marcus, I—"

"I said I don't care!" He stood so suddenly his chair flung backwards, crashing on the tile floor. Aerina jumped and stifled a gasp, shocked at his rare outburst.

He strode to the door and opened it with exaggerated care.

"Get out. We have nothing more to discuss." Marcus controlled his voice with effort. He had been angry about her careless words that had seemed to slip so easily off her tongue. But he'd known tonight would change things. That she'd go back to being a Patrician, and he'd still be a Reaper. Forever on the outside. He was more furious that it had bothered him at all.

He was a killer. He'd killed more people than he cared to remember in any number of ways. He was skilled at torture and intelligence-gathering. There wasn't a time in his life that he could remember giving a shit about anyone. Years of brutal training, of inventive tortures, and tests both mental and physical had made him feel so cold, so empty, that he hadn't thought to ever truly care about something again. And this girl—this naïve, entitled, and inexplicably beautiful girl—had gotten under his armor. It needed to end here, tonight. He couldn't handle another day of the torture; being close to her and not having her.

"I'm not leaving until I've said what I want to say." She stood stubbornly in his white and tan kitchen, hugging her arms around his t-shirt, her chin lifted obstinately. Marcus stared at her, uncomprehending that she was refusing his order.

No one told a Reaper 'no'. Even the Consul himself tread carefully around Marcus.

He closed the door slowly, carefully, and stood for a moment, gathering with effort the remnants of his quickly fleeing control.

Turning back, he walked towards her slowly. She stiffened slightly but didn't move, her expressive blue eyes meeting his defiantly.

Without fear.

He stopped directly in front of her, deliberately using his sheer size to intimidate her. His hand gripped a still-damp curl, letting the silky stuff run through his fingers.

"Then say it," he commanded, his voice gritty and low with the effort to control his anger.

Aerina's mind had gone blank as he had approached. She

knew he was trying to intimidate her, and she admitted to herself that it was working.

The strong, callused hand that gripped her hair had been covered in blood not too long ago. She had seen it herself.

But she wasn't scared.

"I'm sorry. I shouldn't have lied about our relationship to those Patricians. I just wanted to end the conversation as quickly as possible." She searched his eyes for any sign of a reaction. They remained as unreadable, as darkly forbidding, as they always were.

He dropped her hair. "You didn't lie. We have no relationship outside of the threat to your life. Once that is resolved, we can both go our own ways."

Aerina felt a shaft of despair shoot through her. It was hopeless. He was never going to let her in; never going to open up.

"You know that's not true. There *is* something between us. Call it a relationship or chemistry or just lust, it's there whether you want to acknowledge it or not. I feel it. I know you do. You're just too damn scared to admit it." Aerina was tired of dancing around it. She was going to lay her cards on the table. Now it was his turn to either play or end the game completely.

When Marcus continued to stand there, no sign of reaction on his harsh features, Aerina turned toward the door with a sound of disgust.

She was reaching for the latch when his hand on her arm turned her quickly around and she was in his arms. He leaned down, his mouth hovering over hers.

"Is this the relationship you want?" His words sounded harsh, his normally controlled breathing ragged.

She closed the distance between them as her answer, her lips meeting his, open and eager.

His hands moved gently down her body, running over her slender curves draped in his soft t-shirt. She pressed her body against his, wanting to be closer, wanting to feel more of him. Her own hands were under his shirt, moving up his chest. The warm muscles covered in soft hairs jumped and flexed beneath her sensitive fingertips. His strength coupled with amazing control both awed her and enflamed her.

He lifted her up, his mouth still fused to hers, and pressed her back against the door. She wrapped her legs around his lean waist, her arms going around his neck.

She was consumed with the need to be closer, to feel more of him, to belong to him. Her stomach clenched with desire and liquid heat pooled at her center as his tongue explored her mouth slowly, his hands gripping her backside as he pressed her against the door.

His mouth broke free from hers to kiss along her jaw, the sensitive place behind her ear, and down her neck. Her tiny moans of delight sounded unfamiliar to her own ears, as if another girl had taken over her normally composed body.

Her body moved against his of its own accord, trying to get closer; trying to alleviate the burning ache that he was creating.

He broke the kiss. "Not like this, Aerina." His words broke through her haze of desire. He rested his forehead on the door next to her, his breathing harsh. He then gently lowered her to the ground, steadying her when she stumbled on shaky legs.

"Marcus, don't stop," she pleaded, her eyes dark and heavy with desire. She tried to pull him back, but he grabbed her hands, holding them gently in his. He leaned down and kissed her swollen lips gently.

Aerina sighed and leaned back against the door.

"Marcus, has anyone told you what a damn tease you are?" Her deadpan words brought a surprised bark of laughter from Marcus. She smiled in response, realizing she'd never heard him laugh before. It sounded unpracticed but beautiful.

He turned away, adjusting his pants. She pretended not to notice, adjusting her own damp panties.

"So, chess?" she asked. He looked at her in surprise and she was rewarded with a small smile that made his harsh features look younger. Less like a man of death, and more like just a man. She knew he had forgiven her, at least a little.

They played chess and drank; Aerina brewed more tea and Marcus had whiskey. Aerina told him her story of being kicked out of the brothel, and she was rewarded by another smile, the sexy quirk of his mouth that lightened his severe features.

"Why do you think the assassin hasn't tried to attack the Consul again? It's been nearly two months," Aerina asked, moving her pawn forward.

Marcus counted her move with his own, taking her pawn. "He's waiting for something." He paused, looking as if he would say more, but he just leaned back in his chair, waiting for her next move.

"What?" she asked. "What were you going to say?"

He raised a brow at her, slightly surprised she had read him so easily. He debated what to tell her.

"I'm going to be gone again for several days, perhaps longer," he finally said.

"You're going outside the city? To the outposts?" she asked excitedly.

"Yes."

"Can I come?"

"No," he answered simply, not leaving room for argument.

Not that it stopped Aerina. "Marcus, I have always wanted to go outside. I won't be in the way, I'll just—"

"No," he said again, cutting her off.

"Why not?"

Had Marcus been another man, he would have sighed. Instead, he crossed his arms over his chest, leaning back in his chair. Trying to intimidate her into submission.

He should have known it wouldn't work. Aerina was obviously not impressed.

"Well?"

"It's dangerous," he finally said. "There are things out there you don't want to see."

"I'll be safe if I'm with you," she said encouragingly.

"No one is safe outside the city."

"I'm not safe in the city right now. Marcus, you know I won't be safer with anyone else, wherever we are. I'm going outside with or without you," she told him stubbornly. "I've been thinking about it for weeks now. I want to see what's out there. I *need* to see what's out there. Please."

"I'm not going to risk your life over some frivolous desire to explore." His voice turned hard. He was growing angry.

He saw her eyes darken at his words. He'd hurt her feelings. But he didn't care. Outside the safety of the city was a world she wouldn't want to experience. It was too dangerous. The Virmortus he had trailing her would keep her safe.

"Frivolous or not, I'm going out," she said coolly, watching the muscle flex in his jaw at her words.

"You've only just gotten back into the Patricians' good graces. Are you ready to throw that away, and potentially your future, just for a week outside? It would not be worth it," he said darkly.

"I disagree. A week outside would be worth a little extra judgment. They already think it anyway." *A week alone with you would be worth a lifetime of exile,* she added silently. She didn't want to scare him off; he was already jittery enough about their relationship. "You saw how it was tonight. I'm still an outcast; they barely tolerate my presence. What else have I got? I threw away my future as a Patrician; I made that choice, and I can live with it. But don't keep me from things I can experience now, after I made that sacrifice. Please," she said again, her eyes imploring him to understand why she needed this.

Marcus considered his options. He could go without her and hope she would be too scared to go outside alone. Or, he could lock her up in the one of the Virmortus inquisition cells and have his men make sure she was taken care of. Or he could take her with him.

None of the options sounded appealing.

He wasn't going to underestimate her tenacity like everyone else seemed to. She'd find a way, and he would be distracted, wondering about it, instead of focusing on his mission. And, if he was honest with himself, he liked the idea of having her in his sight at all times. It would also get Aerina out of the way so his men could take care of a little problem.

"Hell." This only reinforced the wisdom behind the rule prohibiting Virmortus from marrying. This was a damn nuisance. Women could quickly complicate things.

Aerina smiled widely at his lowly muttered curse. He was going to give in.

"Tomorrow morning. Early," he said shortly. Aerina gave a very un-Patrician-like squeal and jumped up, running around the table to squeeze his neck. He sat stiffly in her embrace but she saw the harsh lines of his face soften.

Slowly, slowly she was learning to read him. And he was letting her.

Chapter 12

"The voyage of discovery is not in seeking new landscapes but in having new eyes." - Marcel Proust

Aerina was ready when Marcus' sporty black e-car pulled up in front of her villa before dawn the next morning. She'd been forced to tell her parents. They would be bound to notice her prolonged absence. Her mother had looked at her as if she didn't recognize her own daughter; she certainly didn't understand. Then she'd sighed and walked out of the room, like she'd washed her hands of Aerina long ago. Her father had just nodded, advising her to be careful.

Even her parents' reaction couldn't cast a pall over her anticipation. Her thrill in the early morning shone as brilliantly as it had the previous night.

He'd told her they'd be gone several days or even a week, so she'd packed a bag. He had gotten out and opened her door, and she gave him a wide smile as she threw her bag in the tiny backseat and climbed in. He didn't return the smile and she guessed he was still irritated over being coerced into taking her.

It made her even happier to know that the coercion had only worked because he cared, at least a little, about what happened to her. He could have told her to go to hell and have fun surviving on the outside. But he hadn't. He was taking her with him.

"White?" he asked as he slid in the driver's seat. She glanced at her attire—tailored white slacks and a short sleeve white button down with delicate ruching around the bodice.

"It's not like I have a lot of other options," she retorted dryly. She'd packed the few Pleb clothes she'd acquired, but felt odd wearing anything but white here on the Capitol Terrace.

They cruised quickly to the Ferry, through the Pleb city, past the docks, and out the South Gate. Anticipation hummed in her chest. She'd never been outside before. The only time she'd left the city had been to visit the Agriculture Terrace, which didn't count.

She felt her heartbeat increase and exhilaration spread through her. Her window was down and the wind whipped her loose hair all around her face, the smell of the ocean filling her nostrils. She laughed for the sheer joy of it, looking over at Marcus.

He looked magnificent, as always, his large frame relaxed in the bucket seat, his arm resting on the steering wheel. He glanced over at her and his mouth quirked up in his version of a smile. Her heart turned over, nearly bursting with the emotion it contained. Nothing could top the thrill of this moment.

The road became increasingly ragged very quickly until it was barely a trail cut through the rocky coastline. She began to wonder how his car was going to take them through the rugged countryside.

Marcus began to slow and Aerina looked over at him questioningly. He pulled over in a small clearing and pressed a button on the dash. The hillside before them slid open like a garage, and Aerina's eyes widened to see the vehicle inside.

It had huge wide wheels, a single long seat, and two thick roll bars. It was the color of the countryside; browns, greys, and greens.

Marcus pulled in next to it and grabbed their bags from the back. He stored them in a small compartment that sealed closed while Aerina eagerly climbed up into the seat through the open side. The long seat had two harnesses and she began to strap herself in as Marcus pulled himself effortlessly into the seat next to her. She tried not to stare at the way his muscles bulged as he settled in beside her.

"Ready?" he asked, and she could swear she saw a devilish glint in his eyes. He was going to enjoy this. She nodded, smiling in excitement.

He scanned his ID chip and the vehicle roared to life, sending another thrill through her already charged body. He backed smoothly out and they were once again heading down the trail towards the south.

It wasn't long before she saw why they needed the vehicle. The trail disappeared completely into a rocky incline. Marcus didn't even slow down, shifting gears as they approached, taking the incline straight on.

Aerina bit her lip to stifle a scream as the vehicle tipped up so far she thought they were going to fall backwards down the hill. But the large tires dug into the rocks and they shot up with bone-jarring force. Marcus shifted again and the engine roared even louder, seeming to growl in protest as it slowly inched them up another outcropping.

Adrenaline pumped through her, making her feel giddy and breathless. She couldn't seem to control the wide grin plastered across her face. She was pressed back into her seat, her feet braced on the metal floor, each jarring bump taking her butt off the seat. She looked over at Marcus and saw his own normally impassive features tight with concentration, his eyes burning with adrenaline.

Just when she thought the vehicle couldn't take any more pressure, the engine roar reached a crescendo and they hit the crest, jumping off the rock onto a smooth peak.

"Balance and serenity." Aerina couldn't stop the whispered words as she saw the other side. The rocky downward incline was even steeper and seemed to go on forever. She looked quickly over at Marcus. He gave her a genuine grin, her only warning, and he shifted again. They lurched forward, hitting the incline at a slight angle. Aerina closed her eyes then forced them open. If she was going to die, she wanted to see it coming.

The vehicle climbed slowly down the hill, angling, shooting forward, lurching over rocks and bouncing through crevices. Her heart seemed to be in a suspended state of defibrillation, beating quickly with each drop then stopping at a sudden lurch forward. It was an adrenaline high like she'd never experienced before.

"This is amazing!" she shouted over the roar of the engine to Marcus, who manhandled the vehicle with the same sexy control he did everything else. He rewarded her with another one of his rare grins. Aerina had finally learned what Marcus did for entertainment.

They hit the bottom of the hill with a jarring bounce and the vehicle jumped forward, the wheels kicking up dust as they sped across the flat, dry ground.

It was almost noon when they reached the first outpost town. They roared in slowly, and Aerina eagerly took in every detail.

The outpost had wooden walls surrounding it, with one large lookout. The surrounding fields were well-tended but scraggily and sparse. The year had been dry.

Inside the walls wasn't any more impressive. The houses were more like old pieces of metal and wood strapped together. It reminded her of the images of shanty towns that had been prevalent in many poor countries before the war.

Unlike the Pleb city, which bustled with energy and culture, here the pace seemed slow. Many people lounged casually, a few slowly sweeping, gathering water from a well, or working on the buildings.

The children were the exception. They ran towards the vehicle, shouting and waving. Aerina smiled, waving back while wondering why they weren't in school. Did this place have a school?

Marcus stopped the vehicle in front of an old but well-kept stone mansion. It looked to be an estate left from the pre-war era, with large glass windows and an impressive entrance.

Vaulting lightly over the side, Marcus grabbed one of the bags he had stored in the back. Aerina climbed down a little less gracefully, looking ruefully down at her formerly neat, white outfit. She understood now why Marcus commented on her white clothes. They were filthy.

Brushing herself off as best she could, she glanced over at Marcus. He looked as immaculate as always, his black armored clothes hiding the dirt and refusing to wrinkle.

A man not much older than Marcus came rushing down the stone steps, a welcoming smile on his face. He was dressed casually, and he obviously hadn't seen a barber recently. But his hair was neatly tied back, his beard clipped close. Beneath all that light brown hair, she could see he was good-looking.

"Marcus! We weren't expecting you so soon after your last visit." The men clasped hands before he turned to extend his welcoming smile to Aerina. "And you've brought a guest."

The statement was more of a question. Marcus never brought anyone with him on his visits. He followed Vick's admiring gaze to where Aerina stood. Even dusty and wrinkled, her hair windblown and her face pink from the sun, she looked breathtaking. In fact, her disheveled appearance only made her look more appealing; more approachable. Less like the cool proper Patrician and more like the fiery woman that lay beneath.

"Vick, this is Aerina Delacroix, daughter of the Senator of Society. Aerina, this is Vick Rain, the 'Mayor' of Vicksburg." Marcus made the introductions quickly, emphasizing *Senator* as if that mattered here.

Vick greeted Aerina politely, with the respect her station demanded, and she laughed off the niceties.

"When I'm this filthy, I think we can skip the formalities," she said, smiling at the sandy-haired mayor. His light hazel eyes twinkled back, and she decided she liked him.

"Shall we?" Marcus' voice was even, but Aerina detected a note of irritation. She preceded both men up the steps and into the cool house. It took a moment for her eyes to adjust to the darker interior, but when they did, she looked around curiously.

The house was very tidy but obviously old, and much of the furnishings were well-worn. Some of the décor was clearly from the pre-war era and she stared in amazement. Albans, particularly the forward-thinking Patricians, did not value anything from the pre-war era. Except for the few mandatory history class visits to the single Patrician museum at the University, she'd never seen relics from the time preceding the Global War.

Old photographs, surprisingly well-preserved, hung in carefully maintained silver frames. A few metal signs with clever sayings were interspersed with a large canvas painting, and artwork made from old glass wine bottles.

Vick invited them to sit, asking if they wanted a drink. Aerina asked for a glass of water, Marcus taking a beer with an Alban brewery label.

Once they were all seated and Vick brought out the drinks, Marcus pulled out his bag.

"What have we got today?" Vick asked eagerly, leaning forward with his muscular forearms resting on his knees, clasping his hands together in anticipation. He looked like a little boy on Peace Day morning. Aerina watched the two men, amused by the strange friendship. Both men were large, well-muscled, and good-looking, but that was where the similarities ended. Marcus was dark, cool, and unreadable. Vick appeared to constantly smile, and his light brown hair and twinkling hazel eyes giving him a boyish charm. His boundless enthusiasm was a stark contrast to Marcus' own careful control. From their comfortable camaraderie, she could tell each respected the other.

Marcus pulled out several carefully packaged holoreaders, the upgraded version with the full teaching module.

"Ahh," Vick sighed in satisfaction. "This is just what we need. The kids have been looking forward to school."

"I can bring another energy box next time, but there weren't any in production," Marcus told him, and Vick nodded.

"Thank you, my friend," Vick carefully took the holoreaders from him. "I'm going to reinvent this town, one small step at a time."

Marcus nodded, sitting back in the worn chair, stretching his long legs in front of him. "What have you got for me?"

Vick leaned forward again, his eyes flicking to Aerina sitting gracefully on her own roughhewn chair.

"No news of raids since you took out that most recent group from Texaco. I owe you for that one; they were becoming problematic." Vick's voice darkened, his face hard for a moment beneath the fur. Then his eyes lightened as if he turned on their switch and he winked at Aerina. Marcus also glanced at Aerina. She had looked over at him in surprise when Vick had mentioned the raiders. Marcus wondered what she was thinking. He'd left behind an ugly scene as a warning for any future raiders that might come across the group. If Aerina knew what he'd done... her look of surprise would no doubt turn to disgust.

If she knew who he really was, she'd never sit beside him so calmly.

He knew she had seen him kill. She'd been to the Training Grounds, per Ramus' report; she'd seen where he'd been raised. She knew who he was, *what* he was. But a tiny part of him, the part he'd thought dead long ago, was afraid. Afraid of her uncovering the truth he'd tried to ignore all these years. That he was unworthy of love. The truth his father had first shown him, and that had been reinforced over the years.

No one had ever loved him. Why would that change now?

"I've been keeping an eye out when I go scouting, like you asked. I haven't seen anything, but a couple whose daughter, Michaela, married one of our boys a year ago visited from New Haven. They told me about an unusual vehicle they saw."

"Unusual?" Aerina asked.

"The Texaco rebels drive some Mad Max-style vehicles; clunky pieces of shit they recommission from the war era."

"Mad Max?" Aerina asked again, feeling lost.

"You know, a pre-war film," Vick paused, considering his words. "Like the theatre but watched on screen or a box called a TV."

"For training, like holofilms?" She was still lost.

"Entertainment."

Aerina cocked her head, trying to remember her history lessons. "Fascinating. Watching a box?"

Vick grinned. "Crazy, I know. But some of those pre-war science fiction writers were eerily accurate in predicting our demise."

"Prophets," Aerina murmured.

"What did these unusual war vehicles look like," Marcus cut in, knowing Vick could talk pre-war history for hours.

"Something armored, fast, and nearly undetectable."

"The Southern Empire," Marcus said quietly.

Vick was silent for a moment, then nodded. "That was my first thought, too. We haven't seen any signs of them for years. Just scouting, you think?"

"It's possible. If you hear anything at all, let me know

immediately." Marcus thought of his recent conversation with Julius. And the last time the Southern Empire had been spotted this far west. Something wasn't right...

"Celeste is making lunch. I hope you'll join us," Vick said, breaking into Marcus' thoughts.

"Oh, is Celeste your wife?" Aerina asked with a smile.

Vick laughed, deep and booming. "No, she's my cook. And also a good friend of my mother's."

"Oh, I see." Aerina laughed with him.

"I don't think we will be able to stay," Marcus said coolly, "We've got a lot of road to cover before tonight."

"Surely a little longer isn't going to hurt," Aerina argued. "And the tiny bit of food we brought is not going to hold us over until tonight. We'll stay," she concluded without waiting for Marcus to reply.

Marcus' jaw clenched, but he nodded curtly. Vick grinned widely, thoroughly enjoying his friend's obvious discomfiture. Marcus had always been a man with no flaws and no weaknesses, but Vick could tell his superhuman friend had finally met his kryptonite. The other man watched Aerina, as if he were both trying to figure her out and as if he were afraid she might disappear if he took his eyes off her.

Poor Marcus, he wasn't going to have an easy time of it. Vick hadn't met many Patricians, but he could tell Aerina was different. She was still aristocracy; that much was apparent in everything from her tailored clothes to the way she held herself.

Vick was still smiling to himself when they sat down to eat. The lunch was simple but tasty; meat, biscuits, and corn. Aerina and Vick discussed the small town while Marcus ate in silence.

"Do you get visitors often?" Aerina asked curiously, tucking a small piece of meat neatly into her mouth, chewing carefully.

"Yes, people come through here looking to trade or just seeking a place to settle down. Some of our residents will move and return to visit friends or relatives," Vick explained.

"No one ever leaves Alba except for the fisherpeople and the Aggies," Aerina murmured thoughtfully. "Well, and Marcus," she added looking over at him. He didn't look up. She wondered why he was in such a bad mood. He'd seemed happier on the drive over.

Vick nodded. "Marcus is the only Alban who's visited our little village. I was invited to the city once to meet with the Emissary; it's quite a different world. I must say, you are certainly different from the other Patricians," he added. Aerina smiled.

"Thanks, I think. Although I must admit it does get me into trouble." She looked over at Marcus again. This time he flashed her a sardonic look.

"I can't imagine someone as refined as you getting into trouble," Vick responded graciously.

"You'll have to ask Marcus to tell you someday about the time he tried to killed me." Vick looked taken aback, glancing at Marcus quickly.

Marcus spoke for the first time. "I didn't try — if I wanted to kill you, you'd be dead."

"Excuse me, I mean the time he *almost* killed me," Aerina corrected with exaggerated politeness.

"Don't make me regret my restraint," he muttered back.

Vick looked between them, fascinated. These two were obviously meant for each other. He was glad for his friend. But he was also a little disappointed. Women like Aerina were rare and he would have snapped her up, Patrician or not.

Aerina thanked Vick for dinner while Marcus headed outside with barely a nod to their host.

"I don't know why Marcus is being such an ass," Aerina apologized. "He's normally not so irritable." Aerina paused for a moment. "Well, ok, I guess he is, but it was still rude."

Vick laughed. "We've been friends for a long time. You don't need to apologize for him. And he *is* particularly touchy today. I think it has more to do with you than me."

Aerina felt slightly offended. "You don't think he likes having me here?"

"Not at all. I think he likes it too much for his own comfort. And he isn't happy that I enjoyed having you here," Vick explained, his perpetual smile in place.

Aerina looked over to where Marcus had crouched down to talk to a few of the children from the town. They were gesturing wildly, obviously telling him a story. He nodded, listening carefully. She found it touching. He probably never interacted with children in Alba; most children were taught to fear Virmortus at an early age. These children had a bad case of hero worship, crowding eagerly around the large man, each vying for his attention.

She hoped Vick was right about Marcus' feelings towards her. She alternated between hope that he was just having a hard time letting down his guard to despair that he genuinely found her to be a nuisance.

"Aerina," he commanded, nodding farewell to the madly waving children as he pulled himself into the vehicle.

"I'm being summoned," she murmured, walking with Vick to the vehicle. He politely helped her up while Marcus stared ahead stonily.

"I'll be in touch. Those new holoreaders have a much greater Com distance. We should be able to communicate with them. If you see anything suspicious, anything at all, let me know," Marcus said tersely. Vick nodded.

"Thanks, Marcus." His voice was unusually serious. Marcus looked over at him and nodded.

Vick winked at Aerina as the vehicle roared to life. She waved as they shot forward, the children running alongside the giant tires.

Aerina glanced back as the small outpost town faded in the distance. She smiled to herself. Vicksburg. What an interesting character he had been. Her eyes slid over to Marcus. He drove staring straight ahead, one hand relaxed at his side, but the other gripped the wheel tightly.

"At first I thought Vick was disgustingly happy, but he's more like you than I first thought. He uses his genial attitude in the same way you use your control—to hide your real feelings."

Marcus glanced at her, surprised at her insight. Vick's youth hadn't been much better than Marcus', and Aerina was right, the other man used his carefree nature to hide his own deep scars.

Just like Marcus used his control to hide his own fear.

The sun was beginning to set when they reached the next outpost. They had followed the coast south and weren't too far from the ruins of old Los Angeles.

Aerina had caught glimpses of ruins from the pre-war and war-time eras. Pieces of old highway that hadn't been reclaimed by the hardy vegetation, old concrete and metal bridges that were twisted and rusty; it was all that was left of the pre-war world. What hadn't been destroyed in the wars was being slowly repossessed by nature.

The next outpost town was more impressive than Vicksburg. The walls were concrete topped with rusty barbed wire. As they drew closer, she realized it was an old prison. She shivered. What a terrible thing prisons must have been. She was glad Alba didn't believe in such a ridiculous form of punishment. Imprisonment didn't just punish the guilty individual, it punished the entire society.

The pre-war era United States would have undoubtedly found Alba's justice system barbaric. But criminals had no place in a society struggling to survive and achieve balance, and the Law of Death was an effective deterrent.

As they neared the entrance to the large compound, the gate slowly rolled open, creaking in protest. Aerina bit her lip, fighting the urge to ask Marcus to turn back. She looked up at the guard tower as they passed through the gate. The man held a large weapon; a gun. Armati did not visibly carry firearms—they were trained in hand-to-hand combat and carried sica blades. She imagined they had guns, somewhere, but she'd never seen one before.

"This place isn't like Vicksburg. You need to do as I say without question," Marcus said in a low voice as they were approached by a group of men.

"I see you brought us something special this time," one of the men called out in a gravelly voice. He was large and very hairy. The grease and grime coating his rather pungent person indicated he did not bathe frequently.

Marcus jumped down, reaching out the shake the man's hand. "Big Jim," he greeted the large hairy man, nodding to the others.

"Who's she?" Big Jim asked, his beady black eyes moving over her slowly. She fought the urge to cross her arms over her chest as he spent an inordinate amount of time staring there.

"She's mine," Marcus told the burly man, his voice low.

"Too bad. She's a beauty. If you ever tire of her, she'd be worth making a trade. And you know I'd treat her good," he said lasciviously while the other men laughed. "I guess you won't be needing anyone for tonight."

When Marcus remained silent, Big Jim circled around Aerina. "They sure do grow 'em pretty in Alba. Is this one of those Patricians I've heard about? She looks like any royalty I'd've imagined." Aerina tried to breathe through her nose to avoid the noxious scent of sweat and unwashed skin that emanated from the large man. He had an annoying way of speaking that rolled all his words together. She looked straight ahead, not flinching even when he stuck his bearded face close to hers. "Well, are you Ari-stock-cracy, princess?" he asked, drawing out the word mockingly. He reached forward to touch a strand of her silky, windblown curls. Marcus' hand darted out, grabbing the heavy man's hand before it made contact.

"She's not part of our business here, Jim." The two men stared each other down for a moment before Big Jim finally smiled, showing his yellow, cracked teeth. Aerina suppressed a shudder.

"Sure, Marcus," he said congenially, his eyes darting back to his cohorts. "Whatever you say."

"Aerina, go help the women with dinner," Marcus ordered curtly, motioning her away. "I'll come get you when I'm done." Aerina noticed for the first time a group of women huddled around a fire with a large pot. She shot Marcus an incredulous look. Didn't this place have electricity? What was she supposed to do with a big pot?

She walked over towards the women without a word, hearing more jeering from the men about how Marcus had already broke her in.

He owed her an explanation. Although, a tiny voice of reason butted in, she had been the one to insist on coming along. And those men.... She didn't even want to think about what would happen to a woman like her without Marcus here.

Probably what had happened to all of these women, she thought as she neared the small group. Without the terrifying group of hairy, unkempt men to distract her, she could now see small fires with cooking pots scattered throughout the large courtyard.

The women were quiet, keeping their eyes downcast as she approached. Their hair was nearly as unkempt as the men, their clothes old and mended. They reminded her of the few wild dogs she had seen on the outskirts of the Aggie Terrace. Wary, a little scared. Desperate.

"Can I help you?" she asked politely. Silence was her only answer. The large pot contained what appeared to be potatoes, a few scraggily carrots, and some unidentifiable meat.

Suddenly, she wasn't as hungry as she thought.

"My name is Aerina," she tried again. One of the women darted a shy smile her way.

"I'm Krista. This is Leah and Jean," she answered, her eyes looking quickly over to where the men sat at one of the crude tables set up under an animal-skin awning.

A woman rushed out of the nearby concrete building, carrying metal cups to the men, setting them on the table. Marcus nodded his thanks. The other men ignored her.

Aerina looked around. Most of the courtyard was filled with men lounging in groups or playing cards while a few used some kind of misshapen ball on the old basketball court.

The women worked, tending cooking fires, hanging up sheets and clothes to dry, and other assorted chores. Children of various ages ran around, screaming and playing.

"Hi Krista, Leah, Jean," Aerina replied warmly, nodding to the women. "Have you lived here long?"

Krista looked over at the men again before answering quietly. "I was born here, but Leah was traded from one of the camps in old Los Angeles several years ago. Jean here was stolen just last year from one of the inland towns."

Aerina was speechless. Traded? Stolen? What were they, cattle?

"I'm sorry, that must have been awful," she said finally, looking over at the other woman.

"It's really not so bad," the woman introduced as Jean said. "My town was larger, and not as well guarded. We had three raids the same year I was stolen. And a food shortage. Here at least we are better protected and there is plenty of food. We even had electricity until our energy box was struck by lightning in a storm."

Aerina winced. "Yeah, the older models had that happen a lot. The newer ones can take a hit and transfer the energy, storing it in the surge coils." The women looked at her blankly. They obviously hadn't learned energy basics like Aerina had. Every Alban citizen knew how to do basic repairs to an energy box. If she were to guess, she would assume these women had never attended a school of any kind.

"What about the camps in Old Los Angeles? What are they like?" Aerina asked Leah, hungry for information. The petite blonde woman shrugged, turning red.

"She can't talk," Krista explained. "That's why her family traded her for food. The camps in the city ruins are basically scavengers. I don't know why they stay in the ruins—food doesn't grow well, and it's still dangerous, even now. Why, just a few months ago one of the skyscrapers collapsed. Big Jim told us all about it. He and some men were out scouting around."

Aerina was shocked into silence for a moment. It was difficult to believe that the world outside of Alba lived like this—basically squalor, like peasants in the Dark Ages.

"Do you like it here, then?" Aerina asked, trying to keep the incredulity from her voice. She watched Marcus get up with the men and walk over to the off-road vehicle, pulling a pack out from the back. They then walked away, not looking towards the women once.

"There are worse places," Krista replied matter-of-factly. "We are just thankful we are well-protected here from raids. I've heard they are becoming more common. Big Jim is always excited to see Marcus—he usually hunts down the raiders when our men can't."

This was the second mention of Marcus killing raiders for the outpost towns. What other new things about the enigmatic man would be revealed on this excursion?

The women chatted quietly; Aerina asking questions about the prison town, the women answering as best they could.

"Krista! Bring our food!" Big Jim hollered from the table they had returned to. Krista hurried to grab bowls and utensils. She had told Aerina that they frequently ate outside since it got extremely hot inside the dormitories. Many even slept outside when the weather was nice.

Aerina helped the other woman bring the food over to the men. Marcus nodded his thanks as Aerina set it down in front of him, but as Krista was balancing a few bowls, one slipped out of her hands and cascaded hot stew on Big Jim's shoulder.

The large man stood up quickly, cursing. He turned towards Krista, backhanding her to the ground. The rest of the bowls went flying.

Aerina gasped, hurrying to help the thin, dark haired woman up. Big Jim was yelling at Krista for her clumsiness, and drew back his foot to give her a kick. Aerina stepped in between.

"What is wrong with you? It was clearly an accident," she said angrily, glaring up at the much larger man. Big Jim turned towards Aerina, a sneer raising one side of his mouth. He lifted his hand but hesitated as Marcus stood abruptly.

"You'd better get your woman under control," the leader snarled instead, sitting back down.

Aerina turned away from him to help Krista up. Looking around the courtyard, she could see everyone had stopped what they were doing to watch the scene unfolding. She knew Big Jim was also aware of their audience. He needed to save face in front of his people.

She tensed, waiting for him to lash out. She carefully kept her body between Krista and Big Jim. Marcus had sat back down, but she could tell from the line of his body that he was coiled to pounce if Big Jim did anything.

It didn't take long. Krista kept her head down, her hands shaking slightly as she collected the spilt bowls. Without looking up, she started to walk back to the fire. Big Jim moved suddenly, reaching around Aerina to grab the other woman. Aerina stepped in his way, and his arms closed around Aerina instead.

The smell was overpowering. The man's bulk was layers of fat over cords of muscle. She felt like he was squeezing the air out of her like a python, one exhale at a time.

Aerina instinctively bit down on the arm wrapped around her chest and Big Jim roared, loosening his grip just enough for her to slip away. He turned on her but before he could lash out, Marcus had grabbed him and sent him sprawling in the other direction.

Immediately the entire group of men jumped to their feet, weapons in hand. But Marcus was faster. He had grabbed Big Jim's weapon and aimed it at the man's head, lifting the heavier man to his feet as if he were a plush toy, wrapping a strong arm around his throat. He motioned to Aerina with a nod and she slipped behind him, out of reach of the other men. Tension bubbled amongst those gathered, waiting to boil over. The entire courtyard was silent.

"Tell your men to drop their weapons," Marcus ordered softly. "I'd hate to see our very profitable relationship damaged because of one ignorant woman."

Aerina ignored that, too concerned to be offended. Big Jim hesitated, and Aerina held her breath, her heart pounding loudly in her ears as she waited for what would happen next.

"Put your guns away, men," he finally ordered. "Marcus is right. We don't want to lose a good trade partner over a stupid woman who can't hold her tongue."

The men all put their guns down. Marcus let go and stepped back, setting his weapon down on the table carefully within arm's reach.

Aerina walked quickly with Krista back to the fire, the other woman keeping her eyes on the ground.

"I'm sorry," Aerina tried to apologize, knowing she had only made it worse now for the small woman. Krista didn't respond, going about fixing another bowl for Big Jim. Leah offered to bring it over to him. The women's earlier friendliness had disappeared and they now ignored Aerina.

Frustrated, Aerina sat on the ground and choked her own stew down past the lump in her throat. Marcus still sat with the men, and he must have told them a humorous story because the table broke out in laughter. He didn't even glance her way, and Aerina couldn't help but feel a little sorry for herself.

She reminded herself again that she had chosen to come. But if Marcus even breathed the words 'I told you so' she wouldn't be responsible for her reaction.

As evening fell and the shadows grew longer, Aerina stayed where she was, her back against the warm concrete of the west dormitory.

The women had cleaned up and the younger children had been herded inside. The heat of the sun had subsided and a late October breeze blew gently, cooling the night. She could smell the warmed concrete, the grasses, and a hint of what was probably the garbage pile outside the walls.

She watched Marcus talking with the men. Raucous, slovenly, and arrogant, the leaders of this outpost were vastly different from Marcus' own immaculate uniform and controlled demeanor. He talked with the group, but was detached. Aerina realized this was how he frequently looked even in Alba. He was always watching, observing; never participating.

Always on the outside.

The men all stood, shaking hands, and Marcus strode towards where she sat. Even after the day of traveling and the scuffle with the men, his black suit looked fresh, and there wasn't any sign of the exhaustion she felt on his contained features.

She sighed at her own pitiful condition—dusty, tangled hair, her clothes more brown than white, and she felt sticky and tired.

"Time to go," he told her briskly, offering his hand to pull her up. She gripped it, feeling the callused strength, and even in her exhaustion that familiar thrill of longing passed through her.

He was already turning away, heading towards the vehicle. She hurried to follow, glancing over at the men as they watched her with antagonism.

Marcus didn't help her up, and she found herself scrambling ungracefully over the high side that didn't open. As the engine roared to life, she had never felt so grateful.

The gates creaked open as they approached, and Marcus drove through them with barely a foot to spare on each side. Soon they were heading down a worn trail towards the coastline.

"I didn't think you'd be able to pull yourself away from your buddies," she commented acerbically as the high walls of the prison shrunk behind them with each turn of the massive tires.

Marcus shot her an unreadable glance as he skillfully maneuvered the vehicle through a rocky dip.

"You need to learn the most important lesson of traveling outside Alba," he finally said coldly. "You aren't there to change these people. They have their own style of living, and as long as it works for them, they are going to keep it. You don't interfere, and you keep your opinions to yourself."

"Are you saying you wouldn't interfere if he were to beat that woman to death?" Aerina asked in disbelief. The Marcus she knew wouldn't stand by and let an innocent person get hurt. As much as he might pretend otherwise, he was a hero at heart. A protector.

Marcus hesitated a short moment before answering.

"If I thought it necessary to intervene, I would use logic and reason first. Most people can be manipulated if one understands what drives them."

Aerina opened her mouth to protest, then shut it. He was right. She could have found a better way to handle Big Jim. It had been quite obvious that he was full of hubris, and she had practically spit in his face.

It was about balance here, just like in Alba. She didn't know why that town had evolved as it did, but it wasn't going to change until the people in it were ready for that change.

"I'm sorry," she finally said. She'd caused trouble for him as well as the women there because of her interference, forcing him to potentially risk their lives and the relationship he'd forged with the outpost for her sake. "I'll try and do better next time."

He looked over at her again, and this time she thought she caught a spark of approval in his shadowy eyes.

"Where are we going now? Won't it be difficult to travel once it's dark?" She held on to the front roll bar as they hit a particularly large bump, lifting her off the seat.

"Yes, the town we're heading to isn't far. I think you'll like this place better," he added drily. "We'll spend the night there."

Chapter 13

"We can easily forgive a child who is afraid of the dark; the real tragedy of life is when men are afraid of the light."
– Plato

Nearly an hour later they reached the coastline. It was beautiful. The sun had just sunk below the horizon but its light still reflected off the distant clouds hanging low over the ocean. Deep blues and purples framed a brilliant golden red where the ocean met the sky.

She could hear the surf far below as they rode on a narrow trail up the hillside bordering the ocean. She glanced forward as Marcus began slowing the vehicle, squinting in the twilight to see what was ahead of them. Strangely symmetrical shapes appeared to contrast with the rocky disarray of the cliffside. The shapes drew nearer and were revealed to be low, square buildings built along the hillside. Lit only by a few dim lights, these structures were barely visible amidst the vegetation and rocky outcroppings, and would be completely hidden from the ocean.

The group in the prison had chosen high walls and weapons to protect them. These people chose camouflage.

Aerina followed Marcus up the hillside, carrying the bag he had instructed her to bring. A shadowy figure detached from the closest structure to meet them.

"Marcus, I could hear that monstrous vehicle from miles away." A slender woman, appearing to be several years older than Aerina, walked forward and hugged Marcus. Aerina couldn't help the sharp sting of jealousy, wanting to pull the woman's arms from around Marcus' muscular torso.

"Debbie, this stop is always the highlight of my journey," he murmured back, pulling stiffly from her embrace. "I want you to meet Aerina Delacroix, a Patrician from Alba."

Debbie stepped forward with a welcoming smile. In the dim

light, she could tell the older woman had dark hair and eyes, and an attractive if somewhat pointy face.

Aerina took her hand, returning the woman's smile. At least she was friendly.

"You must want to get cleaned up. When I heard you coming, I had the guest house opened up. Jana should be finishing up now," she said, turning to walk back up the path. Aerina and Marcus followed behind.

The guest house looked like all the others, a single room with a low, flat roof. An acrylic tub, similar to the ones on Alba, sat in the corner with taps. Aerina couldn't contain a wide smile at the site of the tub and small sink in a kitchenette. They had running water and electricity. It was heaven. She couldn't wait to be clean again.

A large bed sat in the opposite corner from the bath area on a platform. Everything looked clean and tidy.

"I'll let you get cleaned up and then you can meet with the council in the Meeting Hall," Debbie said, gesturing towards the tub. "Please let me know if there is anything you need."

"Thank you!" Aerina said with feeling. "This is wonderful." Debbie smiled in response as she left quietly.

"Go ahead and take a bath if you'd like. I'll just wash up in the sink," Marcus told her, heading towards the small kitchen area. He shook out his armored jacket and hung it behind the door, then pulled the black t-shirt he wore underneath over his head. She couldn't seem to look away from the muscles that rippled in his back as he leaned over the sink, splashing water on his face and neck. A too-familiar heat spread through her body, settling in her core as a throbbing that was difficult to ignore. Her heart-rate picked up, and she suddenly felt overheated and slightly lightheaded. She worried she might start panting like a dog in heat at any moment. Not a very attractive picture. Marcus paused for a moment, glancing back at her.

"Enjoying the show?" he asked calmly with a quirk of his brow. She blushed and turned towards the tub, opening the faucet. Clean warm water rushed out and she sighed in contentment. Glancing over her shoulder at where Marcus was grabbing a clean t-shirt from his bag, she quickly shrugged out of her own dirty, wrinkled clothes and climbed in.

She sank into the warm water with a groan of pleasure, still trying to ignore the way the water felt on her overheated skin. "This is amazing," she sighed. Looking over at Marcus, she saw him standing absolutely still, watching her, the forgotten t-shirt still in his hand. "Enjoying the show?" she asked teasingly, glad to get back some of her own. At least she wasn't the only one desperately fighting an attraction. From the fit of his pants, she knew he at least found her physically appealing.

Rather than look away, as she had, his dark gaze flicked from her creamy skin to meet her own sapphire gaze. His eyes gleamed as he walked slowly forward, still gripping the t-shirt in his hands. The grin faded from her face as she took in the lines of his body, all hard planes and lean muscles.

He stopped directly beside the tub, the air between them nearly crackling with the heated currents. His eyes flicked down over her slender body, covered only by the clear water. Her golden skin gleamed in the low light. Instinctively her arms crossed over her chest and she flushed slightly. She'd never been naked in front of anyone before.

His hand lifted slightly for a moment, grazing lightly over her damp shoulder. She shivered involuntarily, feeling as if he'd branded her, the heat of his hand startling. She bit back a groan, holding her breath as she hoped, prayed, he'd go further. Touch her elsewhere. Anywhere. *There*. The place that throbbed and ached.

She almost cried out with disappointment as he clenched his fists and turned away instead. He strode to the door, wrenching it open and closing it behind him with exaggerated care.

Her head dropped back against the tub and she closed her eyes with a frustrated groan. She *hurt*, dammit. She'd never truly felt desire before, and unfulfilled desire sucked.

Marcus and his damn self-control.

Washing quickly, she drained the tub and threw on a pair of Pleb clothes. Julia called them yoga pants after a pre-war exercise that was popular now. Black and tight, they emphasized her well-shaped backside and long legs. The top was a fitted tank the color of her eyes.

Braiding her hair, she hurried out the door after Marcus. The night was startlingly dark without the Alban city lights to illuminate it. The sound of the ocean filled the air as it often did in Alba, but no other city sounds filtered through the crash of the water against the sand. It was peaceful, and a little bit lonely.

A path was dimly lit by tall torches that appeared to burn using some kind of oil rather than electricity. She followed the steep path up, around several more small houses similar to the one she was sharing with Marcus, and came to a larger building that was rectangular with a higher roof. Light streamed through the windows lining the side and she could see Marcus along with several women inside.

Entering quietly, she hesitated inside the door.

"Come join us, Aerina," Debbie beckoned her forward from her seat at the head of a long wooden table. A total of eight women were seated. Aerina sank slowly into the empty seat beside Marcus. "Marcus tells us that this is your first time outside Alba? This is Sybil, a town primarily of women. We offer a safe haven to any who are persecuted. Very few know of the location of our town, and we hope you will respect our privacy."

"Of course," Aerina murmured, glancing at Marcus. "How did Marcus find you?"

"From a fishing boat," Marcus answered. "I was mapping the coast, making note of the towns and camps. The activity. I noticed a cooking fire and came ashore to investigate."

"We tried to shoot him with one of our tranquilizer guns but he was quick and it didn't penetrate his armor." Debbie shot Marcus a wry look. "Needless to say, he discovered our town but promised to keep it a secret if we gave him information. He also brought us one of your amazing feats of science, the Energy Box." The attractive older woman folded her slender fingers and rested her chin on them. "We've learned much about the world outside of our region from Marcus."

Aerina felt again that familiar twinge of jealousy at the obvious connection between Marcus and Debbie. A leader, confident and assured of her place. Everything Aerina wasn't.

Marcus leaned forward slightly, changing the subject away from himself. He'd humored the women long enough. "What news do you have?"

"Jera saw an old-fashioned all-terrain vehicle when she was tending the inland garden a few days back," Debbie answered, nodding towards a young woman sitting across the table from Aerina. She had large, dark brown eyes and dark skin. A bold chin and blunt nose were marked with several scars crisscrossing an otherwise compelling face.

"The vehicle looked like a re-commissioned war vehicle from the Global War era. It had several men riding, some carrying weapons."

"Ballistic?" Marcus asked. Jera nodded, glancing at Debbie who smiled encouragingly. She kept her eyes down on the table as she continued. "Probably Texaco rebels," she spoke quietly in a voice that was hoarse as if it had been damaged at some point. "They've been a problem around here for several months now. I don't think they've ventured this far to the coast before."

"Aren't you from Texaco?" Marcus asked the young woman. She nodded, keeping her gaze down on her hands.

"We haven't seen any fisherman from the south," another woman piped up. "I found that to be strange. Usually we see at least one or two fishing boats a week. It's been several weeks since one has passed the coast."

"Has anyone been to New Diego lately?" Marcus asked.

"No, we've been staying close to home," Debbie answered. "The last we heard, there was an illness spreading through some of the southern towns. We figured New Diego would be a prime breeding ground for any illness, as filthy as it always is."

"Isn't New Diego built right in the old city of San Diego?" Aerina asked curiously, unable to hold her tongue any longer.

"Yes," Debbie answered patiently. "San Diego was never destroyed in the wars, and much of the pre-war city is still standing. It could be quite a beautiful historical city if it wasn't so full of riff-raff. Sadly, the government was overthrown several decades ago, and it's become a very different place."

They continued to discuss the possible causes of the missing fishing boats. A young blonde woman, perhaps fifteen, brought in some fruit and water, which Aerina was grateful for. The tiny bit of stew she had managed to choke down at the ex-prison hadn't filled her.

Aerina ate while the others talked, listening with interest. Marcus mostly asked questions, the women answering. Aerina determined that these women were the elected officials of Sybil, this tiny town of mostly women. She relaxed into the comfortable, cushioned chair. Her eyes grew heavy in the warm evening air, and before she knew it, a hand was on her shoulder.

"Come, I will walk you back to your room," a shy voice offered. Aerina started with embarrassment. She couldn't believe she'd fallen asleep in the middle of the discussion. Looking up, she saw the younger girl who had brought snacks in earlier. Aerina thought her name was Jenny. Several of the other council members had also retired. Aerina rose with a smile of thanks, nodding to the remaining group. The women bid her good evening, Marcus just watching her with his unreadable eyes.

The evening was humid but cool, the surf heavy in the air around them. The damp breeze woke Aerina up further as she followed Jenny down the dark path. The lights had been turned out, and only the thin moon and Jenny's lantern lit their way.

Aerina tripped over a small rock and Jenny turned, holding the lantern higher.

"Are you alright?"

Aerina nodded, then realized the girl wouldn't be able to see the movement in the dark, and answered "Yes, I'm fine."

"Sorry about the dark. Debbie doesn't like the lamps on after twilight. It is too easy to spot from a distance."

"I understand," Aerina replied, then asked curiously, "So do only women live here?"

"No," Jenny's voice carried over the breeze. "There are some men, and children. Many choose to leave and we help them find a good place to resettle. Once someone leaves, they can't return. Debbie is very strict about that rule."

"How do you keep your population stable?"

"We have contacts, mainly former residents, in several cities and towns. They notify our scouts if someone is in need of our help."

"A refuge," Aerina murmured.

"Yes," Jenny replied, having heard her words over the crash of the surf. "A life-saver for many of us."

They continued the rest of the short walk in silence. Jenny stood at the door as Aerina entered.

"Please leave the shutters closed if you have the lights on, for safety. Is there anything else you need?"

"No," Aerina said gratefully. "This is wonderful. More than I expected. Thank you."

She stood for a moment, watching the small flickering light disappear back up the hill. Turning, she held up the extra lantern Jenny had thoughtfully left with her.

Aerina wondered what it would be like to live every day, every moment, thinking of ways to stay invisible to the world. Albans believed in isolation because it has saved them during the wars, but they certainly didn't hide in the dark like the citizens of Sybil were forced to do.

Turning out the lantern, she settled in the wicker loveseat placed on the porch with a blanket. The night was dark, the whitecaps on the dark ocean below reflecting the little bit of moonlight.

"Aerina."

Aerina started at the low voice calling her name. Her eyes opened to find a dark form crouched low before her. Without being able to see any features, she knew it was him.

"Marcus," she murmured, involuntarily raising her hand to touch his familiar stark features. He didn't move as her hand stroked along his stubbled jaw to where his cheek bones arched above taught cheeks, to his prominent, dark eyebrows. Learning him. Knowing him.

"You're beautiful," she said softly, her eyes going to his dark ones. A hidden fire burned in their nearly black depths, the flecks of gold barely visible in the lantern sitting on the porch boards.

"I remember when I first saw you," Aerina told him, letting her hand trail down his arm, over the t-shirt stretched taut over cords of muscle, to the warm skin of his forearms. "You were young, just a boy, standing with a few other Virmortus on the Capitol steps. Even then you looked more dangerous than the Reapers holding your arms." Aerina tucked her legs up, pulling Marcus onto the small seat with her. He let her, settling into his corner easily, stretching his long legs out and throwing his arm over the back. The seat creaked in protest.

After a long moment of silence, Marcus spoke. "I remember that day. My Conscription. You were even younger than I, but you had the same bold stare. And your hair... I remember your hair. It was glowing in the light of the setting sun, brighter than the sunset itself." His hand trailed down her golden red hair, letting the silky strands fall through his fingers.

Aerina smiled, her scalp tingling and a shiver of pleasure going through her at both his words and light touch. She was inordinately pleased that he had noticed her, too.

"How were you chosen to become a Reaper; a Virmortus?" she asked, hesitant to shatter the moment.

He remained quiet, the callused hand thrown across the back of the couch still combing gently through the silky strands of curls that spread over the back. Then he spoke, his voice distant.

"My mother... died soon after I was born. My father was an Armati and hated me. I didn't know why until I was older. An archaic sin the Laws cannot erase—infidelity. He was constantly finding reasons to punish me. And an Armati only knows one form of punishment," Marcus said bitterly. Aerina bit her tongue to keep from asking questions, not wanting him to stop. She had a feeling he rarely, if ever, told this story.

"When I was five, I started Armati training. It was a relief. The training was harsh, but at least the rewards and punishment were consistent. And I was good, better than the older boys. I finished all the tests earlier and had higher scores." Marcus shrugged, letting her hair drop away and setting his hand on the couch with his normal exaggerated care. "I was a natural choice—no family to protest, high scores, the best fighter. A born killer, they said."

Aerina's heart turned over at the perfectly even, emotionless way he talked about his childhood. He'd never known love or concern from anyone; he was just a tool. A tool of death.

She wanted badly to reach out and touch him, to show that she cared. But she was afraid he would take that as a sign of pity. From the shuttered look on his face, she knew that would be a big mistake.

Marcus sat tensely, forcing his clenched fist to relax, waiting for her response. He tried to read her face in the dark. Pity or disgust? He dreaded either. Pity for the pathetic child he had been, disgust for the machine he had become. He had no illusions about himself—he did what was necessary to preserve Alba.

Nothing matters but your job.

But her opinion mattered. She mattered, and he didn't want to shatter whatever image of him she'd built in her mind. Yet he also didn't want her believing a lie. He wasn't a hero. He was a killer.

Angling her slender body towards the warmth emanating from his large form, Aerina rested her chin on her hand. She could feel the stiff lines of his body pressed against her side, tensed as if ready for a blow. She both marveled and felt overwhelming sadness at his insecurity. An insecurity she never would have believed possible a month ago. Even a week ago.

Lacing her slender fingers with his larger ones, she raised his hand slowly from the back of the seat, gently kissing the light scars that adorned it.

She couldn't see his expression in the dark as she leaned in, settling against the hard lines of his chest, still holding his hand. Bringing his other arm around her, she forced him into an embrace.

He didn't fight. His arms tightened around her of their own accord, fighting off the depth of emotion threatening to overwhelm him.

Resting her head on his chest, she finally broke the silence.

"I was ten when I disobeyed my parents and took my little brother down to the beach to swim. They were often busy, too busy to take us themselves. I remember the day was cool, almost too cold to swim. But I was determined." Her hands unconsciously tightened on his, her voice thinning.

"The water was rough, but we'd already come all that way. Max was scared but he went in. The first big wave pulled him out, so far I couldn't reach him. He was crying; choking. I screamed and swam to him, but the cold water kept most people from the beach that day. I managed to get to him, but I was too cold, too tired, to hold us both up. I remember screaming, the salt burning my eyes and nose, trying to hold onto Max.

"It seemed like an hour passed but it must have only been a few minutes. A Pleb surfer pulled us both out and paddled us to shore. He tried to resuscitate Max, and the Medella arrived to take over. They let me ride to the Clinic with them, holding Max's hand. It was so cold," she whispered the last. Marcus' arms tightened around her, rubbing her back gently as she continued.

"My mother arrived first. I'll never forget the look on her face. And her words. *This is all your fault.* Because it was my fault." Tears flowed freely, soaking Marcus' t-shirt. Her voice cracked as she continued.

"I've spent my life trying to let go of that regret. Trying to run from that one horrible mistake that cost my brother his life. We all have our darkness. But it isn't who I am.

"And it isn't who you are," she finished quietly, looking up at the outline of his features. He lowered his head slowly, giving her time to back away.

She met him half-way, their lips meeting in a soft caress unlike their previous passionate kisses. His rough hands cupped her tear-streaked cheeks as his mouth moved over hers, gently, firmly.

Her breath caught in her chest as sorrow mingled with pleasure. He tasted of salty air and whiskey. Her mouth parted on a sigh and his tongue swept in to lightly mate with hers.

Aerina pressed closer, her arms going around his neck. She

ran her hand over his head, her fingers delighting in the sensation of his close-cropped hair.

As his hands swept down over her heated, throbbing body, she knew this night was theirs. There would be no withdrawing; no stopping.

He stood, lifting her effortlessly and carrying her over the threshold like an old-world bride. The past and future faded to insignificance. There was only this moment; only these two people. A man and woman about to become one in the oldest dance known to man.

Aerina lurched awake, thrashing at the suffocating weight covering her, a hard hand stifling her gasp of fear.

"Quiet." Aerina stopped her struggling at the familiar rumble in her ear, her body tense beneath Marcus' heavy form. He was looking at something outside the cottage. Then she saw it, too. A tiny dancing light moving around the side of the cottage, visible through the shutters Marcus must have opened after she fell asleep.

The beauty of their union a few hours earlier was forgotten as fear surged through her taut body.

Sensing that she understood the situation, Marcus flowed from the bed to squat on the floor, moving silently towards the door in a crouch. Aerina cautiously felt for some article of clothing. Her grasping hands found a piece of cloth — Marcus' black t-shirt.

Marcus stood just to the right of the door and waited; a panther crouched, ready to pounce. The door swung open slowly, quietly, and Aerina could immediately tell the shape was that of a large man. Before he could take more than a step into the room, Marcus slid behind him, garrote wrapped tightly around his neck. The figure struggled barely a moment before going limp. Marcus pulled him further into the cottage and lowered him slowly to the ground. Motioning for Aerina to stay put, he slipped out the door, closing it behind him.

Hell no. She wasn't going to cower in here while he risked his life out there. Her heart pounding so loud she couldn't hear her own footsteps, she made her way in the darkness towards the door. She kept her gaze averted from the dead man laying just out of sight from the door.

Aerina kicked something, the clink making her jump. She reached down for the object. An ElectroMagnifying Weapon. She knew a little about EMWs. They used an electric current to either stun or kill the victim. It could be set to hit multiple targets at once. She'd never shot one, but how hard could it be? Point and squeeze...

Picking it up, Aerina followed Marcus out into the cool, salty pre-dawn without a second thought.

It was dark. The moon wasn't visible, hidden behind clouds, and it was too early for the sun to cast a glow from behind the tall coastal hills.

Aerina stood pressed up against the cottage, trying to make out something, anything, in the complete darkness. She felt terribly exposed wearing nothing but a t-shirt. After a moment that felt like an eternity, she saw another bobbing light some distance down the hill. Near Marcus' vehicle.

She waited patiently as the light approached. The individual was going to walk directly past her on the trail. Should she shoot? Her mind whirled in panic. What if it was set to kill and that was one of the Sybilians? What if it was Marcus?

Marcus wouldn't use a light, common sense assured her. *And it's the same light as the man in your cottage. Not the lanterns the women use.*

The figure was practically upon her, the crunch of gravel loud above the calm of the ocean. Not wasting time on second thoughts, Aerina closed her eyes and pulled the trigger. A small zap and pop sounded, and then she heard a muffled thud as the body hit the ground.

I'm sorry, I'm sorry, I'm sorry, her mind cried over and over as she moved away from the body. Should she stay and watch for any other intruders? The urge was overwhelming to find Marcus and make sure he was alright.

She walked slowly in the dark, not wanting to stumble and give away her position. Adrenaline pumped through her body, making her feel hyper-aware. Her breathing seemed loud to her own ears and she tried to control it, but her heart was pounding so quickly it was hard not to take quick, short gasps.

When she heard a scream a short distance up the hill, she gave up trying to be stealthy and ran. Immediately she tripped over a rock but managed to catch herself. Her bare feet were cut again and again on the sharp gravel but the adrenaline kept it from hurting. She reached a cottage, its outline barely visible in the dark, and peered inside the open door. A figure lay on the floor. A large figure.

Heart in her throat, she rushed forward. The amount of hair covering its head and face convinced her quickly that it wasn't Marcus or one of the women. Turning, her heart stopped when she saw another form in the doorway.

"Marcus?" she whispered. Something whistled past her ear and thudded into the wall behind her. She instinctively pulled her own trigger. The same zap and pop sounded, and she dropped a second body. Aerina inched forward, her foot hitting an object that skittered across the floor. Another knife. The first one was embedded in the wall not far from where her head had been. In the dim light, she could make out the intruder's features. A woman.

Aerina didn't want to see more. She knew the quick glimpse of the woman's features, frozen in the rictus of death, would haunt her. Making her way to the next cottage, she slowly opened the closed door. A feminine gasp sounded.

"It's ok, it's Aerina," she said softly.

"Oh thank goodness," Jenny exclaimed just as quietly. "Marcus was here a few minutes ago. He told me to barricade the door." Aerina could see the other woman was pushing the divan towards the door. She hurried forward to help. When they were close, she squeezed through the crack.

"Where are you going?" Jenny hissed.

"I'm going to help Marcus," Aerina whispered back, ignoring the other woman's quiet protests as she closed the door behind her.

The next few minutes seemed like an eternity as she

stumbled around in the dark. She wasn't sure where the other cottages were, or if she was even on the path anymore. Stopping, she listened to the night. The soft lapping of the ocean against the sand far below was all that she could hear.

Where was Marcus? She felt panic begin to rise in her chest, and she gripped the weapon carefully. She wasn't sure how many blasts it had. Perhaps she was already out of whatever energy it took to shoot it.

Suddenly an arm shot around her throat and she froze, dropping the weapon. She was pulled back against a large, warm body, the arm on her throat a band of steel.

"What the hell are you doing out here?" a furious voice growled in her ear. She sagged against him in relief. Marcus.

"I'm helping," she murmured back. She could feel the warm solidity of his bare chest against her back. He hadn't had time to dress, either. Bending to pick up the dropped weapon when his arm loosened from around her neck, she held it up to show him.

One long finger slowly pushed the barrel of the weapon away from where it pointed at Marcus' chest. Aerina flushed in the dark, careful to keep it pointed at the ground.

"Stay behind me," he ordered, moving forward slowly. She gladly did as he told her. He methodically went through each cottage, checking on the inhabitants, advising them to barricade their doors.

They then headed down the hill to where his vehicle was parked. Marcus cursed silently. The tires had been slashed. Not far from the vehicle was a small body. Aerina's heart froze as she recognized the gleaming ebony skin and small scars.

Jera.

The poor woman's throat had been slit so deeply, it had nearly severed her head. Aerina looked away, the gory scene etched on her retinas. Her heart started pounding heavily, a low buzzing in her ears blocking out everything around her. She couldn't keep the tears that rushed forward contained, although she tried, and one trailed down her face, cold in the early morning breeze.

Marcus continued on, stepping carefully over the body

without a second look. Aerina took a shaky breath and followed him, her eyes still swimming with unshed tears. They could do nothing for the girl now.

Moving around a tall outcropping, they came upon the rest of the assassins. Two men stood around a large armored vehicle, a dim light sitting on the hood. A third man stepped forward, only his outline visible in the early morning dark, holding an EMW to Marcus' head.

"Move and you're dead," he sneered. Marcus didn't hesitate. In a movement that was a blur, he broke the man's forearm, forcing the weapon into his opponent's chest and firing. The force of the current sent the man sprawling backwards. Without hesitating, Marcus threw the weapon at the head of the second man, dropping him instantly. Before the third man could ready his weapon, Marcus was on him, breaking his neck with a twist of his hands.

Aerina stood frozen, gripping her own weapon in both shaky hands, aiming it in the general direction of the fallen men.

"Do me a favor and don't shoot that. I don't want to end up like them," Marcus said dryly, indicating the fallen men. Aerina carefully set the EMW on the ground, watching as Marcus turned up the lantern and began methodically going through the vehicle.

"Won't their friends see us?" Aerina asked worriedly, glancing around.

"No. The seven I killed, plus the two you killed, and these three here are all of them. An Armored Off-road Vehicle only has room for twelve. If there was another AOV here, they'd already be on us," Marcus explained succinctly. He was now going through the men's clothing. He then picked up one man's arm and made a slit on his wrist with his sica blade. Aerina flinched but refused to look away. Marcus shoved his finger inside, moving it around for a moment, and then extracted a small chip coated in blood. It looked a little like the Alban ID chips.

As Marcus moved to the second man, Aerina turned to the one laying on the ground near her. Her sica blade was still in the cottage, but she used the long knife hanging from the dead man's belt to slit open his wrist.

Fighting back the squeamishness, she used her finger to dig around in his wrist. Her stomach turned over as she felt tendon and slick muscle. Finally she felt the chip, extracting it carefully. Looking up, she saw Marcus was watching her with an unreadable expression. Without a word, he walked forward, taking the chip and sticking it in the pocket of his pants.

Grabbing the lantern, they walked back up the hill. Aerina winced with each step, trying to avoid the sharp rocks. Marcus was also barefoot, but he wasn't human, striding forward seemingly unbothered by the rocky path.

When they reached the meeting hall in the center of Sybil, the sun's rays were just visible above the peak of the hillside. The glow of dawn spread slowly, casting its light upon the village.

Just past the meeting house, Marcus knocked quickly. Aerina heard some scuffling and imagined the divan was being pushed back. Then the door was opened and Debbie stood in a thin nightgown that delineated her tall, curvy body.

"They're all dead," Marcus said flatly. "Meet me in the Hall in five minutes. We will be leaving in ten."

Debbie was there in less than three, having just thrown a robe over her thin sleeping gown.

"Who?" Debbie asked first, griping the edges of her robe tightly. The sides of her mouth showed her strain. Their haven had been breached.

Aerina stood silently beside Marcus, still barefoot and wearing only his t-shirt. She couldn't work up the mindset to be embarrassed. She still felt a little horrified but mostly numb from shock. Her hand was stiff with the dried blood from the dead raider's wrist, a reminder of the horrors they had just experienced.

Marcus stood still and tall; a dangerous sight to behold in just his drawstring pants. The group looked to him for leadership, and he wouldn't let them down. Aerina felt a burst of pride, and the other overwhelming feeling she still wasn't ready to name, fill her chest.

Besides Jera, only one woman had been hurt, shot with the

EMW. She was only unconscious—they hadn't intended to kill the women. At least not right away.

"They weren't raiders," Marcus stated grimly. "They were too organized; too well trained. This was an assassination attempt, perhaps a kidnapping. They were looking for me."

"But who?" Debbie asked again, her slender fingers shaking slightly where they gripped her robe.

"The Southern Empire. They are the only ones I know of who wear ID chips like Albans." He opened his hand to show the bloody chips they had extracted from the dead men. "And I recognized their armored vehicle. I need to return to Alba immediately."

"What should we do?" Debbie asked quietly. "What if they return?

Marcus shook his head as he turned towards the door.

"Once I am gone, you won't have anything they want. It's doubtful they will return. But I can't make any guarantees. Let me suggest you begin thinking about a better system of guard and defense. I found you, they found you; it's inevitable that someone else will find you. Nothing can stay hidden forever," he said in an undertone, and Aerina sensed a deeper meaning behind the statement.

"What about the bodies?" Debbie asked, looking surprisingly lost for such a strong woman.

"Burn them."

He nodded to Debbie and motioned Aerina to follow as he strode out the door. He paused suddenly, causing Aerina to bump into his back.

"I'm sorry about Jera," he said quietly. "I'm sure she had good reason to betray you." Without looking back, he continued out the door. Aerina hurried to keep up, wincing as the stones bit into her already sore and bleeding feet.

Once back at the cottage, they dressed quickly and threw everything into their bags. Marcus dragged the body of the dead man outside while Aerina did her best to comb her tangled hair with her fingers and braid it.

When Marcus returned, they both scrubbed their bloody

hands in the sink in silence.

Aerina went to put on her shoes, wincing in pain as she pulled the white moccasins over her bloody soles. Marcus glanced over, dropping to his haunches in front of her.

"It's fine," she said quickly when he moved to grab her foot. He ignored her, looking for a long moment at the torn flesh; at the blood stains on her expertly crafted white moccasins. Carefully, he used the blood-spattered shirt she had been wearing to wipe her foot clean before pushing the moccasins back on. His expression was cold, remote; a contrast to his gentle ministrations.

She followed him out of the room without a backwards glance. The young Patrician who had left Alba just a few short days earlier was gone. In her place was someone new; someone whom Aerina was still figuring out.

Marcus walked past the useless all-terrain vehicle, heading towards the armored vehicle around the bend. Aerina looked away carefully from the three bodies they had mutilated to remove the chips. She would have never thought herself capable of something so grotesque. She was finding new limits to her abilities.

The Armored Off-road Vehicle, which Marcus called a Hillbilly Tank, had large tires like Marcus', but was completely covered in a camo-colored thin metal. As she climbed in, Aerina could feel the clear plastic coating over the metal. Protection against an EMW, she guessed.

They both strapped in with the harnesses. Marcus paused for a moment, staring at the steering wheel.

"You did well today for one who never trained," he finally said. Pleasure welled in her chest at his simple words of approval, only to be crushed by his next statement. "But never disobey my orders again."

She glared over at him, but as quickly as it rose, her ire dissipated. He was used to being in control, of himself and those around him. Whether he admitted it or not, he was beginning to care about her.

He was just going to have to learn to deal with that.

Glancing back, Aerina watched Sybil disappear into the landscape. A strange tangle of emotions twisted inside her as the pivotal place faded from view. Like many of the refugees who had come to that place, she had been reborn there. She'd become a lover; joining herself with a man outside of her class.

And she'd become a killer.

She turned back to face forward, glancing sideways at Marcus as the vehicle sped along the rocky coast towards Alba.

She had no regrets.

Chapter 14

"Security is mostly a superstition." - Helen Keller

Marcus didn't speak to Aerina as they drove away from Sybil. The situation was worse than he thought. He'd known someone on the inside was plotting to change the power structure in Alba and had reached to the outside towns for help. He hadn't realized it was the Southern Empire. The military state spanned much of the old south of the former United States. It was organized. It was powerful. It posed a real threat to Alba.

They must be coming for the Technology. There was nothing else Alba had that would be worth their time.

When he wasn't madly trying to determine the Southern Empire's next step, he thought about Aerina. About the danger he had put her in by bringing her along. He alternated between feelings of pride at her composure throughout the short battle and fighting off fury, with both himself and her, over the risk she had taken.

He'd known trained men who, in a real battle, had crumbled completely. But this slender, fiery girl had ventured alone into the night with a weapon she had never used before and killed two assassins.

She could have died, he reminded himself, his hands curling fiercely on the steering wheel. And he would have been responsible. Marcus always took his responsibilities seriously. Deadly serious. But she was more than just a responsibility. Too much more.

And that made him furious all over again.

His mind, of its own accord, brought up the memory of the night before the attack. The memory he had been trying to block out; to keep in the deep recesses of his mind, only to be brought out and explored on the most lonely of nights; the most hopeless of moments.

Of her, beneath him, her gleaming hair spread on the white

pillow. Her eyes luminous, trusting, and heavy with passion. For him. Her words, the moment before he'd finally made her his.

I always knew it would be you.

It hadn't been the furiously passionate coupling he had always thought, a culmination of the sexual tension that had been building between them for months. It has been something far more dangerous. Their joining had been slow, tender, and raw. Shattering.

Another night like the last and he'd be considering stepping down as Alpha Virmortus.

Nothing matters but your job. The first lesson every Virmortus learned. But it wasn't true. For the first time, something — someone — was more important to him than the fate of Alba.

Once they returned to the city, they were done. There was no future for them, so it was best just to end whatever it was they had now. If they survived whatever was coming, she'd forget about him and marry some upstanding Patrician. He'd go on as he always had — alone.

Marcus ignored the wrenching in his heart at the thought of Aerina marrying and forgetting him. Hardening his resolve, he stared straight ahead as he drove. She would be safe, and he couldn't afford to lose his own focus. Millions of lives were his responsibility to protect; he couldn't allow distractions like her.

Aerina was lost in her own thoughts, unaware of Marcus' resolve. She'd made her own resolution to never go back to the life she had lived before this short trip. A life of leisure and study, of legislative responsibility. A life where she felt like she was always an observer and not a participant. She wanted to experience the darker side; the parts of life that weren't so pretty. That weren't so white.

And Marcus. She wanted something more with him than this limbo they were in together. If she had to lose her status as a Patrician, she didn't care. It had been tough to be an outcast to her caste, but she'd survived it. She wouldn't mind living a new life. Perhaps becoming a Virmortus herself. Anything to be with Marcus.

Lost in her musings, she was unprepared for Marcus to bring

the vehicle to a sudden halt. She gasped, grabbing the bar on the dash in front of her.

Thick black smoke hovered ominously in the distance. Brush fire, she thought, scanning the horizon. It didn't take her long to realize her mistake. They'd come inland to bypass old Los Angeles. The smoke curled from the familiar fortress in the distance, its blackened walls starkly outlined in the early morning sun. Aerina stood through the trap door above her seat and squinted against the bright glare of the sun. Marcus was doing the same. She pressed the button on the side of her sunglasses, using her gaze to indicate the zoom icon on the tiny screen that appeared in her peripheral. The lenses automatically adjusted on her optical command, focusing closely on the old prison.

She wished the view wasn't so clear. Two bodies slumped in the guard tower, another hanging in the barbed wire fence. The smoke was coming from the center of the courtyard, and Aerina could only imagine in the dark recesses of her mind what was burning. Canceling the zoom quickly, she looked away.

Nausea fed by panic rose in her throat and she choked it back. An image of the women cooking dinner and children playing in the courtyard rose, unbidden, in her mind. The babies in their mother's arms.

Balance and serenity...

Taking deep breaths, she sat back down inside the vehicle, fighting back the tears of anger and sorrow welling in her eyes.

A few minutes later, Marcus slid back into his seat.

"Should we go help?" Aerina asked past the lump in her throat. Perhaps people were injured or hiding. Perhaps—

"No one is left." Marcus' voice was chilling in its utter lack of emotion. In its finality. Aerina again felt the panic rising in her chest, a mixture of sorrow and outrage. Horror. *All those children.*

"Buckle up," Marcus ordered in his low voice. The vehicle roared to life and they were speeding again toward Alba.

Aerina tried to stem the tide of fear. This was bigger than anything Alba had faced in nearly a hundred years. This could be war.

She wanted to ask Marcus questions, but kept her mouth closed. His face was drawn in concentration as he maneuvered the large vehicle over the uneven terrain. The ferocity on his features was quite unlike the devilish enjoyment of the few days previous.

It was early evening when the large golden dome of the Capitol came into view. Marcus was on his holoreader with Ramus as soon as they came into range of the ComTower, telling him to put the Armati on alert.

"I'll brief you further when I return," he said, cutting the connection. Not long after, Marcus pulled the large vehicle into the hidden garage. They both transferred quickly into his car.

They passed through the large southern gate and Aerina felt a new sense of pride. This was her home, and she would protect it. She looked at the Pleb city—so full of life, with its packed yet tidy streets and carefully organized districts—with new eyes. After seeing the way people outside lived, she had a new appreciation for how the founders had organized Alba, and the way the government upheld the original ideals.

The people here never worried about their meals, or about protection. Women had rights. Children grew up educated and cared for. It was a place worth protecting. Worth dying for.

Marcus sped down the streets of the Capitol Terrace, his car screeching to a halt in front of Aerina's house.

"Out," he ordered shortly.

"I'm coming with you to speak with the Consul," she protested.

He gave her a look. He wasn't in the mood to be lenient. She realized now that up until this point he had been humoring her because he wanted to. This was a side of Marcus he rarely displayed when he was around her. The side that had almost killed her in the Capitol. The side that had effortlessly slain eight men in the Pleb alley. The side that had hunted down the assassins in Sybil while unclothed in the dark. The Reaper.

Without a word, Aerina pushed out of the car, grabbing her bag from the back. At the last moment, she slowed the car door to a quiet click rather than a satisfying slam. She stood in front of her parents' villa, watching his car zoom towards the Capitol.

Just because he wouldn't include her, it didn't mean she had to be helpless in this. There had to be a way for her to help. Squaring her shoulders, she hurried inside, already on her holoreader.

Marcus stood stiffly before the Senators and the Consul in the large meeting room at the back of the Capitol building. The ocean stretched out below them, calm and blue. The sky was cloudless, the sun shining brightly.

The air was calm with barely a breeze to stir the long filmy white drapes that hung on the sides of the glass doors opening into the courtyard.

The picturesque day was a stark contrast to the ponderous atmosphere inside the meeting room. The Consul had briefly told the Senators the severity of the situation and now they waited on Marcus' report.

He outlined the events of his trip, leaving out the role Aerina played for the sake of her already ashen-looking father. When he described the devastation of Ryan, several Senators looked ill.

"You're sure they're not just raiders?" asked the Senator of Defense. Marcus shot him an unreadable look.

"In a Tank with embedded ID chips and EMWs?" Julius said with disbelief in his tone. "Raiders are from Texaco, a barely civilized and poorly organized region that can barely scrape together enough weapons and supplies to go out and steal what other towns have. No, this is not just raiders."

"I am having a tech team hack into the chips we removed from their wrist. But I am certain they will confirm that it is the Southern Empire."

The room was silent, the name striking an old fear in the hearts of many.

Julius sat back in his chair, his blue eyes scanning the room slowly.

"We all know what they are coming for." Several of the Senators nodded their heads. Marcus looked out the window at the horizon. It was still bare, but the Empire was coming. The secret that Alba had guarded for nearly a hundred years was about to be brought into the light again.

It was sparking a new war. The question that remained was whether or not they would be able to defend it like the founders had.

Or would it fall into enemy hands. And inevitably be the downfall of the world. Again.

Chapter 15

"Only the dead have seen the end of war." - Plato

Aerina waited two long days before seeking Marcus out. During those days, it seemed as if the atmosphere in the city had altered. Perhaps it was the knowledge she was privy to, but the winds of warning blew from every familiar corner. The guards seemed more alert, watching and noting the actions of Pleb and Patrician alike.

The city, rather than a refuge from the outside, seemed to be precariously perched on the mountainside, a clear target from the ocean for invaders, each terrace a small prison rather than a stronghold.

Had they learned anything more? Was war truly coming to Alba? Even the threat of the assassin paled in comparison to the thought that the largest entity in North America, the Southern Empire, might be coming for Alba.

But why? Why would the powerful nation care about a small city-state like Alba? If it was technology they wanted, why not try and trade for it, or merely steal it from the outposts and reverse engineer it? Why come to the city and invade?

Aerina had a feeling that Marcus knew the answer; knew what they were coming for. On the evening of the second day after they returned, she sought him out to get answers to her questions.

The day was dark, the mist from the ocean thick and cold. It was as if nature understood the threat Alba was under and empathized the only way it could.

Aerina walked to Marcus' house. It was late, and her father had just returned from the Capitol. This would be her best chance of catching Marcus at home.

The eerie mist swirled gently, her footsteps muffled. It was so thick, she could barely see the houses lining the streets around her.

She arrived at Marcus' familiar doorstep, and felt her heart jump with excitement when she saw his car parked in the carport. He was here.

She almost walked right in, but after their last departure, she hesitated, knocking instead. Straining, she listened for the sound of approaching footsteps inside. Then the door opened without warning and Marcus filled the frame. The look on his face did not bode well.

Gone was her lover and chess partner, and Marcus the Reaper was back firmly in place.

"Can I come in?" she asked, taking a small step forward. He didn't budge. Their eyes locked; hers challenging, his impassive. He didn't relent this time.

After everything they'd been through, after *that night*, did he really expect her to just give up and leave? Did he not know her at all?

When she again went forward to try and push past him, he put his hand out, stopping her.

"Can we at least talk?" She tried to keep the anger out of her voice. Once she became emotional, he immediately had the upper hand. She had to stay cool; in control.

"We have nothing to talk about," he answered finally, ice in his voice.

"You know that's not true," she responded, beginning to lose the battle with her emotions. Were they both just supposed to pretend nothing had changed between them? Regardless of the status of their relationship, she wanted some answers about the upcoming invasion. "I think I deserve an explanation."

His head came down slightly, as if in acquiesce. "I'm sorry if you got the wrong impression, but there was never a chance of us having any kind of serious relationship—" he began stiffly, only to be cut off by her disbelieving laugh.

"You've got to be kidding. Forget about that." She waved her hand angrily, brushing aside that subject and his asinine explanation. "I meant you need to tell me what in the name of peace is going on outside this city."

The slight narrowing of his eyes was the only indication of

his displeasure, but he answered calmly, "Nothing a *Patrician* needs to concern themselves with." His voice became harder, lower, "You have nothing to do with this. Go home, go to the theatre, go surfing. I don't give a damn, but don't come back here."

Aerina wouldn't have been more hurt if he had plunged his sica blade into her chest. The pain of his words, sharp and burning, spread to encompass her whole body.

"Marcus," she said, a question in her voice, trying and failing to keep the hurt from her tone. She lifted her hand to touch him, needing some reassurance from contact that the Marcus who saved her life, that she played chess with, *made love with*, was still there. "I—"

Marcus' hand shot out, capturing her wrist gently but inextricably. "Don't touch me," he said in a dangerously gentle voice. "Anything you imagined we might have had—any friendship, relationship—it's over. It only really existed in your overly imaginative mind. Don't come here, and don't think for a moment that I would share confidential information with you."

The pain was crushing, threatening to suffocate Aerina. She took one deep shaky breathe, and then another. She would not cry. *She would not cry.* If this is how he wanted it, fine. She could play this game.

But if he thought for a moment that she could go home and pretend these past weeks had never happened, forget about the invasion, and go back to her cloistered existence as a Patrician, he was sadly mistaken.

That Aerina was dead. She'd died the day in the Capitol courtyard with the other dancers. The new Aerina had been reborn over these last few months and had finally matured the night they'd killed the soldiers in Sybil. The night she'd given herself to a Reaper. She wasn't about to back down. She wasn't going to forget.

"Fine," she said quietly, wrenching her wrist out of his grip. He let her go, and she took a step back. "If this is how you want it. I just hope you don't regret this as much as I'm going to," she murmured the words back to him that he'd said the night they'd first kissed.

Because she had a feeling they were both going to regret this.

Turning, a rebel tear forcing its way down her cheek, she walked into the mist without a backwards glance.

Marcus watched the fog close around her, using the last remnants of his self-control to keep from chasing after her. He was doing the best thing. War was coming, and he wanted her as safe as possible. She was small, delicate, beautiful; a Patrician. She'd never survive the battle that was coming unless she stayed protected.

It was best that it ended now, anyway. Before it became impossible to walk away. She deserved better than him.

Stepping back, he shut the door gently. Then he gave in to the urge and put his fist through the plaster wall, breaking through the wooden stud behind. He felt the satisfying crunch of his knuckles against the wood, the sharp pain as his skin broke and blood began to flow freely.

The burning pain from his hand was nothing compared to the agony he felt in his chest.

Chapter 16

"Never was anything great achieved without danger."
-Niccolo Machiavelli

Marcus stood in his office, staring at the Network Grid. Ramus was at the holocomputer, typing in another command, and Consul Julius sat at the long meeting table, appearing to be relaxed, his hands clasped together on the table. But his knuckles were white, and lines of strain rather than laughter creased his forehead.

"They have been in the city at least three times that we know of." Marcus nodded to Ramus, who continued to type furiously.

Most of the dots on the grid blanked out, leaving two dots that were unmoving.

"We have identified two individuals who left the city perimeters under hunting permits. When they returned, their actions did not follow their normal pattern." Marcus nodded again, and a small screen popped up, showing a small version of the grid with two dots standing out in bright red, moving about the city from terrace to terrace before finally moving back to their positions outside the city and remaining unmoving.

"I've dispatched a team, but I am sure we'll find the hunters' bodies, sans ID chips. It is the only way they could get into the city unnoticed for reconnaissance."

"How did their abnormal activity get past your filters? Shouldn't the hunters' behavior have been flagged in the Network?" Julius leaned forward slightly, his gaze watchful.

"The filters were disabled," Marcus replied softly.

"A Virmortus?" Julius asked in disbelief. "How would a Virmortus come in contact with the Southern Empire without your knowledge?"

"There are ways," Marcus responded. "The bigger question is *why* a Virmortus would choose to help the Southern Empire. What would be in it for them? Besides myself and Ramus, none of the Virmortus are privy to the information about the Technology."

"One of the Senators?" Julius still seemed baffled, staring at the grid as if it held the answers. And in a way, it did. Marcus said nothing, just continuing to watch Julius. He was a smart man; he couldn't deny the truth forever.

"Someone else who has been informed of our state secrets. Who has the most viable motive for wanting you dead. The most to gain," Marcus said quietly.

Julius' shoulders slumped as if a great weight had settled on them. He couldn't deny the evidence before him.

"What do we do?" he asked.

"Here's the plan."

Aerina had been unable to sleep the night following her confrontation with Marcus, alternating between crying and pacing angrily in her room.

When the morning sun had risen, cool but warm enough to burn off the mist, she had calmed herself enough to devise a plan.

She dressed quickly, without the normal care she took, throwing her heavy hair into a ponytail. Grabbing her pack and her holoreader, she called one of the few people she knew she could trust.

Stephen opened the door to his villa, motioning Aerina inside. "What's going on?" he asked. He looked as if he was getting ready to head to the sports complex, his lean form encased in lightweight athletic clothes, sneakers on his feet.

"I need a favor," Aerina said. "You work with the Capitol Technology engineers, right?" Stephen nodded slowly, his gaze quizzical. "Could one of them, hypothetically speaking, access the Virmortus files on the Network?"

Stephen's eyes narrowed. "Aerina, what are you up to now?" he asked softly, concern in his tone. Aerina debated for a long moment what to tell Stephen. If she was going to gain his help, he was going to need to know the truth.

She opened her mouth to begin explaining when a voice cut her off.

"I'm ready, Stephen."

Aerina turned quickly towards the familiar female voice. "Helen?" She looked between her friend and Stephen. Helen was also dressed in athletic clothes. "Oh." Stephen had won over Helen after all. She wished him luck with her prickly friend.

"Is this not a good time?" she asked, fighting off disappointment. Helen was probably the last person who should know about her plans.

"What are you doing here?" Helen asked, her eyes narrowing suspiciously. Aerina rolled her own eyes. She never thought she'd see the day Helen was jealous of anyone.

"I just needed to ask Stephen a favor, but I can talk to him another time." She inched backwards towards the door.

"You might as well ask now," Stephen said, lounging against the wall. "I don't keep secrets from Helen."

Aerina was surprised by the jolt of pain she felt at those words. Marcus had no problem keeping secrets from her. The hurt and anger rushed back anew, and she pushed it down into the hidden recesses of her heart with effort. Now was not the time to dwell on it.

She stared at her petite friend thoughtfully. With a mental shrug, she decided if Helen would report her, her position wouldn't be much worse than it already was.

She was still essentially an outcast, and now Marcus would have nothing to do with her. What did she have to lose?

"Can we sit down for a minute?" she asked finally, feeling exposed standing in the villa's entryway. Stephen met Helen's eyes before motioning them both into his office. The girls sat in two chairs facing the large redwood desk. Stephen perched on the edge of the desk, folding his arms and staring at Aerina intently.

Aerina took a deep breath and began telling them the story of her trip outside the city walls.

"You went outside?" Helen interjected incredulously. "With a *Reaper*?"

"Not just any Reaper. The one that almost killed her," Stephen said with dry humor. Aerina waved that off impatiently.

"That's not what is important." She continued the story, telling them of the assassins in the outpost town. "The Southern Empire sent them. And Marcus believes they are planning some kind of invasion, perhaps war," Aerina finished, leaning forward in her chair. Helen looked at her skeptically, but Stephen's gaze had turned thoughtful.

"What do you expect to find in the Virmortus files?" he asked, referring to her original question.

"I'm not sure, but I think they have been in the city. And I know how they got in, and how they are gathering information." She held up her wrist with her ID scanner. "We've made it easy for them."

"The bodies of the two hunters have been recovered. Both ID chips were missing from their wrists, removed posthumously. We recovered them not far from the bodies." Marcus listened to the young Virmortus' report while staring out over the city.

From his vantage atop the Training Grounds, he could see the terraces brightly lit in the early night far below. The fishing boats bobbed with each rolling wave at the docks; above them, the bright and colorful lights of the Pleb Terrace; still higher, the more muted but still well-lit Merchant and Capitol Terraces. On clear nights like this one, he could even see all the way to the Agriculture Terrace that filled the inland valley to the right, and the glowing dome of the Capitol to the left.

The city had grown quickly from the small group of original founders. Initially, most of the citizens had been immigrants, fleeing the destruction and chaos left from the Global War.

Concerned about the city's explosive growth and the balance of resources and control, the second generation leaders had placed restrictions on the population.

When the city had reached three million inhabitants several decades previously, they had stopped accepting immigrants from the outpost towns.

The city was now the largest in North America outside of

the Southern Empire's capitol, exceeding three million citizens.

Three million, one hundred and sixty seven thousand, two hundred and thirty nine, to be exact. That was how many dots lit up the Network Grid. How many people he kept track of. How many people he was responsible for.

How many people could die if the Southern Empire invaded.

"Anything else, sir?" The young man's question brought him from his dark thoughts.

"No, Quintus, that is all," Marcus answered. As Quintus quietly exited the roof, Marcus leaned forward to study the ocean far below. They would come by ship; it was the fastest and easiest approach. An air attack would be easy to counter, using the ComTowers as defense weapons. A land attack would be challenging due to the precarious terrain. The ocean was his weakest point.

At that thought, his eyes traveled to Aerina's villa. He was too far away to make out individual villas, but he knew she was there. He had placed a filter on her ID after the assassination attempt. He always knew where she was.

The ocean might be the weakest point for the city, but she was his weakest point. In his mind's eye, he could still see the expression on her face when he had told her they were over. That they were nothing. She couldn't hide her devastation. She hadn't even tried.

He'd wanted nothing more than to take back the words; to change his mind and keep her close, at least for a little longer.

Then the night in Sybil played again in his mind, the night she could have been killed because of his carelessness. He wouldn't be responsible for her death. She was his weakness, but she also gave him new purpose. He wasn't just saving Alba because it was his responsibility; in saving Alba, he was protecting the one thing that had come to matter to him.

"You know how crazy you sound, right?" Helen looked at her friend with a mixture of concern and derision. The shorter girl looked over at Stephen, their eyes meeting as if to say, *Yeah, she's gone over the edge. Bat-shit crazy.*

"Aerina, you've always had these conspiracy theories about the Alban government, and ideas about the outside," Helen began gently, a little condescendingly, "Are you sure all the pressure you've been under hasn't been....influencing your thoughts?" she asked as tactfully as it was possible to ask someone if they were losing their mind.

"No, I saw the assassins. I cut one of their ID chips out myself," Aerina exclaimed impatiently, trying to keep control of her temper. She rubbed her hand absently on her pants as if the blood from the assassin's wrist still stained her fingers.

"Even if what you say is true," Helen said, the skepticism in her tone indicating her doubt, "You can hardly expect Stephen to risk his reputation, even his very life, to investigate your wild theories. That is the job of the Virmortus."

Aerina looked over at Stephen. Was he really going to let Helen speak for him? The Stephen she'd grown up with would have his own opinion; he would never let anyone control him.

But the older Patrician remained silent, still leaning against the desk with his arms folded. His dark brown eyes were unreadable in the early evening shadows falling in the office.

Aerina felt frustrated anger rising, threatening to choke her. With an effort, she tamped it down. A month, even a few weeks ago, she would have exploded. She supposed she had one thing to thank Marcus for.

"I think you're making a mistake," she said quietly, grabbing the canvas bag she had dropped on the ground. "This is going to affect all of us. I am not going to sit by and be an observer when I can do something to help."

Stephen wasn't her only option, just the best one. She was sure Julia would have connections; someone who would help her get the information she needed.

She walked home slowly. She would need to wait for complete darkness to carry out her Plan B. Just in case Marcus still had a Virmortus trailing her. As she walked, she instructed her holoreader to check her messages.

Two from Julia inviting her to the first performance of their new show, asking her where she'd been lately. One from Lina, inviting her to a party at the University.

Nothing from Marcus. She ignored the sting of disappointment. Not that she'd expected one. But she had hoped...

The man had never called her, not once, during the course of their tumultuous relationship. And if she were honest, he'd never once sought her out, except the night he'd saved her and Julia from the dockworkers-turned-attempted murderers.

Perhaps she'd been deluding herself, thinking he cared for her. He was attracted to her, sure, but that didn't mean anything.

It was devastating to think that the entire time she had been falling for him, he had been merely tolerating her.

It's over. It only really existed in your overly-imaginative mind. Marcus' words replayed again in her head, as they had a hundred times already since he had spoken them.

Did he mean it? Had he just been humoring her? And then when the fun was over, he was done? No, she refused to believe it.

Just don't think about it, her inner voice cautioned. *Focus on discovering what the Southern Empire wants.* Because if Marcus was right, and she had no reason to doubt him, they were coming.

And she was going to find out why. With or without his help.

Her parents were both home when she arrived, a rarity. They were talking quietly in the garden, and Aerina studied her father thoughtfully.

What did he know? Was he privy to the same information that Marcus knew? As a Senator, he must know *something*. He turned and she caught sight of his face.

He knew.

He looked older, wearier. His face was pale and the lines etched deeper than normal. Their eyes locked, his filled with horror, hers filled with determination.

Walking out into the garden, she confronted both her

parents.

"What do you know?" she asked bluntly, not wanting to waste time being subtle.

Their eyes met, and then her mother forced a smile.

"What do you mean?" she asked, folding her hands at her waist. So this is how they wanted to play it. Fine.

"I just wondered if you heard the rumors about the pending invasion, is all," Aerina commented softly. Her parents glanced at each other again. They were probably wondering how much Marcus had told her.

Not nearly enough.

"I'm sure you know a little, since you were with Marcus when...er, during the week he discovered the intel. But we haven't learned much more since," her father said challengingly, as if daring her to disagree.

"I see," she responded, unsurprised. If he did know more, he wasn't going to tell her. She studied her parents for a long moment, both meeting her gaze unflinchingly. Aerina nodded with a small smile. "Alright. I'm going out tonight, it might be late."

Not waiting for their response, she ran lightly up the stairs to her room, shutting the door gently.

She sat on her bed for a long moment, staring down at her hands. She knew what she needed to do; she just wasn't looking forward to doing it. Her parents' response had strengthened her resolve. She was on her own.

Slathering Num cream thickly on her wrist, she grasped her sica blade. *Just do it.* Pressing it to her wrist, the blade cut easily through her soft skin. Blood immediately welled from the cut, and a sharp pain, dulled by the cream, shot up her arm.

She grabbed a towel and laid it under her arm to catch the dripping blood. Now came the worst part. Her stomach twisted squeamishly as she groped around inside her wrist with the fingers of her other hand. Gritting her teeth against the discomfort, her fingers closed over the small ID chip.

She pulled it out carefully, setting it on her nightstand. She wrapped a white hand towel around her wrist tightly to staunch the flow of blood. A small first aid kit sat on the bed. She applied liquid skin to glue the cut together, then a bandage.

That wasn't so bad, she thought, opening and closing her hand. Dull pain throbbed in her wrist, so she threw back a few pain relievers and pulled a light coat on, easing her injured arm through the sleeve.

She rinsed the small chip carefully in the sink, watching as the blood swirled in the glass basin, disappearing through the drain. The silver chip, shaped a little like a bullet, lay in her hand, gleaming dully in the bathroom light.

Setting it in her jewelry box, she closed the lid with a snap.

She was ready.

The night was dark; the moon conveniently covered by thick clouds. Aerina exited through the back Pleb gate, her black clothing blending well into the shadows. The spikes on her boots clicked lightly on the cement walk. Anyone who came across her would immediately know her intent.

She came to the edge of the terrace, near the Patrician tram. A stone wall, about chest height, ran along the edge. She could look out and see the tops of the buildings on the Merchant Terrace below.

Shoving her booted foot into a tiny chink in the stone wall, she hoisted herself up. As she perched on top, she had a moment of vertigo as she looked down at the street far, far below.

I can do this, she told herself. Securing her pack tightly on her back, she grabbed her picks taken from the sports complex and started lowering herself slowly towards the terrace below.

She was about a third of the way down when it felt as if the wind picked up. Her arms were already shaking with exhaustion, and she hadn't considered the injury to her wrist when planning this late night climb.

If she did manage to make it down, there was no way she was getting back up. The distance between the Merchant and Pleb Terraces was even greater than this.

Keep going. Don't look down. The words became a mantra in her head as she focused only on her slow movement. *Find a foothold. Stick your right spiked boot in. Pull out your right pick, stick it in lower. Repeat for the left side.*

Slowly, slowly she got closer to the Merchant Terrace. She had chosen an unused street that ran behind several closed shops. The street was dark, most of the light from the streetlamps blocked by buildings, a small fence meant to contain falling rocks the only thing between her and the terrace.

When her feet finally landed on the uneven bottom of the cliff, she lowered herself down on a large boulder, resting her shaking arms on her knees. It seemed an eternity before her exhausted limbs quit quivering. As the sweat dried on her body, she began shivering in her lightweight black clothing. It had kept her cool and protected during the exhausting climb, but offered little protection from the chill in the night air.

Sticking her pikes in her belt, she stood, tackling the next barrier. The mesh metal fence wasn't much taller than her, and the rungs made it easy to climb over. She dropped lightly on the other side, scanning the deserted road. She would have to take the long way around the shopping district to avoid detection.

The heavy, even fall of footsteps had her heart pounding loudly in her chest. Tucking herself between two shops, she waited with baited breathe for the footfalls to pass by. Her heart was so loud, she was convinced whomever was walking past would hear it.

The footsteps faded away and the night was again quiet. She could hear distant sounds from the active areas near the theatre, restaurants, and nightclubs. The muffled roar of the Pleb Terrace filtered up through the even more muted roar of the ocean far below.

Aerina continued on cautiously, trying to stay in the shadows between buildings as she made her way to the edge of the terrace.

She made it without further incident. Her destination was a small park perched on the cliff's edge where Merchants could come to relax and look out over the ocean. Here, the busy sounds of the Pleb Terrace were even louder, and she could see the bright lights from the city below.

A lone couple sat on a bench, talking animatedly. A lover's

quarrel, perhaps. Aerina waited behind some hedges until she heard the woman stalk off angrily, the man calling out for her to stop and listen.

She waited another minute. Two minutes. The couple did not return, and no one else entered the park. The breeze had now turned into a biting wind, blowing damp air off the ocean, whipping a few strands of hair that had escaped her ponytail around her face.

She either had to go back up the way she came down, or continue down to the Pleb Terrace. Either way, she was going to have to climb again.

Taking a deep breath, she hoisted herself atop the decorative stone wall that edged the garden, jumping down to the slight ledge before the cliff's drop-off. The feeling of vertigo hit her again and she swayed slightly before pressing her back against the cool stone of the wall.

Ignoring her protesting limbs, she began lowering herself down the gentle slope that quickly became a steep slope and then sheer wall.

This lower cliff was slower going. The stone crumbled in some areas, and she had to test each hold before putting her weight on it. Halfway down, her foot slipped and she slid a few inches before she could get her second pick in, the foot dangling over the city below.

Her heart racing, she clung to the cliff for a moment, taking even breaths. Her arms were burning, her legs shaky. But she had no choice. She had to continue.

Stinging abrasions from her near-fall added to her discomfort as she descended slowly, painfully. She was no longer as worried about discovery, and in fact a small part of her wished she would be discovered just so she could get off this damn cliff.

But no one noticed the dark figure hugging the shadows of the cliff. Finally she was about eight feet above the uneven ground. She tried to jump gracefully down, but her exhausted limbs wouldn't obey her command and she ended up tumbling painfully amid the fallen rock strewn about.

She made it. Tilting her head back, she looked up, way up, to where she could see the glowing gold of the Capitol dome. Giddy laughter escaped. She'd done it! She'd actually done it.

Rising on shaky legs, she climbed the fence and then quickly changed into the clothes she'd brought along, leaving the spike boots and climbing picks tucked under a compost bin behind a restaurant.

The sense of elation stayed with her as she walked down the city streets towards the theatre district. It was probably just the afterglow of adrenaline, she thought ruefully.

She let herself into the back of the theatre, heading straight for Julia's office. The last show of the evening was almost over, and she'd wait for her friend there.

What would she tell her? Julia had always been pretty accepting of Aerina and her sometimes outlandish behavior. But this topped anything Aerina had done or attempted to do. She remembered Stephen and Helen's skepticism. It *did* sound rather crazy.

Assassins, an invasion, the end of Alban life as they know it… Cutting out her ID chip and scaling down the cliff.

Yeah, Julia might think she'd lost her mind completely. And what evidence did she have of her claims?

The office door opened suddenly, making Aerina start violently.

"Aerina!" Julia exclaimed happily, giving her friend a sweaty hug. Her light brown skin gleamed with perspiration and exhilaration. The show must have gone well. "Give me a minute to clean up." She disappeared from the cramped office into an even smaller bathroom. The water ran and a few minutes later Julia emerged in warm-up clothes, her face scrubbed free of the heavy stage makeup.

"How has the new show been going?" Aerina asked, standing so Julia could sit at the desk. Julia ignored the gesture, perching on the desk corner.

"Great! I think it's going to be our most successful show yet. Kevin is thrilled," she added, her dark eyes bright with her own elation.

"How is Jamia?"

"Oh, you know; a teenager. Too smart for her own good, chasing boys. Probably pregnant and doing drugs," Julia said dryly.

Aerina rolled her eyes. Jamia was the most level-headed youth she'd ever met. Had she been born to a different caste, she'd probably become a Lead Engineer or even a Senator one day. But as a Pleb, the best she could hope for was a job at an engineering facility, or a secretary position for a Patrician.

Julia swung one leanly muscled leg slowly, her chocolate eyes studying Aerina with interest. "You look…different. What is going on with you? It's like you dropped off the cliff these last few weeks."

"Funny you should say that," Aerina murmured. "Actually, I have a lot to tell you. And a big favor to ask."

Julia arched one delicate black brow. "Ask away."

"Well, let me give you a little background. I recently left the city with my Reaper friend, Marcus—"

"You what?!" Julia exclaimed, sitting up straighter. "You left the city? I don't believe it. What is it like? Was it terrifying? Exciting? Terrifyingly exciting?"

Aerina laughed. "Yes to all." Aerina then gave Julia a quick summary of the events, including the night in Sybil. She could tell her friend had questions, but she remained quiet until the end.

Julia was silent for a long moment before she spoke. "So Marcus thinks the Southern Empire is going to *invade* Alba?" she said, her voice slightly disbelieving.

Aerina sighed. "I know it sounds crazy. We've existed for over a hundred years with barely any contact with the outside world. But I saw the soldiers, the assassins, myself. Saw their weapons, their ID chips. I saw the entire settlement of Ryan burning. I smelled the bodies," she added barely above a whisper. "And I trust Marcus. He wouldn't be concerned over nothing."

"What are the Reapers and soldiers doing to prepare?" Julia asked, looking less disbelieving and more concerned.

"I don't know," Aerina answered. "But I think I know how to find out if the Southern Empire has been in Alba; how they get in and out without being detected."

"How?"

Aerina pulled her sleeve up to show Julia her bandaged arm.

"ID chips. It's how we get around the city, how we pay for things, how we are identified. The Reapers track us on a giant grid."

"I knew it," Julia said darkly.

Aerina continued. "The easiest way to get into the city would be to take someone's ID chip. And then use it to gather information."

"So you want to hack into the Virmortus' Network files?" Julia asked. Aerina was already nodding.

"Yes. Do you know of anyone who can do it?"

"Aerina, why can't we just let the Reapers do their job? It's their Grid; their files. They should know better than us if someone has been doing reconnaissance in the city."

"Maybe you're right. But I can't just sit at home and prepare for Final Examinations, knowing we might be *invaded* at any moment. Wondering if I could have done something to help; to give Alba a better chance at surviving."

Julia stared at her for a long moment.

"Alright. I might know someone who could help."

Chapter 17

"We may stumble and fall but shall rise again; it should be enough if we did not run away from the battle."
- Mahatma Gandhi

The wind was still cold and strong on the walk to Julia's small townhouse, forcing the women to silently huddle in their thin coats. The little brownstone was near the warehouse district where most of the city's supplies were stored. The Armati were quite prolific, strolling the streets and monitoring activity.

Even though she knew it was unnecessary, Aerina was careful to keep her face hidden or averted as they walked.

It was a nice neighborhood, the cobblestone street and sidewalks clean, well-kept townhomes brightly lit, and a few small restaurants interspersed. Quaint would be the description Aerina would choose.

Julia scanned her wrist to open the door, leading Aerina inside the familiar skinny, two-story home. A small living area and kitchen made up the first floor, and two bedrooms were above.

Jamia looked up when the two women walked in. Her blue eyes lit up when she saw Aerina.

"Rina! I haven't seen you in forever," she exclaimed, getting up to give the older girl a hug. "Julia told me what happened. And I heard about it at school. I'm so glad you're ok," she added with a shiver.

"Me too," Aerina agreed dryly.

"Drink?" Julia asked, pulling a bottle of wine from the fridge. Aerina shook her head.

"Water is fine," she said, ignoring Julia's eye-roll. "Jamia, I have a strange favor to ask," she began, before launching quickly into a slightly edited version of her story. Jamia listened with wide eyes, unlike her sister, drinking in every word with excitement.

"Oh. My. Gosh," she said when Aerina completed the tale. "I can't believe you went outside. With a *Reaper*. And were attacked. That's soo unbalanced," she exclaimed.

"I need some information about..." she trailed off, not sure how much to tell Jamia. She looked over at Julia.

"You can tell her. She won't freak out," Julia said, smiling at her younger sister.

"I think I can get some details about the invasion, but I need to get into the Virmortus' Network files to do it. Do you know of someone who can do that?" Aerina asked quickly. She felt a sudden rush of guilt for including Jamia. She was so young; she might not grasp the full ramifications of illegally accessing those files.

Jamia tilted her head to one side. "I could probably do it," she said simply.

Aerina was already shaking her head.

"No, I can't let you do it, Jamia. If the Reapers would find out..." she looked over at Julia for her friend to back her up, but Julia suddenly seemed very busy fixing herself dinner.

"I know. I wouldn't get caught," Jamia said confidently.

Aerina studied the young girl, weighing her options. This might be her only chance to find some answers. And if Julia wasn't protesting... But what if the Virmortus found out. A vision of the dance troupe being executed, without time for explanations, filled her mind's eye, and she shook her head again.

"No, I can't let you risk your life," Aerina said with finality. "I'll have to find someone else; find another way."

Jamia looked over at Julia before glancing down at her hands, idling twirling an over-large ring that looked as if it might have been her mother's.

"Even if you don't come with me, I'll still look into the files on my own. Wouldn't it be better if you were there?" the dark-haired girl informed her casually. Aerina's eyes narrowed. That kind of emotional blackmail was rather unpleasant to be on the receiving end of, she thought, remembering her own attempt at coercing Marcus. Her eyes darted over to where Julia sat at the small glass kitchen table, sipping her wine. At Aerina's incredulous look, her friend just raised a perfectly shaped dark brow as if to ask, what are you going to do now?

"Alright," she relented, ignoring Jamia's look of delight. "But you have to promise you'll be cautious. The Virmortus tend to kill and ask questions later."

"I know," Jamia said simply. Aerina met her midnight blue eyes, seeing she grasped the severity of the situation.

"Where do we start?" she asked.

"I need to use a holocomputer that is connected directly to a Network Database."

"Where would that be?"

Jamia frowned, thinking. "That might be the toughest part. The only terminals that I know of are in the Technology Complex on the Merchant Terrace, and in the Tech labs at the Patrician University."

"Damn," muttered Aerina.

Julia cleared her throat, as if she had been waiting for this moment. "I might be able to get us into the Technology Complex."

Jamia brightened. "That's right. Simon."

"Simon?" Aerina repeated questioningly. She was hesitant to bring anyone else in. More people meant a greater chance of getting caught.

"Yeah, Julia's boyfriend. Er, ex-boyfriend," Jamia added with a sideways look at Julia.

"I didn't know you were seeing someone from the Engineering Caste," Aerina said, eyeing her friend.

Julia sighed. "We dated for awhile — "

"Like almost two years," Jamia cut in.

"What happened?" Aerina asked, fascinated by the blush staining the high cheekbones of her normally unflappable friend.

"You know how it is — a Pleb dating an Engineer? I think the whole process of applying for a caste change was too much for him, and who knows if they would have even approved me. What could I do on the Engineering Terrace? I'm a dancer. And I couldn't ask him to give up his position. Simon *lives* for Network

Database Programming." Julia shrugged, her coffee-colored eyes shadowed. "It just wasn't meant to be."

Aerina looked at her friend with sympathy, thinking of her own pitiful situation. She couldn't imagine how hard it would have been to part ways with Marcus after nearly two years. It was bad enough after two months.

She couldn't imagine Marcus giving up being a Reaper. It was a big part of who he was. And everyone knew Reapers didn't marry. What future would they have really had? Perhaps what Marcus had done was really for the best.

No, her inner voice shouted. They could find a way. She would find a way. She didn't care what she had to give up.

She wanted to ask Julia why the other girl had given up so easily, but held her tongue. It was none of her business. Julia must have had a good reason.

"So you think he will help us?"

Julia and Jamia looked at each other, Jamia grinning slyly. Julia's mouth quirked up at the corner.

"Yeah, he'll probably help us," she said.

"And we'll have to go to the Engineering Terrace," Aerina stated fatalistically.

"Hmm, yeah." Julia looked at her friend's wrist. "I hope you're right about all this. Or you're screwed."

Aerina grinned. "Yeah, no shit."

Julia sighed. "I'll borrow Kevin's e-car. We can try and hide you in the backseat."

An hour later, Aerina was tucked on the floor in the backseat of Kevin's very compact car, in a large duffel bag.

The car began to smoothly glide through the Pleb city, the muffled voices and gentle bump as the car entered the Ferry the only indications of where they were.

The fifteen minute ride was going to seem like an eternity, and she could only imagine what it would look like to an Armati if he happened to check the bag.

Should she try and fight? Play dumb? Tell them her wrist was injured and her chip must have been damaged?

She was still working out different scenarios in her head when she felt the car start up, and a few moments later another gentle bump as it exited the Ferry. They must be on the Merchant Terrace.

Her heart beat with excitement and a little claustrophobia. The duffel bag was closing in on her.

They were almost to the Technology Complex. The hub for all new inventions and programming genius that ran the Network, which kept Alba interconnected and every house and business functioning at optimal levels.

The perfect place to hack the Network.

It was late. Well past midnight. He'd heard the night guard making his rounds twice already. As far as he could tell, no one else was in the Network Database wing with him besides Stan, the security guard who worked the weekends.

Simon sat at his terminal, two holocomputers and one flat screen with a virtual keyboard sitting around him. He was working late. As usual.

Sometimes he would get lost in the code, spending hours that really felt like minutes on an intricate section, reworking and reworking until he was sure it was perfect.

But lately his job had lost much of the fascination and was now just something he did to fill the time. To avoid being in his empty house, facing an empty bed.

Because since Julia had ended their relationship, he just hadn't cared about anything. About the work he loved so much, about going out in the evening, socializing with his coworkers, and certainly not about finding a new bedmate.

He missed her desperately.

Lowering his shaggy blonde head, he rested it in his hands for a moment, blinking his eyes before glancing back up. He stared in shock, wondering if he conjured her with his thoughts.

The object of his lonely nights, his misery, stood before him. Her lean dancer body lounged against the door to the large room housing several terminals, backlit by the dim light from the hallway.

Without realizing it, he had stood, oblivious to the protest of muscles that had been sitting in one place for too long. His tall, lanky body gave him a perfect view of her over the top of his flat screen.

He stepped back from his desk and the holocomputers winked out. He ignored them, walking towards her slowly, a little afraid she might vanish.

"Julia?" His voice came out hoarse; ill-used.

She smiled at him slightly, her witchy brown eyes creasing slightly, her black hair gleaming almost blue in the light. He almost reached out for her, but clenched his hands into fists instead.

Julia took a deep breath, fortifying herself against the pain shooting through her at the sight of his beautiful face.

He looked exactly as she remembered, although there were dark circles under his eyes and he looked like he had lost weight. His tall and lanky form was even leaner, his stubble-covered square jaw even more pronounced, his aquiline nose more prominent in his leaner face.

She drank in the site of him, every emotion she'd felt when she was with him rushing back—joy, lust, *love*, and finally, heartbreak.

"Hi, Simon," she finally replied, straightening gracefully. "I wish this were a more…pleasurable visit, but I have a favor to ask."

She saw his eyes flare before scanning over her body, encased in dark pants and pink t-shirt. She used to come visit him when he worked too late, wearing something scandalous, to seduce him away from his work. And it had worked, every time. They both were remembering those passionate nights.

Simon broke the silence this time. "What favor."

Julia hesitated, glancing around for security cameras. "It could be…dangerous. If you don't want to do it, I understand—"

"Just tell me what you need," Simon broke in a little harshly. Julia began to have second thoughts. What if he was seeing someone else? He didn't owe her anything. It had been three months since she'd ended the relationship. A lot could happen in three months.

Before she could let her nerves get the better of her, she felt a presence behind her. Turning slightly, she saw Jamia and Aerina had come in. Without waiting for her signal. Sighing in defeat, she stepped further into the large room.

"I'll let Aerina explain it," she said.

Simon's eyes went from Julia to the other girls. He skimmed quickly over Aerina and settled on Jamia, his serious features breaking into a real smile.

"Jamia." He opened his arms and the younger girl rushed forward, her petite frame engulfed by Simon's large one. Julia watched a little enviously—she would have liked that kind of greeting. But then she smiled; Jamia had always loved Simon like a brother.

Simon stepped back, his pale blue eyes studying Aerina icily. Aerina cocked her head to one side, studying him in return.

"You're good looking enough, but I'll reserve judgment on whether or not you're smart enough," Aerina said softly; baitingly. "You did let the best thing to happen to you slip through your fingers."

Simon's eyes narrowed. "Aerina—" Julia chided, her face turning pink in the darkened room. Aerina waved her hand, cutting her friend off.

"Forget it. I need you to do something that could be potentially very dangerous, but could also be crucial to the survival of Alba."

Simon remained silent, although Aerina thought she detected a note of incredulity on his face. The dark shadows made it hard to tell.

"The darkness is atmospheric and all, but do you suppose we could turn some lights on?" She walked further into the large, dark room.

Simon finally spoke. "System, please brighten the lights."

The room immediately grew brighter.

"Neat," Aerina said, "I'm still getting used to voice commands, myself."

"I'm glad you approve," he muttered sarcastically. "Can you

tell me what this is about?"

Aerina smiled blindingly. "Perhaps we should sit."

Once everyone was seated at one of the many rolling office chairs in the room, she launched into her explanation yet again. She could tell Simon found her story as ludicrous as Stephen and Helen. She just hoped the presence of Julia would be enough to convince him otherwise.

"You're telling me that you went outside. With a *Reaper*. And you're a Patrician." The tall man's eyes swept over her black-clad form. His eyes narrowed. "Aren't you the one that was almost killed, along with the dance troupe?"

Aerina stiffened slightly in her chair. So much for the Virmortus cover story. She must be more infamous than she thought.

"Yes," she replied, "but that holds no relevance —"

"Of course it's relevant," Simon broke in. He glanced over at Julia and Jamia. "You are endangering all our lives with these crazy plots. I should report you right now," he finished softly.

"Simon," Julia broke in, leaning forward to rest her hand on his arm, "I think we should take her seriously. What if it's true? She is a... close... friend of the Alpha Virmortus. What if we could help discover something that could help save Alba? Aerina may be impetuous, but she'd always been truthful."

Simon was silent for a long moment, staring at the slender hand resting on his forearm. Aerina held her breath, waiting. If he said no, they could try the University, but the risk of discovery would be much higher.

And if he reported her... Well, then the entire game would be over.

"Alright, we can run a few quick scans through the database. But the longer we're in, the better chance we have of getting caught," he cautioned. "There are only a few things I would be willing to die for. And your crazy friend here is not one of them."

"If we're going to work together, could we at least *try* to get along?" Aerina chided. Simon ignored her, spinning his chair around to face his terminal.

Two holocomputers blinked on, a virtual keyboard appearing at his fingertips. He began typing furiously, and Aerina could hear the tiny buzz of the haptic feedback all virtual keyboards made to give the user a sense of actually touching something.

Images began popping up on each screen. One screen looked as if they were in a holographic RPG, a role playing-game in which Simon was navigating through a maze, passing some cube-shaped doors with unusual code on them, selecting and examining others.

On the flat screen, straight lines of command codes appeared swiftly in time to Simon's typing and the tiny buzz of the haptics. The third holographic projection showed the files he selected. Words, documents, voice files, images, and even videos swirled slowly above the projector of the holocomputer, waiting to be selected either by physical touch or Simon's typed command.

Jamia sat next to Simon, her fascinated gaze following his every movement. Aerina met Julia's rueful gaze. Her sister had a bad case of hero worship. It must have been more difficult for Jamia than Julia had realized to lose Simon from her life.

"Ah, I'm in," Simon said softly. On the second projector, a tiny image of the giant grid Aerina had seen circled slowly.

"Can you pull up the movements of Cassandra Redding?" Aerina asked, leaning over Simon's shoulder. He typed quickly and soon a file appeared, a large D blinking in front of the information. Deceased.

"Now, reference that against any recent unusual behavior by another recently deceased or inactive individual."

Simon continued typing, swearing twice before sighing again. "Ah yes, here are two Aggie hunters that were just marked deceased yesterday. They both were at Cassandra's brothel on at least two occasions after never visiting the city previously. Both occasions were only months preceding her...death," he finished slowly, his eyes falling on Jamia.

"Oh please, I know all about how she and the dancers were executed by Reapers," Jamia said. "You don't need to shelter me from the morbid details." Julia just rolled her eyes at her precocious younger sister.

"We've found the connection. But there must be something more," Aerina said in frustration.

"Yeah, why would Cassandra be their choice for an assassin? Why not just try it themselves? And how would she have known about them at all?" Julia agreed.

"There should be a link. What about someone who isn't on the Grid? Someone who knows about it and can erase their ID?" Simon suggested.

"Like a Virmortus?" Aerina breathed. "That's brilliant. Perhaps even a Senator. But why? Why destroy Alba? What would they have to gain?"

"Power," Simon said simply. "Power can be a strong motivator. Perhaps the Southern Empire has promised him, or her, something that is better than what he has now."

"But what does the Southern Empire want with Alba?" Jamia asked, resting her chin on an upraised knee.

"That is the million dollar question, to use a pre-war idiom." Simon began typing again, perhaps digging deeper. The women all remained quiet, considering the question, watching the screens come alive.

The room was quiet but for Simon's quiet typing and the hum of machines. The nearly absolute quiet was what allowed Aerina to hear the smallest scrape on the cement floor. Stiffening, she glanced around the room, looking first towards the door closest to them.

Suddenly the lights when out.

"Damn." Aerina heard Simon's whispered curse in the darkness, the barest of light from the screens sending an eerie glow on his features. She could barely make out Jamia's face, and Julia was almost completely in darkness.

She opened her mouth to ask him what had happened when she felt something, the tiniest whoosh of air, and then rough arms grabbed her.

She shrieked, fighting desperately against the iron hold. Several shadows detached from the darkness around her, and she saw Simon swing a fist at the figure that had grabbed Jamia and pulled her up out of her chair from behind. A moment later his legs were pulled out from under him and he hit the cement hard. Jamia's terrified face was the last thing Aerina saw before she felt a sharp pain in her neck and then everything went dark.

Chapter 18

"Sometimes by losing a battle you find a new way to win the war." - Donald Trump

Aerina awoke with a pounding headache, her back muscles burning with agony. She realized she was in a chair, hunched over a metal table. Straightening with a tiny groan, her hands caught on something. She squinted against a bright light to see her hands chained to a metal ring attached to the table.

"Damn," she muttered, glancing around the room. It was small and empty. The only other furniture was a chair across the table from her. Looking at the stone walls around her, she caught site of a small black circle. The eye of a camera.

This must be an interrogation room in the Virmortus Training Grounds. Too bad Ramus missed this on his tour when she visited last, she thought drolly.

A loud clang as the door opened behind her made her jump. She sat stiffly, waiting to see who had entered. A young Virmortus, dressed in the typical armoured black attire, walked around her. She had a square object in her hand that she fit into some kind of connector on her side of the table.

The woman looked almost her age, typical Reaper with close cropped dark brown hair, impassive grey eyes, and slight scars marring her youthful features. She was short but with an impressively toned physique that more than made up for any lack in stature.

"I like what you've done in here. An interesting mix of pre-war precinct and medieval torture chamber," Aerina said flippantly, leaning back in her chair as far as the manacles would let her. She was still deciding if she was afraid or just frustrated. Surely Marcus wouldn't let her be harmed?

But what about her friends? Scenes of the mass execution in the courtyard flashed through her mind, sending a shaft of real fear through her.

"I don't suppose you can tell me where my friends are, hmm?" she asked, jiggling her chains lightly to gain her attention. "Or perhaps even share what the weather is doing outside?"

A burning began in her wrists and then suddenly pain spread through her entire body, forcing it to jerk straight up in the chair and eliciting a gasp of shock and agony.

Then the pain was gone and Aerina slumped in her chair, shaking uncontrollably. The woman was looking at her now, her face still inscrutable, but she thought she detected a gleam of satisfaction in the blue-grey eyes.

"A simple 'no' would have been sufficient," she choked out from between lips stiff with discomfort, refusing to be cowed.

The Virmortus glanced back down at the torture device she held in her hands, making Aerina stiffen in fear. Nothing happened. She set the device on the table, far out of Aerina's reach, and headed past her towards the door.

"Coward," she muttered as the girl passed by. The Reaper ignored that, and the loud clang indicated the door had shut behind her.

Julia, I am so sorry. Aerina felt the agony of guilt twisting in her gut. Were her friends being subjected to that terrible torture? Poor Jamia, she was so young, surely they would have a little understanding...

What did I do? Panic welled up in her at the thought of her friends suffering and her being trapped in here, unable to do anything. *This is all your fault.* It had been her idea. She had talked Julia into it. Jamia hadn't known better; she was just a child for serenity's sake. And Simon... he'd done it for Julia.

Glaring at the tiny dot she assumed was a camera, she fought the urge to mouth obscenities in the lens. That probably would not be best for her friends at this moment.

It seemed like an eternity passed before she heard the clang of the heavy door. Again, it made her jump before she forced herself to relax as much as possible in the uncomfortable chair.

She looked straight ahead as another black-clothed figure

walked around to stand before her.

Marcus.

Pain lanced through her heart, still fresh from their recent encounter. His rejection. She tamped it down with effort, trying to match his poker face with one of her own. A tingling awareness remained as she studied his familiar features.

He looked every inch the dangerous killer she knew him to be. His dark eyes swept over her own black-encased form, coming to rest on where the manacles wrapped tightly around her wrist.

Had they seen the cut?

Her question was answered a moment later as Marcus pulled back the sleeve of her thin black shirt, revealing the blood-soaked bandage. The wound must have broken open during the scuffle.

His eyes met hers as he dropped her wrist and stepped back slightly as if disgusted.

"Is this really necessary?" she asked, jiggling the chains lightly.

"What did you expect to happen?" Marcus replied in the soft, even tone that indicated he was probably furious.

Aerina sighed. "Honestly, I hoped we wouldn't get caught. But I thought we'd be dead already, so perhaps I shouldn't complain."

"What did you think you were doing." Marcus bit out the words as more a statement than a question.

Aerina answered anyway. "I was trying to find out where the Southern Empire was in the city. And how they came in contact with Cassandra."

"Do you think I am incompetent?" he asked incredulously. "What do you think I've been doing these past few days?"

"I didn't know!" Aerina replied angrily, standing as much as the clinking chains would allow, bracing her hands on the table. "You shut me out! After everything we'd done together. It was over, just like that. No information or explanations. Complete silence. What was I supposed to do?"

"Are we still talking about the investigation?" Marcus asked softly.

Aerina narrowed her eyes. "No one would tell me what measures were being taken. I couldn't just sit around and hope you had all the information. Because what if you didn't?"

"What were you going to do with the information, if you found it?" Marcus asked, leaning back against the stone wall, his arms crossed over his hard chest.

"Bring it to you," Aerina muttered, sitting back down with a thump. She rested her forehead on her bound hands, willing the pounding to subside. Guilt spread. *Did I do it just to be closer to Marcus? Did I endanger my friends because I wanted to show him I could belong in his world?*

Marcus was silent for a long moment before he, too, sat down, his large frame filling the small metal chair. He rested his muscular forearms on the table, clasping his hands together not far from hers.

"What did you find?"

"Where are my friends?" she countered, having overcome the moment of anger. Marcus just looked at her, stone-faced.

"Do you know what this is?" he said in a dangerously soft voice, his large hand moving the small weapon device that had been sitting, untouched, to his right.

Aerina flicked her eyes to the square device, resisting the urge to clench her hands nervously.

"Your colleague was kind enough to demonstrate it for me," she spoke with saccharine sweetness. "But she neglected to tell me what it is called."

"This is a nerve stimulator," Marcus explained gently. "Through the cuffs you wear, it can send electrical impulses to your nerve endings that simulate any kind of sensation programmed into the device. I can make you feel as if your skin is on fire, a bone has been shattered, a limb detached, even that insects are crawling under your skin." Aerina grimaced at the uncomfortable thought. Marcus was watching her intently as he continued, "The beauty of this device is that no actual physical harm is done, so we can interrogate someone for hours on end without worrying about a subject losing consciousness or dying.

Although many of them wish for that outcome," he finished thoughtfully, tilting the device as if considering its many wonderful uses.

Aerina couldn't help being fascinated in spite of herself. "Is it programmed to simulate pleasurable things? Like sex?" she asked, leaning forward to better see the words on the tiny screen.

Marcus' hand closed tightly on the device, his eyes flaring for a moment. Then he gave an unexpected bark of laughter. "Aerina, only you would ask such a question when you are being threatened with torture."

"It just seems to me like it might be an awfully handy device, if you get my meaning." She shrugged, her bright blue eyes challenging his patience.

"I'll be sure to ask the Engineers," Marcus replied dryly, dropping the device onto the table. "Now tell me if you learned anything useful and I won't be forced to display the uses it currently *is* programmed for."

Aerina sighed, searching his dark eyes for any sign that he was bluffing. But she knew Marcus well enough now to know he never bluffed. If she pushed hard enough, he would push back. He'd be forced to carry through with his threat, whether he wanted to or not.

Quickly, she told him what little they had learned before they had been captured by the Virmortus.

"Whoever met with Cassandra and the Southern Empire men must be able to access the system to hide their own ID," Aerina said.

Marcus studied her for a long moment. She fought the urge to squirm under his gaze. Then he stood fluidly, walking past her towards the door without a word.

"Marcus," she said quickly, "what about my friends? Are they ok?"

Chained, facing the back wall, she couldn't see his reaction, but she heard the heavy metal door cranking open.

"Marcus!" She let the desperation seep into her voice. She had to know. Surely he couldn't be so cold as to deny her this small thing…

"They are fine. For now," was the low reply before the loud door protestingly closed.

Marcus walked down the cold grey hallway of the interrogation wing to the room holding Simon West. He looked through the small viewing pane at the lone inhabitant. The tall, lanky man sat hunched over the table, staring stonily at the camera eye on the back wall.

"He's good," Ramus commented, coming to stand next to Marcus. "The tech team just finished reviewing his hack, and in the half hour it took us to get to the Technology Complex, he got into our files and managed to isolate the same IDs we discovered. He referenced those with Cassandra's profile, even though it's been removed from the shared Network. If we don't kill him, we could use someone like him."

Marcus nodded absently, looking across the hall at the two rooms holding Julia and her younger sister. "He shouldn't be too difficult to persuade. We know his biggest weakness," Marcus murmured, watching the beautiful Eurasian woman shift uncomfortably in an attempt to hide the earring she had jammed into the electronic manacle lock. No wonder she and Aerina had become such good friends. They were two of a kind.

He forced himself not to look into the room where Aerina sat. When the alarm was triggered in the Network that the files were being accessed, they had hoped to catch a Southern Empire agent. But when they had entered the large building, and he'd seen the figures darkly illuminated by the large screens, the same mixture of rage and admiration he'd felt on the Capitol Terrace the day he'd almost killed Aerina came rushing back.

In fact, those feelings were fairly common when he was around the maddening woman. He personally had taken her in, admitting to himself it was because he didn't want anyone else harming her. He had been enraged even further when he'd seen what she had done to her wrist. If they weren't on the cusp of war, he'd be forced to kill her for that offense alone. As it was, he was tempted to keep her locked up, preferably in his villa.

Pushing those distracting thoughts deliberately from his

mind, Marcus turned to Ramus.

"This is Simon West's lucky day. He's about to be enlisted. His first assignment is to crack into the Southern Empire ID chips."

Ramus nodded, entering the Engineer's room.

Marcus didn't wait around. Ramus knew what needed to be done here. He wanted to personally oversee the Electronic Grounders they were setting up on the ComTowers that would be the best defence against air attack or any EMWs. The anti-ballistics had already been installed the previous day.

The Empire had to know Marcus would find out about their decimation of the prison town of Ryan. They were through being subtle. It wouldn't be long before they attacked. He would be sure the city was ready.

After what seemed to be an interminable wait, Ramus had come in and released Aerina from the electronic manacles.

"Where are my friends?" she began badgering him immediately, trying to remain calm and polite. Ramus, however, was as stoic as Marcus, escorting her politely out the door and down a long, grey hallway. The other interrogation rooms were empty and dark. The large, ebony-skinned man held her elbow gently but firmly as they walked towards a sliding door.

He propelled her through the open door and into a small elevator. She pulled her arm out of his grip, standing far to the left as the cab descended. As the door opened again, Ramus motioned with exaggerated politeness for her to proceed him out.

They were in the main section of the Training Grounds, the familiar front walkway before the large pit. The pit was empty of trainees. Aerina wasn't sure if it was night or day, as they had no windows here deep in the mountain. Just harsh, unrelenting artificial lights casting long, eerie shadows far below.

Ramus entered a short code followed by a retinal scan and the main exit opened, revealing the short white hallway that led out.

"I'm free to go?" Aerina asked, glancing behind her. Where

were Julia and her sister? And Simon?

Ramus smiled slightly and nodded, turning to head back down the hallway toward the large office. He was brought up short by Aerina's sharp words.

"I'm not leaving. Not until I know where the others are."

Ramus slowly turned to face Marcus' girl. He could see the appeal she held for his friend; smart, impetuous, loyal. Unafraid. A fascinating combination. He'd known Marcus since they were children, rising together in the ranks. He'd never seen Marcus care about anything the way he did this girl.

Over the past several years, since Marcus had become the Alpha Virmortus, he'd worried that his friend had stopped feeling anything at all. But this girl was capable of inciting more emotion from Marcus in a short time than he'd seen in the other man since they were children.

And it was about time.

"I'm afraid it is none of your concern," he finally answered, waiting expectantly for her response. He wasn't disappointed.

"It is going to be your concern," she replied before dashing back the way they came. Ramus smiled, following more leisurely. There were few places she could go without the proper credentials.

He was unprepared for her to scramble over the low wall that divided the walkway from the pit below. The pit was dug into the mountain wall but it wasn't smooth. The slight girl had found a rough section with enough hand and foot holds to quickly lower herself several feet into the pit.

He debated what to do.

"Shit." He was going to have to go after her. If she fell to her death, Marcus would never forgive him.

Climbing over the wall, he quickly began lowering himself after the surprisingly agile girl. She started heading right on a diagonal, which would bring her up close to the office. Ramus sighed inwardly as his muscles flexed and relaxed, following. He'd grown up rock climbing this wall and the surrounding landscape. Did she really think she could out-climb him?

"What the hell is going on?" Ramus glanced up at the source

of the dangerously low voice. Marcus had returned from overseeing the defence installation.

"Just teaching her a few new tricks," Ramus called sarcastically to his friend and leader.

"Aerina, get the hell up here before you fall and kill yourself," Marcus called in a lethal voice, throwing his own leg over the wall.

Aerina had stopped moving when she heard Marcus' voice. This wall was more difficult to climb than she had first thought, particularly without picks or her spike boots. She clung to a small outcropping, her arms shaking. Damn. She might actually fall.

Ramus reached her at the same time Marcus did, both grabbing an arm. Marcus lowered himself just below her, while Ramus remained beside her. They helped guide her slowly up the wall, Marcus catching her once when she would have slipped.

When all three were again on the stone walkway overlooking the pit, Aerina grimaced sheepishly at the two large men. "I imagined that going differently in my head."

Marcus' eyes narrowed angrily, while Ramus fought back a smile.

"What, precisely, were you hoping to accomplish?" Marcus asked in his low, dangerous voice. It had long ago lost the ability to strike fear in her, Aerina told herself. Almost convincingly.

"I was hoping to find out where Simon, Julia, and Jamia are," Aerina said, shrugging. "I thought if I could just get a little time, I could convince Ramus to..." she trailed off, refusing to look away from Marcus' stony gaze.

"Convince him how?" Marcus asked softly. "In the same way you convince me to abandon reason and listen to your pleas?" He took a step closer, running a long finger down her cheek, his gaze lowering further to the gentle swell of her breasts outlined by the tight black material of her climbing suit, then further still to her long, slender legs encased in the form-fitting black pants.

Ramus glanced away from the intimate scene, still fighting a smile at the obvious sign of Marcus' jealousy.

"Stop it," Aerina hissed, slapping his hand aside, refusing to back down. Marcus' jaw clenched and he stepped back, glancing at Ramus.

"Just one smirk, G, I dare you," he murmured to his friend, using the nickname from their training days. Ramus threw his hands in the air as if in surrender.

"I'm going to see how Si—er, how the tech guys are coming along," Ramus said pointedly, turning away. Marcus turned back to Aerina.

"Go home, Aerina. A Virmortus is waiting outside to escort you and replace your chip." With that, he dismissed her, turning to follow Ramus.

"I'm not letting them reinsert the chip, Marcus. They will have to kill me first," Aerina quietly warned him. She wanted to reach out and touch him. To have his arms surround her in comfort rather than anger. To quit being at odds with one another, for just a moment.

"And I'm not leaving without my friends. Like it or not, I'm involved in this." She watched his stiff back, willing him to turn and face her. To talk to her.

He did. But his harsh features were as unreadable as always. "Your friends have been escorted home," he informed her calmly, adding in the same even tone, "And you will have your chip reinserted, willingly or not."

"I'll just cut it out again," she threatened rashly.

"It might be a little more difficult if it's inserted into your neck," he murmured silkily. Aerina blanched, her hand involuntarily going to her throat.

They faced each other for a moment. This wasn't really a battle worth fighting. She'd tried and failed to gather information. They knew now. Why not let them put her chip back in? It went against her nature to concede, but she was learning to pick her battles.

Maybe she was maturing, she thought dryly.

"Fine," she said at last. "Thank you for not hurting Julia and her sister. And Simon," she added as an afterthought.

"Do you think I did it for you?"

Aerina flushed. "I know what you're trying to do. And it's not working," She took a step towards him until they were almost touching, tilting her head back, her blue eyes meeting his challengingly. His hands came down on her shoulders of their own accord, his fingers gripping her tightly.

She rose on her toes as his head lowered to meet her, their lips touching lightly then with more force. The familiar rush of desire settled in her stomach, spreading slowly lower. The pain and animosity faded, leaving behind only the familiar longing. The heady rush of pleasure; the exhilaration of love.

His mouth moved over hers with surprising gentleness, contrasting the force of emotion she could feel contained in his large frame. He practically shook with it. She revelled in the rush of pleasure and the knowledge that she still had this power over him. The same power he had over her.

A commotion down in the pit interrupted them. Several Virmortus came in through a door directly below and headed towards another door on the other side. Marcus stepped back, the moment gone.

"Go home, Aerina," he said quietly after the group had disappeared. He touched her mouth with one blunt finger. "There can never be anything more between us than this." He turned and walked away.

She, too, turned and headed towards the exit down the short white hallway.

"I'm not giving up," she murmured to herself. "But I can wait."

The door opened and she stepped out into the early morning sun. It was a new day; a bright morning. But as a Reaper stepped forward to politely motion her to a black military e-vehicle, she couldn't help but notice the ominous dark clouds gathering on the horizon. A storm was coming. She hoped Alba would be ready.

Chapter 19

"The danger of the past was that men became slaves. The danger of the future is that man may become robots."
- Erich Fromm

Marcus stood behind Simon, watching the other man work. Simon typed furiously, pausing only momentarily at odd times as if considering his next attack before resuming. His blonde, shaggy head was bent low over the holoscreen that had been merged with a flat screen. Lines of code ran alongside the projection of files that were quickly becoming visible as Simon delved deeper. Under his long fingers, the virtual keyboard came alive, giving up the secrets embedded in the small ID chip held in the scanner.

His skill had been immediately apparent. He'd quickly bypassed and shut down a built-in defence system programmed to wipe the disk upon unauthorized access. That little defence had been what kept the Virmortus tech team out. How had so much talent been overlooked? Marcus made a mental note to review their recruiting process when all this was over. Simon would have saved them precious time.

He supposed he owed Aerina for that one.

It hadn't taken the lanky Engineer long to crack the code on the Southern Empire ID chips, and he was now decoding the stored files.

Marcus studied the most recent file Simon had managed to access. If he didn't have the information in front of him, he would have a hard time believing it. Hell, even with it right there he could still hardly believe it.

"Holy shit," Ramus muttered next to him. Marcus couldn't help but agree. "How long have they had access to our Network?" Ramus asked.

Simon shook his head. "I don't think they have a direct link. Even with the alarms disabled, you would have noticed someone accessing the Network and poking around. This is a screenshot of the file system, particularly the tracking subfolder of your security," Simon explained as he began typing again.

"Can you access a time or date stamp on the screen shot that might tell us when and who accessed the system to get that information?" Marcus asked, leaning closer and resting his hand on the desk to better see the code.

"Already working on it," Simon said, still madly typing. His exhilaration was almost palpable. This is what he lived for.

"Ah, here it is," Simon murmured almost to himself, satisfaction in his voice. A time and date appeared on the holoscreen. A date Marcus remembered well. Founder's Day. The day of the attempted assassination and Aerina's near-death.

"I'd say that is either one hell of a coincidence, or this confirms our suspicions," Marcus said, straightening.

"You mean Aerina was right in thinking that the assassination was connected to this potential invasion?" Simon asked, a note of surprised admiration in his voice. "I'll admit, when she and Julia came to me, I thought she was as crazy as the rumors claimed."

"Then why did you risk so much to help her?" Ramus spoke up from where he leaned against the back wall, curiosity in his tone.

Simon shrugged his wide, lean shoulders. "I would do anything to win Julia back," he stated quietly, unashamedly. "I guess that makes me just as crazy."

Marcus looked at the other man with new respect. It might be crazy, but at least he went after what he wanted, without regret.

"Aerina's not crazy, just dangerously inquisitive. And smarter than I give her credit for," Marcus said quietly, clenching a fist in renewed regret. He never lied to himself, and was quick to admit when he was wrong. Like now. He was beginning to think he'd made a mistake in pushing her away. Glancing at Ramus, he saw his friend giving him a slightly amused and sympathetic look. He narrowed his eyes and made a rude gesture that had Ramus bursting into surprised laughter at the un-Marcus-like behaviour.

He would worry about their relationship, which he finally admitted to himself did exist, when this situation was over. Not only was Ramus never going to let the issue go if Marcus continued to dwell on it, but if the Empire successfully invaded, the matter would be irrelevant. They would all be dead.

"Keep unlocking the files; at least we'll know what they know," Marcus instructed brusquely. He wanted to check in with the perimeter guards and the progress of the new ComTower installation that would allow him to reach some of the outpost towns by Com device.

"Sure thing, boss," Simon replied sardonically. Marcus glanced back before nodding and continuing out the door. Simon might not have been raised with the strict rules of Virmortus respect drummed into him, but he also didn't seem to harbor any ill-will about being pressed into service. In fact, the blonde man seemed excited about his new role.

He *did* owe Aerina for this one. Suddenly, he felt eager to pay off this debt.

Aerina walked into her house, the Reaper escort close behind her.

"Please, come in," she said facetiously. He remained impassive, as he had during the short ride to her house in his military vehicle. As juvenile as it might be, she had to admit that she'd enjoyed prodding him almost as much as she did Marcus.

Something about the Reapers' stoic demeanour just begged her to find some crack. So far, she'd been unsuccessful in getting any kind of rise out of this small red-haired man of death. He was certainly fit, but otherwise seemed quite innocuous with his small stature and unusual red hair. She knew his harmless aura was just an illusion. No one survived Virmortus training unless they could kill effortlessly.

Leading him up to her room, she was glad her parents were not around to ask questions. If Alba still existed after her graduation, it would be a relief to find a villa of her own. This experience had helped open her eyes about her parents. She was never going to be the girl they wished, the perfect Patrician. And as long as she was here, in this house, she was never going to get out from under the burden of blame they'd placed on her those many years ago.

This is all your fault.

The Reaper took the small cylinder from its place in her jewelry box, spraying it with a disinfecting mist before inserting it into a tiny gun that she had seen used on newborns.

Stoically she held out her undamaged wrist, repressing the fleeting thought of trying to bash him with a discarded shoe laying on the floor and making a run for it. She didn't want to hurt him, and besides, what would be the point? They already knew about her defection. She was hardly going to hide in the hills. The whole purpose was to uncover the truth.

Nevertheless, she couldn't help the shiver of premonition that went through her at the sharp pain of the cylinder being injected. The tiny click of the gun sounded like electronic manacles closing around her once again.

Without saying a word, the red-haired Reaper packed up his things and headed towards the stairs.

"Thanks for all your help, and the delightful company," Aerina called after him as he descended the stairs easily. His only response was the gentle click of the front door as he exited.

Leaning on the window sill, she looked out over the ocean far below, letting the cool breeze blow her hair. It was early afternoon, and she hadn't eaten since...well, she couldn't even remember.

Heading down to the kitchen, she selected a simple salad from the Dispensare. It blinked at her—none was available. She selected granola and milk instead.

She wondered why the cook hadn't refilled it. Having the Dispensare automatically refilled was just one of the many things she took for granted. She'd never really thought about it until she'd started spending time with the Plebs. As a child, staff had always been around. Tending the garden, fixing her food, even babysitting.

How would her life have been different, had she been born a

Pleb? Would she even now be working in a shop, or perhaps tending someone's garden? Would her restlessness be abated by the physical exhaustion of menial labor? Or would her mind still wander, imaging what lay outside the walls? Pondering what worlds were there to be discovered down the coast, and across the once-easily traversable ocean?

The *what ifs* of life were a waste of time. She hadn't been born a Pleb, and she *did* want to know the answers to her questions. Dread of the impending invasion lay heavy in her gut, but a tiny part of her felt exhilaration. Some of the answers to her questions might at this very moment be traveling closer to Alba, bringing possible destruction but also liberation from the constant questions and wondering. From the limbo that seemed to hold Alba suspended, unchanging.

Change was coming on the wings of military drones, in the wake of war ships, and in the dust of the armoured vehicles that were coming to spread destruction and perhaps another, more sinister motive.

Grabbing an apple, she took a big bite. A twinge shot up her wrist from the tiny wound where the chip had been reinserted. Removing this one was going to hurt even more.

Aerina walked down the familiar street as a surprisingly cold wind whipped from the north. Stopping, she knocked lightly on the door she had left not more than forty-eight hours earlier. It cracked open immediately, revealing Stephen's good-looking features with a slightly grey cast.

"Are you alright?" Aerina asked as he glanced around quickly before pulling her through the partially opened door. She shot him a quizzical look as he shut the door and pushed the lock button above the latch. When she'd finally checked her holoreader that evening, which had been returned by the delightful red-headed conversationalist who had escorted her home, she'd found several messages from Lina, her mother, and one from Stephen, asking her to come immediately. She'd deleted the others. Highly curious about what he had wanted, she'd come right over.

She'd spent the day after the Reaper had left on the Pleb Terrace, visiting Julia and Jamia. She'd needed to see for herself that they were alright. They waved off her profuse apologies, assuring her they hadn't been harmed in any way. They also had been escorted home by a Reaper, and Simon had left Julia a message that he was fine, working with the Virmortus tech team.

Aerina's pride, and her feelings, were bruised at hearing that. She'd practically begged to be included and Marcus had chastised her and sent her home like a naughty child.

A familiar anger began rising, the anger she used to cover up deeper emotions, and she struggled to control it. It wasn't fair, she wanted to cry out. Somehow, it sounded childish even in her own mind. So she had listened to Julia's brief story about their hours in the Virmortus interrogation rooms, assured herself again they were unharmed, and left to throw herself a small pity party. She'd been about to partake in the popular Pleb technique of drowning one's sorrows in liquor when she'd seen the unexpected message from Stephen.

She'd been relieved — the clear liquid she had been about consume smelled horrendous, a little like the counters smelled after they had been disinfected. She couldn't imagine how consuming that liquid would make her feel any better.

"Does Helen know I'm here?" Aerina asked half-jokingly as Stephen remained silent. He shot her a look that had her shrugging. Not everyone appreciated her humor.

"I want to show you something," he said, motioning her to follow him into his office. The shades were all drawn, a dim lamp casting long shadows. He had a few screens up on his desk, reminding her of a much smaller version of Simon's setup.

"After you left the other day, I kept thinking about what you said," Stephen began, sliding his large form easily into his chair. Aerina perched on the edge of the desk, waiting for him to continue, studying the screens. It was gibberish to her. "I know you're a little crazy when it comes to politics, but you don't make things up. So I did a little checking around — and found this." With a dramatic flourish that was unlike Stephen, he spun his flat screen around so she could see it.

"I hate to ruin your dramatic reveal, but what does it mean?" Aerina squinted at the screen. It was line after line of information, intermingled with code.

Stephen sighed, turning the screen back.

"It's the Network. And it has a virus," Stephen said. The meaning was still a little lost on Aerina, but she could hear the seriousness in Stephen's voice.

"Like a sickness? What does a virus do to a computer?"

"In the Pre-war Era, viruses were commonly used on computers to steal information or just cause damage," Stephen explained patiently. "I haven't found yet what specifically this virus will do, but I do know it has a timer to activate some malicious code. And it's set for three days from now."

"Do you think it's related to the invasion?" Aerina asked intently.

Stephen shrugged. "I don't know, but no one has ever introduced a virus to our Network before. It seems like a strange coincidence, if what you claim is true."

"We need to tell Marcus," Aerina said, standing quickly and turning towards the door. Stephen rose just as quickly, grabbing her arm.

"Hacking into the Network is a death sentence. Just let me find a little more information and we can decide what to do," he said uneasily. "We don't know what the Virmortus will do when they find out I've been in their files without authorization."

"They might already know," Aerina said impatiently. "This is important—three days isn't long. We need to find out what the virus is going to do. And the soldiers need to know something might happen in three days, to prepare." She pulled her arm out of Stephen's light grasp.

"Dammit, Aerina, I said wait," Stephen said, lunging around the desk and grabbing her again, this time with both hands.

"Stephen, don't worry, they won't do anything. You have valuable information." Aerina tried to reassure him, meeting his worried, dark eyes. He looked more like his sister Lina than ever with his normally confident demeanour shadowed by apprehension.

"Just give me the rest of tonight," he pleaded, his grip bruising in his distraction. Aerina hesitated. An entire night was a long time when they might only have three days. But Stephen had trusted her enough to call her — she owed him that, at least.

"Alright, we'll go in the morning," she conceded, mentally crossing her fingers. If she couldn't convince him, she might need to take the information to Marcus herself.

Stephen's tan face lit with relief and he pulled her off the ground in a bear hug. "I knew I could trust you."

"Get your hands off her." The deadly quiet voice from the doorway had them both gasping and turning. Stephen dropped his arms slowly, meeting eyes even darker than his own; eyes that promised death.

Marcus took a silent step into the room and Stephen stiffened, squaring his shoulders in challenge. The two men eyed one another as if combatants sizing up an opponent.

"Stop it," Aerina said sharply, stepping between them. "As flattering as I find your little display of jealousy, this isn't the best time for you to finally be honest about your feelings." She saw Marcus' jaw tighten and could almost swear a light flush darkened his taunt cheekbones.

Stephen's eyes widened slightly and he shot a warning look at Aerina as if to tell her to quit provoking the beast. She didn't take her eyes from Marcus' hard stare. "We were just going to call you," she added, taking another step away from Stephen to lean against the desk. Marcus' brow raised faintly at that. "Stephen found something that you need to see."

She motioned to the computers behind her. Marcus cast a long look at Stephen before striding forward to look. Stephen remained silent, merely stepping aside to let Marcus past.

"You're in the Network," Marcus commented, his voice still dangerously low. Stephen stepped forward, pointing to a few lines on the flatscreen.

"This is what I found. A virus," he said, his voice aloof.

Marcus began firing questions in his low voice, Stephen answering succinctly.

Aerina rolled her eyes as she looked at the two dark, virile heads bent over the screen. She couldn't decide if she was flattered or disgusted by the men's behaviour. The blatant show of possession was so unlike Marcus, she was still in shock. She'd have to decide how she felt once the surprise had worn off.

Marcus stepped back from the desk, taking his Com device from his pocket.

"Call Tech Office," he commanded, his eyes falling on Aerina as he waited in silence for an answer on the other end. Aerina tried unsuccessfully to read the expression in those familiar obsidian depths.

"Yes, I've got her and the party that accessed the system. Get Simon; we might have found something important that needs to be dealt with immediately. I'm scanning in an ID; you'll be dealing with Stephen."

Marcus disconnected. "They'll be calling you. Tell Simon what he needs to know and then a car will pick you up to take you to the office."

"Yes, sir," Stephen replied sardonically. Aerina smiled sympathetically at her friend, understanding how he felt. She then glanced over at Marcus to find him watching her, his eyes hot with anger. He banked the flames and turned away quickly, heading towards the door.

"Coming?" he said finally without looking back, merely pausing in the doorway. Aerina sighed and followed. "Good luck," she murmured as she passed Stephen. "I won't tell Helen if you won't," she added jokingly and was rewarded with a smile.

Marcus held the door open to his car, the lines of his body straining with impatience. The urgency of the coming deadline weighed on all of them. Aerina slid in quickly, her dark clothes blending with the seat color. Her hair was the only bright color, its golden-red luminescence gleaming brightly in the dimly lit night.

The sleek car shot into the night. Aerina turned to look at Marcus. "You knew it was me in the system." It wasn't a question, but Marcus nodded anyway.

"I'm glad," she said simply. "Stephen was anxious about

going to you with the information. I don't know how long he would have convinced me to wait. Do you think it is important?"

Marcus nodded again, his eyes remaining on the dark streets of the Capitol Terrace.

"You can admit it, you know. I won't gloat," Aerina said finally as the silence lengthened between them. Marcus looked over, shooting her a sardonic glance. She smiled beatifically back.

"I'm impressed. You managed to not only bring Simon in, you motivated Stephen to uncover a virus that might have taken Simon another day or two to discover," Marcus admitted freely, his low voice holding a note of admiration. Aerina felt warmth spread through her quickly at his approval.

"So you admit I can be useful?" she prodded.

Marcus remained quiet for a moment before saying softly, "You're more than useful." Aerina looked at him quickly, her smile fading. Her slender hand slid slowly across the seat to touch his callused one where it rested on the console. He still looked straight ahead, but turned his hand up to clasp hers. They remained that way, driving in silence, until they reached Marcus' villa.

"Aren't we returning to the Training Grounds?" Aerina asked in surprise. Marcus shook his head.

"I've been awake for over twenty four hours. I need a few hours rest before heading back," he said as he pulled himself out of car. Aerina followed, noting the deep grooves and shadows on his face she hadn't noticed earlier. She wanted to ask why he hadn't brought her home; why he had changed his mind. Afraid to break the fragile connection, she remained silent.

Aerina stepped into his villa ahead of him, hearing the door close with a quiet snap. Even before looking at Marcus' face, she knew what was going to happen.

Since the first time, she had known it was only a matter of time until they made love again. Whatever was between them was too great to ignore, as much as Marcus might want to.

She felt him come up behind her, his hard, warm chest pressed tightly to her back. His arms—strong, bearing scars of his experience—slid around her slowly as if giving her time to step away.

She didn't move, enjoying the feel of him around her for a long moment. Then it wasn't enough; she needed to be closer. Turning, her arms slid around his neck. His normally cold dark eyes were burning, hot with desire.

He ran his hands down her arms, her sides, then up her slender back, sending shivers down her spine. His fiery gaze followed his hands and her light coat dropped to the ground, unnoticed. Her shirt followed and she stood in only her white lace bra and slim jeans.

Heat spread from each spot his hands touched, turning her center liquid and making her knees weak.

"Tell me you want this as much as I do," he rasped in her ear, his lips moving gently along her jaw.

"You know I do," she gasped in response, pressing her body against his, trying to get even closer. She revelled in the feel of his rough woven vest against her hyper-sensitive flesh. "And I won't regret this as much as you do. I won't regret it at all."

Her words released the floodgate of Marcus' control, and his hands shook lightly as he ripped her bra off roughly, dropping it in the pile of her forgotten clothes. He dropped to his knees, his hands cupping her small, firm breasts reverently.

Aerina breathed a gasp, letting her head fall back as his rough thumbs ran over the hardening tips. She gasped again as his hot mouth closed over one nipple, his tongue running over the peak. He then kissed the inner curve of each breast before moving lower, kissing along the sensitive part of her ribcage, lower still to her abdomen. He inserted his fingers in the waist of her jeans, running them along her smooth skin before unbuttoning them and jerking them down.

He gazed up her nearly nude body for a moment before lifting her effortlessly in his arms, leaving her clothes behind in a heap and carrying her to the divan, lowering her gently.

"You're so beautiful; so elegant and delicate. I'm afraid I'm going to break you," he murmured as he lowered his own body over hers, careful to keep his weight off her. His large form was shaking. Aerina froze for a moment, scanning his eyes and making a shocking revelation.

He was scared. Scared of losing control. Scared of harming her. Suddenly, reassuring him was just as important as assuaging the desire that was burning her alive.

"I'm not as fragile as I look," Aerina said, pulling him closer. She arched against him, groaning in frustration at the layers of clothes he still wore. She wanted to feel his skin against hers; feel his heat pressed against her core.

She struggled with the zipper of his vest, jerking it off. With his help, they switched positions; she straddling his lean hips. Running her hands up under his shirt, she let her hair fall forward, screening them from the room around them. Their eyes met and she smiled. "Just lay back and enjoy," she instructed. "I promise to be gentle." He smiled in return, his eyes still gleaming with banked fire. His large hands clasped the couch arm behind him, shaking lightly with the effort to hold onto his control.

She slid her hands under his snug shirt, feeling the ripples and grooves of his muscled chest. His breath hitched in his chest; her own came in heavy pants.

The passion between them exploded as powerfully and impressively as any ballistic weapon, burning the night around them. They made love with a desperate passion that both embraced and denied the coming shift in their world.

For this night, this moment, it was just them.

They held each other as if this night was the last moments they would share. Aerina didn't know if they had a future together, or even if they had a future at all. But here, held secure in Marcus' arms as the night blanketed them in darkness, she didn't care. This moment was enough.

Chapter 20

"The supreme art of war is to subdue the enemy without fighting." - Sun Tzu

The low buzz of Marcus' holoreader brought Aerina from a restless sleep. Quickly clearing her head of strange dreams, Aerina sat up in bed.

Marcus talked in a low voice in the kitchen to whomever was on the other end of the Com. "I'll be there in a few minutes."

Throwing the covers off, Aerina stood, watching Marcus stride back into the bedroom area, selecting a fresh set of clothing from the Wardrobe. The room was silent but for the silent whirring of the wardrobe bar as it delivered the uniform he had selected.

Black, naturally.

"Get dressed," he instructed brusquely, pulling on his slacks as Aerina stood dumbly. A wave of relief rushed over her. He wasn't going to leave her behind this time.

Hurriedly, she pulled on her own wrinkled clothes, pretending not to notice Marcus' sculpted form as it disappeared beneath his clothing. Her body still ached deliciously from their fervent lovemaking. She tried to ignore that, too.

They both remained silent throughout the short trip to the Training Grounds, each lost in their own thoughts. Aerina didn't bother asking what had happened; she would find out soon enough.

Marcus glanced over at an unusually silent Aerina. He hadn't let himself hope to have another night with her; he couldn't have imagined it would be even more soul-shattering than the first time. But every moment together seemed to build their bond even stronger. He accepted that he would never be able to completely separate his own soul from hers. He didn't understand it, but it existed. Call it love, call it passion, or just plain obsession. Whatever the word, it was something so powerful, it scared the hell out of him.

He was done pushing her away. He was going to keep her as close as possible; protect her as best he could. She was the only person he truly cared about; the only person who truly cared about him. He wasn't going to lose that. He wasn't willing to lose *her*. He might not deserve her; he might not be worthy of love, but for her, he was willing to spend the rest of his life trying.

Once in the underground garage of the Training Grounds, they exited the vehicle quickly, taking a flight of stairs to the main level. In Marcus' office, a small group of people alternately sat and stood. Aerina's eyes were drawn immediately to the familiar woman seated at the long meeting table.

Debbie gave them a wan smile. Another woman Aerina recognized from Sybil, Portia, sat beside her. Two other Virmortus stood near the door, no doubt the ones that had brought Debbie and her friend in. The Consul himself sat at the meeting table across from Debbie and her friend.

"She would only speak with you," Ramus said quietly, coming up to Marcus and motioning to the attractive older woman. Marcus nodded and sat in the chair next to Debbie.

The millions of lights on the Network Grid twinkled like stars, many of them unmoving in the early hours of the morning. Aerina looked away, focusing again on the tall, dark-haired woman seated at the table.

"You were right, Marcus. The Southern Empire is coming," Debbie said quietly, ignoring the rest of the room. "No one can stop them," she continued, her voice hitching on a sob.

Marcus leaned closer. "What happened, Debbie?"

Debbie began to cry softly. "We spotted the ship early this morning. We could see the lights of their ComTowers. Portia and I tried to contact you, but our Com device wasn't working so we used your old vehicle to come and warn you." Debbie stopped on a gasp as she tried to stem her sobs.

Marcus waited patiently, his eyes never leaving Debbie. Aerina felt a lump rising in her own throat, guessing what the woman was unable to say. The room was deathly silent as everyone listened to her quietly gasping sobs.

Finally, she regained enough control to continue. "We were a few miles away when we heard it. It looked like a lightning strike. Each bolt seemed to strike a home, or an individual, I don't know..." Debbie broke off, but got herself back under control. Portia rested her hand gently on her friend's arm.

"I've never seen anything like it," Debbie whispered. "Everything was melted, blackened, warped. And the smell..." Debbie stopped again, her eyes seeming to shiver with the horror they had witnessed, her nostrils quivering with remembered repulsion.

Marcus looked over and met Ramus' gaze. Aerina couldn't keep silent, speaking the question on everyone's mind.

"What could do that?"

Marcus glanced over at Aerina with a look that told her he had been expecting her question. "It is like the EMWs, but much stronger. It is the weapon of choice for the Southern Empire. Essentially a controlled electrical current; harnessed lightning."

Silence followed Marcus' brief explanation. Terror was nearly palpable.

"Don't we have something like that?" Aerina finally asked.

"Not as powerful or with such a great reach. But we do have the Technology to fight them," Marcus said, his eyes locked on Julius. The older man just shook his head, his blue eyes worried.

"Not now, Marcus," he ordered, his voice harsh.

"We don't have the time to wait. By the time you make a decision, we'll all be dead," Marcus replied, his voice so low and even, Aerina had to strain to hear him. Aerina glanced around. Everyone else looked as bewildered as she felt, except Ramus, who stood leaning against the back wall, his face impassive.

Both Marcus and Julius stood, leaving the room. Perhaps to continue their argument; Aerina didn't know. She sat down in the seat vacated by Marcus, beside Debbie. Resting her hand on the other woman's, she murmured how sorry she was, knowing words couldn't begin to alleviate the slender woman's grief.

Debbie looked smaller; her statuesque form seeming to have sunken in on itself with the weight of grief. The other woman, Portia, seemed to still be in shock, her dark eyes staring ahead, swarthy skin pale.

Suddenly, the office seemed to be pressing in on Aerina, the stone walls suffocating her. With one final pat on Debbie's cold hand, she rose and walked to the door, bursting through with a suppressed gasp. The heavy weight of grief lifted slightly in the bright hallway overlooking the Pit. The large space was again eerily silent, the normal inhabitants no doubt out patrolling the city or outside the walls. Preparing.

She jumped as a buzzing interrupted the heavy silence. It was her holoreader. Putting one hand to her thumping heart, she held up her wrist where the reader was clipped, letting a small image project. It was Lina calling again. Her friend must be wondering what had become of her. Slowly, she cancelled the call. She couldn't talk to her friend right now and pretend like everything was ok.

And her parents... what did they think? They must know she was up to something. It hurt to think that they wouldn't talk to her about what was going on; that they didn't even seem to care what was going on with her.

Shaking her head as if to physically clear the unwelcome thoughts, she turned, walking further down the hall. She knew both Simon and Stephen were here somewhere, working to uncover more information. Marcus was coordinating the defence with Julius and Ramus....

And then there was her. Where did she fit? Aerina had a moment of sorrow, feeling the same sense of not belonging she'd felt her whole life. Of being on the outside, looking in. What was her place?

Forcing down the rising sadness, Aerina straightened imperceptibly. She would do what she'd always done—she'd forge her own role. Create a place for herself.

What better time than now. It was the end of their world, anyway.

Marcus re-entered the large office, his eyes quickly scanning the inhabitants. Debbie and Portia still sat at the table with the two silent Virmortus standing guard. Ramus was gone, no doubt in the tech room.

And Aerina was gone. He felt unease rising; now that'd he given up on pushing her away, he felt an inexplicable need to keep her near. It didn't take her long to find trouble.

"Max and Vin will take you to a villa where you can rest and get cleaned up," Marcus said quietly to Debbie and Portia, motioning to the two guards. "Let them know if you need anything." Debbie nodded mutely, rising. Marcus hesitated only a moment before turning and striding out.

The panic subsided a few minutes later when he walked into the tech room to see Aerina standing behind Stephen, watching characters fly over the flatscreen. Simon worked similarly at a nearby station. Her eyes rose to meet his, their blue depths gleaming. Vibrancy emanated from her, beginning with her glowing hair, her sparkling eyes, and the healthy glow of her skin. She was breathtaking in her vitality, and Marcus felt a rush of something indescribable. More than passion. More than mere love.

It was like the first time he had seen her, this recognition. She was the center of a cyclone, the world swirling around her, pulling at her, and she remained in the epicenter of it all. In the chaos but somehow apart.

"Hell." The blunt four letter word interrupted Marcus' thoughts and he walked over to where Simon sat hunched over a virtual keyboard and surrounded by numerous screens of various display-types. He stared intently at the holoscreen where a large red warning symbol blinked.

"They're in the Network."

"Shut it down," Marcus ordered harshly.

"But—" Stephen began to argue, hurrying over from his station. Everything was connected to the Network: holoreaders, Com devices, holocomputers, e-cars, even the climate-control, wardrobes, and dispensares in homes.

"Better that it's shut down than they have control," Marcus said. When Simon also hesitated, his fingers hovering over the keys, Marcus pushed him aside and typed in the command himself.

The entire building went dark for a long moment before the emergency offline back-up kicked on, and lights and devices began to recharge.

"I didn't know there was an offline backup," Stephen said, breaking the horrified silence. A wave of relief swept through the small group gathered in the tech room. Marcus just watched the screen as it began slowly restarting the city-wide systems. It was now running through an old cable network that hadn't been used in decades, but so far seemed to be running smoothly.

"Don't hesitate when I give a command," Marcus ordered softly, his voice no less deadly for its quiet restraint. Simon nodded, his jaw stiff. "Hesitation in a kill can be deadly for you, even if it's just killing the Network." Marcus lightened the mood with his uncharacteristic humor. Aerina gave him a small smile, a note of approval gleaming in her eyes.

The mood lightened, and even Simon grinned.

"Can we get a lock on their digital signal?" Marcus asked, and the two men returned their stations, all business once again.

One of the Virmortus tech team, an older woman that was short and a little rounded, hurried over with a small device.

"I've been continually scanning for signals, and a new one came in. I've pinpointed the origin to several hundred miles south of here," she said brusquely, her voice gravelly and surprisingly deep. Plugging the device into Simon's station, a new holoscreen popped up, displaying a topographic map on which a tiny beacon blinked.

"It's in the water," Ramus said from his post near the door.

"The ship," Aerina murmured, quiet until now. Marcus looked up quickly, nodding.

"Yes," he affirmed aloud. "It must be the ship that destroyed Sybil."

"An armada or a lone wolf?" Ramus muttered the question almost to himself.

"They probably thought they could take Alba with a single ship," Marcus replied. "When we defeat it, they'll no doubt come with more." He looked at Aerina as he spoke and she just raised an eyebrow, knowing he was keeping valuable information from them all. The secret the Consul knew and was trying to protect. The secret that was drawing the Southern Empire to their shore.

The stocky tech woman frowned, making her already fierce features more forbidding. "Even after shutting down the Network, they're still locked on something. They are downloading information from somewhere." Simon and the woman both leaned in, studying the characters flying across the flatscreen.

"Our ID chips," Aerina said softly, her fingers pressing against the tiny fresh wound on her wrist. She knew it was her imagination but she could almost feel the chip burning in her.

"Damn," Stephen said in awed horror. "Each chip has its own Network uplink. It is only one-sided, but shutting down the Network won't stop the ID chips from being online. They can access the information stored in the chips, they just won't be able to upload anything, or interact with the chips."

"But they'll learn how many of us, where we are, and demographic information that is invaluable in war," Ramus muttered in disgust. "They're using our own technology against us."

Marcus was silent, staring at the screen as information passed through the digital connection, streaming their world's secrets to the enemy.

Turning, his onyx eyes fell on Aerina and he walked forward slowly to where she stood beside Stephen's station. Taking her small hand in his large, callused palm, he slowly turned it over, gently pushing back the sleeve until the bandage covering her recent self-inflicted wound was revealed.

Aerina watched him in silence, waiting to see what he was going to do. The enormity of the situation was slowly sinking in. The reality of it all was overwhelming. It was still difficult to believe, even after she'd witnessed the violence on the outside and after seeing Debbie and Portia's devastation.

"Call the General. Tell her to contact the Armati across the entire state and issue an emergency ordinance — all citizens must have their chips neutralized."

Ramus immediately left the room to follow Marcus' order.

Without the Network, no one's Com device would work. They would need to rely on old fashioned phone lines, a few of which were installed for an emergency such as this.

"Keep monitoring their digital activity," Marcus ordered. "I'm going to check in with the perimeter watch, then I'll be back here. If anything comes up, contact me on this." He opened a small box and tossed a simple two-way radio to Simon. "Try to keep communication to a minimum."

The tech team nodded. Marcus grabbed Aerina's hand and strode towards the door. He wasn't about to let her out of his sight. She struggled to keep up with his long strides as he pulled her along the hall and down the stairs towards the lower level where his e-car was parked.

Opening her door, he tucked her in unceremoniously before sliding his own large frame in. Pulling out his sica blade, he reached in front of her to open the storage compartment, removing a first aid kit. Grabbing disinfectant, he poured it over the knife quickly.

"Marcus?" Aerina asked nervously as he grabbed her hand, but didn't pull away. She'd trust him, even with a garrote around her neck. He wouldn't hurt her.

She was still reminding herself of that when the knife pierced her skin. She couldn't repress the gasp as the pain shot up her arm. It was over in a second, the damn ID chip she'd already removed once sitting in his palm.

"You could have let a Medella do that," she muttered as he swiftly bound the wrist. "I look like I'm suicidal," she added dryly, studying her matching wrist bandages.

"This was quicker," he said brusquely by way of explanation, a quick twist and quiet beep indicating the chip had been deactivated.

"My turn?" she asked, eyeing his wrist. Marcus' mouth curled in his version of a smile.

"Sorry, I don't have one," he said, starting up the car with a wave of his hand.

"But you just—" She stopped as he turned his hand over and showed her the small card he held in his hand.

"Kind of unfair," she muttered, slowly rotating her sore wrist. Marcus shrugged, driving with his normal relaxed control.

"Just call it a perk of being the Alpha Virmortus."

Chapter 21

"Life isn't about finding yourself. Life is about creating yourself." – George Bernard Shaw

The e-car took an old road that wound up the mountain, stopping finally in front of a tall tower. A lookout.

"I've never noticed this," Aerina said, sliding out and following Marcus, having to almost run to keep up with his quick pace.

"It's designed to be hidden. We call it the Crow's Nest," Marcus said, scanning his wrist—no, card—and they stepped into a small elevator that quickly ascended.

Two men turned when they entered, both looking surprised to see Aerina. But like true Virmortus, they hid it almost immediately, nodding respectfully to Marcus.

"Our Com devices are down. Remy was just going to head to the Training Ground to contact you. Look." The taller of the two, so thin he looked almost emaciated, motioned out towards the water to the south.

Marcus slipped on his sunglasses, zooming in. Aerina did the same, clapping a hand over her mouth to stifle the gasp that she was sure was very un-Reaper-like. She would hate her boyfriend's colleagues to think she didn't fit in.

Boyfriend. She liked the sound of that. If she was going to die soon, which might happen by the looks of the giant warship that was barely visible on the distant horizon, she wanted to have had a boyfriend.

Although the title *Reaper lover* had a nice ring to it.

Pushing aside the foolish thoughts that flooded her mind to hold the near-hysteria at bay, she looked over at Marcus to try and read his expression.

He didn't look worried, but with Marcus, that didn't mean much. His harsh features were composed. He was probably determining the next course of action.

The enemy had been spotted. They were coming. Wrapping

her arms around herself, she turned back to look out at the familiar ocean. The old friend that had given her an escape; that had embraced her regardless of who she was. It almost felt like a betrayal as it was the sea that was bringing death to her home.

Marcus conferred briefly with the guards in the Crow's Nest, handing each a two-way radio like he had given the group in the Training Grounds.

Aerina continued to look out over the ocean, her eyes scanning the familiar coastline. She refused to focus again on the large ship waiting just out of sight to the naked eye.

She sensed the brief but curious gazes the Virmortus were sending her way. She ignored them. Marcus, being Marcus, offered no explanation of who she was.

As they were preparing to leave, Aerina turned back, the manners bred in her forcing her to introduce herself to the two men.

"I'm sorry for being rude; I'm Aerina De —"

"We know who you are," the tall, thin man interrupted her politely. "It is an honor to meet the Alpha's woman, Miss Delacroix," he finished, bowing his head without offering a hand. The other man also bowed his own head in greeting. Aerina smiled her thanks, glancing over at Marcus. He said nothing, just stood by the exit to the elevator silently with his thick arms crossed lightly over his chest. As if he had all the time in the world to wait.

As the elevator doors closed behind them, Aerina turned to Marcus.

"Your woman?"

He shrugged in response. "Aren't you?"

Aerina felt warmth spread through her at his matter-of-fact question. As if there was no doubt in his mind about her belonging to him.

"Yeah," she answered simply, unable to keep a small smile from spreading. He looked over at her from where he leaned nonchalantly against the elevator wall, his large hand clasping gently on the back of her head, pulling her in for a quick, hard kiss.

They rode the rest of the way down in companionable silence, each lost in their own thoughts. As the doors slid open, revealing the parked e-car and rocky terrain, Aerina almost hesitated to leave the pseudo-security of the elevator. The view of the ocean was quickly becoming obscured by a thick mist that blew in. Not an unfamiliar site, nevertheless it seemed a foreshadowing of what was coming.

As if sensing her unease, Marcus grabbed her hand in his, pulling her towards the vehicle. Aerina skipped a few steps to keep pace, liking the new, more demonstrative side of Marcus.

Their doors clicked close, sealing them in the silent interior of the e-car. Marcus sat facing forward, his hand on the steering wheel. Aerina looked at him questioningly.

"I need you to trust me." He continued to look straight ahead, waiting on her answer.

"Ok," she answered, reassuring him and asking a question with that single word.

The vehicle came to life with a low roar, the powerful e-car turning easily onto the rocky road heading back down the mountainside. "Whatever happens, just trust me," was his only reply.

The dull afternoon light filtering through the haze disappeared as they dipped into the tunnel that would take them around into the Training Grounds. Aerina sighed and leaned back in the leather seat. Marcus apparently hadn't changed much, after all. He played his cards close to his chest.

At the Training Grounds, Marcus left the car sitting in the underground garage. Aerina followed him up a long flight of stairs and down a long hallway that seemed to go to the very center of the mountain.

The hallway ended at a thick door that looked impenetrable. Marcus typed in a long code before placing both hands on a biometric scanner. A long beep sounded and a red light began flashing a countdown. Marcus entered in another long code and followed that with a retinal scan.

Finally the door clicked, opening slowly. Marcus looked at her once before stepping through. Aerina followed hesitantly, wanting to ask what the hell he was doing. She knew it would be pointless. He'd tell her when he wanted.

So she blindly followed his large form into a narrow room holding several safes. Low lights blinked on upon their entrance, one flickering as if it might not have been used for a long time and needed to be replaced.

He moved purposefully to the center safe, dialing in the combination on the old-fashioned tumbler dial. The only sound in the room was the buzzing of the flickering fluorescent light and the soft click of the safe dial.

After a final click, the safe door opened silently. Aerina peered around Marcus' broad shoulder, desperately curious about what lay inside. Cool mist flowed out, indicating the interior of the safe was refrigerated.

It was filled with vials. Aerina moved forward slowly as Marcus moved to a second safe, dialing in another code. Aerina hesitantly reached her hand out to touch a vial. It contained an amber-colored liquid. Slowly lifting one from its stand, she held it up to the light. It writhed and glittered, as if alive. A shiver of premonition traveled quickly down her spine, sending goosebumps across her flesh.

The second safe opened as easily as the first. Looking up, she saw the second safe contained more vials and an old-fashioned computer storage device. A hard drive, they had been called.

She couldn't hold back any longer. "What...?" she asked, holding up the vial. Marcus picked up the hard drive and then moved next to her at the first safe, taking a rack of vials. The first he slipped into a small pack, the latter he set gently into a lined cooler case he had brought in preparation.

He then smashed every other vial, the amber liquid pooling on the floor, slowly turning a deep muddy brown. Aerina lifted shocked eyes. "Why did you destroy them? What was it?" Marcus didn't answer, pressing a few buttons on the inside of the safes. Their lights winked out, the slight hum stopping.

Groaning in frustration, Aerina took the sack containing the hard drive while he lifted the small cooler.

"It wouldn't kill you to give me a small explanation," she

complained, following him out of the room. "The suspense is killing me. And apparently the Southern Empire knows about this little secret so you may as well spill it to me. I can hardly be more of a threat than them."

Marcus' mouth curled up. "Don't underestimate yourself."

"Mar-cus," she drew out his name in frustration. She was so focused on giving Marcus her best beseeching gaze that at first she didn't notice the small group waiting for them just outside the entrance to the long hallway. When Marcus suddenly stopped, Aerina did too, looking over in surprise at the group of Patricians.

The Consul and several Senators, including her father, stood with Armati guards in the entrance, as if they would block her and Marcus' exit. Aerina slipped the long strap of the sack she carried over her head, gripping it tightly. She had a feeling this was going to get ugly.

"I told you the Technology was not an option, Marcus. What are you doing?" Julius snapped, his athletic frame taut. Aerina met her father's concerned gaze, his eyes imploring her to listen to the Consul. She let her own eyes fall away, glancing up at Marcus. He stood tall, his muscled legs braced slightly apart, the vials gripped firmly in a deceptively relaxed arm.

"My job," Marcus replied curtly, his face impassive.

"Your job is to follow my orders," Julius said, his normally gracious voice hoarse with restrained anger. "I thought we agreed that the Technology wouldn't be part of this!"

"My job is protect you and the people of Alba. If this is the only way, then I'll use it," Marcus replied unapologetically, his dark gaze traveling over the group gathered before them.

Aerina stood silently, watching the Armati shift nervously before her. They were unsure; uncertain who to follow. And none of them looked thrilled to tangle with Marcus.

"Aerina," her father murmured in a low voice. "Please, listen to the Consul. You don't know what you have in your hands."

Aerina glanced quickly at Marcus' still form. He didn't even glance at her, but she knew he was waiting for her to make a decision. He wouldn't stop her from leaving, although he might take the pack from her.

Her mind flashed back to the night at the Graduation Ball, when she'd denied a relationship with Marcus. This was a pivotal moment—if she sided with Marcus now, things would be infinitely different. She wouldn't be just associating with an undesirable caste. It would mean going against the Consul. Disregarding his direct command. She would be a traitor.

I need you to trust me.

The world around them was changing, and no matter which way this game of chess played out, she wanted to be on Marcus' team. Not only was he the best chess player she knew, she loved him.

No questions. No doubts.

Smiling somewhat sadly at her father, she shook her head. Their blue eyes, so similar, met in a new, shared understanding. They might be on opposite sides of this issue, but for once, each understood the other.

"I'm sorry, sir," Marcus said quietly, moving forward. The Armati nervously stood their ground, moving as if to stop the large man. But they were no match for a trained killer; an unstoppable force. Like a tsunami, Marcus melted around them, his movements nearly a blur. When he was done, the group of seven lay on the cement floor of the hallway, unmoving.

Aerina looked at Marcus with horror-filled eyes. "Are they—?"

"No, they're just unconscious," Marcus told her shortly, grabbing his two-way radio from his belt, speaking rapidly. "I need seven unconscious bodies removed from the Vault level and put in interrogation rooms."

Ramus' deep voice crackled back in affirmation of the order.

"Let's go," Marcus ordered, already walking away.

"They will just obey, even though it is the Consul himself?" Aerina asked in disbelief, pausing a moment to crouch by her prone father. His chest rose and fell steadily, and a weight lifted from her own chest. Glancing up, she met Marcus' watchful gaze.

"They'll follow my orders."

Within minutes, they had reached the main level where the tech room was located. Aerina's heart still raced after the confrontation in the vault hallway. What would happen now? Her life had been changing so swiftly over the past month it seemed she barely had time to acclimate to a new norm before it changed again.

And here she was, officially a traitor. Although it might be more accurate to call this a military coup, as it seemed like Marcus held the power, and the Consul would find himself soon imprisoned by his own special forces.

Marcus paused in his office to put the vials in another refrigerated compartment hidden in the floor, tucking two in his vest. Aerina remained silent, although questions bumped around in her mind, trying to force their way out.

As they walked quickly down the long hallway to the tech room, Marcus' radio crackled loudly in the silence, making Aerina jump.

The mix of multiple voices intermingled with shouts from down the hall, making everything unintelligible. Aerina struggled to make out the panicked words and strings of profanity through the two-way and the shouts that were growing louder as they approached. Marcus had started running and Aerina found herself following, terrified about what was happening.

Amid all the chaos, she heard the muted yet unmistakable booms of artificial thunder, and she knew. They were under attack.

Ramus came running from the tech room and Marcus turned back, both men bursting out onto the small balcony connected to the office.

Aerina arrived a few moments later, her breath coming in gasps. It caught in her throat at the sight that met her eyes outside.

Lightning bolts of energy cracked through the hazy midday air to be met by Grounders shot from the city's perimeter. The bursts of light were so bright, it hurt Aerina's eyes. The men had already put on sunglasses, and Aerina followed suit. The resounding booms were deafening; she could feel the compression waves in her chest.

Marcus stood for a long moment, taking in the sight, before he picked up his two-way and began barking orders. Ramus had picked up his own two-way and was relaying his own commands.

Aerina was deaf to their quick, low voices. She walked forward slowly as if in a haze, unable to take her eyes from the battle unfolding before her. Her slender body had begun shaking, probably in shock, and she gripped the balcony rail tightly. She blinked quickly, as if she could clear her vision and the organized chaos before her would disappear.

Between the EMW strikes, a ballistic missile with a fiery tail came streaming towards the Capitol, to be met in the sky by an anti-ballistic flare. The brilliant streams of light glowed eerily in the wet haze hanging over Alba, and the artificial thunder was strangely distorted. A loud drone flying in the distance caught her eye a moment before an Alban EMW strike brought it down; a melted and warped metal mass was all that was left to hit ground just outside the Merchant Terrace.

If she wasn't seeing it with her own eyes, she'd never believe it was possible. That Alba was capable of such defenses. That the Southern Empire actually existed. That battle would come to her perfectly peaceful State.

"Aerina."

Aerina glanced back to find Marcus watching her intently. She realized it hadn't been the first time he'd called her name.

"Are you alright?" he asked in a low voice, barely audible over another thunderous boom of a countered EMW strike.

"I will be," she answered with a small smile, reassuring him that she wasn't going to freak out. The last thing he needed now was a hysterical woman to deal with.

"There's nothing we can do here. Let's go back inside," he said quietly, taking her hand. She was embarrassed to realize he had to practically peel her grip away from the rail. She gripped his hand tightly, letting him lead her back into the office and down the hall to the tech room.

The room's inhabitants looked up as they entered.

"Is it bad?" Simon asked, looking at Aerina's pale face.

"It's going to get worse," Marcus said. "They're just testing our defenses. We can't know what weapons they might still have, waiting to use," he finished grimly. He gently pried the pack containing the hard drive from Aerina's grip.

"Simon, is the link still open with the enemy?" Simon nodded. "Good, I need you to upload this software to our system and use the link left open to infiltrate their network."

Simon was already nodding, his fingers working the keyboard, crafting a worm that could find its way through the open link into the heart of the Southern Empire's system.

Marcus grabbed a Medella kit, pulling out a syringe and slipping one of the vials into it.

"What are you doing?" Aerina asked, trying to keep the panic from her voice.

"I'm going to use the Technology the way it was used the first time it started the Global War to stop this war," Marcus told her grimly.

Aerina felt the panic continue to build. Whatever Marcus was doing, she knew there was no going back. As he moved to put the needle in his arm, Aerina grabbed the wrist holding the syringe.

His dark head shot up, obsidian eyes meeting her panicked blue ones.

"Don't do this. We can defeat them without it," Aerina begged, uncaring that the small group in the room pretended not to listen.

Marcus' eyes met hers as he paused, patiently waiting for her to regain control of her emotions.

"One mistake, one good strike, and they have us," he murmured, his voice quietly reassuring. "Do you think I would defy the Consul on whim? This is the only way or this Technology will belong to the Southern Empire, and we'll be another Sybil. Another Ryan."

Aerina gripped his wrist tightly, his words ringing true. Marcus had never lied to her. This was their only chance. Slowly, she let her hand relax and fall away. A moment later, the amber liquid in the vial was disappearing into Marcus' arm. Into his body.

The only sign of discomfort was a slight tightening in Marcus' jaw. The familiar tell she'd come to know well. One of the millions things she loved about him.

If anything happened to him…

Fighting down the panic that was again threatening to drown her, she focused blindingly on the screen in front of her, breathing deeply.

Flexing his arm, Marcus lightly set the syringe on the desk, looking to Simon.

"It's uploaded to our systems, but I'm having trouble getting into the—dammit, dammit, dammit!" The lanky man, his boyish features darkened with stubble, cursed loudly. He hunched even further over the virtual keyboard, typing quickly.

"Damn," he cursed again. "They've closed the link. We're out."

Marcus echoed his sentiments quietly.

"Stephen, you're up," he said quietly, looking at the other large man in the room. Stephen looked up from his station in surprise, standing quickly.

"What do you need?"

Aerina marveled at the change in her friend. His quietly arrogant ennui was gone, and in its place a nearly childish excitement radiated from his handsome face.

Marcus held up a second syringe, already loaded with a vial. "You're going to have to trust me. This is going to change your life."

"I think it's already changed," Stephen answered dryly as he strode forward to take the needle from Marcus. Marcus just watched him inject the liquid into his own arm, hissing as it flowed through his veins.

"Damn, that stings," he said through clenched teeth. Marcus' mouth quirked up at the corner. "Don't be such a little girl," he murmured, gaining surprised looks from the room.

"I'm going with you," Aerina said, stepping forward. Marcus was already shaking his head.

"The fewer people, the better. I need Stephen because he might need to help me navigate their software, or shut them down if I can't."

If he couldn't. Because he died trying.

The feeling of panic filled her chest again, a sharp pain in her heart. What would they do without Marcus? What would *she* do without him?

"Marcus, please, I won't be in the way. I—"

"No, Aerina," Marcus said again, pulling her into his arms without regard for the small audience. He kissed her, his mouth moving over hers gently, then with more force. Aerina relaxed slightly in his embrace, opening her mouth to feel the heat of his breath flow into her. After a moment that was too brief, he set her back gently.

His large, callused hand touched her cheek where a lone tear had escaped in spite of her efforts to contain it.

"I'll be back," he told her, stepping back and looking to Stephen. The other large man had busied himself securing the hard drive in a small pack that attached to his belt.

As the two men moved towards the door, Stephen paused beside Aerina, looking carefully ahead.

"Tell Lina... Everything is going to be alright. And tell Helen..." he trailed off, shooting Aerina a grin. "On second thought, better not tell her anything just yet." Aerina gave him a half smile in return, stepping forward to hug him tightly. He returned the squeeze, kissing her quickly on the cheek. Then he followed Marcus out the door.

Marcus left Aerina behind, standing in the tech room of the Training Grounds, looking more beautiful than he'd ever seen her. In her dark Pleb clothes, her hair mussed, face smudged, and dark circles under her eyes from little sleep, she'd stood bravely by his side. Defying the Consul for him; even her own father. And she had been willing to follow him up against an army of unknown magnitude, armed only with a weapon she knew nothing about.

He didn't know how he'd gotten so lucky to have the love of a woman like her, but if he survived this, he was never going to let her go again. Whatever changes happened to Alba after this battle, he was claiming Aerina, however she'd have him. Wife, partner, lover.

When he'd faced Julius in the Vault hallway, he'd known he wasn't defying the Consul just for Alba. He wasn't using the forbidden Technology they had all sworn to safeguard just to protect the city, or even the millions of inhabitants. He'd been swayed to betray his most important duty for her. For Aerina.

Saving her had become the most important thing in his world. He'd save Alba, and in doing so, he'd be saving Aerina.

"Get ready for a crash course in the Technology that changed the world," Marcus said softly as he pulled open the door to his car. "Hopefully not literally," he added beneath his breath, then almost smiled. He was starting to sound like Aerina.

"I'm ready," Stephen said with barely repressed enthusiasm.

Marcus sat down slowly and looked at the car steering wheel, imagining the engine turning on. Nothing happened. Relaxing his mind, he then imagined the ignition panel, seeing it in his head, then thinking of the ignition code embedded in his ID card.

The car rumbled to life, and he looked over at Stephen with satisfaction. The other man was eyeing him curiously.

"So, what was that?"

"Turn my car off," Marcus instructed brusquely, then grabbed the other man's arm as he reached over to hit the off button. "Without using the switch."

Stephen glanced at him curiously, looking back at the off switch. A look of surprise crossed his face, then concentration, and the car went silent, the engine going silent.

"Holy shit," Stephen breathed. "That's amazing. It's like the car's computer is in my head. I could see it. *Control it.*"

Marcus turned the car on again, mentally entering the code to open the underground garage and driving out. He closed it behind them. It was simple; almost as if an afterthought. As if the computer was really in his head; functioning within his neural pathways.

The two men drove in silence through the deserted streets. The terrified citizens had been ordered inside by the Armati patrolling. A few of the soldiers stationed near the Capitol nodded to Marcus as he passed. In a state of emergency, he was king.

Stephen seemed bursting with excitement, his eyes darting quickly. Finally, he burst out, "Every holocomputer, every holoreader, every villa system… I can access it. I can hack in, open files, send commands. It's amazing. It's like *I* have become the Network." He turned to look at Marcus, his eyes widening even further. "That's what we are going to do. Hack into the war ship. Control it."

Marcus nodded, parking the car near the Patrician tram. The trunk opened, and he began pulling gear out.

"Why can't we just hack their network from here?" Stephen asked, warily eyeing what Marcus was removing from the trunk. Climbing equipment.

"We need to be close enough to access their network. Unless they reopen their signal, I don't think we'll be able to get in from this distance with our Network down. Once we're in, we can piggyback off their network to ping whatever towers or satellite signals they're using," Marcus explained, handing him a pair of spike boots. "Suit up."

Stephen began pulling on the boots, looking wryly at his white slacks and white button down shirt. "I wish you would have mentioned mountain climbing was part of the job description," he complained good-naturedly. Marcus tossed a Virmortus vest at him.

"This should help a little," he told the other man, eyeing Stephen's fit form. "You shouldn't have any trouble. Aerina made it all the way down to the Pleb Terrace."

Stephen snorted. "I shouldn't be surprised she'd try it. But Aerina is not your average gentle Patrician lady."

Marcus' mouth quirked at the corner in agreement as he

slammed the car trunk lightly. The sound was drowned out by another boom of a countered strike.

"I hope you're in as good of shape as you look," he told Stephen grimly, all humor gone. "We're going to move fast."

Stephen nodded silently, his face equally somber. Grabbing their picks, the two tall men—one elegantly lean, the other powerfully muscled—began a controlled yet hurried descent towards the ocean.

Aerina stood in the tech room beside Simon, listening absently to his muttered cursing. Her thoughts were on the two men who might at this moment be heading towards their death.

"Their strikes are getting faster," Simon told Ramus, his voice loud in the muted atmosphere of the tech room. "Our defenses can hold up against their current voltage, but if they come too quickly for the Grounders..."

Aerina's eyes met Simon's for a long moment. Both had the same thought.

Julia.

The Training Grounds were protected, hidden back within the mountain. But the terraces were exposed; the Pleb city a large target of dense populace. A single strike could be devastating.

"I'll get her," Aerina told him quietly, resting a slender hand on his taut shoulder. He relaxed slightly, nodding. Aerina turned to the door, only to be brought up short when a tall, ebony form glided in front of her.

"Where are you going?" Ramus asked lightly, his dark gaze belying the casualness of his question.

"To get Julia," Aerina answered shortly, her eyes darting to where Simon sat hunched over his station.

"I can't let you leave, Aerina. If Marcus knew you were out there—"

"He won't," Aerina cut in. Her slender form was stiff and tense, bracing for an argument. Ramus smiled slightly at her tenacity.

"The Ferry isn't working. How will you get down to her?"

Aerina opened her mouth, then shut it. He was right. Even if she could climb down the mountainside again, it was doubtful she would be able to get both Julia and Jamia back up with her.

"Isn't there any way to communicate with the lower terraces?" she asked in frustration.

"I can radio an Armati to check on them, but they won't be able to come here," Ramus told her gently. His radio crackled and he turned away, responding to the distorted voice coming from the small speaker.

Aerina absently smoothed the end of her long ponytail, thinking. She wanted to see what was going on outside.

As she exited the tech room, she could feel Ramus' eyes on her. But he was conferring with a few of his men, and didn't follow.

Out on the balcony, Aerina could see the intensity of the battle had increased. The strikes were more frequent, coming nearly on top of each other. Each strike was countered by Grounders, but it almost seemed to her that the time between the flash of lightning and the countering streak of light was a millisecond longer than before.

Or maybe she was just freaking out a little.

She looked out over the city-state. The fog had thickened with the coming evening, covering the city in its damp embrace.

She worried about Marcus. About Julia. About her parents, Stephen, Lina, Helen... She hated standing here, doing nothing. Feeling so helpless. So useless.

When the boom and pop echoed through the city, Aerina thought it was just another countered strike. Then the smell rose on the fog. The smell of melted metal and charred wood, of burning. Death. Smoke curled within the wisps of grey moisture in a macabre dance.

"Julia," Aerina murmured, her heart frozen in her chest as she stared hard at the Pleb city far below. A circular section of the city glowed red-hot, the inner circle a black hole of burnt rubble.

Ramus and several others, including Simon, burst onto the office balcony. Ramus was barking orders into his radio. Simon walked slowly to stand by Aerina, his hands curling tightly around the rail.

"It was countered on the ground." Simon's voice was raspy as if he was barely holding himself together.

Aerina reached out to place a comforting hand on the tall man's back, but withdrew before actually touching him. Nothing would help until he knew Julia was alright.

"We're going down," Aerina said firmly. "Turn on the Network. We're getting the injured citizens here, to the Capitol Terrace. Ready the clinics."

Ramus looked at her thoughtfully, the radio still held aloft in his hand. The Virmortus' dark eyes traveled to where Simon stood, poised to return to the tech room and follow Aerina's orders. She could see him weighing their options. He nodded his cropped head slowly.

"Yes."

Stephen and Marcus carried two longboards into the surf, their grey wetsuits blending with the heavy mist as they paddled slowly towards the distant ship. Flashes of artificial lightning eerily illuminated the fog-shrouded city.

The city had looked abandoned as they descended the cliff, the Armati following directions to keep citizens indoors.

The ship grew larger as they approached, the hulking sides with a flattened top looming in the fog like a small floating city. Unlike the silent Alban city, the ship bustled with activity. They were preparing for an invasion.

Marcus stroked steadily beside Stephen, both men cutting quickly through the small waves.

"We should be close enough. Let's try to get into their network without boarding the ship," Marcus said in an undertone. Stephen nodded, sitting up on his board.

"Stay low!" Marcus said, pulling the other man down. "Their radar is going to catch us eventually and we don't want to make it easier for them."

"I think it already did." Several small boats ejected from the ship's side, heading straight toward the two men. Marcus calmly pulled several weapons from his wetsuit, and Stephen fumbled to follow suit.

Marcus stood absolutely still in the small, below-level room on the war ship. Stephen stood beside him, brow furrowed in concentration.

They'd been captured by the Southern Empire.

Several bodies had been floating in the water after the confrontation, but Marcus and Stephen had both been taken.

"Don't harm them; they're carrying the device," the leader had ordered. He'd stood before Marcus, a small, somewhat pudgy man in his late fifties. He hadn't aged well. His jowls hung low, and deep lines had creased the commander's face.

His control over the ship and its crew was obvious. They reacted quickly, almost fearfully, to every order.

They'd been taken to this interrogation room, stripped and searched and beaten. It had finally been determined that the "device" had been injected intravenously, and a tech team had been summoned to determine the best way to extract it. Both Stephen and Marcus wore collars. If they stepped outside the room, they would be rendered unconscious.

"They were ready for us; for our Technology," Stephen muttered. "Their firewall is quite impressive."

"Can you get in?" Marcus was able to see the firewall but didn't have the knowledge to hack in.

Stephen smiled, his swollen, split lip cracking open and a bead of fresh blood seeping out. "Of course. I just need a little more time."

"We might not have much of that." Footsteps echoed in the tiled hallway outside.

A large man stepped into the room. He was tall but what once might have been muscle had given to fat. Like the leader, this man's jowls hung low, and a large belly swayed when he walked. A nicotine stick hung from his mouth. He couldn't have been older than Marcus, but he appeared to have aged much more quickly.

Marcus was again caught off-guard by the apparent lack of concern over health this society seemed to have.

"Well, my men have told me that the only way to recoup the device is by removing your blood, as that seems to be where it's currently housed," the large man drawled, releasing a puff of vapor. Neither Marcus nor Stephen responded to the deliberate taunt. The large man seemed disappointed.

Marcus could see Stephen working on the virtual plane, but was unable to help him. The firewall was holding strong. He needed to give the other man more time.

"Are you certain that is going to get you what you came for?" Marcus asked quietly. The large man puffed deeply on his nicotine stick, his already beady eyes nearly disappearing in sweaty folds as he frowned in consideration. Then his brow cleared and a slow smile spread across his clean-shaven face.

"I do believe they're nervous, after all, Geoffry," he spoke jovially to the smaller, edgy man standing by his side. The small man flashed a false grin, shifting from one foot to the other.

"It would be a shame if you screwed up after coming all this way. Your general doesn't seem like a man who tolerates screw-ups," Marcus said evenly, his eyes on the obviously nervous Geoffry.

The small man shifted again, his eyes widening slightly and pupils dilating in a sure tell of fear. Obviously the general was not a very nice man.

"Bring in the team," the large man commanded, his thick lips still parted in a smile. He was looking forward to whatever they were about to do.

"Um, sir," Geoffry began nervously.

"What?" barked the large man impatiently.

"Perhaps we should que-question them," Geoffrey stammered. "Before we kill them."

"Nonsense. He's just trying to stall. Once we have the device we came for, we can obliterate this useless city and head home. It's damn cold here, and the mist makes my knee ache."

Geoffry said nothing, just continued to shift nervously as two men came in carrying chairs. They then took up positions near the door. At least the soldiers were fit, unlike their leaders, Marcus thought in disgust, mentally cataloguing and dismissing the two men as a threat.

Marcus assessed the situation quickly. He could easily neutralize the soldiers. Fatty and Geoffry would be no problem. The real issue was the collar. If Stephen couldn't get into their network, they'd be stuck in this room even after killing the men.

He shot Stephen a look. The other man just shook his head slightly, pressing a hand to his temple as if he had a headache.

Two men in lab coats entered the room carrying syringe kits and large bags. To collect their blood, no doubt. As the first man opened a kit, pulling out a syringe, Marcus moved quickly. He had to buy them time.

The syringe made little sound as it struck the man's artery, a thin line of blood pumping quickly from his neck with each heartbeat, arching across the room. The man's eyes were wide in shock as Marcus released him to use the same syringe on the second medical man.

The two soldiers rushed forward to subdue Marcus, but he was ready for them, taking one down with a well-placed kick, breaking the other's neck with a twist of his hands. He finished the first attacker by collapsing his windpipe with a boot to his throat.

Geoffry cowered behind Fatty as Marcus paced forward, his dark eyes locked on the obese man's beady green ones. He never made it to his target. Fatty must have a remote that gave him control over the collar.

No wonder he was so arrogant, Marcus thought as blackness sucked him down. His last thought was that hopefully the useless effort had at least bought Stephen a little more time.

Chapter 22

"We came equals into this world, and equals shall we go out of it." - George Mason

Aerina tapped her foot impatiently, urgency building in her chest as they cruised towards the Ferry. Ramus drove the car with the same easy grace that Marcus did, the familiar sight sending another shaft of worry through Aerina's already overloaded heart.

She pushed the thought of Marcus to the back of her mind. If she dwelled on those concerns, she'd become a useless blubbering mess. And people needed her help.

It had probably been less than fifteen minutes since the EMW strike had hit the Pleb city, but it seemed like hours. Each minute crawled by in desperate intensity as Aerina waited for Simon and the tech team in the Virmortus headquarters to turn the Network back on.

She and Ramus had already stopped at the Capitol Medella Clinic to order the clinicians to ready their supplies and head to the Ferry.

A few had been hesitant to leave the false safety of the clinic, but a surprisingly large number had begun readying supplies without question or complaint. It had warmed Aerina's heart to see the eagerness of the Capitol health workers, who were essentially of the Patrician caste, to help the Plebs.

The Ferry perched on the edge of the Capitol Terrace, the large glass-enclosed structure looking more fragile than ever amid the periodic strikes and counter strikes flashing around it.

Like an old world lighthouse, it was lit from within, shining through the fog that still lingered over the dark city. A beacon of hope. And a target for the enemy.

As they neared the edge, Aerina couldn't help but stare at the distant warship, wondering. Was Marcus aboard? Was he at this moment working with Stephen to neutralize the ship? Or was he captured.

Or dead. His body floating in the fog-shrouded surf...

"Don't." Ramus' voice cut through her increasingly morose thoughts. His large hand settled on hers, an unusual display by the taciturn man. Aerina shot him a thankful half-smile.

"What's taking so long?" she asked.

Ramus leaned forward slightly, scanning the area around them before answering. "They're making sure everyone's chips are removed or disabled. No sense in sharing even more information with the enemy than we already have."

Aerina nodded her understanding, but it didn't alleviate the sense of urgency that continued to build with each passing moment. Already it had been too long. People were injured; dying. Every second mattered.

The Medella were pulling up in the specially built emergency vehicles that could each carry several individuals to city clinics. Mobile Clinics were fully equipped with much of the life-saving technology that was needed in emergency situations, including the synthetic blood that had been a recent breakthrough.

Aerina did a double-take when she noticed Helen riding shotgun in one of the vehicles. Glancing at Ramus, Aerina hopped out of the car and jogged over to her friend. She barely winced at the loud boom of a countered strike over their heads.

"What are you doing here?" Aerina asked as Helen lowered her window.

"I studied medical as my secondary focus," Helen said matter-of-factly. "The extra help might be needed. Lina is coming, too. She told me you would probably be in the car leading the charge. She was right, I see."

Aerina smiled at her friend, surprised at the unexpected support of the Patricians. Right now, they were all just Albans, fighting a common enemy. Bonded together by stronger ties than occupation or caste.

"I'll see you below," Aerina murmured, jogging quickly back to Ramus' black military vehicle. She waved to Lina further back in another van, hoping her friend didn't know about

Stephen.

As she slipped into the passenger seat, she heard Ramus' low-voiced exclamation, "We're back up." Then he added more loudly out the window, "Let's head out."

"Holy shit." Marcus awoke to Stephen's quietly breathed words. His vision was blurry, his head pounding, and every muscle in his body ached. With careful focus, he was able to take in his surroundings.

They were still in the small room they had been held in, and two new men in lab coats were busy prepping a small table for another attempt at extracting the Technology.

Fatty stood near the door, several extra guards stationed around him.

Stephen was strapped in a chair next to him, metal bands cinched tightly around their arms and legs, making it impossible to move.

As Marcus' mind began to clear, he was able to see why Stephen was so excited.

The Alban Network was back up, and with it, the open connection to the Southern Empire's network. A back door through the firewall.

Marcus met Stephen's gaze. The other man was silently asking what he wanted taken out first. Marcus looked over at Fatty. The man gripped the remote tightly, his beady eyes scanning the room. He'd have to be the first this time.

Marcus looked up at the lights for a long moment, then at the electronic chairs. It was easier to have everything on a shared network. And now it was going to make Marcus' job much easier, too.

Stephen nodded, and a few moments later, the lights went out, while at the same time Marcus felt his bands retracting into the chair.

He was across the room before the whirring of the bands' motor had quieted, feeling Fatty's large frame before him. A moment later, the large man lay on the ground, unbreathing, and Marcus held the remote in his own hand. In his mind's eye, he could see Stephen working quickly to shut down as many of the warship's systems as he could.

The lights started to fire up from the emergency back up, but Stephen was quick to shut those down and the room was once again shrouded in darkness. In the moment of clarity, Marcus was able to see the two lab techs cowering against the wall, and the guards looking around uneasily.

They were easy to neutralize, their skills nothing compared to what the Virmortus were taught. Technology could not be used as a crutch, because technology could fail. It was one of the most important lessons a Virmortus was taught. It was a lesson learned by the world during the Global War.

Apparently the Southern Empire hadn't learned that lesson quite so well.

"Let's go," Marcus said quietly, mentally scanning the map Stephen had shared with him. It was amazing, this technology. It was like he had a computer built into his mind, the amazing natural processer of neurons merged with the store of information and control from its machine counterpart.

Keeping a hand on the wall, they exited the total blackness into the equally dark hallway.

The Ferry was bursting with Mobile Clinics and Patricians that had gathered to help their fellow citizens. Aerina sat in Ramus' car, tapping her foot, shifting continually.

"You're making me nervous," Ramus said with quiet humor.

"Sorry." Aerina tried to force herself to sit still.

"When we reach the bottom, we will assign a section of the area to each Mobile Clinic. Armati will be meeting us to assist in search and rescue," he told her, his hand on the door handle as they both felt the Ferry click into place on the Pleb Terrace.

Aerina stood beside Ramus as he instructed the gathered citizens, using a map of the sector to show each group which area they would be responsible for. His calm confidence settled on them, and each face held determination; hope.

The caravan of vehicles split up as they neared the market

area that had been hit. Aerina bit her lip until the metallic flavor of blood filled her mouth. The formerly bustling city center, which lay near the Pleb beach, was a heap of stone, melted metal, and unrecognizable rubble scorched black. And the smell. It was all sulfur, so strong it seared her nostrils.

How could anyone have survived this?

The horror of it all struck her anew. It seemed as if the fog in the air had settled in her mind, making everything distant and muted.

From her distant place, she watched the team closest to her rush from their Mobile Clinic, the armed soldiers leading the way. Pleb citizens waved them down, huddled around bodies lying prone on the burnt ground. One older man limped towards the MC, one leg twisted and distorted as if it had melted in the blast.

Reality came rushing back, breaking through the fog, the scene before her clearing, sounds growing louder. Throwing open her door, she rushed after Ramus, following cries for help into the heart of the city.

Aerina's holoreader beeped. Her heart lifted. Julia had responded to her message. *We are ok. Helping the injured.*

She worked, lifting rubble, searching for life amid the devastation. Other Patricians, including Helen and Lina, worked alongside her. The minutes passed quickly, the labor keeping her mind from the two men absent from the scene.

"Aerina!"

Aerina turned towards the sound of her name, relief flooding her as she saw Julia rushing towards her. She pulled her friend into a tight embrace.

"Jamia?" she asked, pulling back to see the other woman's dirt-streaked face.

"She's fine, helping at the emergency clinic set up in a warehouse," Julia answered, turning with Aerina to view the destruction. "What is going on? No one knows for sure."

Aerina opened her mouth, then closed it again. "It's a long story," she said finally. "But we'll defeat them. Marcus has a plan," she added reassuringly.

Julia shook her head. "If anyone could do it, it would be your Reaper. But this is not your normal threat. This is war, Aerina. We've never known war."

"Have faith," Aerina said quietly. "He's more than just a Reaper."

"I hope you're right."

Marcus and Stephen waited just below deck, backs pressed against the cool metal of the hallway wall.

"The systems are shut down," Stephen said in a barely audible voice. "Simon is uploading the worm right now; it should go from the ship's network to their command center back east. Now we just need to get the hell off this ship."

Marcus nodded. "Once we're off, I'll set the weapons to fire on the ship. We need to wait until the worm is completely loaded, in case we need to use the hard drive." He held the sack with the small hard drive containing a second copy of the powerful software that would spread through the Southern Empire's network, wreaking havoc on their technology and possibly opening it for control remotely by Marcus and Stephen.

The silence stretched for a moment as they waited for the sound of pounding footsteps just outside to pass. The ship was in chaos.

"This is more excitement than I'd ever guessed I'd see," Stephen finally commented wryly, breaking the silence.

"And I never thought I'd use all the skills I was forced to learn," Marcus agreed quietly.

Marcus heard Stephen turn to look at him in the darkened hallway.

"You know," he said softly, "I always wondered why the Virmortus were necessary, and had even thought of proposing to dissolve the group."

"They were protecting the Technology. It was the founders' reason for creating the group," Marcus said quietly.

"If they were so worried, why didn't they just destroy it?"

"They created it. Perhaps they couldn't." Marcus pressed back further against the metal wall behind him as footsteps sounded loudly above them, his voice dropping even further. "Or perhaps they knew a day would come when they would need it."

From the strange connection between Marcus' mind and the networks around him, he could "see" that the worm was now uploaded; it was already hard at work attacking the remaining firewall between the ship and its host servers back in the Empire.

"We're clear. Now for the hard part," he muttered, sliding closer to the opening to the lower deck.

"Straight over the side?" Stephen asked, moving carefully to the other side of the hallway so he, too, could look out at the chaos not far from their hiding spot.

Men were inspecting the large EMWs and ballistic weapons out on deck, some shouting, others looking baffled. Most men had removed the headgear they had been wearing, as they no longer transmitted orders but a loud, unending beep.

It was about a hundred feet from the storage hallway in which they hid to the side of the ship. Once to the edge, they would need to dive carefully over the side. Hitting the water from this height at the wrong angle could result in broken bones, a concussion, or death.

"Ready?" Marcus asked.

"No," Stephen replied, tightening up his gear, "But let's do it."

"You go first. I'll detonate a small ballistic on the far side to draw attention. As soon as it implodes, head towards the side and don't stop. For anything," Marcus instructed succinctly. Stephen nodded, unnecessarily tightening the strap to his pack again.

The explosion.

All the men on the deck turned toward the sound.

Stephen took off running, his long legs carrying him quickly across the deck. Marcus took off behind him.

Sixty yards.

Marcus glanced up at the upper deck as he ran.

Forty yards.

Outside of the control room stood the little general. He

looked at them in fury. He knew exactly what was happening.

Twenty yards.

He was lifting his weapon. A small EMW. Not on the network.

Ten yards.

Stephen was already climbing the side, getting ready to throw a leg over the high metal rail.

Marcus braced himself for the burning shock, sparing a last glance at the general.

But it wasn't Marcus he was aiming at.

Stephen.

Marcus reached for the other man, but he was a few yards short.

The low pop sounded and Stephen stiffened up before going limp, his body tumbling over the side just out of Marcus' grasp.

Marcus didn't bother looking back again. Without hesitation, he leaped to the side, vaulting over and diving after Stephen.

The other man's body was hitting the water far below as Marcus cleared the side. The sensation of falling stole Marcus' breath away as the misty air raced past his face.

He kept his eyes on the spot where Stephen's body was slowly sinking below the rolling waves. A moment later, his own body hit the water as he slid into its icy embrace with barely a splash. Using the force of his dive, he propelled under the water to the spot where Stephen's body had disappeared.

Seconds passed that seemed like hours as he searched the muffled darkness. The pressure inside his lungs grew as the used air strained to escape, his throat tightening with the effort to hold in the last bit of oxygen.

Just as he was about to head up for air, his hand touched something solid and he grabbed hold. Kicking up, he dragged the impossibly heavy dead weight towards the surface.

His head broke the surface and he gasped in air, dragging up Stephen's limp body until the other man's face was above the water.

Stephen was limp, and Marcus couldn't feel a pulse.

Ignoring the sinking fear that Stephen was already dead, Marcus began slowly kicking in the direction of the distant shore. Wading through the myriad of commands in the network, he finally found what he was looking for, and a covered lifeboat was forcefully ejected from the starboard side in which they floated.

As it hit the water, Marcus began stroking powerfully towards it, opening the back hatch as he neared.

Aerina stood beside a Medella, holding a bandage tightly around a melted, bleeding stump that had been a young girl's arm.

"Perfect, just like that," the Medella murmured, expertly tightening the bandage, glancing continually at the unconscious girls' face. The girl, not much older than Jamia, had passed out from shock a moment after Aerina had uncovered her from the melted rubble of a small café. She had tried to grab Aerina's hand, only to realize the entire appendage had been burned off.

Aerina looked away, her eyes taking in the shocking scene around her. Other Medella worked methodically and tirelessly around the large square where the heaviest damage had been done. With the Medella were citizens that had rushed to help.

Everyone was covered in the black char that stained much of the debris, wearing masks either acquired from the Armati or makeshift masks of clothing tied around the nose and mouth.

It was impossible to tell who was Pleb, Merchant, or Patrician. At this moment, everyone looked the same. Dirty. Exhausted. Determined.

Aerina looked back down at the girl the Medella worked on.

"Are you ok?" the doctor asked as she finished wrapping the cleaned and cauterized stump. Aerina looked up quickly, nodding.

"Yes, I'm fine," she answered quietly, realizing it was almost the truth. No matter what happened — to her, to Alba, to Marcus — the world around them was indelibly changed. She no longer felt lost; like an outsider looking in at the world around her. She knew where she belonged. That nothing, no one, was perfect. And that was ok.

Looking up again, she realized that it had been surprisingly quiet for at least ten or fifteen minutes. Not a single strike had fired since Julia had returned to the emergency clinic. A rush of excitement filled her as she looked out at the distant ship. Perhaps Marcus and Stephen had succeeded.

As she watched, the ship exploded before her eyes. The brilliant flash of light was nearly blinding, and she instinctively shielded her eyes, the loud blast shaking the ground beneath them.

Everyone stopped what they were doing to watch the ship remnants going up in flames as burning pieces carried high into the air began raining down into the ocean.

Aerina's heart was frozen in her chest and she couldn't seem to move.

Marcus.

She realized she was gripping the unconscious girl's hand and forced herself to let go.

He got out. He got out. She repeated the words in her head, refusing to believe he had still been on the ship.

But she knew he would have detonated the ship while still on it if he thought it was the only way.

He's too quick. Too smart. Too strong.

Another long moment of frozen silence followed. Then a loud cheer broke out, spreading like a wave throughout the city. As the resounding noise faded, everyone began turning back to their gruesome work of recovering bodies and tending to the injured.

"She's ready for a stretcher and we'll send her to a recovery room," the Medella said quietly, waving to an Armati. Aerina couldn't look away from the burning ship, her eyes desperately scanning the hazy water for a sign of...something. Anything to give her a glimmer of hope.

"Aerina?" the Medella said gently, her hand resting on Aerina's arm. "Do what you can. And let the rest go."

Aerina stood for another moment in silence before nodding. It was good advice.

Do what she could.

Let the rest go.

Turning to help the doctor lift the girl onto a waiting stretcher, she heard shouts from the beach. Spinning back around, she took a step forward.

A large lifeboat was beached and a familiar figure was climbing out swiftly, a large form over his shoulders.

Marcus.

Without realizing it, Aerina was running towards him, along with several others.

She met his ebony eyes and her steps faltered briefly. The darkness she saw there was shocking. Then she looked at the figure he carried, now in his arms as he lowered the body gently to the sand.

Stephen.

Stumbling forward, she raised a shaking hand to her mouth.

Falling to her knees beside Stephen she touched his familiar face. It was unnaturally cold. No life beat beneath the surface, his bright blue eyes staring blankly at the grey sky above.

Suddenly she was catapulted back to a long ago day. Another familiar, lifeless face pulled from the water.

Max, just breathe! Please take a breath, please! I'm so sorry. I shouldn't have taken you swimming. I'm so sorry!

"This is all your fault!" *Her mother screamed over and over.*

All your fault.

An anguished scream brought her back to the present, to the numbing pain spreading through her limbs. She saw Lina drop to her knees beside her brother.

The sounds around her faded to a buzzing silence as she was gently pushed aside by medical workers who checked Stephen's pulse, hooking him to a machine and telling everyone to step back. From a distance, she watched his large body jerk as they tried to restart his heart.

Lina was forcibly held back as the doctors worked, and the other woman's anguished gaze went to Marcus as he stood silently over the scene.

"You bastard! You did this to my brother. You forced him to

help you and now he's dead!" Lina lunged at Marcus, her tall frame allowing her to easily reach his head, her fisted hand connecting solidly with his cheek. He stood, unmoving, as her other fist connected again. Two Armati pulled her back and she collapsed between them, her body wracked with soul-wrenching sobs.

Aerina watched the scene as if from a distance, her arms wrapped tightly around her middle, her gaze still on Stephen's lifeless form. Scenes from her childhood flashed before her, of Stephen helping her and Lina with homework. Standing up to bullies. Teaching her how to surf. Serious, responsible Stephen.

Her eyes finally focused, rising to meet Marcus' empty gaze.

His eyes met hers unflinchingly, as if in challenge. She stared at him uncomprehendingly as wave after wave of sorrow washed over her. She needed Marcus. Needed him to hold her. To tell her everything would be ok.

But he was pulling away. He was blocking her out, turning back into the unreachable man he'd been before.

Then through the haze of her own pain, she realized something. He was afraid. Afraid of feeling emotion. Of caring. He felt responsible, and he expected her to hold him responsible, too. Like Lina did.

Without thought of the people around her, she rose unsteadily in the sand and practically fell into Marcus, wrapping her arms around his stiff body and letting the tears fall unchecked.

After a long moment, his stiff body seemed to collapse and his arms went around her, nearly crushing her in their hold.

She didn't care, wishing she could get even closer. Resting her forehead on his chest, she wept. Sobs wracked her body — tears for Stephen and Lina, for the people hurt and dying around them, for the life they had all lost. And she wept for herself. For the brother she'd lost. For the friend she'd taken for granted. The parents who'd pushed her away in their grief. The life she'd given up. For the man she loved.

As her tears slowed, she squeezed Marcus and stepped back. Turning to Lina, she stepped forward to embrace her friend. Her sister.

But the other woman turned away, a look of hatred crossing her face. Kneeling, Lina gently brushed hair back from her brother's pale face, kissing his cheek gently. Helen was crouched on Stephen's other side, her hand holding his. Tears streamed silently down her soot-streaked face. The Medellas were slowly packing up their gear, some already moving on to other patients.

Stephen was dead.

And she was just as much to blame as Marcus.

More so.

And Lina knew it.

This is all your fault.

The words that her mother had spoken on the day of Max's death, the words that had haunted her since, echoed again in her mind. But for the first time, she accepted the guilt without letting it crush her.

Do what you can.

Let go of the rest.

Chapter 23

"Change is the law of life." - John F. Kennedy

Aerina felt like the fog had descended in her mind. She stayed with Marcus, watching Helen leading a broken, weeping Lina away. Ramus came, conferring with Marcus. The Consul still needed to be dealt with and the future of Alba needed to be decided.

The warship was gone, but it was only the beginning of the changes for Alba.

With Ramus overseeing the continued recovery and relocation, Aerina went with Marcus back to the Capitol Terrace. They made the journey in silence, their hands clasped tightly. Aerina refused to release Marcus' hand, needing that reassurance.

Marcus went straight to the interrogation room holding Julius. The Virmortus standing guard nodded respectfully as Marcus strode past, their eyes lingering curiously on Aerina.

She ignored their long stares, determined to see this to the end.

"Marcus?" Julius asked quietly as they both entered, his demeanor difficult to discern.

"It's over," Marcus stated, sitting before Julius at the table. Aerina stood near the door as unobtrusively as possible.

Julius said nothing, waiting for Marcus to continue. Even with everything between them, the men still understood one another, possibly better than anyone else.

Marcus gave a quick and concise summary of events, shocking Aerina with the hopelessness of the situation he had overcome. Julius sat quietly, his manacled hands clasped lightly in front of him on the table as he listened.

When Marcus finished, Julius finally spoke.

"They won't stop here."

"No," Marcus agreed.

Julius sighted. "Those damn founders should have destroyed the Technology when it first nearly destroyed the world."

"They still would have come looking for it," Marcus said matter-of-factly. "We could never prove it was gone. But we can use it to survive. And perhaps study it; find out how it can be better controlled."

Julius sighed again, staring towards the wall for a long moment.

"Alright, you had your fun, now cut me lose," he instructed, lifting his bound hands. Marcus' mouth quirked in his version of a smile and the manacles opened and slid into the table.

"Enjoying your new skill, hmm?" Julius murmured dryly, rubbing his wrists. Marcus just smiled again and the door slid open.

"Aerina," Julius nodded to her politely and she bowed her head respectfully, still a little in shock over the casualness of this encounter. She had expected a little more drama, similar to the confrontation in the Vault hallway. Certainly not this friendly conversation. Her confused gaze met Marcus'. He just shook his head, the slight smile still on his face.

The Consul rose. "Well, Marcus—"

"I hate to wreck this cheerful scene," interrupted a sneering voice from the hallway. "But I'm afraid not everything is resolved. We need to talk about my mother." Aerina looked over quickly to see Niko standing with an EMW held to his father's head. The heir's bodyguard stood behind him, another weapon trained steadily on Marcus.

"I wondered when you'd make your move," Marcus said calmly, widening his stance slightly, letting his arms hang loosely at his side. Aerina recognized that stance. He was preparing.

She saw the bodyguard's hand tighten slightly on the weapon and her own muscles tensed, ready to move.

"Do you even know the truth about your mother?" Marcus asked softly.

"I know enough," Niko snapped. "The Southern Empire came me about what Father had done to her, and told me they would help depose him if I got them information." His pale blue eyes darted to Marcus and back to his father, gleaming with unholy delight and rage. He'd waited years for this moment. "You murdering, arrogant bastard. You think you're so smart. So *mighty.* You never treated me like your son. Mother respected me, cared about me, until you *killed* her." Remembered sorrow twisted his face in an angry grimace, his hand tightening on the gun. Aerina could see from the way Julius flinched that the weapon was pressed tightly to his head. Niko opened his mouth to continue, years of pent-up rage needing to be purged.

Then the lights went out.

Aerina stood frozen in the darkness, hearing a small whistle followed by a thud and a high-pitched shriek. She listened for the telling 'pop' of the EMW, afraid to even breathe in case someone fired.

Then the lights came back on and she blinked against the brightness. As her gaze focused, she saw two men on the ground. Niko was slumped against the door, struggling to remove a throwing knife from his shoulder. His bodyguard appeared unconscious.

Relief rushed over her tingling nerve ends, making her dizzy. Marcus walked over to Niko and his accomplice, scooping the EMWs from the ground. He clicked on the safeties, and removed the small generator pack.

Julius stood beside the open door, rubbing his head where the weapon had been pressed a few moments before. "I'll do my own dirty work this time." He walked forward slowly, his hand outstretched. Marcus paused, dark eyes narrowing slightly as he studied the Consul.

He gave Julius the ties he was going to use to secure the captives. The Consul took them and stood before his son.

"Son, you surprised me today. I didn't think you had it in you. You've been quite a disappointment to me." Niko didn't even look up at his father's words, his blood-slick hand still gripping the handle of the throwing knife in his shoulder. Julius continued regretfully. "I'm sorry about your mother. And for this." Julius grabbed the knife from Niko's shoulder, plunging it into the young man's heart. Before the echo of Aerina's gasp faded in the barren room, Julius had turned on Marcus, an EMW in his hand.

Marcus stood, unmoving, meeting Julius' guileless blue eyes.

"I'm truly sorry about this, Marcus," Julius said regretfully, his lean finger tight on the trigger. "I would have made you my heir, but I could never maintain the balance if a killer was to take over the Consulship."

"You were just pretending to be unconcerned about Marcus' defection?" Aerina asked, trying to keep her voice calm. Inside, emotions rampaged. Fear, horror, shock.

"He wasn't worried about my defection because he already planned to kill me," Marcus responded quietly, his eyes still intent on Julius. Was he waiting for his chance to strike?

Julius smiled. "You always were too smart for your own good. You see, my dear," he directed his explanation to Aerina, but kept his eyes on Marcus, "The Virmortus have been growing more powerful with each passing generation. At this point, the Consulship is more of a figure. Without Marcus' backing, I am powerless. He knows it. Many of the Virmortus know it. And the Senators know it. How can I rule without power?" Julius asked rhetorically.

"You contacted the Southern Empire to kill Marcus," Aerina breathed, her eyes moving from Julius' serene features to Marcus' unreadable ones. Had he known all along?

"Yes, I'm afraid I had no choice. And it was time to ally ourselves, perhaps even open trade. My wife found out, but Marcus took care of that little problem. Tell me, Marcus, because I've been dying to know. How did you find out about me?"

"The man you sent after Aerina. Anyone will talk, with the right incentive," Marcus finally spoke, embers of anger burning deep in his dark eyes.

Julius looked surprised for a moment, but his weapon never wavered. Aerina shuffled her feet slightly. The Consul didn't seem to notice, his eyes locked on Marcus.

"That is a little surprising. I suppose I should have questioned him myself before I killed him. Unfortunately, my plan did backfire a little. The Southern Empire learned of the Technology, thanks to Niko here, and of course they wanted it. I agreed to a trade once Marcus was dead, but when they failed to kill him in Sybil, they gave up and decided to just take it," Julius' even voice grew hard, his face contorting. Aerina was shocked to see the change in him; watched him struggle to bring himself back under control.

"Once again, Marcus saved the day. Oh, I know they'll be back. But now I know how to use the Technology against them. And without Marcus, the Virmortus will be easy to dissolve.

"Now stop stalling and tell me, Marcus, and I'll spare your girlfriend here. She can escape into the desert. Where did you hide the vials? Because I know you didn't destroy them all."

"They're gone. All that's left of The Technology is coursing through my veins."

"I don't believe you. But I don't need you conscious to extract it. I truly am sorry, Marcus," the Consul said again, "You were like a son to me." Then he laughed.

Aerina lunged forward as the Consul's finger tightened on the trigger, throwing herself between him and Marcus. Her body was braced for whatever burn or shock would come from the weapon, her nerve endings screaming in anticipation.

Marcus caught her before him, gently setting her aside.

Her own surprised gaze met that of the Consul's.

"What...?" Julius muttered, his finger repeatedly squeezing the trigger, his eyes going wide as Marcus began to walk forward.

Before the older man could run, Marcus gripped his arm tightly, grabbing the weapon with his other hand. Julius moved to strike Marcus, his attempt easily blocked. Marcus drew back one large fist and threw his own punch, knocking the Consul to the ground.

He stood over his former leader, casually holding the EMW down at his side.

"When I determined the traitor was someone on the inside, I had all the weapons changed to require a biometric scan. Only a few can now fire or authorize any weapon in Alba," Marcus explained quietly.

Julius sat up slowly, angrily swiping blood from his dripping nose.

"Bastard. Who has authorization?" he demanded.

"I do," Marcus answered softly, raising his arm and pulling the trigger. Aerina let out a soft shriek as the gun popped and arced. She instinctively looked away. When she looked back, the Consul still sat on the ground, cowering. The Virmortus traitor behind Niko's body lay frozen in the rictus of death, a knife he had been about to throw still spinning slowly on the stone floor where he had dropped it.

"I'm done here," Marcus called, and Ramus appeared. Aerina stood stiffly, still in shock, trying to assimilate what had all just happened.

"Tell Aerina why you tried to have her killed, while we are tying up loose ends."

The Consul glared at them both, and Aerina thought he wasn't going to answer. A look of disgust crossed his face. "I started getting blackmail threats after those dancers were killed. Someone knew about Niko's connection and dared to blackmail *me*." He glared at Aerina. "I thought for sure it was you; that the stupid little hooker had told her friends something. But I learned later it was the sister. It was too late to do anything; Marcus was having her watched."

Ramus took the sullen Consul away, leaving just Aerina and Marcus in the interrogation room.

He turned slowly, walking forward and laying his hands on her shoulders.

"Don't ever do that again," he ordered, his voice sounding gruff.

"What?"

"Step between me and a weapon."

"I'm not going to just stand by and watch you die," Aerina retorted.

"And I can't watch you die," Marcus responded, his voice cracking. Jerking her forward, his arms went around her in a crushing embrace. Aerina let a small smile cross her face, hidden as it was against his chest.

Real love was madness, but it was an insanity she would embrace.

Aerina took Marcus' e-car, scanning the ID he gave her to start it. He had promised he wouldn't be long.

Many things needed to still be done. The battle had been won, but the war was only beginning.

She drove slowly through the empty streets. Rather than the atmosphere of quiet seclusion that normally permeated the evening, the terrace felt abandoned. Lonely.

Aerina turned down the back street, away from her villa. She pulled the e-car into Marcus' carport and let herself into his villa using the same card.

She was home. This was where she belonged.

Without hesitation, she stripped out of her filthy, char-covered clothes and rinsed off in his shower. The weight of the day, the sorrow of Stephen's death, and enormity of all that had happened made it impossible for her to do anything other than collapse into Marcus' neatly made bed. She had barely pulled the thin coverlet over herself when she fell into an exhausted slumber.

Chapter 24

Life is a series of small choices. Even when we feel fettered and unfree, there is always a choice. Every moment, every breath, is a choice. And in this, is freedom.

Marcus drove towards his villa in one of the Virmortus vehicles, watching the sun set over the ocean. The day had cleared up, barely a cloud or mist to impede the view of the brilliant globe lowering against the dark waves.

This one day had changed Alba forever. But like the original founders, they would rise from the ashes of the city to forge a stronger one.

They would use this attack to strengthen the bonds between citizens, and Marcus intended to relax the strict divisions between castes. They could only survive the coming onslaught if they banded together.

He thought about Aerina, unable to keep his mind from wondering where she was sleeping. Had she gone home? He didn't dare let himself hope that she'd found her way back to his villa. Not in the face of the growing divide between the Virmortus and the ruling class.

He had personally released her father and the rest of the Senators. They had made it clear they did not approve of his leadership, but none had been bold enough to confront him. The city belonged to the Virmortus now. To Marcus.

The founders had hidden the Technology away, hoping to keep it concealed from the world. That had been a mistake. They should have used the intervening years to perfect it, study it, learn how to better control it.

Marcus would not make the same mistake.

Aerina had been right in her final thesis, which he'd read. *Change is always imminent; if you don't seek out change, it will find you unprepared.* He wouldn't let it catch Alba unprepared again.

As he neared the far side of the terrace, it was a struggle to turn the car east, away from the Delacroix villa.

He would give her time. Time to adjust to the changing city. Time to mourn Stephen. Time to find out exactly what she wanted.

As the carport door slowly lifted, he braked hard. His own car sat in its spot.

She was here. Where she belonged.

She'd made her choice.

She'd chosen him.

Visit Lindsey's website and enter your email for an exclusive sneak peek of the second book in
The Secret of Alba Series,
Patrician.
www.lindseywinsemius.com/my-books

www.ingramcontent.com/pod-product-compliance
Lightning Source LLC
Chambersburg PA
CBHW061549170626
46811CB00001B/142